THE LICK

BRIAN D. ALI, JR.

The Lick
Copyright © 2020 by Brian D. Ali, Jr.

Master Plan Publishing
P.O. Box 214886
Auburn Hills, MI 48326
www.masterplanpublishing.com

Publisher's note: This is a work of fiction. Names, characters, places, and incidents either are the product of the author's imagination or are used fictitiously. Any resemblance to actual events, locales, or persons, living or dead, is entirely coincidental.

This book contains an excerpt from *Pradaceous* by Brian D. Ali, Jr. This excerpt has been set for this edition only and may not reflect that final content of the forthcoming edition.

Edited by Hillary Crawford
Proofread by Kristen Corrects, Inc.
Cover art design by Elite Media
Author Photo by Zanyita Ali

ISBN 9781735750903
First edition published 2020
Printed in the United States of America

When I looked around, I was surrounded by three walls and a metal door. I had a million worries, and no hope. I had no family, except a wife and a mother. I was certain that I had run out of chances. I fell asleep, and awoke years later with a story.

Brian D. Ali Jr.

For Zanyita and Baby Bryant

Prologue

"Ain't this a bitch? I can't believe this shit."

Lesson was talking out loud to himself. He couldn't believe what the fuck was going on. The U.S. Marshals had kicked in his door and arrested him. Lesson found himself standing in a holding cell at the Livingston County Jail in Howell, Michigan, waiting to be booked on a conspiracy charge.

Someone in his circle had cooperated with the federal government, and a sealed indictment had been handed down, charging Lesson with conspiracy to organize an armored truck heist.

Lesson could not believe that Team America was really trying to make this bullshit charge stick, without any physical evidence. What Lesson really wanted to know was where the fuck the government was getting their information.

Lesson was not in his right frame of mind. Before his arrest, he had learned that his fourteen-year-old son, LJ, had been shot, and his little brother, Learn, was taken to Henry Ford Hospital in critical condition, from being shot in his arm and neck by Lesson's long-time nemesis, Juman.

Chapter One

Lesson was fuming on the inside. He felt like his family was cursed. Every fucked up thing imaginable had happened to his family in the past year, and now he wanted revenge.

First, he needed to get a bond. Lesson hoped his wife, Ashanti, was in her right frame of mind when she contacted Brittney Storm. Lesson was referring to one half of his legal team from Wise, Storm, and Associates, who were his legal representation. Anthony Wise was the brains behind their legal empire, and Brittney Storm was the attractive mouthpiece. Lesson knew that once Ashanti got in touch with Brittney, she would call her partner, Anthony. Together, Anthony Wise and Brittney Storm were two of the best lawyers in Michigan. They didn't take just any case. Wise, Storm, and Associates only took on heavyweight cases. Either you had to have a bankroll that didn't stop rolling, or the case had to make sense, where it would give the firm the notoriety to bring in other heavyweight cases due to the exposure.

Every federal judge in the Eastern District of Michigan, including state judges, feared their work ethics. If there was a loophole to be found, Wise, Storm, and Associates found it. If there was ever a team that could get even a guilty muthafucka off who was caught with his hand in the cookie jar, Wise Storm, and Associates was the cream of the crop.

The city of Howell was the worst place to be if you were a minority. Howell was where the first chapter of the KKK started

3

in Michigan. It sat between Detroit and Lansing, the capital of Michigan.

Lesson wanted to make a phone call, but was reluctant. If somebody was cooperating with the government, it had to be somebody from the inner circle.

Lesson thought about his lick team, which included four other members. The team had known each other for years, had been doing robberies together for the past two years, and as far as Lesson was concerned, everybody was solid. Lesson knew that his father, Tha Pope, would die before he rolled, and his little brother, Learn, was raised under the same rules. That left Jameer and Big Goob, but Lesson could not believe that either one of them would ever talk to the police under any circumstances. This left Lesson to believe that the police were either trying to set him up, or see if he would let something slip while using the jail phones.

Lesson knew that Ashanti stayed on point, but with the tragedy of her stepson and brother-in-law getting shot, he didn't fully know if she was capable of following his instructions. He couldn't count on her to contact his legal team, which were his strict instructions if a situation like this was ever to arise.

Lesson knew that Ashanti would bounce back out of her funk—he just didn't know when that would be. She was dealing with so much and she was now in charge. Ashanti would first try to contact Brittney, because she trusted her the most.

He figured by now, Ashanti probably had already made contact with Brittney, but since he was out of the loop, he was semi-stressing. He did not have any information and did not know what was going on.

Lesson was standing against the wall and thought about Ashanti some more. Over the past year, he had put her through the wringer. She was basically going through the same drama that he was going through, right now. She had just given birth to a son three months ago and found out today that her stepson, LJ, had been shot.

He hoped she was holding up. Lesson knew he was a lucky muthafucka, for real. Ashanti was there when the U.S. Marshals fugitive squad busted into their suburban home and took her husband. During all the turmoil, Ashanti held herself together the best she could. She knew she needed to be strong for Lesson and their children. She was already in an emotional state before they ran up in her crib; however, she didn't let her personal situation affect the role she needed to play for her husband, like most hustlers' wives or side bitches would've.

She didn't act a fool and try to get attention at the worst possible time. What Ashanti did was play her roll to a T. Ashanti wasn't the complaining type, although she did complain to her husband when that nigga was out of pocket.

Lesson was a smooth brother, and for the most part, she didn't know what he was out in the streets doing. For years, she had suspected that he was fucking a few bitches here and there, but she never caught him. She never had proof, until recently.

Ashanti was well taken care of. She didn't want for anything. The streets were good to Lesson, and Ashanti benefited from his success. However, Lesson was still a street nigga—and Lesson's mom, Rocci, told her that there was a different set of rules for a street nigga.

Ashanti knew that in a matter of days, Lesson would be standing in front of a federal judge, asking for a bond, and he expected to be back in the world. That's why she needed to get in touch with Brittney, to make sure that happened. Lesson knew that if he had to choose who he wanted to handle his affairs, Ashanti was the perfect choice.

He had groomed her for moments like this. Lesson learned at an early age that he could not place too much trust in a bitch, because hurt feelings could mean life and death, and Lesson had to learn that lesson the hard way. Lesson had almost been killed when he had gotten shot by Savage Keith over his baby momma, Nesh, and her pillow talk. Lesson told himself that he would never trust a bitch again, the way he trusted Nesh, but Ashanti proved to be the biggest asset he could ever have. That's why he made her his wife.

Lesson made her prove herself over and over again, and Ashanti always passed every test. Ashanti proved that she could take a punch. During the arrest, she stayed silent and recorded the entire arrest on her Samsung Galaxy S10 phone. Ashanti wasn't stupid.

With all the white-on-Black police brutality happening around the country, if something was to happen, even if they didn't believe her personally, they would believe the video recording.

You never know with these white folks out here in Hicktown, USA. They played dirty when it was time to be dirty. Lesson knew that the racist-ass crackers were waiting on him to use the phone to try to obtain more evidence on him.

Lesson was sitting on a cement bench, thinking about his arrest, going over different scenarios in his mind. He looked up and noticed multiple deputies walking by the holding cell he was in, pointing at him like he was some type of celebrity. If only these muthafuckas really knew who he was. They definitely wouldn't be staring at him like that, he thought.

If Lesson had been a real-life celebrity, he wasn't flashy like former NFL player Antonio Brown, or even the look-at-me type of dudes. He didn't crave attention like Kanye West or Kim Kardashian West. The way Lesson made his money, he had to stay under the radar.

If Lesson was a celebrity, he would be a private celebrity. He played a big role in keeping his family together, and he meant everything to the people closest to his heart—his parents Rocci and Tha Pope, his brother Learn, Ashanti, and his kids Lovely and Lesson, Jr., who everybody called LJ.

He was not the person who they were portraying in the media, who had committed a serious crime in this bullshit Hicktown. They made it seem like somebody had gotten hurt, or guns were pulled on people. What they didn't say to the public was that the money was simply handed over to the team who committed the heist.

The town was so small that it was like the media craved attention. Hell, this small town *needed* to have a spotlight flashed on it, a town that nobody seemed to care about.

Lesson was a Black man in a small predominately white town, and because of that revelation, it was supposed to be game over for him, or at least that's what they wanted to portray. However, in order for that to happen, they first would have to deal with Wise, Storm, and Associates.

Lesson knew that once his legal team started to break down the case, Hicktown would wish that they left well enough alone in the first place. Lesson didn't give a fuck how long they stared at him or pointed. He knew he wasn't going to entertain them by talking to them.

If they wanted a conversation, then they had Lesson Day all fucked up—at least that's what he was thinking. He wasn't a five o'clock FOX News or TMZ type of nigga. He didn't aspire to be judged by public opinion, especially by muthafuckas who sat on the couch eating TV dinners, shaking their heads, watching the news—day and night—saying that guy was crazy, or that nigga was dumb as fuck.

If anything, Lesson was a special breed. The type who if the news did put his business on their segment it went unsolved. Shit, the way the news was portraying Lesson Day, every white deputy who walked by the holding cell had a certified reason to be looking at him all funny and shit. But damn, this pointing and staring had gotten old really quick. Lesson wanted to check these muthafuckas in the worst way, He was thinking about his son and his little brother, as well as getting a bond. Lesson knew they wanted him to act a fool.

As Lesson was contemplating his next move, this short funny looking deputy turned the TV up loud enough for everyone in intake to hear. Lesson positioned himself directly in front of the holding cell door to make sure that he could see and hear what the fuck was going on.

Lesson couldn't believe what he was seeing—these muthafuckas had his face blasted all over the entire screen.

BREAKING NEWS: "FOX News Veronica Starr is reporting. The United States Marshals

Fugitive Unit just apprehended a suspect who they immediately turned over to FBI Special Agent Dave Opperman. The United States Marshals are claiming that the suspect was the mastermind in a bank heist that shook a community in Livingston County. Police say an undisclosed amount of money was taken in less than thirty minutes. No money was recovered during the arrest. However, United States Marshals say they believes that they have the person in custody who they believe help set up and participate in the heist. This is Veronica Starr reporting live for FOX News. We have Special Agent Dave Opperman here now. Do you have anything that you would like to add for the public, sir?"

Lesson watched reporter Veronica Starr and Special Agent Dave Opperman stand side by side in front of the Livingston County Jail in Howell, Michigan. In the background, he could see civilians going in and out of the building. Special Agent Dave Opperman knew that this was his moment and careers were made during times like these. He perked up for the camera to catch his best view, grabbed his belt to pull up his slacks, and spoke into the microphone.

"To anyone who's planning on committing any type of crime in the eastern district of Michigan, I personally want you scumbags to know that we will take you down. We work hard for our communities and joint law enforcement agencies will work together to bring you to justice."

"Veronica Starr reporting for FOX News at five o'clock. Special Agent Dave Opperman, can you tell the community the name of the suspect you apprehended and, after about a full year of investigations, how you broke the case wide open?" she said.

Dave Opperman looked directly into the camera and said, "Veronica, the suspect's name is Lesson Day, and because of the pending investigation, we cannot provide any details at this time. We ask the community to stay calm, have patience, and rest easy. Trust that no matter how long it takes, law enforcement will do their jobs."

"Well, there you have it. This is Veronica Starr reporting for FOX News."

Lesson could not believe this shit. This was not the attention that he craved. Lesson was the low-key type. He built his reputation off of being inconspicuous and smarter than the next man. He had put in mad work over the years. His father, Legend Day, AKA Tha Pope, had made sure that he was battle-tested.

Lesson was known throughout the city because of the moves he made over the years and his father's ruthless past. At an early age he learned that in order for a man to stay out of prison, a man can't be throwing rocks at the penitentiary. Most niggas literally stood outside of the penitentiary with a brick cocked back in their hands, like they were the legendary Detroit Tigers Pitcher Justin Verlander. It didn't matter if there was a camera pointing directly at them. They would still throw that brick, because most young niggas actually wanted to go to prison to up their status in the hood.

That was not how Lesson got down; he wasn't like that. Lesson learned early to let his flunkies throw the bricks at the penitentiary—and the crazy thing was, he didn't have to do too much convincing. These young niggas were eager to do it, just to prove themselves.

Lesson knew how to lead, and a real leader can't lead from behind the walls of the penitentiary. He wasn't the leader who sat on the inside, contemplating on how to get the dope sack in through visitation or playing poker and stressing. Lesson needed to be in the world. Shit, only a fool would want to be in prison.

Some niggas are just dealt bad hands, but most of the niggas in the joint were in that muthafucka, because of their impatience and stupidity. Lesson sat on the brick bench, shaking his head.

Damn this shit is bad. Where the fuck is Brittney? he thought.

The other guys in the holding cell kept looking up at Lesson. That's when he realized that he wasn't just thinking to himself, but talking out loud.

Man, I'm in this bitch tripping. Calm down, Lesson, he said to himself. Lesson couldn't believe he was in here right at the exact moment that his son had died, over some flimsy fluke-type shit. Or was it really some fluke shit?

Lesson whispered, "Ain't no reason in crying over spilled milk. What's done is done. I'm gonna find out who took me away from my family."

At this point, Lesson didn't know if he was talking out loud or in his mind. All he knew was that he had to get out of this cell. He had too much shit going on in the world.

God, I don't know what you are doing but you know you got me fucked up, I'm in this bitch at the wrong time.

Lesson had been in too many situations where he had to be on point and out-think the next muthafucka. Being in this punk-ass jail was no different. Now Lesson had to think, really think, to get himself out of this predicament.

Lesson was light-skinned with a full body of big visible tattoos except on his neck. The Mexicans who he let tattoo on him showed the fuck out. He was six feet tall and 205 pounds with brownish black eyes. He was what you would call muscular, but not to overbearing. He kept one-carat diamonds in each ear. His hair tapered his waves and stayed spinning just like his little brother and his pops.

Of all the places he could have been locked up at, why in the fuck did they have to bring him to this hoe-ass racist jail? Of all the rumors he heard about the city of Howell, he knew that he probably would never walk out of the jail without at least an assault charge.

"Inmate Day, step out for processing."

Those words knocked Lesson out of his thoughts.

"Hey dude, I think they're calling you," another inmate said to Lesson, pointing at the speaker on the wall.

The inmate looked like he had seen better days. The white guy was dirty as hell and shaking like a stripper. Lesson knew what that dance meant. If the white guy didn't get out of there soon, this muthafucka was gonna detox right in the holding cell all night.

Lesson heard his last name being called over the intercom again. He stepped out of the holding cell and presented himself.

This short-ass deputy stepped out of the control room in intake and headed over to the finger scan area. He strolled around with his chest poked out like he just benched 350 pounds. The little muthafucka could not have been more than 130 pounds. The little man thought he was top shit. Maybe he was in this hoe-ass jail, but Lesson didn't think twice about the little deputy.

If little man thought he was impressing somebody with those goofy antics, then he had Lesson fucked up. The only thing that would impress Lesson at this point would be to hear his name being called for release.

"Over here, inmate Day, and keep your hands at your sides where I can see them. Don't make any sudden moves neither, boy," Deputy Biehl said.

"What you say, man? I can't hear you from all the way down there, especially when you talking all that boy business," Lesson said, looking at the top of little man's head.

"I said, don't be moving your hands all over the place, motherfucker," Deputy Biehl repeated again.

He was looking for a reason to call the Special Response Team.

"Man, what the fuck is your problem? I'm not looking for what you looking for. Just process me and put me back in that holding cell over there," Lesson said and nodded in the direction of the cell he just came out of, "so I can make this bond real quick." Lesson was trying to defuse the situation.

Deputy Biehl looked directly at Lesson and said, "I hate mother fucking people like you, thinking you can talk your way through life."

Lesson just stared at the top of the little man's head for a few seconds, but could not stop himself from making a sly remark. "Is counseling apart of your job description, because I didn't know that you made that much to turn keys and save the world with yo mouth," Lesson said. "Now if you aren't big enough to just do the job that you've been assigned to, then maybe you should let one of the other bigger deputies handle it."

Lesson threw that comment in there about the short muthafucka's height. Lesson knew that most short muthafuckas always have height issues and he tried to subliminally strike a nerve.

Deputy Biehl definitely had a little man's complex and little man's syndrome. He stood at five-foot-two on a good day. He wanted to prove that he was larger than life and that he was one of the big boys. He wanted to be respected like a man of average height, but what he never learned was that respect didn't come from height or acting hard. Respect came from the respected. Deputy Biehl hated Black men and women and the niggas hated him. Lesson knew he would go zero to one hundred really quick for his respect, and to prove his point. However, in order to get the bond he was looking to get, Lesson knew that he had to chill, at least for now.

Deputy Biehl processed him, fingerprinted him, stripped him out, and placed him in a new cell to await his court hearing for his bond.

Chapter Two

Thirteen months earlier – October 2019

"Pops, where you at, OG? You know we still got this meeting set up for tonight." Lesson left a message on his father's Samsung Galaxy S10. "Hit me up, Pops. You know I got Goob and Jameer on deck. We all waiting on you, so get at me."

Lesson hung up and poured himself three fingers of Rémy 1738 and threw it back. He breathed easily through his mouth.

"*Damnnn*, that Rémy is smooth as fuck going down," Lesson said to Jameer. "You get you a sip of that, lil homie?" He pointed to the bottle.

"Naw, Lesson, I don't like drinking on an empty stomach. It gets me too drunk," Jameer said, rubbing his stomach. "Shit, I'm trying to fill this muthafucka up with some grub, you feel me?"

"Hell yeah, I feel you. I'm starving, too," Lesson said all serious and shit. "Hit up Big Goob. The food should be here within the hour. I told him to grab the usual from Asian Corn Beef. You already know Tha Pope ain't gonna be on time, so we might as well get comfortable," Lesson said to Jameer. "When Tha Pope arrives, he's gonna make me go over this plan a million times, until he says it's bulletproof."

Lesson was sitting lazily on his Lazy Boy. Jameer was on the other Lazy Boy. To the untrained eye, you would've thought both men had just finished an eight-hour shift at the General Motors plant. They were at one of the houses Lesson owned in a suburb near the east side of Detroit, in Clinton Township.

"You know what, Jameer? Tha Pope gonna be here. He be doing his thang, but Ima be real with you. When it's business on the floor, Tha Pope shuts all that extra shit down," Lesson said to Jameer.

Lesson waited on the return call. He knew his pops would hit him back. OG was probably in some pussy. That nigga stayed in some wet-wet. While Lesson was waiting, he thought about his pops and all the game Tha Pope had given him throughout his life. Lesson fucked with his pops heavy.

Whenever Lesson had a lick lined up, he took it to his pops to see what he thought. Lesson valued his father's opinion. Even if the lick was some bullshit, his father always heard Lesson out. His father was a better version of his son and he knew the game better than anyone. Within two minutes into any plan, his father would either say he's in or he's out.

If Tha Pope said he was out, then that was that. There wasn't any talking him into it, because it wasn't gonna happen. Lesson could never get him to reconsider. Tha Pope told Lesson years ago to never bring a lick to him that wasn't complete, because a plan with holes in it meant going upstate to an old farm, built up with bricks and steel rooms, bars, and wire gates. That's what Tha Pope referred to as the prison yard.

However, if Tha Pope was in, then you could bet your ass that the lick team was gonna make it home safely. In the last year, Lesson had to leave a few big licks on the table because he never hit a lick without Tha Pope.

Tha Pope knew that he trained Lesson well when it came to planning. He instilled in Lesson that you couldn't just think about the money factor, because if the lick was good, then the money would come. But if you fucked up and something went wrong, because of faulty planning, then you got no money and, at the very least, a decade upstate.

If Tha Pope said he's out, then Lesson was out too, simply because his father was never wrong about his No. 1 rule: Never bring a lick to the table that wasn't completely researched.

To Lesson, his father was his father, but to the streets, his father was called Tha Pope, and he was legendary. Lesson asked Tha Pope when he was younger why everybody called him Tha Pope. His father just shrugged and said, "Young Lesson, remember these words, all right son? The lesson of your life is to figure out why I'm called Tha Pope in the streets, and when you figure it out, Ima let you run the family business."

Tha Pope told that to Lesson when he was twelve years old. Now eighteen years later, Lesson knew the answer, though it had taken him years to figure out. True to his word, Tha Pope gave the business to Lesson five years ago.

For as long as Lesson could remember while he was coming up and making a name for himself, the streets called his father Tha Pope, because Tha Pope could either bring peace or destroy your life in a matter of minutes. But the streets would say anything and Lesson had learned that as well. Tha Pope's real name was Legend Day, but he made the hood call him Tha Pope, because having a name like Legend was worse than having a name like LeBron James or Michael Jordan for his two sons.

Tha Pope didn't want them to have to live up to his name. He was twenty years older than Lesson and twenty-five years older than Learn. At fifty years old, he had light brown smooth skin. He was six feet tall and 190 pounds with the waves still spinning. The hoes were still sweating Tha Pope like he was still a young nigga, and it wasn't because of the bag he kept full or the whips that he was still driving.

Tha Pope was still fucking bitches, because that's what he liked to do. It wasn't nothing to see Tha Pope pull up with something bad in the passenger's seat. Tha Pope was fucking bitches ages twenty to forty-five. He was still sharp as a freshly sharpened No. 2 pencil, but he knew that he was getting older, so he let his son run the business.

When Lesson was young, he made him that promise, and Tha Pope never lied to his sons. Tha Pope had seen so much shit over the years, it was a wonder that he wasn't forced to take that trip to hell, or hell on earth, referring to the grave or prison like the majority of his homies from the eighties.

The city of Detroit wasn't no hoe. Anybody who was from there knew how fucked up the streets were. You either survived or you died. You either survived or you got life in the joint. Tha Pope knew that he outlived the stereotype for Detroit niggas, which was the twenty-five shake. That's when either you are dead by twenty-five or doing twenty-five years.

Tha Pope had his own vision of his twenty-five shake and it didn't have shit to do with doing twenty-five to life. By the age of twenty-five, Tha Pope had two boys, so getting killed wasn't an option, and neither was going to prison. Everybody always asked him why he named his boys Lesson and Learn, and he would tell them that was a Lesson they were not trying to Learn.

Tha Pope always schooled his two boys in Streets Economics 101. He would tell Lesson all the time that his little light ass was gonna Learn. He would say to Learn that it was time to Learn and he would teach him a Lesson. Both boys respected their pops dearly. All three men would walk through hell with gasoline drawers on for each other.

Chapter Three

Lesson's phone started blowing up. "Bitch, my momma ain't no hoe, bitch. My daddy ain't no hoe. Quit trying to play me like a hoe. Count money all day, count money all day, count money all day. Ma, ma, ma money all day, every time. My line ring it's ten-point-five. The money phone." The lyrics of Detroit local rapper Icewear Vezzo Joint was Lesson's ring tone for his pops.

"Yooo old nigga, what up doe?" Lesson joked to his dad.

"Young nigga, you know ain't nothing old about a Detroit nigga like me, except these old money bags, and I keep adding to the vault, so you might as well call me New Money. You dig?" Tha Pope told Lesson. "Son, when is you gonna learn that if it wasn't for me, you wouldn't have so much game yo self." Tha Pope continue to stunt a little bit. "Lesson, you know I got money put up for a rainy day or to fuck up, and if you don't believe me, we can go fuck up the Pantheon Strip Club tonight. You know I'll shut that bitch down and have all them bitches on dick. They know who up and who been up, you dig?" Tha Pope was smiling hard. He loved fucking with his oldest boy. "What's up son? You good, my nigga?" Tha Pope asked his firstborn.

"Yeah Pops, I'm straight. What's up with you?" Lesson shot back. "What you getting into tonight, besides talking about going to the Pantheon Strip Club? You gonna have to take a rain check on that, Pops. You must have forgot we got that meeting coming up," Lesson reminded his pops.

"No doubt, I remember, my nigga. I was just knocking some rust off. I was in the gym sweating like a muthafucka," Tha Pope told Lesson.

"What gym you was at, Pops? I woulda fucked the gym up with you. You know I like to show off, Pops," Lesson said while looking down flexing his arms.

"Naw, young buck. Nigga, I was at my home gym, fucking the shit out of this lil freak. She was on dick, heavy bad bitch. She was shaking all that ass, fucked me up."

Tha Pope was laughing to himself. He knew Lesson would never catch him on his belt count. Since he was fifteen years old, Tha Pope had fucked just about everything that was worth fucking in the city and Metro Detroit area. Tha Pope had seriously fucked up happy homes. He knew that when he died, it would probably have something to do with some pussy, because he loved it too much.

"Lesson, did you learn something from yo pops with that shit I just dropped on you?" Tha Pope asked.

"What's that, Pops?" Lesson asked him. "You still bragging on them busted-up-ass hoes you be fucking?" Lesson was laughing, knowing damn well his pops was something like a playa, and he wasn't about to slide his dick up in nothing less than an eight-piece. "Or was you trying to tell me that you added to your belt count?" Lesson laughed.

"I mean, you said it not me, Lesson. I see you on point. Let me tell you about my new lil sweet thang. After I worked her out for about forty-five minutes, she said she thought that she loved a nigga. I couldn't believe it. The dick still good. That shit fucked me up, Lesson."

"Damn, Pops, you let her put that ratchet pussy on you like that? Because that's what it sounds like to me. Shit, Pops, it sounds like she fucked you up."

Lesson was trying to hear what his pops was gonna say next, because if Tha Pope said anything about that he was about to settle down, then Lesson would have to give that nigga a reality check. That would be something Lesson would never forget. He knew that only the woman to ever fuck Tha Pope's head up was Rocci Day, Lesson's and Learn's mother. To this day, she still had Tha Pope's head fucked up. They still fucked around a little bit and Tha Pope didn't play when it came to Rocci. He didn't give a fuck if she let another nigga hit, but as soon as she called Tha Pope, he was chasing that nigga away. And if Tha Pope was called to intervene on some domestic-type shit, that's when it was a problem.

"Pops, you me that yo sweet thang ain't got you booed up and shit, man, like that Ella Mai song." Lesson kept jabbing at Tha Pope.

"Lesson, you got me fucked up. See, that's what I'm talking about. I can't even talk to you about who I'm fucking, because yo inexperienced ass can't handle it," Tha Pope joked.

"I'm just making sure, Pops," Lesson said. "Man, you gotta stop this shit. You out here making me look bad. I can't keep up with yo old ass, OG. I can't keep trying to compete with the shit you out here doing. These hoes gonna want the same type of treatment from me, Pops, that you giving them," Lesson said. "But for real, Pops, what time you coming through? I got the team ready to go."

Tha Pope looked at his presidential Rolex that had diamonds all around the face. "Ima be over there in thirty minutes," Tha Pope said.

"All right, I got Goob out getting the corned beef sandwiches and shit from Asian Corned Beef. He should be here about time you pull up," Lesson said and hung up.

"Yo Lesson, what's up with Tha Pope? I heard y'all talking and shit. He was knocking off another sweet thang, wasn't he?" Jameer asked while still sitting in the Lazy Boy, watching FOX News. "Dog, your pops be getting mo pussy than me," Jameer said seriously.

Lesson just laugh and said, "Me, too."

"Why you laughing?" Jameer asked.

"When you said Tha Pope get mo pussy than you, I thought the same shit, how he gets mo pussy than me, too. He been that way since I was a little nigga," Lesson said. "Tha Pope's retirement package is a lil different, compared to muthafuckas his age. Most OGs retire and go to Florida once they get their chicken up. But Tha Pope is happy with some fresh pussy," Lesson said. Ay, Jameer, you got those building plans I told you to grab?" Lesson asked.

"Yep, I got that and the highlighters," Jameer responded quick as hell. He wanted Lesson to know that he was all the way on point. "You know I'm always on point, big homie. I was ready when you said get ready. If this job don't get the okay, it ain't gonna be my fault," Jameer said, referring to how much respect Lesson had of his father's opinion. Jameer knew that Tha Pope had to give the final okay in order for Lesson to move forward. He also knew that Lesson could say fuck Tha Pope's opinion, but Lesson wouldn't do that.

"My nigga, you wanna know why I been fucking with you for so long?" he asked Jameer.

"Why is that, big homie?" Jameer shot back.

"You wanna win, just like me, and you don't wanna be the reason that we can't get no money," he said. "And you realize that in order for us to get money, I can't have any slip-ups, because if I do, Tha Pope gonna tell me how I fucked up and wasn't all the way prepared. I hate to look stupid in front of my pops, especially over preparations. You feel me, Jameer? Tha Pope told me a long time ago never to bring nothing to the table unless it was ready," he said. "And till this day, I still stand by that motto."

"Ay, Lesson, cut that Madden on." Jameer was referring to the NFL game they both loved to play on Xbox One. "We can get a game in while we're waiting on the food and Tha Pope. If you scared, then I'll just play a professional live somewhere in Cali or something," Jameer said.

"Fuck you talking about, Jameer? We can play three-minute quarters. Bout time I beat that ass, the food and Tha Pope should be here," Lesson said.

"No doubt you already know I'm trying to get that $100 you cheated me out of the other day," Jameer said, trying to get Lesson to bite on the bet by throwing the controller in Lesson's lap.

"Shit, my nigga, you know I don't play Madden for less than a hundred. My skills can't be wasted for less than that, and that's too cheap as it is." Lesson faked like he was Detroit Lions QB Matthew Stafford throwing a fifty-yard pass to Detroit's new star, WR Kenny Golladay. "Crank it up, lil homie. Since you don't like money, I'll spend yours for you," Lesson told Jameer.

Twelve minutes later, Lesson had his bank roll out, peeling off five twenties, his face looking tight. He couldn't believe Jameer won on a comeback play with Green Bay Packers QB Aaron Rodgers. Lesson had Stafford and they were up fourteen points. He knew he had the win in the bag, so he figured he would just go on cruise control for the rest of the game, but this lucky-ass nigga, Jameer, came back and won with Aaron Rodgers. Lesson couldn't believe it.

"Yo, Jameer, you lucky as fuck, my nigga," Lesson said.

"Naw, nigga, I'm hungry as fuck," Jameer said as he reached out to grab the cheese from Lesson. "I already told you about going against the Green Bay Packers with Aaron Rodgers," he said. "Shit, I would've beat your ass with Brett Favre. Hey Lesson, I gotta ask you some serious shit, for real. Do I gotta count this money, because you know that we don't do short money in this bitch." Jameer was rubbing it in.

"Yo man, take your wins whenever you can get them, because you know it might be a month before you win again. You know, for every ten games I win, you win two."

Lesson teased his lil homie, trying to get in his head, because he was mad as fuck that he had lost. Lesson kept going. "Shit, I'll take those odds any day, Jameer."

"Big homie, even the warriors lost after a while. LeBron fucked up their first run, then Khawai took them down with that busted-up ass Toronto Raptors squad. He did that after LeBron left the crown to go to the Lakers. I'm the super team killa," Jameer said while fanning himself with the five twenties.

Jameer had smooth, creamy black skin. He looked identical to the hip hop artist Akon, but Jameer didn't like that comparison, and he would check the shit outta anybody who called him that. He was five-foot-nine, a stocky 185-pound build with a tapper ceaser haircut. Out of the entire lick team, Jameer was the easiest one to get along with.

As they were talking, they heard Goob pull up. He had a 2019 black Kettle GT Mustang hollering out front. Goob wanted everybody to know that he just pulled up. He knew that his muscle car was the shit, that's just how Goob was—all flashy and shit. He had the loudest car on the streets, ain't no question about that, and if you asked him, he had the fastest car. Goob had a personal mechanic who he called White Boy Rick who used to work for the professional Hendricks Motor Sports Racing Team.

Whenever Goob bought a new Mustang, he would hit White Boy Rick up and within days, Goob had the fastest car in the city. Goob wasn't just about talk either. You catch him at the light and he would try you. That nigga would even try the hook, referring to Detroit Police Road Patrol. If they acted like they wanted to smoke, he would smoke their asses.

While he was smoking a nigga on the road, somehow he would get some video footage on his Samsung Galaxy S10. He could drive and film the shit. Big Goob was a YouTube legend.

"That's got to be the food. All that noise out there, it ain't nobody but Goob showing off," Jameer said to Lesson.

Lesson pulled the blinds back and peeked out of the window. "Hell yeah, that's that nigga," Lesson said, shaking his head. "I'm hungry as fuck, but tell me this, Jameer, why the fuck is this nigga Goob so fucking hardheaded? This nigga don't be listening to shit. Why do I gotta tell this nigga the same shit everywhere we go? I keep telling him we ain't in the city. He can't be waking up my white neighbors, smoking that loud, and bumping local Detroit rapper T. Grizzly at one in the morning on a week day, knowing damn well these white muthafuckas be going to work early as fuck. That type of shit be having they nosey asses looking at us every time we leave this muthafucka, or come in this muthafucka," Lesson continued his rant.

While Lesson was still looking out of the window, Goob's black ass was getting out of his whip. He reached in and grabbed three big-ass plastic bags. When Lesson saw the food, he stopped being so angry—that's how hungry he was, and the damage was already done. Lesson's stomach was rumbling just thinking about the corned beef egg rolls and his big man corned beef sandwich that he was about to fuck up. He knew he wasn't about to play with that food, once it came inside.

Lesson tried to think about the reason he didn't eat all day and couldn't figure it out. He chalked it up to the fact that he just let the day get away from him while preparing for the lick that he was about to put on the floor. Lesson worked hard, just to get to this point, where he could deliver the plan to the lick team. But first he had to eat, or he wouldn't be able to deliver the plan without thinking about food.

Lesson told himself the reason why he lost the game against Jameer a little while ago was because he was hungry and smiled.

"Yo Jameer, you know I lost that game because I was hungry and thinking about food the entire time," Lesson said.

"If that's what you wanna tell yourself, big homie, I'm cool with that, as long as I got these five twenties in my pocket." Jameer was patting his right front pocket to let Lesson know that he was holding the winnings.

As Goob was walking up to the front door, Jameer snatched it open and threw a playful punch at Goob's head, but Goob slipped it.

"You know you to slow and little to try to go at a heavyweight like me, Jameer," Goob said, rearranging the food in his hand so he didn't drop the shit. "Man, you be frustrating the shit outta Lesson with all that playing and shit. How many times he got to tell your ass to go on stealth mode whenever you come out here to his burb house? You do realize that this ain't Detroit and we are out here for a reason, don't you?" he said, shaking his head at Goob.

Goob blew air out of his mouth like he was frustrated. When he finally spoke, he said, "Why do this nigga think that I gotta act like a suit and tie nigga, when I ain't never wore one in my life or owned one?" Goob asked Jameer. "Dog be tripping sometimes."

"You don't have to act like a nigga either, Goob. And on top of that, out here ain't nothing but suit and tie muthafuckas. Maybe you need to look around and realize where the fuck you at," Jameer said seriously, because he didn't want him to fuck his chicken up.

"How many years have Lesson been fucking with me?"

Jameer didn't answer, because to him it was a rhetorical question.

"Exactly," Goob said. "Lesson gonna be all right. I always do my part, and right now, my part is to get this food in the door so all four of us hungry-ass niggas can eat, Jameer. But for some reason, somebody blocking the door like the left tackle who plays for the Detroit Lions, Taylor Decker. And you know he wasn't worth the first-round grade the Lions gave his always-hurt ass. Since you don't look like a big-ass white boy, get yo little ass out of the way, Jameer," he said. Big Goob smiled at his closest friend. "I mean, unless you aren't as hungry as Lesson said y'all was when he was blowing me up."

Goob was a big nigga and super strong. He was dark-skinned, six-foot-four and 240 pounds, with black eyes with a high top fade. He didn't have an inch of fat on his entire body. If you had to compare him to anybody, it would be the new NBA phenomenon, Zion Williamson.

"Goob, come in here, my nigga," Lesson said. "Goob you know I hear you talking all that shit, but this ain't the time to be on joke time. Bring that food in here. Let's bust that shit down, then get to business. You got Tha Pope's order?" he asked. "Because you know he don't do delivery and he about to pull up at any moment."

"Yeah, I got everybody's shit, Lesson. I didn't even have to tell my bitch. She already knew what we wanted. It's the same shit we been going to her to get for the past two years. Getting the same shit, my nigga," Goob said sarcastically to Lesson. Even though he was playing, Lesson picked up on it. "You know I always do my job. Everything you ask me to do, I do it."

Lesson stroked his beard and nodded at Goob. "You don't do everything I ask you, Goob," Lesson said.

"My nigga, I know you ain't talking about the Mustang," Goob said. "My ride ain't hurting nobody, Lesson. You be acting too tight, when you about to put a lick on the table."

Lesson waited a minute, grabbed his food, opened the wrapper to his sandwich, took a hungry nigga's bite, then took a sip of his strawberry lemonade EverFresh drink, and said, "Goob, you do handle yours, but you still a hardheaded-ass nigga, and once I realize that you can't follow a single direction, no matter how small you think it is, Ima have to cut ties with you, my nigga, because ain't nobody who's a part of the lick team bigger than the team."

"What you talking about, Lesson? I know you ain't talking about the Mustang, Lesson. What good is having toys if we don't play with them?" Goob said, looking hurt that Lesson was seriously scolding him for revving his engine. But knowing that he fucked up, Goob just took the verbal beating.

Goob was hungry as fuck, but he couldn't eat while Lesson was showing him how he fucked up.

"Goob, fuck the dumb shit," Lesson said. "Before you started coming around here, these white muthafuckas only acknowledged me when I came in contact with them, and that's if I was leaving or coming in this muthafucka. Now they think we are friendly enough to be commenting on your ride anytime we speak, which means that they are paying too much fucking attention to me, Goob," Lesson said, taking another bite out of his sandwich that was now a third gone.

Lesson thought, *Damn this shit is good as fuck. Them muthafuckas who opened that corned beef joint was onto something, for real.*

"Goob, we are not nine-to-five niggas. We are straight-up hustlers, and I can't have these white folks catch onto the slightest hint why we are coming out here," he said. "But since we can't get past go with this car shit, don't drive the Mustang to any more meetings, because you're careless when you're in that muthafucka. You want to many people to see you, when I don't want nobody to see me, you dig?"

Lesson was staring big Goob directly in the eyes.

30

"Lesson, come on, man. You taking this shit to far," Goob said. "You know the Mustang is my baby," he added, shaking his head.

"It's not about all that, Goob," Lesson told him seriously. "You ignored an order, just because you think it ain't about nothing. I can't have that happen with a detail, because then my worries would be about more than muthafuckas paying attention. My worries would be about going to prison," Lesson explained. "So if you bring that whip around again, then don't show up, because I'm not gonna let you work the job. And on top of that, Goob, you seem to care more about the whip than you care about getting this money."

"Why you talking about taking Goob off a job, Lesson?" Tha Pope was looking at Lesson, waiting for answers. Everybody was shocked that they let Tha Pope sneak up on them like that. They were all too caught up in eating and the topic at hand, and they were embarrassed, because they were too sharp to be caught slipping by the OG.

"It ain't about nothing, Pops. Me and Goob got an understanding out of a misunderstanding, ain't that right, Goob?" Lesson asked.

"No doubt, big homie," Goob responded.

Tha Pope was already grabbing for his sandwich that he knew was in the bag. He didn't think nothing of how Lesson shut his question down. If it was important, he knew Lesson would bring it up later. Once he got his food, he sat down next to Goob, shaking his head, while opening the wrapper to his big man corned beef sandwich.

"Goob, this bet not be about the Mustang, my nigga," Tha Pope said.

Jameer was staring at Tha Pope like, *How the fuck this nigga know what the deal was?*

"Pope, you must have been ear hustling for a while," Jameer said.

"Naw, little nigga. I know Lesson, and only thing that would get him to say that to Goob is that fucking car," Tha Pope said. "Niggas like us shouldn't have a car like that. It's bad enough that it's too fucking fast, but that muthafucka is loud as hell. We all have fast whips, but nobody's shit is as loud as Goob's, and when you bring a car like that around white folks in white suburbia, it stands out like a muthafucka."

"Pope, how the fuck you be knowing everything before a muthafucka tell you the business?" Jameer asked amazed.

Tha Pope bit into his sandwich and said, "Jameer, when you get to be fifty years old, young playa, you gonna be wiser than Tha Pope, no doubt, my nigga."

Tha Pope was just as hungry as everybody else, because for the next ten minutes, everybody ate without speaking.

Lesson got up from his Lazy Boy. "That's what a nigga need at least twice a week. If a nigga don't eat corned beef, then he ain't a real Detroit nigga," he said while dapping Goob up.

"All we eat is soul food and corned beef," Goob said.

Jameer, not wanting to be left out, jumped into the conversation. "What else, bro?" He was looking at Tha Pope, trying to get him to comment.

"Buffs, young nigga. We stay buffed the fuck up," Tha Pope said. "If you are from the city of Detroit, niggas betta have at least a pair of Cartier glasses."

They all were pounding fists and laughing. That was how the lick team was. One minute, shit was tense; the next minute, niggas was having a good-ass time.

"Let's get down to business, gentlemen," Lesson said.

All the men came into the kitchen and assembled around the countertop, which was made of white pearl. Four large building plans were spread out by Jameer, who had given everybody a highlighter, just in case they needed to highlight a particular area on their plans.

Lesson told everybody to look at the plans and tell him what they saw.

"I see a big-ass building that looks like a factory," Jameer said.

"Lesson man, I'm not with hitting a lick on a rim shop," Goob said. "But seriously, I don't know what the fuck I'm looking at."

Tha Pope was silently studying the plans, going over every detail. He couldn't figure out what the building was, until he noticed the street it was located on. They all were using their highlighters at some point on their building plans to get a better understanding of what they were looking at. Lesson was watching Tha Pope, because he knew that he would be the one to figure it out first. Lesson wanted to know if Tha Pope would go for it, once he realized what it was.

"Lesson, what the fuck you got us looking at a Wal-Mart for?" Tha Pope asked. "Ain't this a job that would need more than four people? And even if we had more people, we would need professionals. The surveillance is too high-tech, Lesson. You would have to spend a fortune to overtake the surveillance. You think Goob and Jameer are ready for a job of this magnitude?"

Tha Pope knew the boys were ready for whatever Lesson had planned, but he wanted to make sure Lesson knew that with this type of job, Lesson had to tie up all the loose ends.

"Pops, I've been training my guys for years. If they ain't ready for this now, then they will never be ready," Lesson said, looking at his pop.

Tha Pope admired his oldest boy and he knew how smart Lesson was. He knew that for Lesson to bring this type of job to him, he was ready. Tha Pope couldn't wait to hear the details, even if he didn't approve the job. He wanted to hear the intellect of his oldest boy and he had a silent admiration written all over his face.

Tha Pope stood against the wall and said, "All right, Lesson. Let's hear the Lesson plan, and it better be good, since you wanna start playing high-stakes poker all of a sudden. I guess $150,000 or $200,000 ain't enough for your ego anymore. You wanna start upgrading. But remember this, Lesson, when you upgrade, no matter if you win or lose, you take the team up with you, or down with you. So let's hear it, Lesson."

"My niggas, we been hitting licks for a minute now—big licks and little licks—but they all been planned out to a T," Lesson said to the three men standing at or around the countertop. "If I was to bring something to the table, I know that everybody would have faith that I did my homework. Over the last year, we probably have split about $800,000. That should've netted each of us $200,000, but that ain't shit compared to this lick. After expenses, I can guarantee each person a cut of a half a mil a piece, for a few hours of work."

Before he finished, he was cut off.

"Half a million is $500,000! You talking about $500,000 that I don't have to split with anybody?" Goob asked.

"Yeah, that's what I'm talking about. You and Jameer will split one million between the two of you," Lesson said. "All you gotta do is do the job I got lined up."

Jameer was watching and scratching his head. Lesson didn't tip his hand to Jameer the entire time they were by themselves.

"Lesson, with that type of chicken, I can open a business and go legit," Jameer said.

"So what's the entire take, Lesson? How much will be in the entire pot altogether?" Tha Pope asked.

"At least three and a half mil, maybe more," Lesson shot back.

"So who else gets a cut of the pie? Because from my math, son, that's still one and a half mil just sitting there that's not accounted for," Tha Pope said.

"Pops, I told you that's everybody's cut, after expenses," Lesson told his pops while looking into his eyes. "I got to buy an armored truck from Florida and bring it up to Michigan, then fix it up and paint it, plus uniforms. And I gotta pay for a spreadsheet on the time, the exact time pick-up is supposed to happen, for the original armored truck to come pick up the money. And I gotta pay my hacker to jam the security system so Wal-Mart's entire system is shut down. And I gotta pay for that window to keep it shut down for twenty-five to thirty minutes, and on top of that, I gotta get uniforms and Brinks ID cards," Lesson explained to the entire team.

Lesson wanted everybody to know that this was a professional job—and to pull it off with minimal problems, it was going to cost a lot of money to make a larger amount of money.

"How do you know that when the system gets jammed that Wal-Mart security is not gonna shut down the pick-up until the system is back up?" Tha Pope asked.

"They're not gonna do that. They know the armored truck can't be sitting around, because the risk of a robbery. Plus, the truck is on a time schedule and to be idling like that could cause the truck to get knocked off. They know that, Pops. Wal-Mart will not stop the pick-up unless corporate tells them to stop it. Everything will be on a time schedule," Lesson said.

"What about the real truck, Lesson? What if they show up as well?" Jameer asked. "That would be a hell of a blow up, I assume."

"That's what the expenses is for, lil homie. We will have a twenty-five to thirty minute window to make it happen. That should be more than enough time. All Goob would have to do is load the money into the armored truck," Lesson said.

"What about Wal-Mart security? Won't they know that we aren't the regular Brinks guys who come to pick up the money?" Goob asked.

"That's a good question, Goob. The thing is, different security personnel come whenever the regulars can't, and since this is the holidays, a different face shouldn't be a problem. Remember, it's the same company, same type of truck, just different people," Lesson said. "All we are gotta do is trick Wal-Mart into giving the money to the first armored truck they see."

Lesson was prepared for all the questions. He knew the lick team would fire his way and he covered everything.

"I brought this to the table now. I wanted to see if you guys wanted to sign on. I'm prepping for the first Monday after Black Friday, which is called Cyber Monday. If we do it on that date, then that would give us about thirty to forty days to complete prep," he said. "However, I want you guys to know that this is only a rough draft. I wanted to reel y'all in first, to get the green light. And Pops, Learn is in Miami right now, closing the deal on the armored truck. He's registering it to a fake security company down there, using a P.O. Box as the official address. I'm sure nobody is paying attention, because the armored truck is considered salvaged."

Learn was five years younger than Lesson, but looked exactly like him. If you didn't know Lesson and Learn personally, you would think they were twins. Lesson really didn't know how Tha Pope was gonna take this information, because he didn't like Learn working jobs.

Tha Pope always had a thing that if something went wrong, somebody from the family had to be out there holding the fort down. But Tha Pope didn't want to throw shade on Lesson's plans. Tha Pope knew that Lesson would never intentionally put Learn in a fucked up situation. He knew the love his two sons shared for each other. If Lesson was the peanut butter, Learn was the jelly. If Lesson was the oil for the engine, Learn was the transmission fluid.

Everybody was deeply in thought. They weren't thinking about the money like most money teams would—they were thinking about the information Lesson had shared with them. What they all realized was that Lesson and Learn had the jump on the lick for a while now. That was the only explanation as to why Learn was already down in Miami. This lick was moving along. They all knew that the only reason Lesson brought the lick to the table was out of respect to the team; however, they also knew that Lesson was a smart-ass nigga and that only a dummy knew that only a dummy would not agree to sign on.

The lick was well planned and thought out, and wasn't even finished prepping. The lick team knew that Lesson had put the majority of the work in and worked out the details. They also knew that he had already stressed over the lick and fool-proofed it. If Lesson had given each of them $500,000, it was because they were family and they had been putting work in with him for years. None of them would earn this money any other time. Lesson could've given everybody $100,000 and everybody would've been happy, but Lesson wasn't like that. Lesson was paying them for the work they put in over the years.

Lesson and Learn could've done this lick solo and pocketed three and a half million, but they brought it to the team and there wasn't any denying that Lesson, Learn, Tha Pope, Jameer, and Goob were a family when it came to putting a lick down. With the exception of Tha Pope and his boys, they didn't hang out together outside of doing a lick.

Jameer and Goob had been close friends for years. To Lesson, they were just workers, but when they all worked together, it was as if they were a family. They did thorough jobs and went about their life until Lesson called. However, to each other, Goob and Jameer were as tight as a lug nut tightened onto a rim of a car. Goob spoke his mind, as soon as reality set in that he was about to be papered up.

"If this lick goes as planned, I'm done throwing rocks at the penitentiary and taking all these chances," he said. "Lesson, my boy, you delivered on your promise. You told me if I stick with you that you would get me in a position to start my own business and leave the hood. I'm about to put the streets in my rear-view, no bullshit—invest right and do the damn thang."

"He's right, Lesson," Jameer said with gratitude. "If I can't go straight with $500,000, then I'm all the way in the way. You delivered, homie. We gonna run through this without a hitch and start wearing that suit and tie Goob is always talking about how he ain't never wearing."

Jameer had to throw a shot at Goob, because almost two hours ago, he was complaining about playing with his 2019 GT Mustang and the entire time, Lesson was trying to get them niggas out of Detroit.

"Fuck you, Jameer. You know I love the Mustang, but you right, bro. Lesson was right from the beginning. Here I am playing and had to be taught a lesson from the big homie Lesson," he said.

After a while, everybody started gathering their shit to leave. Lesson and Tha Pope were dapping the team up. Jameer left first, then Goob followed him out. Both men were shadow-boxing in the dark, walking to the car. Tha Pope was just about to leave when Lesson stopped him.

"Hold up, Pops. You got a minute or two?"

Tha Pope leaned against the door. A slight breeze came through from the Michigan weather. October showed promise of a cold winter ahead. Lesson had his Diane wave brush in his hand and was brushing his waves.

"What do you think, Pops? You think this is the one?" he asked. "Me and Learn have been working hard as fuck, that's why you haven't seen him in the last few weeks. I mean, Pops, we done went over every possible scenario. We even did a test run, using a rented U-Haul van. It went off like a hitch."

"Son, it looks good and sounds like you and Learn did all the dirty work, but always remember this, son: No plan goes as planned. You should know that from experience. With that being said, I believe in you and I believe in Learn, and from what I saw, ain't no way I'm not getting a piece of this cake. I would've joined just for the fun of it, no bullshit, my nigga. However, the bonus is the chicken at the end," he said. "But Lesson, how thorough are your contacts, because you definitely will need to make sure the drop goes as planned and the security goes as planned. If those go off without a hitch, then the plan is foolproof."

Tha Pope looked Lesson directly in his eyes.

"All my contacts are on point, Pops. If they weren't or if something changes, then we will have to abort the lick," Lesson said.

"I'm proud of you, son. This is bigger than my biggest lick when I was running shit," he said.

Lesson stared back into his father's eyes and got serious. "Pops, don't be proud of me while we doing all this talking. Be proud of me when I bring the team back home from the war and we counting that chicken."

Lesson gave his pops a hug and Tha Pope looked down at his wrist to check the time. It was dark outside. The presidential had the night lit up like a disco ball.

"I gotta hit the road, Lesson. Make sure Learn is good," Tha Pope said and he was out the door.

Chapter Four

Learn had on overalls, the kind the diesel mechanics wear in the wintertime. Learn was responsible for getting the truck registered and back to Michigan. He had been in Miami for about two weeks, and he fell in love with the city. Learn knew that he was coming back to Miami as soon as this lick was complete. He definitely wanted to find a few Miami bitches, maybe even a wifey.

The Cuban who Learn purchased the big truck from for $30,000 told Learn not to be fooled by the truck's exterior. He told Learn that the big truck had strong bones. Learn drove this hunk of junk up from Florida. He took I-75 north, all the way back to Detroit.

Man, Lesson got me all the way out here, for real, driving this raggedy piece of shit back to Detroit, Learn was thinking.

"I know this bitch is gonna break down," he said to himself. "Man I just hope if it does break down, it's closer to Michigan than Florida." He couldn't believe that he let Lesson talk him into driving it back, instead of getting it towed. Lesson told him he wanted him to drive it, because if he got it towed, the muthafucka who towed it would remember it if the lick made the national news.

This stupid-ass Cuban done lied to me. Learn thought about what the Cuban had said after he took the $30,000 for the big truck. "My friend, this truck has strong bones."

Strong bones my ass, Learn thought.

When Learn made it to Ohio, he started to relax a little bit, because he thought he was going to make it all the way to Detroit.

However, right after he refueled the big truck up outside of Dayton, Ohio, that muthafucka broke the fuck down, and there was nothing he could do about it except call for a tow. Learn had no other choice. When he got to the truck stop, Learn didn't know what the problem was. Shit, he didn't even know if they were going to be able to fix this piece of shit, but the white boys knew what the fuck they were doing. They had the big truck on the road within three hours.

They asked a few questions about what he planned to do with the truck, and for two seconds, Learn was caught off-guard by the question. He wasn't expecting to have to answer a question like that, but he quickly recovered. He told them that he was going to turn the big truck into a home on wheels. That must've been the right thing to say, because that blew those white boys' minds. They talked among themselves until they finished working on the big truck. It just needed a battery and a minor tune-up, and Learn was back on the road.

For the rest of the ride, the big truck drove smoothly. He made it to Detroit in record time. The worst thing about the trip was the stares he would get on the highway from the big truck being a hunk of junk.

Learn drove to a building that Lesson told him he bought for $25,000 on the east side of Detroit. The building was located on E. Jefferson Avenue. The building was a forgotten beauty—all it needed was a little T.L.C. like so many abandon buildings or houses in the city of Detroit. If someone was to put money into abandon properties, maybe there could be a resurgence for jobs and population. But with the crime levels so high, most owners had opted to move their businesses to the suburbs, which led to buildings and warehouses going into foreclosure and decaying.

Learn was happy as fuck to be finished with the trip, and he was excited to see the building that Lesson purchased. Lesson had a real estate agent named Jessica who he did a lot of business with. Learn knew from all the deals Lesson got from Jessica over the last two years that he wanted to get involved in real estate like his big brother. After this lick, Learn was gonna fuck with her as well to purchase some property.

As Learn pulled up to the building, he couldn't believe it. *What the fuck is this shit?* He was expecting to see a nice building, just in a bad location, but what he saw at first glance was a building that was in the middle of a former neighborhood that was now deserted. It looked like a bomb had just went off. The neighborhood had missing houses and abandoned, boarded-up homes.

Learn was surprised that Lesson bought this piece of property, because once he was finished with it, he would never be able to unload the property, even Learn knew that. As Learn was pulling up to the gate, he saw Lesson's car on the other side.

Lesson was sitting in his car, smiling. He was happy as fuck to see that his little bro had made it.

Learn had never been to the building before and really didn't know what to do, so he stopped and waited. Lesson exited his fire-red 2019 SRT Dodge Charger, smiling at his little bro. Lesson had a remote in his hand, hit a button, and the gate started opening. Somehow, Lesson had installed an automatic gate opener. Lesson was waving his hands like the man on the ground at an airport directs airplanes. Learn followed Lesson's directions and pulled the big truck inside the gate and straight into the building. To Learn's surprise, the look on the inside did not compare to how the outside looked.

The inside actually looked like some type of mechanical shop for trucks. Once the big truck was all the way inside, Lesson pulled the chain on the garage and locked the door. Learn shut the big truck down and climbed out with a manila envelope in his hand.

"What's up, bro?" Learn asked Lesson, shaking his hand and hugging him at the same time.

"How was the vacation, bro?" Lesson asked.

"Man, fuck you, bro. You sent me out there to work, bro. Do you know how much pussy I missed out on?" he said. "Dog, Miami has all the bitches. I wanted to put this Detroit dick down on them hoes, but I had a job to do. You told me Miami wasn't a pleasure trip, so it was all business for me, but yo, check this out." Learn pulled some papers out of the manila envelope. "This is the registration for the truck and the company name that you told me to put it in. Bro, listen to this shit: When I first gave them Cubans $30,000 for the truck, I thought you lost your mind, bro, throwing away money like that. Then I'm driving this big muthafucka up here, praying it didn't break down," Learn said, looking all serious at Lesson. "And guess what the fuck happened, bro, when I got to Dayton? That muthafucka broke the fuck down," he said all animated and shit, waving his arms like he was frustrated. "I didn't have no choice except to get it towed to a truck shop, but they got me back on road in two or three hours. They asked me what I planned on doing with it, and I made up some shit saying Ima turn it into a motor home. And them white boys was geek the fuck up, like man, it has a strong engine and solid foundation. Like I know what the fuck they was talking about, but I was in that bitch agreeing and shit, bro, and I was back on the road, bro. But Ima tell you like this once. You put your mechanics on this joint, it's gonna do what it supposed to do."

Lesson was nodding at his bro. All their lives, his little bro had followed directions and always got job done. What Learn didn't know was that he had the most important job out of everybody. Without the big truck, they would be on their asses, and the job wouldn't be able to get done.

"Good shit, bro," Lesson said to Learn. "And I told Pops you were in on the lick."

"What he say, bro?" Learn asked. "You know he don't like all of us working together at the same time."

"But what could he say, bro?" Lesson asked. "He know If I bring you in, then it had to happen, and I don't trust another nigga like I trust you, because you is the only nigga that think like me. We think alike, bro. But for real, when I put Pops up on the lick, it blew his fucking mind. You know how Pops don't want a muthafucka thinking they can read him, but I read him like a book, Learn, and we put that fire back in him with this lick. That's what he told me, bro. You know how big the Wal-Mart franchise is, right? Ain't nobody ever knocked off a Wal-Mart the way we are about to do the damn thang. We gonna get all that money from the week leading up to Black Friday, so on to Cyber Monday. And I'm low-balling shit by saying three and a half mil. We gonna get that entire bag, bro," Lesson said, rubbing his hands together like they were cold.

"When is your truck crew coming to get this muthafucka together?" Learn asked, looking around the building. "And I didn't know you had this joint. Outside, it look like Iraq, but inside, it's definitely a truck shop. Bro, how much you say you paid for this spot, $25,000, right?"

"Yep, I paid a small penny and it ain't mines, bro. I bought it for my white boys who is about to put this truck together for us. Ima give them the deed. All they have to do is get with Jessica and it's a wrap. Only thing I want them to do is fix this truck up in the next ten days and paint it how I want it painted. After that, their debt is paid. The building will be theirs," he said. "Shit, they was making house calls to fix trucks to get their paper. I just established them. Watch, bro, they are about to put the truck in the game. They assured me that they will work day and night for the next ten days and we will still have four extra days to spare, just in case. We good, bro," Lesson said.

As they were talking, two white boys came inside the building from a side door, with coffee mugs in their hands. One was fat with long stringy hippy hair and the other was tall and skinny with hippy hair. The fat older one's nametag read *Stevie* and the tall skinny kid's nametag read *Bradley*.

"Lesson, thanks, bro," they both said at the same time.

"We could never do enough to repay you," the fat white boy said.

"Just complete the job at hand by the deadline and we square," Lesson said, handing the older guy the deed to the building. "You remember Jessica?" he asked the younger white boy.

"Yeah, you're talking about the real estate lady, right?" the older one said, while holding the deed.

"Yeah, her. Get with her and she will help you transfer everything," Lesson said.

"But, Lesson," the skinny white boy said. "That's not enough. I mean, to be fair, we are gonna totally finish the job in record time, but we feel like we're taking advantage of you. And on top of that, you're paying for all the parts for the truck. All we're doing is providing labor."

"Dude, don't worry about it. You guys are my buddies. Maybe if my truck breaks down, I can bring it back and you guys can cut me a deal on the price," Lesson said.

"No way, man," the fat white boy said, walking over to the big truck and inspecting it. "You will have a lifetime of free maintenance from us, brother."

"Well, in that case, thanks. I'll hold you guys to that offer," Lesson said.

"All right, Lesson, let us do the job you paid us for. We have a lot of work to do," the skinny white boy said. "And when are you gonna tell us how you want it painted? You know I'm the best painter in Michigan."

"I know, that's why I got you both working on my truck," Lesson said. "And I'll tell you in seven or eight days. Is that okay? Y'all should be finished with the exterior and interior by that time, right?" Lesson asked. Both white boys nodded. "Okay guys, Ima talk to you in about a week."

Lesson turned to walk out and Learn jumped in step with him, heading for the door that led outside. Once they got outside they felt the winter weather coming in. Both brothers knew that once the Great Lakes got cold, Michigan was gonna be frozen for the next four months. But right now, it wasn't too cold yet. They were both from Detroit and they knew how unfriendly Michigan winters were.

"Lesson, why you pull them white boys chain like that, bro? You be fucking me up acting like they helping you, knowing damn well we need them more than they need us," Learn said.

"That's the thing, Learn. They don't know that and since they don't know that I really need them, they gonna bust their asses for me so they can pay their debt off for the deed that I had already given them for the building."

Learn shook his head, letting Lesson know that he understood. Learn just couldn't let it go through. "I'll invest $25,000 any day if it leads to three and a half mil. If only they knew," he said, laughing.

"Good thing they don't," Lesson said. "Then they would've been more expensive," he said, as both brothers reached Lesson's Charger and climbed in.

Soon as Lesson cranked the ride up, he peeled out of the warehouse driveway, fishtailing onto E. Jefferson Avenue, with Detroit rapper 42 Dugg featuring Yo Gotti's 2019 hit slapping through the speakers.

Chapter Five

As Lesson walked into the law offices of Wise, Storm, and Associates, he looked around and admired the decor. It looked nice and expensive. The couches and chairs appeared as if they were recently polished or waxed, because they had an impeccable shine to them. Lesson never understood why all top-notch legal offices in America had furniture that always had to look the same and were expensive, uncomfortable leather. He wondered if it was an unwritten rule to have this specific look. To top it off, there was always a shelf of legal books that he knew cost a fortune. Were the books simply a conversation starter for when a certain type of client who came into the firm?

He wondered if Anthony Wise and Brittney Storm read any of the legal material that they had on display. There were also multiple magazines on the coffee table.

The secretary secretly watched the nicely dressed Black gentleman staring at the decor in the office. She wondered, like so many others who had come inside the office staring, what he was thinking at this exact moment. Would Lesson head to the bookshelf and pretend to scan the books, or would he settle for a magazine? The secretary never got tired of the awe each client showed when they walked into the firm's offices.

As Lesson walked up to the desk in the reception area, he noticed that Wise, Storm, and Associates had a different receptionist sitting behind the reception desk. Lesson had on one of his favorite suits, a tailor-made cream-colored three-piece Gucci suit with the collar opened from the third button down, black cufflinks, a black Gucci hanky in the pocket, and black gator shoes. His suit and shoes cost $5,500.

"Hi, my name is Lesson Day. I have an eight o'clock appointment with Anthony and Brittney," Lesson told the attractive white lady who he assumed was the new secretary, giving her a full view of his thirty-two pearly whites.

Her nametag stated her name as Cindy. Cindy tried to speak, but could not formulate the right words, because she was tongue-tied. She placed her hand over her mouth and coughed to clear her throat.

"Sorry," Cindy said to Lesson. She took a sip of her lukewarm mint tea. Cindy was a very petite, short, attractive young white woman. To say anything else would be an understatement. At twenty-four years old, she was on the right track to becoming a paralegal. She had long, flowy blond hair with reddish highlights, and stood five-foot-one and was 112 pounds with ocean blue eyes.

"Yes, I see that you have a standing appointment and you are early, Mr. Day. Please have a seat and I will send a message to Mr. Wise or Ms. Storm for you," she said.

Picking up the office phone and calling her boss, she said, "Mr. Wise, you have an early Mr. Day here for his eight o'clock with you." She spoke quietly and professionally into the phone. Cindy nodded her head several times to whatever Mr. Wise was telling her on the other end of the phone, then she hung up.

"Mr. Wise said he would be out to get you in five to ten minutes, Mr. Day. He's just wrapping up a conference call in the south of France," she said. "Can I offer you a cup of coffee or some type of beverage?" she asked.

"No thanks, I'm just fine, Cindy. I'll wait on Mr. Wise," Lesson said.

Lesson turned around and headed toward the polished couch and picked up a *Fortune 500* magazine that had Donald Trump on the front. He unbuttoned his suit jacket and sat down on the couch.

Cindy was following Lesson with her eyes as he headed to the couch and made himself comfortable.

Damn he is sexy, Cindy thought, *and he must be important to have an appointment with this firm.* She noticed that he dressed professional, but not like the older white guys who normally came into the firm. *This guy had...* She couldn't think of the word, then it came to her: *Swag. And he didn't act like he was entitled.* Cindy had never been around a lot of African-Americans. From how they were depicted on television and the internet she vowed to stay away from them, but this guy was definitely different. He was breathtaking. She was instantly turned on by his presence.

Lesson was thumbing through the magazine, caught up in his own thoughts. Lesson had big aspirations. He knew what he wanted, and right now, he wanted to have a company in the magazine that he was holding in his hands.

He knew that he was smart enough to make it in the white professional world. All it took was money to have white America accept him, but Lesson didn't know if fate would derail his plan of trying to raise the capital to start the type of business that would take him to the top.

Lesson said to himself, *I can do this. I'm doing it now. It starts right here, in this office.* Lesson looked up to scan the room. He felt important just being there. Lesson was not there to talk about a pending criminal case—he was there to talk business and contracts.

He noticed Cindy staring at him. He thought he made eye contact with her, but she kept staring, so Lesson waved. *She must've been daydreaming about something pretty important*, Lesson thought.

Cindy realized she was caught staring at Lesson and just smiled. That smile did it. This man's smile was powerful. *Oh my gosh, what is wrong with me?* Cindy thought and her cheeks instantly became flushed. She was embarrassed.

Lesson just sat there smiling at her. *How long was I daydreaming?* she thought. *He must think I'm some type of creep or something.*

Mr. Wise interrupted her thoughts when he waltzed right in the reception area like he owned the place, exuding power. Hell, he did own the place.

"Lesson…good to see you, my boy," Mr. Wise said, dragging each syllable like they were old friends. Mr. Wise grabbed Lesson's hand and gave it a strong shake. Mr. Wise was a large white man who graduated from Harvard University. He had a hard-looking face, and for fifty-four years old, he looked damn good for a man who spent a lifetime with his head buried between chapters of books. He stood at six-foot-one and was 235 pounds with slicked back salt and pepper hair that was slightly balding at the center. He only wore tailor-made black or gray suits that he called his power suits. He was one of the most powerful men that practiced law in Michigan.

Mr. Wise did not respect people—he respected money, and Lesson was an up-and-comer. Ever since Lesson hired the firm, Lesson kept his billing balance paid. Not once did the firm have to remind Lesson of a past due balance. Lesson was paying Wise, Storm, and Associates $650 an hour.

Mr. Wise and Ms. Storm didn't think Lesson could pay that amount per hour, but Lesson fooled them both. As long as Lesson had money, the firm would back him and keep him out of jail, or advise him on all of his legal matters. Most Americans did not understand that white rich Americans stayed in just as much trouble as the average American from the urban communities. The only difference was that white rich Americans either rubbed shoulders with the people who made the laws, or defended the laws. And for the right price, anything could disappear.

"Hello, Mr. Wise," Lesson said.

"Now, Lesson, you know how many times have I told you to call me Anthony," Mr. Wise said. "Come on back to my office, son, and sorry to keep you waiting. I had a client on a conference call and the client always comes first." Anthony said this while wrapping his arm around Lesson and guiding him toward his office. "We have a lot to talk about."

Lesson followed Anthony into his office, passing Cindy on his way. He winked at her, which made her flush again.

As both men entered Anthony's spacious office, a desk area was on one side and an informal seating on the other side, where several Lazy Boys sat facing each other across a fancy coffee table. Anthony assumed the position behind his desk, indicating Lesson's appointment was going to be formal. When both men were comfortably seated, he asked, "Lesson, what can I do for you, son.?"

Lesson exhaled, then spoke using his white voice. "Anthony, I'm in the process of purchasing a twenty-five-unit apartment building near Midtown, right at the center of the revitalization in downtown Detroit. You have the Detroit Lions, Tigers, Pistons, and Red Wings all within five minutes of the building, not to mention Motor City Casino," he said. "Most of the tenants are young, white millennials who are starting families and want to be in the city. Each unit has either two or three bedrooms. I'm pretty much thinking about charging $2,000 or $2,500 per unit each month. Each unit will have access to a state-of-the-art gym, have access to an indoor swimming area and we will also have a parking structure. My question to you, Anthony… Is this a good idea to invest in this type of project?"

"Well, Lesson, you always surprise me. When I first met you, I thought you were out of your league hiring me, but after our one-year anniversary, and you never missing a payment or complaining about me over-billing you, what I realized was that you are an ambitious and focused young man and you could very well become a millionaire ten times over in the next five years or so," Anthony said, leaning back into his chair, twisting an expensive Cuban cigar in his hands. He nodded to a cigar case, silently offering Lesson one. Lesson shook his head no and Anthony continued. "Because of the location, I think it would be a good investment if you had the right person drawing up the contract who would be able to look into the history of the investment. We would mainly want to know if there are any unsettled lawsuits pending. And assuming that the owner would want at least eight million for an investment of this magnitude."

Lesson was digesting all the information. Anthony was right about everything; that's the only reason why Lesson continued to nod his head in agreement.

"I think I'm gonna have to invest about $250,000 into the project after purchase, but besides that, I know the realtor who I'm good friends with and I can get the project for two million," Lesson told Anthony.

Anthony sat up in his chair extremely fast.

"Lesson, you're telling me that you can get a twenty-five-unit apartment building in Midtown for two mil?" he asked. "Hell, I don't care if there are lawsuits pending. I would definitely jump on that immediately, Lesson, because with an investment like that, after you put a little money into it, I could have my people sell it for you for at least five to eight million. Son, when you invest, the trick is to turn a profit and I think—no, I know—that I'm associated with the right people who would want to own that type of real estate. So I'm asking you now, can the firm do the contract for twenty points on a dollar and I'll do the rest, meaning I'll find a buyer and finalize all the documents?"

Lesson was looking at this greedy white muthafucka smiling at him, trying to work him. Lesson's smile was matching Anthony's, without revealing his inner feelings. There was no way that Anthony thought Lesson was stupid. Anthony did not know how Lesson made his money, but he had an idea that Lesson was a drug kingpin. That would be the only explanation as to how Lesson made money.

Lesson wanted to check the shit out of Anthony for trying him, talking that shit about twenty points on a dollar. However, he really could not blame Anthony for trying to sham a stupid deal on Lesson. After all, Anthony was known for winning on every deal. Lesson knew that everything was about money with him. If, for any reason, Anthony thought that Lesson was a low-life nigger, he would never attach his firm to Lesson. But Lesson knew that

Anthony saw potential in him, on top of the dollar signs, and a smart man would not disregard potential.

"You can have the contract, Anthony, but not for twenty points. I'll give you ten points if you have a buyer ready to go for five mil or more. I know that the property would be able to be sold for north of eight mill, so ten-percent of at least eight mil is a very generous piece of my pie. Twelve months after purchase, the property should be available for purchase, and maybe your contact can start a bidding war. How does that sound, Anthony? We can shake on it now, and as soon as I'm ready, I will have my realtor send over the paperwork to complete the deal," Lesson said to the greedy attorney.

Anthony started brushing imaginary lint off of his Gucci suit, trying to appear like this wasn't a big fucking deal he could possibly be closing. *This fucking guy is a smart cookie*, Anthony thought. *Hell, I tried to lock Lesson in for twenty points—that would've been fucking amazing—but ten points is no chump change. Now, close the deal.*

"Lesson, you drive a hard bargain, son, but I think we can take you up on your offer, because Lesson, it's a damn good offer," Anthony said, cheesing.

"So, let's get down to the real business pertaining to why I came to your office," Lesson said, sitting up and getting serious.

Anthony was taken aback. He was confused. The investment property was a big deal, and he thought, *What could possibly be more important and bigger than that?*

"What's up, Lesson? What's on your mind?" Anthony asked.

"Since this conversation is privileged, and you were talking about points on the dollar, I'm thinking of bringing about two to three million in cash to you, maybe even more," Lesson said. "I want to know what kind of deal I can get from you to turn a type of paper into legal currency attached to an account. I need you to clean it and deposit it into an account for me, Anthony. Can you do that, and we can negotiate the points?"

"So you are asking me to break the law, is that what you're asking me, son?"

"Are you talking to me like you're law enforcement, because I find that type of questioning disrespectful, Anthony," Lesson said seriously.

"No…no, son. I'm not saying it like that. Lesson, I just want you to know what you are asking of me." Anthony was trying to clean up his last statement. "I can do it, Lesson, but not for cheap. I can clean up money for you within the hour, no questions asked. The cash will not be of your concern once you bring it into my office. However, what I would ask for is twenty-five points, no questions asked and that's non-negotiable. All you would have to do is give me an account number, but I prefer that you start a new account for that type of funds to be deposited."

"Twenty-five points? That's mighty steep, Anthony, but like you said, no questions asked," Lesson said. "I'll agree with your terms. You have a deal. So for two mil, I would give you $500,000 and for four mil I would give you one mil and so forth, if there's more money—is that correct?" Lesson asked. "I can do that. Let's shake on it, Anthony." Both men shook hands. "Anthony, next time you see me, I will have the funds readily available, if that's okay. So clear out a closet in advance."

"Sure, Lesson. I'll get right on that," Mr. Wise stated.

After Lesson left, Anthony called Brittney into the office. Brittney was the other partner for the firm Wise, Storm, and Associates.

"Did you hear that, Britt?" Anthony asked her.

"Yeah, it appears you were right about Lesson. He is not the typical Black loser. He's extremely ambitious like you said when you brought him on. We can either take home $250,000 apiece or $500,000 without reporting it on our tax returns. Maybe more. What a great year this is turning out to be," she said, smiling. "I just might purchase the vacation home I was planning to buy on the coast of Alabama this year."

Chapter Six

Lesson hit the garage door opener as he pulled into the driveway to his home in Chesterfield Township, Michigan. Chesterfield Township was about thirty to thirty-five minutes outside of Detroit city limits. Lesson put a $75,000 down payment on the $350,000, four-bedroom, five-bathroom ranch-style home two years ago. The house was located in the Emperor Village neighborhood. Lesson still owed over $250,000 on the home. However, his mortgage was so cheap and Lesson was paying the bare minimum monthly.

Lesson pulled his fire-red Dodge Charger all the way in and noticed Ashanti's 2019 black Chrysler Town and Country minivan was in her usual spot. He was glad, because he wanted to see her and his daughter, Lovely.

Lesson had been working extra hard trying to put together the Wal-Mart job and make sure that all the details were ironed out to perfection. Lesson knew that he was neglecting his family, but he felt that to give them the world, something had to be sacrificed. It was either they live in Detroit and he could be home daily, or he worked hard at setting his family's future up. And sometimes that meant staying away from home for days or weeks at a time.

Lesson and his family were the only Black family who lived in a three-mile radius. At first, Lesson was worried about moving his family around so many white folks, especially when his family was from Detroit. But in Chesterfield Township, the white population wasn't racist. They felt that if the Days had enough money to move out there, then they belonged and were accepted.

Lesson's daughter was well-dressed and Lesson did not bump his music too loud. He respected the community and the community respected him. Nobody in his community would ever be able to suggest that Lesson was nothing except a hard-working, family man.

Lovely was a standout soccer player. She also played volleyball and tennis. Ashanti was a soccer mom. She went to all Lovely's sporting events and volunteered at Lovely's school. Every Tuesdays and Thursdays, Ashanti worked out with three other women at L.A. Fitness. Afterward, they went to Rizzoli, their favorite Italian eatery where they could eat out and gossip. Lesson was proud of his family.

Lesson did not have to look over his shoulder out here in the suburbs. He could relax; his neighbors had no clue what his occupation was. They thought he worked for General Motors.

As Lesson got out of the car, he stretched and yawned from being seated for the past hour, driving.

"Daddy, where have you been? You missed my basketball tryouts," Lovely said, looking sad, breaking her father's heart. Lovely had baby-smooth skin, just like when she was first born. To Lesson, she was still the little girl he brought home ten years ago. Her complexion was caramel, just like her mom's. She was tall for her age, standing at five-foot, with thick, long wavy brown hair with black eyes. She looked like a baby version of her mother.

"Baby girl, you know I can't be at all your games. Daddy has to work, baby," Lesson said as he reached down, hugging his daughter.

"Daddy, you never come to none of my games or tryouts, so when you say you can't come to all of my games, what you really mean is that you can't come to none. But if it was LJ, you would come," Lovely said, referring to her older brother.

"That's not true, baby. It just seems like I go to his games more. I didn't have to work when I went to his events, baby."

Lovely was pouting. She had tears in her eyes. Lesson knew how sensitive she could be and that this was her version of a serious conversation. Lovely knew what she said was breaking her daddy's heart, but she didn't care, because he had hurt her as well by missing one too many of her sporting events. Even though she was ten years old, Lesson picked his baby girl up. She wrapped her legs around her father's waist and laid her head on his shoulder. Lesson was rubbing her back as he walked into the kitchen.

"Lesson, put her ass down. She's too big for you to always be babying her like that. She's ten, Lesson," Ashanti said. She had her hands on her hips in an *I'm not joking, Lesson* type of way.

Lesson put Lovely down, but he still had his arm around her shoulder. Lovely shot her mom a death look. She couldn't believe that her mom would stop her dad from showing her attention when he hadn't been home in almost a week.

"Little girl, if you don't fix your face right now, I'm not playing with your little-too-grown ass, Lovely," Ashanti said.

"Daddy, tell her to stop," Lovely said, looking up into her father's eyes with tears in her own.

"Lovely, you know I can't do that or Ima be in trouble, too," Lesson said, squatting down so he could be eye to eye with her. "You are growing up fast, baby girl, and you have to respect your mom and dad equally, okay? I can't always come in to save the day when it comes to your mom, but anybody else I can."

"Lesson, stop, because what you are doing is sending this little girl the wrong message," Ashanti said to her husband.

"Listen, girls," Lesson said and grabbed Ashanti's hand with his right hand and Lovely's hand with his left. "Both of you ladies are my two favorite women in the world and both of y'all have to get along at all times, or it's gonna hurt Daddy, because Daddy can't take sides, okay?" Both ladies nodded. This conversation was more meant for Lovely than it was for Ashanti and Ashanti knew it, so she played along. Lesson still made it appear as if he was talking to both women equally.

"Lesson, Lovely is gonna break some little nigga's heart in the worst way," she said. "That's why I'm trying to break her outta that shit now, Lesson. You spoil her ass entirely too much and she's gonna want some little nigga to do the same things for her ass and he's not gonna be able to live up to those expectations that you set. And when he don't do it or can't do what she wants, it's gonna fuck him up, because she's not gonna want him."

Lesson didn't want to hear that bullshit, but deep down he knew that Ashanti was right.

"Lovely, go finish your homework, then you can come back out here and hang out with your father, because I know he wants to see you."

That was all Lovely needed to hear. She hugged he father and left.

"What up, boo?" Lesson asked Ashanti, grabbing her waist, pulling her to him, then reaching around palming her ass. Ashanti had her hands wrapped around Lesson's neck and kissed him. It felt good that her nigga had his arms wrapped around her.

Ashanti had the fattest ass. That's what drew him to her in the first place. When he saw her walk into the strip club ten years ago, Lesson knew that he had to hit that, but what he didn't know was that he would end up leaving his baby momma for her, after she got pregnant with his daughter. Lesson knew he better stop, because if he didn't, they were gonna fuck right there in the kitchen, or he was gonna make Ashanti drop that sloppy head on him to put his little man back in check.

"You know you can't be playing with me, boo, after over a week without me being up in that, Ashanti."

"Whose fault is that, Lesson? You the one who has been missing, nigga," she said.

"Whose fault is what? Are you talking about me taking care of my family and hustling?" he asked. "Oh, my bad for trying to keep you and Lovely out here in the burbs."

"You can do both, Lesson. It ain't stopped you before," she said, kissing him, sliding a little bit of tongue inside Lesson's mouth in the process. There was something about Ashanti that he couldn't get enough of. It wasn't always about the pussy with Ashanti, but he couldn't front. The pussy played a hell of a role. Ashanti challenged his mind, too. She thought like Lesson and she wanted Lesson to win. She knew if Lesson won then Ashanti won, and their baby won.

Ashanti was twenty-nine years old, five-foot-seven and 170 pounds. She had caramel-black eyes and thick, long wavy brown hair that she either kept braided or in a ponytail. Ashanti was what a street nigga would call a *badddd bitch*. She was another level of fine and knew it.

Ashanti let Lesson go and said, "You need to control your hoes, Lesson. Straight up, nigga."

"What you talking about, Ashanti? You know I don't play with shit like that," he said. "This jealousy shit ain't for me and you, baby, you know I'm not out here disrespecting you."

Ashanti rolled her eyes and thought, *Yeah right, nigga, that's what you saying now, until I catch your ass.*

"Lesson, I'm talking about Nesh," she said, referring to Lesson's baby momma. "That bitch won't let me pick up LJ. I'm tired of the bitch, Lesson, for real. Ima have to beat that hoe's ass again. I'm trying to chill, because the kids are older and I don't want them to see that shit, but I'll fuck that bitch up and you know it, Lesson."

"Chill, baby, you going too hard," he said, wondering what Nesh said, and if it had to do with what happened at Nesh's family barbecue last summer. "You acting like you still a Detroit bitch. Leave that petty shit for them hood-rat hoes. Ima handle her ass when I make it over there," he said, reaching over and kissing her neck.

"*Stopppp*, Lesson," she said in her whiny voice, trying to fake pull away.

"I know what you need, baby. Ima give you some of this dick tonight, once Lovely goes to sleep," he said, licking Ashanti's neck. He knew that was her sport. She pushed him back for real this time, because he was making her pussy too fucking wet playing with her.

"I knew you knew what's wrong with a bitch," she said, smiling. "Nigga, you ain't been handling your business and my toy ain't cutting it no more, Lesson."

"It betta cut it until I have time to lay this dick down," he said, smiling. "Because those are your only options, other than your fingers."

Ashanti rolled her eyes as Lesson headed downstairs to his office in the basement and called LJ.

Chapter Seven

"Me think me can do job good for you. All sizes you request fit, huh? You no fit you, Mr. Jones," the small Filipino clothing designer told Goob. He could barely understand her, and that was pissing him off. She was referring to his uniform not fitting. "Me fix fast, Mr. Jones."

She had introduced herself as Sue Li when Goob first arrived. All her teeth were rotten to the core and he noticed that her hygiene was extremely bad, but the designer pieces that she showed him was enough for him to hire her.

Goob was getting agitated in the small sweat factory. It smelled like used kitty litter, and he felt like he was locked up just being inside there. Sue looked dirty, she smelled dirty, and the stank bitch kept touching him as she talked. He wanted to get the fuck up out of there. Sue had to fix his order on each uniform three times already.

"What the fuck is wrong with this stupid bitch?" Goob mumbled. "I been here all fucking day. I'm giving this bitch all this fucking money. Two-hundred-fifty dollars per uniform, but that's about to change if I'm not out of here in the next hour." He was literally talking to himself.

"Hey, Sue," Goob said, stood up, and started pacing in the small space. If an employee or customer was watching, they would think he had a few marbles loose, or that he was about to nut the fuck up.

"Mr. Jones," Sue said, rushed up to Goob. "See problem?" she asked, touching his arm.

Goob yanked his arm away. "Yeah, see problem," he repeated. "*You* is the fucking problem." He was pointing at Sue. She became scared. Goob was a big man and Sue did not understand the problem.

"Sorry, Mr. Jones. Me help you how?" she asked. Goob realized he was making a scene and scaring the small rotten-mouthed woman.

"Are we almost finished, Sue?" Goob asked as he looked at his watch and tapped it, showing Sue that he was pressed for time.

"Finish thirty minutes, Mr. Jones," Sue said and clasped both of her hands in a praying motion and returned to the back of the shop to finish.

Goob looked around the small sweat shop and was not impressed. The interior and exterior were run down. It reminded him of a third-world business, but he couldn't deny that for what it was worth, they did great work.

He was in St. Louis getting the uniforms for the lick. Lesson wanted him to go as far as he could out of state to get the uniforms so they would not raise suspicion. Goob felt the fourteen hours it had taken him to get to St. Louis was enough distance, and he knew that the Filipino family members who owned the sweat shop were probably all illegals who never would watch the news.

Chapter Eight

"What's up, son?" Lesson asked LJ. He immediately got to the point of the call. "Why haven't you called Lovely and your stepmom?"

Lesson was leaning back in his office chair, shuffling papers around.

"Been busy, Pops, with school and football," he said. LJ was lying in his bed, on his back with his Bluetooth in his ear, tossing a football up in the air.

"You beat anybody in Madden lately?" his father asked. That got lil Lesson's attention and he became excited.

"You know can't nobody beat me except you, dad. I just beat this guy who was supposed to be a pro in Texas." Little Lesson was referring to playing live.

"So again, why haven't you called your little sister, nigga? You know she looks up to you and you telling me this shit about you playing the game," Lesson said. That made his son feel bad.

"But, Dad," LJ responded.

"Naw, don't Dad me. When we get off this phone, you call your sister, boy. You hear me?" Lesson said firmly.

"Okay, I got you, Dad. Ima call her. And Ima call momma Ash, too," he said, referring to his name for Ashanti.

"What was the score?" Lesson asked.

"Huh?" little Lesson asked.

"What was the score on the game you won with the professional player, and who did you have?"

"Twenty-four to fourteen, and I had Detroit Lions. He had Kansas City Chiefs. Dad, he thought he was on to something, because they had that super bad QB Patrick Mahomes who won the NFL MVP last year. Stafford and Kenny Galloday lit him up, Dad," Little Lesson was excited talking about his win.

"You know what, Little Lesson, I just lost a game the other day with Stafford against Aaron Rodgers. Make sure whenever you are up, you keep your foot on whoever you are playing, on their neck," he told his son.

Little Lesson was a good kid. All he wanted to do was play football and play Madden on his Xbox 360. He was just starting to get into girls and they were taking over his mind. Lesson Junior was thirteen years old and already five-foot-nine. Lesson thought his son would outgrow him, because he was shooting up so fast. He was 170 pounds and all muscle. His coach showed him how to work out and he stayed with it. He was light-skinned and he looked exactly like his dad, except he had hazel eyes and his waves were a little deeper.

"You still wearing them skinny jeans, son?" Lesson was throwing a jab at LJ's clothing attire.

"Everybody wears them, Dad. It ain't about them being skinny jeans, Dad. It's about how much they cost. All my jeans are $200 and up. You know I'm one of the freshest guys in the school. They be on me, Pops."

"Who be on you?" Lesson asked his son.

"The girls be on me. I can't walk nowhere. They be touching my waves and always trying to grab my hand, and if I show one girl attention, another one will get jealous," Little Lesson said as he put the ball down and turned onto his side and started brushing his hair as he talked to his father.

"You got you some pussy yet, boy?" Lesson asked him. Lesson Junior got quiet. "Don't get quiet now, when I ask you about fucking. I heard how y'all be taking to each other when you are with your homies. You know you can tell me." Lesson was smiling, because he really didn't know if his son had got himself a little taste, but he knew for a fact that his boy was straight. He wasn't a fruitcake and that's all that mattered.

"Lesson Junior, get yo lazy-ass down here and take this trash out," Lesson heard Nesh say on LJ's end of the line. "And do it now, LJ. Why do I gotta keep telling you over and over to do the same thing."

"Listen to your momma, boy, and put her on the phone when you go down there."

Lesson Junior jumped up and went downstairs. He did not want to hear his mom's mouth, because once she started, she wasn't gonna stop. When he reached her at the bottom of the stairs, he handed her his cell phone.

"Dad wants to talk to you. I was talking to him when you called for me," LJ told his mom. He handed her the phone as he passed her, heading for the kitchen to grab the trash.

"What the fuck you want, Lesson? It's your fault he acts like this, because you are not here in this house raising him."

"What are you talking about? I'm not there, Nesh? I'm always around. I take care of my son. Stop all that bullshit," Lesson told her.

Nesh went to the couch and curled up while talking to her baby daddy. "I'm talking about here, Lesson. I mean, home. You just left your family and started another one, like your first family never existed. I would've given you a daughter, baby," she said seriously.

"Nesh, what has it been, ten-plus years since that bullshit went down? You don't remember what happened when we were twenty and I was giving you the world, but I was young, dumb, and fucked up, and fucked around and got Ashanti pregnant. You knew that shit was a mistake, because I told your ass a million times, but you couldn't handle it. You didn't want to fuck with me no more. You don't remember that shit," he said. "You don't remember all the shit you caused behind your hurt feelings. You fucked a nigga on the other team, and almost got me and your brother killed pillow talking. If it wasn't for Tha Pope showing up when he did, I would've been dead. I'm still fucked up to this day behind how that shit went down. Every time I look in the mirror and see this scar on my stomach, it's a reminder of what happened. You showed me that you wasn't wifey material at that point, because when shit went bad, you gave up on a nigga, and you would've let me die over your hurt feelings. You lied all the way until the end, Nesh, and then you protected the nigga. Tha Pope spared the nigga, because he was a young nigga and Tha Pope said that could've been any hood nigga in that situation. What would you have told my son that happened to his father, if that hoe-ass nigga would've killed me? But you seem to forget about all that every time we have this conversation. So stop with the games, Nesh, and be glad I spared yo ass and I'm still taking care of your ass," Lesson said.

Chapter Nine

Lesson, Learn, and Skeet headed to Eastland Mall to buy Jordans and a fit for the club. Every week, everybody was in 007 Strip Club and niggas had to get fresh to be up in that bitch. There were all types of bitches in that joint, and not just strippers. It was popping and making a name for itself as the hottest spot in the city.

Niggas and bitches were coming from all over, just to get in that muthafucka for a few hours, just to give their money away. Lesson, Learn, and Skeet pulled up to the valet in Lesson's pearl-white 2008 Chrysler 300. Lesson was twenty, Skeet was seventeen, and Learn was fifteen. Lesson had to pay $100 just to get Learn and Skeet in, because they were both underage.

Once inside, they got a table in the cut. Lesson ordered six bottles of Moet and a fifth of Hennessy. When the strippers saw the bottles at the table on display, they came at them in flocks. Lesson, Learn, and Skeet each had $1,500 apiece, all in singles. They were in that bitch having a ball. They were fresh as hell, throwing singles in the air and making it rain, just giving it away. Everybody had two bottles apiece. Lesson knew that once the bottles were gone, they were out of that bitch.

They each had a bad bitch shaking that ass either in front of them or on their lap. Niggas were just relaxing. Lesson looked up and in walked this caramel, thick-ass chick with a fat ass. She had braids in her hair. Lesson got up and made a beeline in her direction. He knew that if he wasn't the first nigga to sweat her, one of these thirsty-ass niggas in this bitch was gonna take her ass to the room, and since he never saw her before, he wanted her.

"What's up, beautiful? Can I be your friend?" Lesson asked Ms. Thick, not yet knowing her name.

Ms. Thick was with two other girls and both of them were laughing. They told Ashanti not to wear those boy shorts going to a club on the east side of Detroit, because of all the attention that they knew that she would get. Ashanti had on a red *bite me* tank top, black boy shorts and all red air max. Her hair was in eight braids that went down to her ass.

"Maybe," Ashanti said to Lesson asking if he could be her friend. "That is, if we can sit at your table and you don't try to fuck me in the club."

"I can guarantee one of the two," Lesson said, looking her up and down licking his lips.

Dayuumm, this light-skinned nigga is fine. Ashanti was thinking about the nigga's offer. She noticed that a lot of niggas were looking at her and her girls, but this nigga whose name she didn't know seemed cool. *Fuck it,* she thought, *we gonna just chill with them.*

"I don't make guarantees, baby, but I'll give you one thing and not the other, because when you don't know what the future brings, how can you guarantee anything?" Lesson asked and winked at her.

"So again, what part won't yo guarantee, sir?" she asked.

"Well, beautiful, there's more than enough room at my table. I got my brother and my nigga with me. Both niggas are cool. If you and your girls are cool with that, the other thing is I'm not gonna try to fuck in the club. It's too much going on already in this bitch, but I can't guarantee that I won't try later on tonight."

The way he was talking was fucking her up. She was feeling this nigga and she didn't even know his name.

"Yes, you can be my friend, at least for now," she said, messing with him. "My name is Ashanti and this is Tia and Staci."

"Hello, ladies. I'm Lesson," he said, shaking Tia's and Staci's hands, but when Ashanti put her hand out, Lesson pulled her into a hug and whispered in her ear, "That was for all these niggas in here. They just saw us hug, so you are pretty much taken while you are in here tonight, Ashanti."

"Umm, Lesson. Can you tell me your real name?" she asked Lesson as they made it to his table.

"My name is Lesson, straight up, and this is my brother, Learn, and my right-hand man, Skeet." Lesson introduced his crew to the girls. Ashanti, Tia, and Staci were all nineteen.

Ashanti couldn't believe his government name was Lesson and he had a brother named Learn.

"So are these really your names, sir?" Ashanti asked again.

"Believe it or not, my dad named us Lesson and Learn, honest to God." He raised his right hand like he was getting ready to go on the stand.

"Damn, that's sexy and original as fuck," she said.

They all partied for a while, then everybody left to go home. Before the night was over with, Lesson had so much fun with Ashanti that he called her at two in the morning and asked if they could hook up.

•••

Thirty days later, Ashanti told Lesson she was pregnant and he knew she wasn't lying, because her pussy was so good he blew all in it.

Lesson was in a relationship with his high school sweetheart, Nesh, at that time and her brother Skeet was Lesson's right-hand man. Lesson and Nesh had been a couple for the past six years, since both were freshmen in high school. When they were seventeen years old, Nesh got pregnant with their now three-year-old son, Lesson Junior.

Lesson knew he couldn't keep the news from Nesh, so he broke the news about Ashanti being pregnant. Lesson tried to tell Nesh it was a mistake, and he wasn't fucking with Ashanti like that, and how he barely knew her, but Nesh tripped all the way the fuck out.

Lesson had never seen her act like that. Nesh told Lesson to make Ashanti have an abortion, and when Lesson didn't do it, Nesh started fucking with this nigga from around the way, who the streets called Savage Keith. Lesson knew Savage Keith from a distance, but not from up close. They hung out in two different circles, but they shared a mutual respect for each other—at least that's what Lesson thought.

Both niggas were known throughout the city. Lesson would be in the club and Savage Keith would salute him when he was with Nesh, but the truth was, Savage Keith was really saluting Nesh and the joke was on Lesson. As Nesh continued to fuck Savage Keith, she started pillow talking and gave Savage Keith all the details of Lesson's weed house that was doing $2,500 a day. Unbeknownst to Nesh, she had given Savage Keith the blueprint to rob her baby daddy.

Savage Keith and his crew robbed Lesson's weed joint right after Lesson dropped off a shipment of ten pounds. As Lesson was leaving, Savage Keith and another nigga who was masked up forced Lesson back in the house; it caught Skeet and Mac off-guard. Savage Keith had the other masked man tie Skeet and Mac up. Lesson gave them the pounds, but Savage Keith wanted more. Nesh told him that Lesson had the bag and Savage Keith wanted it.

"Where's the rest of the chicken, bitch-ass nigga?" he asked, pointing the AK-47 at Lesson's head.

"That's it, bro. Take it. You got that," Lesson said.

"Yeah, nigga. I know I got that, but I want the rest of that, nigga. So come off it or Ima smoke yo ass, nigga."

"Nigga, you can have the bread. This is it, my nigga. I spent it on the package," Lesson said.

"Nigga, you got at least ten bands in here somewhere. Where is it at?" he asked.

When Lesson heard that statement, he thought about Nesh. He always joked with her that if his spot ever got raided, he would offer the raid team ten bands to let them go. Lesson told Nesh he always kept at least $10,000 in that bitch.

"Shoot that nigga, fam," the other masked man said. "Shoot that nigga, and let's get the fuck outta here."

Tha Pope was riding past Lesson's spot to tell him that his homie said he would front him ten pounds on the strength of Tha Pope, if he would add an extra C-note to the ticket for each joint. As Tha Pope pulled up, he noticed the front door to Lesson's spot was open—and that was odd, being that Lesson just got a shipment in of some fire weed. As Tha Pope was walking up to the door, he heard niggas talking crazy, putting the press on his son. All Tha Pope heard was "Shoot that nigga."

Tha Pope pulled his .45 Smith and Wesson from behind the small of his back and let it holla. Boom…boom…boom. Tha Pope started shooting in the house and hit a masked man in the left shoulder. The masked man started firing back recklessly. Boom…boom. The gunfire scared Savage Keith and he pulled the trigger by mistake—boom—and Lesson yelled. Savage Keith had shot Lesson in the stomach at point-blank range.

Savage Keith and the masked man took off running. Tha Pope could've run them two young niggas down, but he was more concerned with Lesson's condition. He heard him yell and knew he was hit. When Tha Pope came inside to see how much damage was done, he saw Lesson on his side, bleeding.

"Hang on, Lesson," Tha Pope said and cut Skeet and Mac out. They carried Lesson to Tha Pope's black 2008 CL 500 Benz. Skeet and Mac didn't ride with Tha Pope to the hospital, because they had to shut down the spot and clear the guns out of that bitch.

On the way to the hospital, Lesson told his pops that Nesh set him up. He knew it was her, because they were looking for ten bands. Lesson told his father that he thought she did it, because he got another bitch pregnant. He didn't know all of the details on how she help set him up, but he planned to find out. And when he did, somebody was going to die.

Chapter Ten

"Fuck you, Lesson. You don't run shit, nigga. I can find a nigga who's better than you anytime I want to," she spat back at him. I'm still a bad bitch nigga, and you know it."

"Bitch, when you do that, Ima have my son over here with me," he said.

"Bitch, I don't give a fuck what you do, but Ima tell you like this: Ain't no muthafuckin' way you gonna play house with my son in the same house," he said.

"Listen, Nesh, I didn't call for this same bullshit. I called because you need to cut that shit out with Ashanti. You can be on bullshit with me to a certain extent, but I'm not about to let you disrespect her or Lovely by keeping Lesson Junior away from them."

"Lesson, you talking all that high and mighty shit, but when you was in this pussy over the summer, you wasn't talking that shit about Ashanti then," Nesh said. "But it'll break your little precious Ashanti's heart for her to find out that you was still fucking the shit out of your baby momma, ain't that right, Lesson?" she asked.

This bitch think she's got me in the bag, Lesson thought. He knew that he didn't want her to break the news to Ashanti, because that would crush Ashanti, coming from a bitter bitch like Nesh. So Lesson had to figure out a way to tell Ashanti on his own time that he slipped up and fucked Nesh a few months back. Lesson was feeling like deja vu was happening all over again. He had gone through this same shit ten years ago and it left him with a hole in his stomach.

Lesson sat in his chair, shaking his head, because Nesh was right. He had fucked up by fucking her back in the summer, after her family's barbecue.

Lesson reminisced on that night. Lesson had shown up to Nesh's family barbecue at Metro Park. Her whole family was there, as well as everybody who was anybody who knew Nesh's mom and pops. Everybody loved Nesh's family. Even though he wasn't kicking it with Nesh like that anymore, Lesson was still cool with her mom and dad. They were like his extended family, because Lesson Junior was their grandson. Lesson had known them most of his life. Nesh's little brother, Skeet, was Lesson's right-hand man, still to this day.

They had four barrels cut into barbecue grill. All over the park, you could smell food being barbecued. They had beef and pork ribs, steaks, chicken, hamburger patties, and dogs on the grill. The music was lit and everybody was having a good time. Everybody was dancing and drinking. Lesson was drinking Rémy 1738. He was tipsy and lounging in a chair, talking shit to everybody he knew.

Nesh walked over to Lesson, and asked, "You want some more, baby?" Nesh was referring to the glass in Lesson's hand, because it looked like it needed a refill.

"Hell yeah, baby. Thanks, Nesh."

Nesh grabbed the neck of the chilled bottle from the ice igloo and filled Lesson's red cup to the brim. It wasn't every day that she got to kick it with Lesson. After what went down ten years ago, she was lucky Skeet and Tha Pope didn't kill her for what she did to Lesson, but nobody understood her side of the story. She didn't know that Savage Keith was planning to fuck over her baby daddy and was using her during her emotional stage. All she wanted to do was fuck off on Lesson like he had been doing for years. Nesh simply wanted to get her lick back, but shit spiraled out of control and Lesson almost died after being shot by Savage Keith during a robbery. Lesson hated her for years, so for him to be with her right now, just relaxing, reminded her of when they were younger.

"What you trying to do, Nesh? Get me drunk or something?" Lesson joked with her.

"Maybe, nigga, that way you won't be so uptight. I just want you relaxed for a change."

Nesh was wearing an all-white Burberry cat suit that left nothing to the imagination. She had on fourteen-carat gold hoop earrings, a gold bracelet, and a gold watch. The gold bracelet on her ankle set off the all-white and gold Air Force Ones. Nesh was a bad bitch and she knew it. She definitely didn't have to try hard to look the part. Her weave was whipped to the core and she was having a good time. The apple CÎROC was hitting her just right. It had her extremely mellow and she was slow winding like a snake in front of Lesson.

Lesson could not take his eyes off of her. He was thinking about when they were younger and how she used to be his bitch. Everybody who knew him knew Nesh, and everybody who knew Nesh knew Lesson.

It started getting dark and Nesh was still dancing and the snake was pulling Lesson in.

"Lesson, you remember this?" Nesh asked and sat on Lesson's lap and gave him a lap dance.

It was pitch black outside and nobody could see the seduction in the dance, but Lesson could feel the pressure from his manhood rising, and it felt good to him. Lesson was beyond tipsy, but not to the point where he couldn't drive if he had to get out of there.

As everybody was leaving, Nesh asked Lesson to take her home. When they arrived at her house, Nesh and Lesson were caught up in a debate about who was the better president, Donald Trump or Barack Obama. Lesson wasn't ready for it to end, so he came inside.

As soon as they walked through the door, Lesson realized he had made a mistake, because Nesh had his ass up against the wall, kissing, tonguing the fuck out of him, and massaging his dick from the outside of his pants.

"I know you missed this pussy, Lesson. You can tell me, I won't tell on you," Nesh said, already knowing the answer. Lesson had his hands all over Nesh's ass, squeezing each cheek. He had to slap that ass a few times, being that it was so phat. *Slap...slap...slap.* Nesh's ass was bouncing like it had a mind of its own.

"Mmmm, Lesson," Nesh was moaning into Lesson's mouth with each slap.

The tingle from the slaps was making her pussy moist. Lesson reached and pulled the straps of the body suit down off her shoulders, and the farther it came down, the more exposed Nesh's body became. Her 34C cups were staring him in the face. Her black nipples were as hard as marbles.

Lesson took each breast into his mouth, one at a time, while squeezing the other nipple. Lesson remembered that was Nesh's thing and she was going crazy from Lesson's touch. He pulled the entire suit off, but one leg got caught on her right foot. Lesson pulled off his shirt as Nesh was opening his belt, pulling at his jeans. She had his dick in her hand and was massaging his monster. It was hard as fuck in her grip.

Nesh got on her knees and took Lesson in her mouth. She missed sucking Lesson's dick and he missed sexing her. When she took his balls into her mouth, Nesh started making suction noises. He lifted up on his tippy toes, because he had to stop her or he would bust. He snatched Nesh up by her hair and bent her over the couch and started fucking the shit out of her doggy-style until he came.

"I love you, Lesson," Nesh said as he stood behind her pounding away.

"I love you, too, Nesh," he said as he busted into her.

Chapter Eleven

Lesson knew he was fucked and he didn't know how to tell Ashanti that he had slipped up. Lesson thought that if he didn't think about that night, when he fucked Nesh after the barbecue, that maybe Nesh would let the shit go.

They both enjoyed their one-night stand and Lesson always took good care of her. He had made sure that Nesh didn't want for shit, but he also knew that he wasn't supposed to fuck her ass ever again, because of what happened in the past. Not to mention what would happen if Ashanti found out.

This bitch Nesh literally almost got me killed and I still gave into the pussy, Lesson thought. He knew that was the difference between him and Tha Pope. When Tha Pope said he wasn't doing something, he never back-tracked.

Now this bitch was acting crazy, and her antics were getting worse as the months passed.

"I gotta fix this shit," he said out loud to nobody in particular, but Nesh had heard him.

"What do you have to fix, Lesson?" Nesh said to him.

"Listen, bitch. Cut all this bullshit out, before I come over there and fuck you up. Don't act like I won't fuck yo ass up, Nesh. What happened to you, the old you?" Lesson asked. "You had a nigga fooled when we was younger, acting all ladylike. Or was this how your attitude always had been? Or did me getting Ashanti pregnant really fuck your head up? You know what, don't even respond, because I don't give a fuck. Listen, Nesh, don't fuck up a good

83

thang you got going for yo ass over your mouth. I already be doing too much for your ass for you to be acting like this every time you don't get your way, Nesh."

"Lesson, if you didn't want to be with me, then why you fuck me in the first place? Why did you tell me you love me? You fucked me without a condom on, knowing the consequences, Lesson. What if I'm pregnant? You made me love you again, nigga," she said.

"Nesh, stop playing. All them niggas you've fucked over the years, and you talking about one little fuck we had while we both was drunk? Bitch, I barely nutted in you, and if you was pregnant, you would've told the world. Get your shit together, Nesh, because you got me fucked all the way up. I got too much on my mind right now to be playing baby momma games, you hear me?"

"Lesson, when are you coming over here? We need to talk, bae, I'm serious," she said.

"I got a few business moves I have to make in the next few weeks. After that, we can talk, but for now, chill out with that bullshit, Nesh."

As they were talking, Lesson was on the computer punching a few keys.

"Drop my son off Monday over to his grandma's and Ashanti will come pick him up. Lesson Junior needs to be spending more time around his baby sister, Nesh," Lesson said. "Ashanti will take him to school for the next two weeks and when I bring him home, we can kick it, okay?" he said. "Check your account, Nesh. I just put three bands in your account. Go get your hair and nails done. Relax your mind a little bit, baby, all right?"

"Lesson, when you come over, I need you to look at my car and maybe take it to the shop," Nesh said, referring to the 2018 Chevy Malibu Lesson brought her last year straight off the lot after he hit one of his licks. "The service light keeps popping up then going off."

"I got you, Nesh. I'll do it when I come over there, but if the problem becomes major, take it to the dealership on your own and charge it to my account," Lesson told her.

Chapter Twelve

When Lesson and Learn walked into the truck shop on E. Jefferson, they were instantly amazed by the shop's progression. Bradley and Stevie had really fixed the place up and brought all of their equipment.

"Bro, you always know how to find the right people," Learn said.

"Bro, don't give me so much credit. We have to see how far along the truck is," Lesson said. In his hand, he held a sealed manila envelope. "We only have about six days before showtime, and we don't have time to spare for any major setbacks."

The new owners named the place E. Jefferson Trucking Service. In the eight days that Stevie and Bradley worked on the big truck, they also transformed the inside of the old building into a real truck shop. They already had other trucks lined up inside and out of the shop—it appeared to be a hit. These white boys knew their way around every make and model of all diesel trucks. If a truck was broken and someone brought it to E. Jefferson Trucking Service, they would get it back on the road in record time.

Lesson noticed Stevie standing on a ladder, the majority of his body leaned inside the open hood of an old big rig BMW semi-truck. He was tightening a nut with a long-handled socket wrench. Stevie had a dirty light-colored rag hanging out of his back pocket and his pants were hanging halfway past the crack of his ass.

"That's a sad sight to look at," Learn mumbled. "Bro, when do you think was the last time that muthafucka took a shower and washed his ass? I can smell his ass from over here." They walked up on Stevie. Stevie was consumed by the task at hand. Lesson tapped Stevie on his leg to get his attention.

"Whattttt? Can't you see I'm working here?" Stevie yelled, annoyed.

"You busy, dude?" Lesson asked.

When Stevie heard Lesson's voice, he cocked his head to the side and said, "Lesson, is that you?"

"The one and only," Lesson said.

Stevie jumped to attention and pulled his head from under the hood. Stevie started descending the ladder. Once he made it to the bottom, he reached out to shake Lesson's hand.

"What's up, boss?" he asked.

Lesson took one look at the out stretched hand and saw that it contained dirt, grit, and grease. Lesson balled up his fist and reached out to bump Stevie's hand. Stevie realized how dirty his hands were.

"My bad, dude," he said and bumped Lesson's knuckles. Stevie was smiling. "Follow me, gentleman, to our paint room. I have something to show the both of you. We named this section of the shop our panic room. We both agreed that any truck that comes in this room has a deadline for completion."

As they were walking in the direction of the panic room, Stevie realized he hadn't greeted Learn.

"What's up, dude," Stevie said to Learn and Learn nodded back. "You guys are going to be impressed, believe me. Bradley is working on the truck in the back, while I take care of the new orders in the front of the shop."

Stevie opened the double doors leading to the panic room, and the big truck sat in the middle of the floor, looking completely different compared to eight days ago. Bradley had on his welding glasses and sparks were flying all over the place, mainly jumping off the floor. There was a burning odor and smoke filled the room. There was a crackling sound from multiple pieces of steel being welded. Bradley was welding the kickboard onto the step of the big truck, so a person could either get into the truck or get out. When Stevie touched Bradley's shoulder, he jumped.

"You fat motherfucker, you scared the bejesus out of me." Bradley noticed Lesson and Learn. "What's up, guys." Bradley put down his welder. "Would you like a tour?" They both nodded. "Okay, Lesson, the body was completely rusted and busted, so we stripped this bad boy literally down to its bones and welded every inch of the truck. Literally, everything you see is relatively new patchwork."

Bradley was walking around pointing at sections of the body on the truck where they had done work. Lesson examined each detail that was shown to him.

"It definitely helped that you said we can buy as much materials as needed to get the truck back on the road, because we needed everything we could get," he said. "The picture you showed us of how the inside of an armored truck should look was extremely helpful. We welded and painted a security gate and placed it inside. Now, Lesson, I don't know if you will be impressed or unimpressed, but we didn't have a lot of examples to work with when we started. So we used the photos you gave us as an example and tried to do our best. However, we think that we were able to duplicate the gate as close to the photos as possible."

Bradley opened the back of the cab and Lesson was dumbfounded. Even Learn was left speechless. The truck looked like a duplicate of a Brinks Security transport currency truck. Lesson knew that this truck could've fooled him—that's how good their work was.

Now it was Stevie's turn to impress, and without a doubt, that's what he planned to do. He pointed to the LED lights in the front and back of the truck and showed Lesson how he welded the bumper on the front of the truck. He lifted up the hood and showed how he changed all the wires and did another tune-up.

"Listen to this, Lesson," Stevie said as he climbed into the truck and cranked it up.

Tink...tink...tink...tink...vroom. Lesson could not believe this was an older diesel truck. The engine hum was extra low, almost silent, without giving it gas.

Next, he showed Lesson the new tires he had installed. Two in the front and four in the back.

"These tires are pothole-proof," he told Lesson. "You won't need new tires until 2021, Lesson, depending on how much driving you do. So what do you think?"

Both mechanics stood nervously next to each other and waited on Lesson to respond. Learn was amazed. He couldn't believe how these two greasy white boys had done it. They definitely were talented.

Learn knew that these two guys would be in business a long time and he figured that Lesson knew the same thing. That was the only reason why Lesson would buy these guys a building. It was the right move on Lesson's part. He scratched their backs and they worked hard for Lesson.

"Good work, guys. I can't complain. You did a fantastic job. That's why I hired you guys. And I just want to say thank you. I really believe that we can meet this deadline," Lesson said. "What do you think, Stevie? All you have to do is paint it, right?"

"Yep, Lesson, we're pretty much finished, once Bradley finishes whatever he's doing."

"Yeah, Lesson, this is it. I'll be done in the next ten minutes," Bradley said.

Lesson opened the manila envelope that contained several pictures he had printed out. He pulled them out and handed them to Stevie and Bradley.

"You see these details right here?" Lesson asked both mechanics. They nodded in unison. "I want the paint job exactly like this." He was pointing to the Brinks sign. "You will pretty much have to duplicate the entire paint job, down to the exact color. I don't want the color to be lighter or darker. It has to be the same, you understand? And nothing extra, guys, okay?"

"Sure, Lesson," Stevie said. "So we have two days, is that right?"

"Yes, that's correct. Can you guys finish the paint job within two days?" he asked. "And will it be dry in that timeframe?"

"How about three days? We can do it in two days, but we want perfection. We know that you don't settle for just good enough work, so can we get an extra day?" Bradley asked.

Lesson was anticipating a delay and one day was doable. "Yeah, we can do it, but Ima need it on Friday. I know that's a busy day, right after the holiday, and it being the holiday weekend, but a job is a job until it's complete, right, fellas?" he asked, giving Stevie the envelope. He watched him take the photos out. Bradley took them in his hand and placed them back inside manila envelope.

"Sure, Lesson, no problem. Lesson, the paint job is gonna cost about two thousand dollars on top of the seventeen thousand we already used out of the twenty thousand you gave us for parts."

Bradley reached inside his wallet to give Lesson the thousand dollars that was left.

"Y'all can keep that," Lesson said, referring to the final thousand dollars. "You guys earned it, and I'm not taking no for an answer, okay? Guys, go buy some new rags and some uniforms with E. Jefferson Trucking Service printed on them. It'll make you guys look more professional, and make sure you get the unis with your name printed on them as well."

"Didn't think of that one, Lesson. That's a good idea," Bradley said.

Chapter Thirteen

Rocci was in her kitchen fixing the food for her two sons. She hadn't seen them the past few weeks and knew something was going on. That would be the only explanation why they hadn't come home to visit.

She started to go to Lesson's house, way out in Chesterfield Township, but that was too far for her to be driving. What made the drive worse was the fact that she would have to drive back home. There was no way she was going to do that, unless it was for an emergency. She knew from the conversation she had with Ashanti that Lesson was out handling business. Even she was missing Lesson.

So Rocci decided to let him be so he could focus on whatever it was that he was working on. Rocci had a special place in her heart for Lesson's wife. That girl there kept her oldest boy grounded. She knew that Lesson really was in love with that girl. That was the reason why Lesson moved her and Lovely to the suburbs to get them all away from the city life.

Lesson had told his mom that he didn't want Lovely to be raised the way he was raised, and he wanted her to go to better schools to have a better chance in life. Rocci didn't agree with Lesson's ideology about Detroit being that bad of a place to raise kids. Hell, Rocci was raised in Detroit, as well as all her family. Besides, the family who moved out of town; Lesson was the only person she knew who moved away to the suburbs.

She couldn't deny how it had done wonders for her daughter-in-law Ashanti. She noticed that Ashanti was thriving in the suburbs. She didn't even go to the clubs anymore, and if you knew Ashanti over the last ten years, even Lesson couldn't keep her out of the clubs. But that had change once she and Lesson moved.

She was now a part of so many social groups. They pretty much had consumed the majority of her time, and those white ladies accepted Ashanti. They had never met anyone like her. She was definitely the life of the suburban mommy movement.

Rocci was definitely impressed. *Damn, I should've told Lesson to bring Ashanti and Lovely over*, she thought. Her grandbaby loved her and she loved her back.

Nesh called earlier in the day and Rocci told her to bring LJ over. Nesh had told her that Lesson wanted her to drop LJ off on Monday, but Nesh said she would bring him today. Nesh asked if Lesson was coming. Rocci said he would be there later. Nesh said she needed to talk to Lesson, but Rocci shut that shit down with the quickness. She told her that after she dropped LJ off, she had to keep it moving. She would not be allowed to see her baby's father today.

Rocci knew that Lesson didn't want to see Nesh right now, and Momma Rocci would acknowledge her son's request. Rocci thought they had been getting along for the past year, but something had happened recently, and she was going to figure out what the problem was. Her grandbaby was too important to her to be in the middle of any type of drama.

Rocci knew that she could never deal with what went down between Nesh and Lesson, because the drama ended up getting Lesson shot. Rocci thought Lesson was going to die—and when he pulled through, her baby was left with an ugly scar that covered most of his chest. She had to nurse him back to life and fatten him up again.

After Rocci found out that Nesh had set her son up over Ashanti being pregnant, she asked her baby's father, Tha Pope, to kill Nesh, but Tha Pope said if Lesson wanted Nesh dead that was his call, not hers. Lesson told his father to let her live. That's the only reason Nesh was alive today and Rocci knew it.

Over the past few years, Nesh and Rocci became cool again. Nesh wanted the relationship that they once had when she and Lesson were going through high school together. Rocci always looked at Nesh like the daughter she never had, and she knew how much Nesh loved Lesson.

Rocci never wanted to believe that Nesh wanted Lesson dead, but a line was crossed when Lesson got shot by Savage Keith and he almost died because of Nesh's carelessness and insecurities. Rocci didn't blame Nesh for being hurt, but she blamed Nesh for Lesson getting shot.

Nesh eventually told Rocci her version of story about how Lesson was shot, and Rocci believed her. Hell, Tha Pope believed her as well. Lesson was their son and Lesson chose Ashanti, even after it came out that she didn't intentionally set Lesson up. So when a side had to be picked, they would pick Ashanti, because that's who he had chosen to spend the rest of his life with.

Rocci knew that Lesson still had strong feeling for Nesh and it was only a matter of time before the pot boiled over, and Nesh and Ashanti got into it again over Lesson. Rocci didn't like what was brewing. Because LJ's mom was Nesh, and Lovely's mom was Ashanti, Rocci didn't want the children to take sides.

So when Rocci called Nesh and told her to bring her grandson so all her men could be together, it broke Nesh's heart. Nesh knew that back in the day, Rocci would've forced Lesson to talk to her, but since Lesson was shot, Nesh felt like an outcast to the family that she was once a part of. Nesh didn't realize there was nothing Rocci could do. Rocci's hands were tied and they'd stayed tied for the past ten years. Lesson told his mom what he wanted and she wasn't going against him.

Rocci was fixing the meal that her boys loved growing up: greens, candied yams, cornbread, potato salad, and smoked ribs with warm carrot cake for dessert. She was almost finished when Tha Pope arrived.

Rocci loved Tha Pope, but that nigga couldn't keep his dick in his pants. Tha Pope had been cheating on Rocci since before her boys were born. Tha Pope never got caught slipping, but Rocci was like a private investigator and she knew he was cheating. She chased every bitch she could away from Tha Pope, but that still didn't stop him.

After her boys were grown, they kicked it off and on. Sometimes she would be in bullshit relationships that never lasted, because Tha Pope was always around. Most men felt threatened by Tha Pope, so after a while, they would leave. Tha Pope kept a few bitches to get him off, but he always came back to Rocci.

She heard him pulling up in his 2019 yellow Stingray Corvette. She opened the door for him, even though he had a key. When Tha Pope walked in he smelled his woman's cooking and it made him fall in love with her all over again.

"What's up, Rocci," he asked, hugging her and kissing her on her lips. She let him kiss her for a second and pushed him back.

"Nigga, don't be kissing me like that. We know your lips probably been between some young bitch's legs earlier today," she said, shaking her head.

"Rocci, yo ass is something else. So you gonna go there, for real? That's how we gonna start this day off? Come here, girl," he said and pulled her back into his arms. She didn't resist and he kissed her again. It don't matter what I do with my mouth, Rocci. On my own time, it's my mouth. What won't change is my feelings for you, baby. You will be my heart forever," he said. "Shit, Rocci, ain't no telling what you been doing with your mouth, baby. You had your share of a few niggas over the years."

"I have had a few niggas and fuck buddies, Pope, but it's your fault that I was put in that position. I was perfectly happy with you and you fucked it up," she said.

Rocci was fifty years old, the same age as Tha Pope. She was five-foot-six and 180 pounds and had a fat, round perfect ass that was still popping to this day. She didn't work out. She was simply gifted with a body of a thirty-five-year-old. Rocci kept her makeup on point and ate healthy. Not a strand of hair was out of place. She kept her hair in short hairstyles and her complexion was the color of olive oil. When they say Black don't crack, they were referring to Rocci. Rocci wasn't aging like the Susan Summers, Lisa Rays and The Stacy Dashs. She was blessed and the young hoes stayed asking her for beauty advice. Rocci would tell them what worked for her was not drinking, popping pills, and doing hard drugs.

"Pope, let me finish this food," she whined. The more Tha Pope touched her, she would melt, and she had to back the fuck up. Tha Pope was looking like a light brown snack that she could eat at any moment, and would not stop eating once she started. She knew why so many bitches stayed on her baby daddy's line, but that shit became too much for her as she got older. Tha Pope didn't realize that all those twenty-five and thirty-year-old bitches he was fucking were making her feel like she had to compete, and instead of competing, she just stopped eating her snack.

"What are you doing over here anyway, Pope? I was waiting on Lesson and Learn," she said. "I was fixing all this food for them. I didn't know that you were going to show up."

"Baby, there's not enough food for the daddy of the family?" he asked, disappointed.

"I'm not saying that, Pope. I just didn't know you was coming over. You need to start checking on me a little more," she said.

"I'm still in the same spot I always been in for the past twenty years. Shit has been a little busy lately, Rocci. I'm in the process of working a job right now, so I'm trying to stay focused."

"Are the boys in on the job, Pope?" she asked. "Because they have been busy lately, too."

"Is that what they told you?" he asked, trying to deflect the question and see if they had told their mom about the lick in progress.

"Pope, stop playing with me. Those are my boys as well as yours, and if something was to happen, you would expect me to try to pick up the pieces and hold shit together, and I would be all alone, Pope, so tell me, are they in on the job?" She was still in his arms and it was feeling good to her. Tha Pope liked having his girl asking him questions and act like she still was in love with him after all the shit he put her through over the years.

"Rocci, those boys are grown men and they are both smarter than I have ever been."

"You still have influence over them, Pope. Those are your sons," she said.

"That's true, but not entirely. I stay in their business, because I love them two young niggas, and I do jobs mainly with Lesson, because I try to look for a weakness in the boy's planning, but Lesson doesn't make mistakes, Rocci. He's so smart I'll be glad when he hit it big and jump in the league with those rich white people, you understand," he said. "So when you say that I control shit, I really don't, baby. I told Lesson when he was younger, if he could figure out why the streets call me Tha Pope, then I would let him run shit, and he figured it out, baby. That's when I knew how smart he was. I work for Lesson, baby," Tha Pope told her, which shocked her at first. "Baby, Lesson respects my opinion, so he will ask me for my opinion about a lot of things that he thinks I'm more familiar with than he is. Don't be scared, Rocci. This job that Lesson put together has been planned out. Every T has been crossed and every I has been dotted. This is one of smoothest and safest jobs I've been a part of in the last twenty-five years."

"Pope, who told you to come over here?" she asked.

"Learn told me that you was cooking and to show up. He told me that they were coming at around six p.m. That's why I'm here early so I can spend a few minutes with you before the boys come over," he told her, grabbing her ass.

They began kissing harder. Pope was thinking about a quickie and Rocci was thinking the same. Learn walked into the kitchen, followed by Lesson.

"Look at their asses, bro. For two people who say they don't want to be together, every time they are alone together, it's the same shit. They always booed up," Learn said. "What up, Mom? You want us to come back in about twenty minutes?"

"Yeah, Pops, you want us to come back?" Lesson asked Tha Pope, smiling.

"Nigga, if it wasn't for us being booed up, y'all wouldn't be in this kitchen having this conversation," Rocci said to Learn, breaking away from Tha Pope and going to hug her youngest son. She gave him a kiss.

He tried to pull back, saying, "Hold up, Mom. I don't know where your mouth's been." Learn was joking, shaking his head and laughing like a baby trying not to be kissed.

"Boy bye," she said and kissed him anyway.

"What's up, Momma?" Lesson asked, hugging and kissing her. "It smells good in here. If we didn't show up in time, Pops was probably gonna make you burn the food." Lesson turned around and threw a jab at his father that Tha Pope slipped easily. Learn was standing next to Rocci laughing.

"Lesson, you still too slow, young boy. I'll still be able to tap that ass when I'm fifty-five. At that point you can have that title. I still got it like pretty boy Floyd Mayweather," Tha Pope said.

"You sure you not talking about Roy Jones, Jr., Pops? He still thought he had it, too, but kept getting knocked out in the end," Lesson said, laughing at his own joke. "Back in the day, Roy Jones was that nigga with them gloves on."

"For real, Lesson? You gonna compare me to Roy Jones, Jr., late in his career? That's how you gonna do play your father?" Tha Pope asked, looking hurt. "Father Time catches up with everybody.

Look at Shaq and Kobe. Nobody would've ever thought them two niggas would've gotten old. Shit, it just caught up with Carmelo."

"I don't know about Carmelo, Pops. I think they are freezing him out like they did Allen Iverson," Lesson said.

"I got title for five more years," Tha Pope said and threw two quick jabs that looked more like Mayweather compared to Roy Jones Jr.

"All right, Pops, you got that," Lesson said.

"Grandma, it smells good in here," LJ said, appearing out of nowhere, holding a duffel bag that contained his clothing. As he walked into the kitchen, everybody started hugging him. Lesson was watching the love his family was showing to his son. It reminded him of when he was younger.

"What's up, Dad?" LJ asked as he went to his father and hugged him tightly. "I called Lovely. Ima start calling her more. I was slipping, Dad. We supposed to go to the movies next week and watch that new *Lion King* movie."

"Good, son. She loves you and you gotta protect her. She getting older and the boys are starting to like her," Lesson said.

Learn looked at his nephew and asked him, "Do you want to play the game?"

"I don't know, Uncle. You can't play that good," he said. "And it's not gonna be fun if I slap your team around and knock you off by thirty or more," LJ said.

"Nigga, go out to my car and grab the black bag with game in it." He tossed LJ his keys. "If I lose, LJ, I'll let you drive my whip," Learn said, referring to his identical 2019 SRT Dodge Charger, the same make and model as Lesson's, except his was all white.

"You might as well just take that boy driving right now, because Lesson Junior is about to beat the brakes off of you," Tha Pope said.

Everybody knew that Learn was gonna be mad as hell all throughout dinner after losing to his nephew. Twenty minutes later, Rocci called everybody into the dining room.

"My controller needs new batteries, that's why I lost so bad, because of the delayed reaction," Learn said as they sat down.

"Dad, what did you tell me when I get the up on my opponent?" LJ asked his father and answered the question at the same time. "You said not to take my foot off of their necks, right?"

Tha Pope was smiling. All his boys were shit-talkers and he knew that Lesson Junior had the family genes. He was already a serious shit-talker at thirteen, just like Lesson and Learn. And they all got it from Tha Pope.

"How much you beat your uncle by?" Tha Pope asked his grandson.

"Forty-four, and Uncle Learn cut the game off on me. I was going for fifty," LJ said, laughing.

Learn was hot. "If you keep it up, I'm gonna make you sit on my lap when we dive the Charger."

"I'm not sitting on your lap, Uncle Learn," he said. "I'm about to jump on I-94 when I get finished eating."

"Boy, you are not about to drive on the freeway. Learn, do you hear me? Don't let my grandson drive on the freeway at thirteen years old," Rocci said.

"You heard her, LJ. And when grandma speaks, it's final," Learn said, laughing.

After the meal, Lesson Junior helped his grandma clear the table and get the kitchen back together. Tha Pope, Lesson, and Learn went downstairs to chill on the couches in the basement. Tha Pope poured both his sons three fingers of Hennessy apiece, and they toasted to success.

"Lesson, what's the final plan, son?" Tha Pope asked.

The three men assembled around a large drawing pad on an easel that Lesson set up. He ran them through their individual roles once more. Lesson explained to the men that he would do the same for Goob and Jameer, once they completed their task. He told the Tha Pope that Goob should be back soon from picking up the uniforms in St. Louis.

"He called me not too long ago and said the unis are all the way on point. He should be back in Michigan within the next few hours," Lesson said.

Learn cut in to tell Tha Pope about the big truck. "It's crazy, Pops. This nigga, Lesson, is a genius. He found these white boys who do professional work. The truck is gonna look identical to a real Brinks truck. Pops, Lesson had those white boys duplicate the truck on the inside and out. It fooled me, Pops. Wait until you see it for yourself," he said. "You will be impressed as well. The only thing that's left to do is have Jameer pick up the guns. Each weapon had its serial number removed. None could ever be traced."

Lesson felt that they would not physically have to use the weapons, but would need the guns to play the role as real armored guards.

"The .38 specials are same kind of firearms that all armored drivers and security carry. We will all have in earpieces to be able to communicate with each other, so we can stay on top of everything, if something was to arise. Jameer will be picking those up tomorrow from Best Buy. Jameer should have that shit complete by lunch time," Lesson said. "I still have to get the info for the pick-up time. The original armored truck will arrive after we are done, which means that we have to be there exactly thirty minutes early. I talked to my hacker and he's gonna jam Wal-Mart's system exactly at the requested time. He has already hacked into their security system, just to make sure that he's able to switch the time. He told me that he wants to wait until the night before, just to make sure nobody notices the change, and he assured me that even if they did notice, he can still change the time at the last minute. So every step is covered."

Lesson threw his glass back and swallowed what was left of the Hennessy. "Learn, it's gonna be a sight to see when Pops puts on that uniform," Lesson said to his lil bro.

"You know he's not gonna wear that uniform, Lesson," Learn said. He was trying to get his pops to respond. "We got some extra tight pants for you, Pops, since this will be the first real job in your life. We gotta make you look professional."

"Don't worry about me, Learn. For the type of money that Lesson is giving us, y'all could paint these uniforms on and I'd still wear that thang," Tha Pope said.

"Pops, if the uniform is painted on then you wouldn't have to wear it, right?" Learn asked, trying to be funny.

"Okay, so you're a real smartass," Tha Pope said, grinning.

Chapter Fourteen

Lesson was on a Native-American reservation in Mt. Pleasant, Michigan, at the world-famous Soaring Eagle Casino, meeting with this computer tech guy who had the skills of a talented hacker. He drove the two hours and thirty minutes from Detroit just to meet his guy.

Why does this muthafucka always want to meet in these far-out-ass places? he thought. Lesson wanted to grab some food, so he went to the all-you-can-eat buffet. Lesson was going to pay the inflated price of twenty dollars, which was kind of expensive for a single buffet order. He was in line, waiting to be seated, when he saw the variety of foods. That's when he realized why they charged so much.

Lesson had them fix him a well done T-bone steak and went to the buffet to grab six jumbo deep-fried shrimp and a perfectly roasted lobster tail. After about thirty minutes of nonstop eating, Lesson was stuffed and had to take a piss.

On his way to the restroom, he walked past the fancy dessert bar and a freshly made strawberry shortcake caught his eye. There were other desserts, most of which he didn't know the names of, but he couldn't front. He was going to make room to try at least one.

Lesson knew he still had a lot to do in the next four days pertaining to the lick, but it wasn't so much that he thought he had to start rushing. What he wanted to do was finish with the preparations in the next two days. Lesson knew that even if his plan was perfect, he would still worry about something. This was that type of job—where he couldn't become complacent. He had too much riding on it being successful and too many of his loved ones' lives were at stake. If he failed, somebody would either die or go to prison.

Everyone knew the stakes were high. Jameer, Tha Pope, Learn, and Goob all signed up at their own risk. The potential risk of danger was high, but the reward outweighed the risk for everyone involved. If something was to go wrong, he didn't know if he could stomach the loss.

Lesson knew there were two people who he couldn't lose—his lil bro and his father—so the stakes were super high for him. Lesson's phone vibrated and he answered it.

"What's up?" he asked.

"Hey, Lesson, how did the shrimp from the buffet taste?" Dorian asked.

"So you are watching me?"

"No, not really, but I can't be too careful, Lesson. A lot of people want to figure out who I am and I prefer to be the smartest guy in the room, if that makes sense, dude," he said. "If you want, you can go to the front desk at the hotel lobby and ask for a key card under the name of Bishop Johnson and I'll meet you up in the governor's suite," he said.

Lesson was already walking toward the front desk. Once his turn came, he asked the guy in a Soaring Eagle blazer who looked to be probably Native-American for a key card under the name of Bishop Johnson.

"Sir, you are in suite 8808. That's on the eighth floor, sir. And you can use the elevators by the wall," the man said.

"Thank you," Lesson said, grabbing the key card.

Soaring Eagle Casino and Resort was a more exclusive casino compared to all of the other casinos in Detroit, including Greektown, Motor City, and MGM Casino and Resort.

Lesson was thinking of Ashanti and how much she would enjoy a few days up here to relax. Yeah, I think Ima surprise my wife and bring her up here real soon and let her chill out for a while, he thought.

When Lesson reached suite 8808, he inserted the key card and walked in to the suite. Dorian was sitting at the dining table, which seated eight. On the table was a Mac laptop, a printer, and a copy machine. Dorian was on his laptop, clicking away.

"Hey, Lesson. What's up, dude? How do you like the suite?" he asked. "Once we are finished up, it's paid up for the night. You can use the suite, just in case you want to relax."

Lesson walked up to Dorian, placed his hand on top of the kid's head and tussled his hair. "You know you didn't have to spend your money on this expensive-ass suite, Dorian. We could've used a regular room," Lesson said, knowing Dorian was trying to impress him and how he was too strapped for cash to be renting suites. Dorian was a preppy-dressed, skinny, pimple-faced white kid who, at nineteen years old, was nothing short of a genius. He could've been at Yale right now, but Dorian didn't believe in the U.S. government. He thought the system was corrupt, so he made his money by hacking into other people's ideas, inserting software and firewalls, then reselling them using fake names and server accounts.

Lesson and Dorian met about a year ago when Lesson noticed this Arab store clerk harassing the little guy. Dorian was upset that the clerk would not accept his fake ID so he could buy liquor. Lesson was inside of the liquor store in the suburban town of Farmington Hills, buying liquor when the owner of the store— who happened to be the clerk—started harassing the little pimple-faced eighteen-year-old kid, telling him that he was going to call the police if he didn't leave the store immediately. After Lesson got his liquor, he saw the kid in the parking lot, fuming. Lesson gave him a fifth of apple CÎROC and walked away.

Dorian remembered Lesson's license plate number and in-boxed him on Facebook, telling him thanks for looking out, that he's really good with computers, and if Lesson ever needed something that involved computers, he could help. Lesson was shocked that the little kid who he gave some liquor to had somehow found him. Lesson took that gesture serious and stayed in touch. Whenever Lesson needed something that involved computers, he called Dorian, who proved to be a valuable asset to him.

"What's up, kid? How have you been?" Lesson asked.

"I'm okay, Lesson. Just working. Trying to make a few dollars and stay ahead of the cyber police," Dorian said.

"Did you buy that house you were telling me about in Taylor?" Lesson asked.

"Not yet. They want sixty-eight thousand dollars and I haven't raised that type of funds yet, but I'm working on it, Lesson," he said. "I still have my apartment though."

"How about you do this job for me and if you do a great job, I'll buy the house for you, kid," Lesson said.

"I thought you were gonna give me thirty-five hundred dollars for this information?" Dorian asked, not wanting to lose out on the money that he needed today.

Lesson realized that Dorian was seriously in need of cash right now. Lesson reached into his pocket and pulled out and knot of cash that had a rubber band around it and tossed it onto the table.

"I'm still giving you the money, but I want to buy you that house, and like I just said, there will be no need for you to pay me back if you do a great job for me. What do you think about that, Dorian?" he asked his little friend. "But Ima tell you now, this information that I'm asking you for has to be all the way on point—not good work, but great work, kid," Lesson continued. "So if it's not great work, then you can kiss that little house in Taylor goodbye. However, if your hacking skills are as good as you say they are, then you will get the bonus, which would be you being a homeowner," Lesson said.

"How many times do I have to tell you, Lesson, that hackers don't like to be called that, and my skills are really that good. I'm one of the top five professional computer experts in Michigan," he said. "I got you, Lesson. Now, let's get down to business. You see this?" Dorian asked, pointing to all types of codes on the computer. Lesson leaned over him and tried to figure out what he was looking at, but was clueless.

"Yeah, I see, but don't understand," Lesson said. "What am I supposed to be looking at?"

"This, right here," he said, pointing to the screen, "is their security spread file. This is the shit we talked about, Lesson." Dorian was trying to talk cool for Lesson. "It shows all the times for the movements for shipping and receiving. You see this right here?" he asked, pointing to a security file. "Inside of this file is the movement schedule. This file is off limits to everyone except the owner of Wal-Mart #987 and Stanley, who is head of security.

Now, when I took a look inside this file, at first I couldn't get all the way inside, because they installed a firewall to block anyone who didn't have the proper authorization, which ultimately could've alerted security that someone was trying to access their file," Dorian said.

"Were you able to get inside of the file, Dorian?" Lesson asked, sounding hopeful.

"Yes, that wasn't a problem. Once I got inside, I secretly installed a software that cloned the owner of Wal-Mart #987's computers, as well as the chief of security's computer. It showed the time for a cash deposit pick-up that was scheduled for Cyber Monday. However, it didn't detail how much cash would be released, but I did get the time for the scheduled pick-up, which is at nine thirty a.m. Cyber Monday. Was this what you were looking for?"

"Not exactly, kid, but close enough," Lesson said. "Now tell me this, Dorian. Say that you want to manipulate the time for the pick-up to say nine a.m. Could the software you installed complete the task without alerting the Wal-Mart security team?" he asked.

Lesson already knew the answer, because they had talked about this issue previously, but since they were face-to-face, Lesson wanted to look into Dorian's eyes to make sure he wasn't sending the lick team on a wild goose chase. There was no question that Dorian could handle the job; however, all cylinders needed to fire at the same time.

"I can do it, if that's what you want," Dorian said.

"Say I want to change the time for the pick-up. Let's say maybe thirty minutes earlier than the scheduled time, from nine thirty a.m. to nine a.m., but the trick would be that I would only want to change the pick-up time in the Wal-Mart computers. Can you manipulate that?" he asked.

"Yes, that would be no problem," Dorian said. "It would only take a click of the button."

"Also, can you make sure that nothing changes in the Brinks computer? I want the Brinks computer timeframe to stay unchanged. I want their scheduled time to stay the same for the scheduled pick-up to be at nine thirty am."

"Of course, Lesson, I can do the job, however, I would have to stay live inside their computer from eight forty-five a.m. until nine thirty a.m. literally, but what I'm really trying to say is that it really will not be a problem. I can do the job for you, Lesson, and if anyone noticed the change, I will change it back, immediately. That's why I need to stay in every computer system live," Dorian said.

"Okay, and what about the computer system shutdown," Lesson asked.

"What do you need me to do?" Dorian asked.

"What I need from you is simple. You keep the Wal-Mart system jammed to the point whereas no data will be going in or coming out, okay? Their computers have to stay down for about one hour and thirty minutes. I want them to have to wing it, when it comes to the pick-up. They know they can't stop the pick-up, no matter if the system is down. So can you jam all incoming and outgoing data?" Lesson asked.

"I can do anything, anytime, anywhere, when it comes to computers," Dorian said assertively.

"After nine thirty a.m., I want you to reset the system back to its normal settings. Is that okay, Dorian?" Lesson asked.

"Yep, I can handle the job, Lesson," Dorian said.

Chapter Fifteen

"How fucking long have we been out here in Columbus, Ohio?" Juman asked frustrated to his homie, Savage Keith.

"It's been a while, man. No bullshit," Savage Keith said.

They were upstairs in Savage Keith's duplex safe house, sitting at the table, counting money. Downstairs on the first floor was Savage Keith's trap house. Savage Keith had eight cameras inside and outside of the trap. He saw everything coming and going, and he kept an eye on his workers. The cash flow was pumping.

"Not a while, bro. We been out here like over ten fucking years," Juman said.

Juman always became agitated when he thought about the events that led up to Savage Keith and him coming to Ohio. They were Detroit raised, not Ohio niggas. If Lesson's bitch-ass would've just given them the money, then Lesson would not have gotten shot and they would not be running from the bounty that Tha Pope put on their heads.

Tha Pope actually played fair. He could've had a hit squad hunt them down, but he settled for making them leave the city and state. Tha Pope knew they were young dummies and Lesson didn't die. Word on the streets was that Tha Pope put a bounty on both of their heads, telling them to stay out of Michigan and that they could live. But if anybody saw them in the city, then they could collect the fifty bands apiece on their heads.

Tha Pope found out about Savage Keith's right-hand man, Juman, after Tha Pope sent a squad to go grab Savage Keith. By

BRIAN D. ALI, JR.

the time the squad was assembled, Savage Keith and Juman were long gone. He put two and two together and he learned that Savage Keith's right-hand man was on the run with him. Tha Pope put another fifty bands on Juman's head with the same restrictions.

The money was good out in Columbus—that's the only reason Savage Keith didn't complain about being out there. But he missed the "D." These Columbus niggas were all right, but weren't right in the head. Savage Keith had to drop a few niggas of over the years for thinking they were sweet. Pretty soon, word got out that if you fucked with Savage Keith the long way, he played fair. But if you fucked him over, then he fucked over your family.

"Dog, it's been ten years. I'm tired of sneaking in and out of Detroit. I'm trying to go see my fam and my baby momma. Shit is too much of a hassle to have them come down here when we could ride up north," Juman said. "I don't give a fuck about Tha Pope. That old nigga don't have the pull that he had back when we was younger. Fuck that nigga. I heard that Lesson is eating real good. My baby momma said he dropped that new 2019 SRT Charger this year. She said she don't think he stay in the city anymore, because nobody see him like no more and she said his bitch, Ashanti, is missing in action. She don't hit the clubs up no more and you know that bitch used to live in the clubs, especially if that club was popping."

"Juman, you can't leave well enough alone. You don't think that Tha Pope know that we are down here, getting money, and just left us alone, as long as we don't hit the city?" Savage Keith asked. "That nigga used to run shit real heavy in Detroit. Just because his name ain't ringing like that no more don't mean he don't got power, and definitely don't mean that he don't got the bag. Juman, you know as well as me, a bitch nigga can get a muthafucka clapped if he had the bag. Bag money make niggas move on niggas."

"So what are you trying to say, Savage Keith? You don't want to go back?" Juman asked.

"Naw, I'm not saying that. You know I want to go back, but I don't want to die either, Juman. You know that when the squad comes, we won't be able to see them. The bounty still stands on our heads, bro, and they will be able to see us, bro." Savage Keith tried to talk some sense into Juman. "So what, you want to sit down with the nigga and ask him can we come back like he's our father? Fuck that nigga like I said. He's Lesson's and Learn's father. Nigga, my pops died before I was born. I don't answer to nobody."

Juman started breaking down the dutch. He had some loud he wanted to blow. "What, you scared of that old nigga, Savage Keith? Don't tell me that you lost the Savage and your name is just Keith now."

"Nigga, you know I'm not scared of God. You wanna talk that shit like shit don't stank. Nigga, shit stank. I'm not a dumb, stupid nigga either. The only thing that I'm scared of is the shit I can't see. We haven't been in the city in ten years, nigga. We don't even know who's on Tha Pope's team now. And if you think this muthafucka ain't still in use," Savage Keith picked up his nickel-plated 9 mm and put it Juman's face. "Look, nigga, this bitch is still smoking from that bitch-ass nigga I had to lay down the other night."

Juman knew he was playing with fire. The streets called Savage Keith a Savage for a reason, and if he pushed Savage Keith hard enough, Savage Keith would prove his gangsta, even though he didn't have to. Savage Keith was right. Tha Pope was more powerful.

"I'm about to put a play down, Savage Keith. You with me, bro?" Juman asked Savage Keith.

"Have I ever not been with you, Juman? Right or wrong, when it's go time, we go," Savage Keith said.

"And if it's time to die, we die," Juman said.

"But they betta be worth it, my nigga, because I'm content out here getting this money," Savage Keith said.

Chapter Sixteen

Lesson and Learn entered E. Jefferson Trucking and headed to the panic room where the big truck was located. As soon as they walked inside, they noticed Bradley and Stevie wiping down the big truck. It looked like they just finished a wax job, because the truck was sparkling. Both mechanics appeared to be proud of their work. They looked up and saw Lesson walk in with Learn.

"So what do you think?" Stevie asked. "We were waiting on you guys."

Lesson looked at Learn and asked him the same question. "What do you think, Learn? Is the paint job identical?"

"Y'all muthafuckaz are good," Learn said, and that made both mechanics smile.

"We did our best to duplicate the photos you gave us. The finished product is not identical. However, to the untrained eye, it looks perfect. Was that what you were looking for, Lesson?" Bradley asked.

"Dude, I think you both earned the deed to this building, and whenever I need work done on a big truck, I'm gonna bring it here," Lesson said. "Stevie, I forgot to ask you, did my real estate agent, Jessica, finish all the paperwork with you?" he asked, referring to the building.

"Yeah, she came by last week, right after you and I talked. She was great about helping us transfer the deed into our joint company name," Stevie said. "When do you want to take the truck?

We can deliver it for you anywhere you want it to go, if that's what you want us to do."

"That's okay, Stevie. I still have my key. We will come pick it up within the next few days. Have you installed a security system yet?" Lesson asked.

"Not yet," Bradley said. "But we're in the process of doing that as well."

Learn jumped into the driver's seat and cranked the truck up. Bradley lifted the garage up halfway to let some of the fumes out. Learn was sitting there getting the feel of the big truck. Learn remembered when he first went down to Florida to purchase the truck. He couldn't believe the transformation. Learn was one hundred percent sure that if this rebuilt truck drove by the original owner, he would not even recognize his old truck. That's how good of a job Stevie and Bradley did.

Once the lick was complete, Lesson instructed Learn that he would be responsible for burning the big truck in an undisclosed location, which would be inside an abandoned factory. Learn thought, What a waste.

Chapter Seventeen

"Aye, what you say?" Juman asked.

The music was beating hard as hell in his 2018 black SRT Charger with five-percent limo tints. If the police tried to stop him, he was going to outrun them. He had a glock on his hip and Savage Keith had his stainless steel 9mm sitting in his lap. He was driving through Monroe, Michigan, on I-75 north, headed back to Detroit.

"I said, turn that shit all the way up," Savage Keith said.

They were listening to Peezy's "Balling Ain't a Crime." Juman and Savage Keith were both feeling good. Juman had been trying to recharged Savage Keith's battery for a few years now. Juman knew that if he kept testing Savage Keith's gangsta and challenged his manhood, he would be able to pull that Savage back out of Keith.

Savage Keith knew that the right move was to stay away from Michigan, but the more Juman brought up going back home, the more the city started to appeal to him. It was calling his name. He had been gone for ten years. The streets never stopped talking about the shit that went down. Nobody could believe that Savage Keith tried to rob Lesson, knowing the consequence would be death if Tha Pope was to find out.

Word on the streets for the past ten years was that Tha Pope ran him and Juman out of Detroit and put the clamps on the old crew. Tha Pope made sure that Savage Keith's old crew could not get any more money in the city, but he showed mercy on them and let them stay around.

The truth was that Tha Pope did run Savage Keith out of Detroit, but it wasn't because he was scared. Tha Pope was simply more powerful than Savage Keith was ten years ago. The streets knew that he would bust his gun and lay who-the-fuck-ever down. Savage Keith's old crew members he used to run with ten years ago were no doubt killaz, but Tha Pope was more organized and powerful. Savage Keith could not compete with a forty-year-old street legend when he was only twenty years old and fresh in the game making a name for himself. However, over the years, Savage Keith thought about going home and told Juman that if he came back to the city, he would come back right and wreak havoc on Tha Pope and his family, and secure his name in the book of legends.

Savage Keith knew the only way for him to come back home was to take out Tha Pope and scare Lesson to the point that he would jump out of the game. Savage Keith was gonna give Lesson the same deal that Tha Pope gave him. Leave the game and Michigan with a lifetime bounty on his head, or get buried. Savage Keith didn't want to kill Lesson if he didn't have to. He would let the streets do it for him. With all those young dummies out there who were starving, Savage Keith knew that once he eliminated Tha Pope, and once he dropped fifty bands on Lesson's head, somebody would kill him sooner or later for the come-up.

On one hand, Savage Keith wanted Tha Pope dead for running him out of Detroit and Michigan for the past ten years, but on the other hand, he respected Tha Pope for not killing him for shooting Lesson in the stomach. Tha Pope could've taken the bounty off his head, but he kept a lifetime bounty out there, and because of that, he had to die. However, not before he took everything Tha Pope had. Savage Keith knew that Tha Pope had that old money and he wanted that chicken to jumpstart the engine that would lead to him taking over the city. Once Tha Pope was dead and the streets attached his name to the murder, he would become legendary in his own right. The streets would talk about him forever. There was only one Savage Keith from the "D," and he was coming home, right or wrong.

When it was time to ride, Juman rode. Juman could've cut ties and gone out west to start his life over, but he held it down from day one. Now it was Savage Keith's turn to return the favor and cement Juman's name in the game, right next to his own. And in the process, if they got knocked off trying to make it to the top of the game, then so be it. They would die together as day-one homies, who came up from the mud together. Nobody was going to stop his gun from smoking this time.

Savage Keith was in the passenger seat, rolling up a dutch. He had an ounce of sour diesel from Cali sitting between his legs, stanking up the Charger. It was late November and the branches were bare on the trees, but it felt like it was summertime to them.

"You ready to take over the city?" Juman asked. Savage Keith lifted his gun from his lap. *Click, clack.* Savage Keith slid a round into the chamber.

"Ain't no question," Savage Keith said. "It's our time, my nigga. You stayed loyal and we got good money down in Columbus."

"Yeah, nigga. The city is up for grabs. Niggas done got too comfortable. If we take Tha Pope's bag and add it to ours, then run down to Arizona and grab a plug, nothing can stop us from running the city. Everybody knows the biggest bag runs Detroit," Juman said.

Chapter Eighteen

"Baby, you ready to go over to your grandma's house?" Ashanti asked. "Lovely, guess who's over there waiting for you, baby?"

What Ashanti didn't know was that LJ already called her and said he was staying over at her grandma's for the weekend and he was coming over to their house after his weekend visit.

"I already know, Mom," Lovely said. "LJ is over there. We already talked."

Lovely couldn't wait to go over her grandma's house. She loved her family, especially Grandma Rocci and Granddad Pope. Grandma always had a fresh carrot cake sitting on the counter and she would cut a piece for Lovely and put it in the microwave to warm it up. When it was good and hot, she would take it out and add a scoop of vanilla ice cream to it. Lovely loved it every time her grandma would tell her little things about growing up in Detroit.

"You ready to go baby?" Ashanti asked her baby girl.

She started thinking about Lesson and the streets of Detroit. It had been a while since she had been there. She used to go to the city every weekend and chill in all the clubs that were popping, with her best friends, Staci and Tia, but Lesson warned her that she was being too predictable and wanted her to stop going out. He wanted her to grow up. Lesson told her that she didn't have to be in the clubs every week. He told her that when she showed up on the scene, the city was supposed to have missed her.

She hated to give up that part of her life, but her daughter was getting older and Lesson was right. Ashanti knew that she was safe and nobody would fuck with her on the strength of who her husband was and that Tha Pope was her father-in-law. Ashanti couldn't even flirt with a nigga without Lesson finding out, not that she would disrespect Lesson like that anyway. However, she knew who she married and how much love Tha Pope, Lesson, and Learn each had in the city.

She loved talking to Rocci, because Rocci was a bad bitch herself and had gone through the same shit when Tha Pope was running the city. Rocci would tell her when she started to complain about being smothered, when it felt like she no longer had a life, or that she knew the type of nigga she married. When she chose to have a baby with Lesson, she had to accept the bullshit, the same way she accepted the glitz and glamour.

Rocci reminded Ashanti how she loved fucking up malls, buying red-bottomed Jimmy Choo and Chanel shoes. That was the good part of being a street nigga's wife. The bad part was when Ashanti had to think about Lesson catching a quick nut with a bitch he didn't give a fuck about, but wanted to fuck, because she had a fat ass.

Rocci remind her that she loved living in a $350,000 house in the suburbs with no worries, but she hated being away from the city. Momma Rocci would tell her that she had to accept the good with the bad and the bad with the good. Rocci would tell her that things would never be perfect while her man was in the game. When a woman is in love with a street nigga, they have to accept the life, play by the rules of the streets, and hope their nigga matures enough to leave the hood once he makes enough money to get out.

"Yep, Mom, I'm ready. I'm grabbing my iPad and purse now," Lovely said. "Can we stop at McDonald's and get breakfast?"

"Yeah, since it's on the way," Ashanti said. Ashanti and Lovely jumped into Ashanti's minivan and headed to Rocci's house.

Chapter Nineteen

11/28/19

Monday, 8:30 a.m.

Tha Pope was in an all-white rented U-Haul van with the logo attached to the side. He was parked about two hundred yards from Wal-Mart on Highlander Road and U.S. 23, in Hartland, Michigan. He was positioned in the parking lot of the Taco Bell, right across the street from the lick. It was eight thirty a.m. and he didn't have to worry about the employees wondering what he was doing in the lot. They didn't start showing up for work until nine thirty, and by that time, he would be gone.

Tha Pope's job was to have extra eyes on the lick and pick the guys up after the job was completed. He could see the entire front entrance of the Wal-Mart. He was looking for something that appeared to be out of place, but so far everything looked good. He also was flying a four-foot electric DJI Mavie Pro Apple Drone. The battery was fully charged and he could fly it for seven straight hours. It was equipped with a camera so that he could take photos or run live video feed. Inside of the U-Haul van was a nine-inch HD monitor that was connected to the drone. He could see everything clearly.

Tha Pope was flying the drone with ease like he was a pilot flying planes in and out of an airport. The drone would allow him to see the Brinks truck arrive from at least 350 yards away. If the real Brinks truck arrived, he had to either try to reroute the truck or make a diversion. Under no circumstances would he allow the real Brinks truck to enter the front entrance parking lot of the Wal-Mart before the job was complete. Too many lives were at stake.

At the last moment, before everyone headed out, Lesson instructed Tha Pope not to wear his uniform, just in case something went wrong and they needed him, because he needed to pose as a civilian. Lesson had equipped Jameer, Goob, and Learn, as well as himself, with an earpiece to be able to communicate with each other. They all were given code names for their prospective teams.

Lesson's team would be called Red Wing. His team consisted of Learn, Goob, and Jameer. Tha Pope was also equipped with the same device and his code name would be Blue Wing. The third and final team and person who was equipped with the same device for radio traffic was Dorian, the hacker. His code name would be Black Wing.

Each team would use their earpieces to not draw attention as a walkie talkie would. No one was supposed to use radio traffic except Lesson, Tha Pope, and Dorian, unless an emergency was to emerge. Blue Wing initiated the first radio traffic.

"I'm all set to go on this end. The bird is in the air and I have a line of sight on Red Wing's location. Over."

Chapter Twenty

Monday, 8:40 a.m.

Learn was in the driver's seat, comfortably sitting behind the wheel, waiting for Lesson's instructions. The big truck looked like it had come from the Brinks company lot.

Learn was nervous and excited at the same time. He was responsible for driving the big truck and keeping the truck under control, no matter how the situation unfolded. Learn had on his uniform with his .38 police special in a holster on his right hip. He wore a Brinks baseball hat and a pair of chrome Oakley sunglasses. To the untrained eye, he looked like an extension of law enforcement.

Jameer wore the same uniform as everyone else. He was positioned in the back of the big truck, along with Lesson and Goob. His assignment was simple. Once the truck pulled up, he would exit the rear of the truck, followed by Lesson and Goob. They would then unholster their firearms and set up a perimeter around the rear of the truck and wait for the Wal-Mart security to bring the currency out.

Next, Goob would re-enter back into the rear of the big truck and load the currency. Lesson would sign for the pick-up and everyone would re-enter the rear of the truck, secure the door, and drive off.

Everyone knew their roles and was prepared. Lesson heard radio traffic from Blue Wing saying he had line of sight on the location and was set to go.

"Roger that, Blue Wing. Stay in position. Over."

Chapter Twenty-One

Monday, 8:50 a.m.

"Black Wing, are we all set to go? Do you have eyes on your end?" Lesson asked Dorian, referring to the magic that Dorian was supposed to work on his computer.

"Red Wing, everything is a go," he said. "I have line of sight on the computer and nothing has changed."

Dorian inserted a software that shut down all of the computers that were connected to the store and inserted a temporary firewall inside of Wal-Mart that was connected to their security team and the deposit pick-up.

"The scheduled time for Red Wing pick-up is scheduled for nine a.m. The real deposit pick-up is still scheduled for nine thirty a.m. Everything is a go on my end, and I will stay live until you tell me to go silent. Over," Dorian said, enjoying being a part of something, and being in so much control to manipulate confidential files, hack computers, insert firewalls, and play with traffic lights. The icing on top of the cake was when Lesson told Dorian he would buy him a house if he completed his job without a hitch. This was a dream job for Dorian and the house was a bonus. Lesson had proved to be a good friend to him and he was trustworthy.

Lesson had given him all types of freelance assignments over the past year. Lesson never tried to play him or underpay him. He always paid him upfront and overpaid him for jobs he had taken less pay for in the past. What Lesson did not know was that if he had asked him to do the job for free, Dorian would've done it, no questions asked.

"Black Wing, this is Red Wing. Are you still in control of the traffic light at the U.S. 23 intersection? Over," Lesson asked.

"Red Wing, I read you loud and clear. I am one hundred percent in control of the traffic light. Whenever Blue Wing instructs me to switch the traffic light to red, it will change immediately. Over," Dorian said, referring to when Tha Pope contacted him directly over radio traffic. He would change the traffic light, and he could and would do it at a moment's notice.

Chapter Twenty-Two

Monday, 8:56 a.m.

Lesson banged on the wall in the back of the big truck to get Learn's attention. It was four minutes until pick-up, and Learn had just pulled into the parking lot of Wal-Mart and headed toward the front entrance to position the big truck in front of the store, exactly where the real truck would've parked.

"Yeah, what's good?" Learn asked.

"Take it easy, bro. Everything is good. We are in a good spot and we are right on schedule," Lesson said.

"All right, bro. Easy breezy, right?" Learn said.

"Jameer, you good?" Lesson asked. Jameer nodded. "What about you, Goob? You ready?" Lesson noticed a few sweat beads forming on his forehead.

He nodded. "As ready as being ready can be," Goob said.

"Blue Wing, are you in position? Over," Lesson asked.

"Roger, I'm in position and the bird is still hovering. Don't worry about me, Red Wing. I'm a vet. Over."

"Black Wing, you still with me? Are you on point and in position? Over," Lesson said to Dorian.

"I'm a professional, Red Wing. I can do my job in my sleep. Over."

Lesson never became nervous for a job he master-minded. As long as he was in control, he could relax. He had everyone in position, according to their skill sets. It was time for the action to happen and he was ready to get it over with.

"Okay, guys," Lesson said to everyone. "It's 8:58 a.m. In two minutes, their security team should be headed our way. Stay ready, gentlemen, so we don't have to get ready. Over."

Chapter Twenty-Three

Juman and Savage Keith pulled up to the drive-thru at the McDonald's on Gratiot and East 7 Mile Road. They smoked the sour diesel and were hungry as fuck.

"Man, get me two Egg McMuffins and hash browns," Savage Keith said.

"I got you."

"It feels good to be back in the city, don't it, Juman?"

It was wintertime and they had their windows down smelling the air like they both were just released from Jackson State Prison. In the ten years they were gone from the city, it looked like an atomic bomb had been dropped onto the center of their neighborhood. All the streets were the same, but houses were missing in bunches, and it looked like a third-world country.

"Welcome to McDonald's. How may I help you today?" the McDonald's employee asked through the intercom of the drive-thru window.

"Yeah, let me get two Egg McMuffins and hash browns, and two Sausage Egg McMuffins with hash browns," Juman told the employee. "Super-size that order with two extra-large apple juices."

"Will that be all?" the attendant asked.

"Yeah, that's it."

"That'll be $22.78. Please drive around to the window," the employee said.

THE LICK

As Juman was reaching for his change and grabbing his order, through the drive-thru window he saw a familiar face ordering food on the inside.

Chapter Twenty-Four

Monday, 8:59 am.

Lesson, Goob, and Jameer exited the rear of the big truck and set up a perimeter around the rear of the truck. They each had their guns unholstered in their hands, pointed toward the ground. They were in position, waiting on Wal-Mart security. A Livingston County Sheriff Deputy squad car pulled up next to the three men standing outside the big truck and stopped.

"Morning, gentlemen," the deputy said after rolling down his passenger-side window.

"Be cool," Lesson whispered. Everyone heard him. "Morning, sir," Lesson said to the deputy.

"What a brisk morning. There's a chill coming off the Great Lakes. I think we have a big storm brewing," the deputy said.

"Yeah, this will be a cold winter," Lesson said, making small talk. "Because the summer was extremely hot."

"Ab-so-fucking-lutely," the deputy said. "That's Michigan weather for you, if you didn't know it. You guys making a pick-up today?"

"Yep, we gotta remove all the holiday money. It's a pretty big order today," Lesson said. "And I couldn't turn down the overtime."

He looked up and saw the Wal-Mart security team ushering out three steel carts with eight money bags on each cart. The security team looked bored.

Man, get the fuck outta here, Lesson thought, referring to the deputy.

"Okay, gentlemen. I'll let you get back to work. I'll be around if you need me. Just give me a hoot and I'll skip right over," the deputy said and tipped the brim of his hat. He pulled off as the Wal-Mart security team was edging closer to the big truck with the money bags. It was now nine a.m. exactly. *On fucking time,* Lesson thought.

Chapter Twenty-Five

"What you want, Lovely? Just get something quick, okay? And grab something for your big brother," Ashanti said. "You know we have to get him something, too."

"Okay, Mom. Get LJ two Sausage Egg McMuffins and one medium orange juice," Lovely said. "And get me the same thing. Thanks, Mom."

"Baby, are you gonna eat both of those Sausage McMuffins by yourself?" Ashanti teased her.

"Yep. All of it, Mom," Lovely said.

Ashanti ordered the food and a small hash browns for herself.

"Mom, you think when we leave Grandma's we can go to the mall? You know they still have all those after Black Friday sales. I need some shoes, and LJ needs some stuff, too," Lovely said, trying to manipulate her mom into taking her and LJ to the mall.

"We will see, baby. If it's not too late when we leave Grandma's, okay? You know she's gonna want to spend some time with you, baby, and we may end up staying for the weekend," Ashanti said.

She reached down and hugged her daughter and noticed how big Lovely was becoming. She already stood next to her shoulder. She couldn't believe ten years had flown by that fast. Ashanti grabbed the McDonald's bag and gave it to her daughter, but not before reaching inside and puling to pull out her hash browns. After Ashanti scarfed down the hash browns, they rushed out to the minivan, because the wind was blowing hard. As Ashanti pulled out of the parking lot, she never noticed that she was being followed.

Chapter Twenty-Six

"Is that Ashanti?" Juman asked Savage Keith.

At the mention of Lesson's wife's name, Savage Keith's high was instantly blown. They were back in Michigan to put down a play on Tha Pope and Lesson, and he couldn't believe that God blessed him with a gift like this as soon as he made it to the East Side.

Savage Keith nearly broke his neck trying to get a good look at Ashanti. "Nigga, that's the bitch and she still *badddd* as fuck, my nigga. She looks better than she did when I first saw her in 007 Strip Club ten years ago. Remember how thick she was back then, my nigga? Look at her ass now," Savage Keith said.

"What she needs is a real nigga, not a playing street thug like Lesson's hoe ass," Juman said in a predatory way.

Juman quickly whipped the ride into a parking space. Savage Keith didn't have to tell him that they would be following her. They were going to wait as long as it took for her to come out of Mickey D's. After a few minutes, Ashanti and a young girl who Savage Keith didn't recognize and thought to be no more than twelve years old came running out and jumped into a new minivan and pulled out. Juman instantly started following her.

"Don't lose that bitch," Savage Keith said. That right there is our come-up, you dig?" Savage Keith was rubbing his hands together, exactly the way Johnny Manziel, who won the Heisman, used to do when he was the star quarterback at Texas A&M. He looked at Juman and said, "This is my money dance." He grabbed his gun and smiled a devious smile.

Chapter Twenty-Seven

Monday, 9:01 a.m.

"Morning, fellas," Lesson said, extending his hand to shake the chief of security's hand. His nametag read Stanley Mickelson. The Wal-Mart security team consisted of an eight man security team to deliver the funds to the armored truck. Goob holstered his firearm and re-entered the rear of the truck to collect the money bags.

"Morning," Mickelson said, accepting Lesson's hand, shaking it firmly. "Mighty chilly out here, ain't it?" Mickelson pulled his collar up on his jacket to try to shield his neck from the wind. "Where's Ole Riley?" Mickelson asked.

"Took the holiday off, I guess. He wanted to spend time with his family," Lesson said.

"Our system is down so we could not confirm the pick-up, but I knew you guys would be on time. Riley is always on time, just like you guys showed up early today," he said. "I thought we set the time up for nine thirty a.m., but seeing how big this currency pick-up is and the holidays, I guess I overlooked it. When I looked at the schedule on the printout, it said nine a.m., so me and my guys had to rush, and with the system being down, we didn't want you guys sitting. No telling how much money you guys are carrying and Wal-Mart doesn't want to be responsible for a delay if something was to happen, you catch my drift?" Mickelson said, winking at Lesson.

Lesson thought that Mickelson was a real-life cornball. He wondered what types of jokes and winks Mickelson would make once he realized how much money he actually gave away. Lesson let him talk. He was gaining a lot of information while letting Mickelson run off at the mouth. Lesson averted his eyes to scan the perimeter of the parking lot and noticed Jameer was doing the same thing. They looked the part and were playing their roles to a T. Lesson looked at Goob's big ass struggling to stack up the first of the eight bags from the cart, and immediately started loading the second cart. Goob was sweating AK-47 bullets, but was getting the job done.

"Here you go," Mickelson said and handed Lesson a clipboard for his signature.

Lesson accepted the order form attached to the clipboard and signed his John Hancock. He noticed that the delivery was for twenty-four money bags for the amount that indicated $4,780,000. He couldn't believe it. Here he was, a nigga from the city of Detroit, and he had put together the lick of the century. Lesson was a great poker player and he had to conceal his excitement.

"How much is in the load, Stan?" he asked, just making conversation. Lesson started talking to the chief security like they were old friends.

"You didn't see the amount on the paper?" Mickelson asked, smiling.

"I saw it. I just wanted you to confirm it," Lesson said.

"Well, if you insist. It's almost five million."

"Wow," Lesson said. "That's a pretty big penny, but nowhere near my biggest load this week. Would you believe it if I told you we picked up about ten million from Greektown Casino last night? It was an emergency pick-up. They said they couldn't hold any more currency."

"No shit! Ten million? I bet that scared the shit out of you, buddy, driving that amount of cash around," Mickelson said.

"No, not really. It was just a heavy load on the truck. We would drive sixty miles per hour and it felt like we were only going forty-five. Took a while to get back to base."

He looked up and noticed Goob. His underarms were soaked and the sweat was dripping down his face like a rainstorm. Lesson noticed the security team watching Goob handle the bags. Lesson didn't want Mickelson to look at Goob sweating so hard, being that it was twenty-two degrees outside. It was basically freezing and this guy was sweating bullets.

Chapter Twenty-Eight

Monday, 9:18 a.m.

"Red Wing, this is Blue Wing. Over. Red Wing, this is Blue Wing. Over."

There was panic in Tha Pope's voice. Tha Pope was trying to get Lesson's attention, but Lesson was silent. He saw the truck still sitting in front of the Wal-Mart, but Lesson, Jameer, and Goob were out of his line of sight, and he didn't have time to maneuver the drone into a better position. He also didn't want the Wal-Mart security team to see the drone and become suspicious. Red Wing was concealed behind the truck. From the air view, Tha Pope noticed a Brinks truck three hundred yards away and about fifty feet from the traffic light.

"Black Wing, do you read me? This is Blue Wing. We have a problem. Over." This was Tha Pope's first time breaking silence and reaching out to Black Wing. He was instructed by Lesson not to speak to Black Wing unless it was an emergency, and it was an emergency.

When Dorian heard his code name being used by someone other than Lesson, he knew something had gone wrong. "This is Black Wing. Over."

"Black Wing, on my dime, I'm gonna need you to turn the traffic light from green to red and keep it red until I say change it to green. Over," Tha Pope said.

"No problem, Blue Wing. Just tell me when and I'll hold it until you say change it. Over."

Lesson heard Tha Pope call out a distress call and he knew that the real armored truck had arrived early. He looked down at his watch—it was now 9:20 a.m., and Goob still had two bags left to load. He wished he could speak to Tha Pope and Dorian and try to direct the issue, but he trained his guys for this moment and they had to improvise. Lesson knew Goob heard the radio traffic, because he started moving a little faster, but Lesson could tell that he was more tired than he realized from the weight of the money. Each bag weighed about 250 pounds.

Chapter Twenty-Nine

Ashanti pulled up to Momma Rocci's house and they went inside. Rocci greeted and hugged her granddaughter and her daughter-in-law.

"Where y'all been hiding?" Rocci asked. "Y'all must love the suburbs better than the city, because I can't get y'all to come visit a lonely old lady no more. I was just telling Tha Pope the other day that he has to come check on me more."

"You know you can come out to our house, Grandma. It's so big and there's a lot to do out there," Lovely said.

"I know, baby. I guess Ima have to start coming out there. It's just so far. I end up being so tired once I make it there," Rocci said.

"It's not even an hour away, Mom," Ashanti said to her mother-in-law. "You just don't like being around those white folks, but the white folks out in Chesterfield Township are a different breed. If you got enough money to live out there, then they will accept you and their men...OMG...love a Black bitch. I always catch them staring hard."

"Girl, you betta watch your mouth around my grandbaby," Rocci said to Ashanti.

"Now Momma, you know damn well we are not raising a boogie girl. Her genes are from Detroit and we gotta keep her wise, even though she stays in the suburbs," Ashanti said.

"You damn right, girl," Rocci said and high-fived Ashanti.

Lovely was smiling, because she was finally a part of an adult conversation. She was like a sponge. She soaked up everything she heard. That's how smart she was and she didn't act out her thoughts; she thought about the lessons she learned. Lovely knew that she was being taught things the white way and the Black way. She knew that there was a difference between what she learned in school and learned from her family.

She didn't like any of the boys in her school, but she had them all wrapped around her finger, exactly the way her mom had her father wrapped around her finger. It wasn't her fault the boys in her grade were all lames. She could tell that some of her girlfriends were jealous of the attention she received from the boys, but that wasn't her problem. That's their problem to solve on their own, she thought.

"Girl, what are you thinking about?" Rocci asked, trying to snap her out of whatever daydream that took her away from planet Earth.

"I was thinking about eating this McDonald's and the carrot cake that I know you have ready for me, Grandma," Lovely said, lying through her teeth.

"Where's Lesson, Mom? We picked some food for him, too," Ashanti asked.

"Ashanti, what did I tell you about feeding my grandkids that poison, girl?" Rocci asked.

"It's not gonna hurt them. You ate it too when you were their age."

"LJ is down the street at his friend's house. He should be back in an hour or so," Rocci said.

Chapter Thirty

Savage Keith and Juman had followed Ashanti to a house not too far from the McDonald's. The house was big compared to all the other houses. Juman looked at the house and figured it had about four to five bedrooms, so there was no telling how many people were inside. However, he noticed only one other car was sitting out front.

When Ashanti and the little girl got out of the car and headed inside, they were met at the door by the one and only Rocci Day, Lesson's and Learn's mother, who was also Tha Pope's wife. Savage Keith couldn't believe it.

"We hit the lottery, my nigga," he said. "All we gotta do is snatch these two bitches, and Tha Pope and Lesson will come to us."

Juman was smiling at Savage Keith. "Let's watch the house for a minute and if nobody shows up, then we can either wait on somebody to leave or we can knock on the door and go in that bitch," Savage Keith said after a few minutes checking out the area.

"You the boss, nigga. I'm down for whatever," Juman said.

Savage Keith grabbed another dutch and broke it down. "We gotta get faded for this one, my nigga."

Juman and Savage Keith were passing the blunt back and forth to each other, getting higher and higher. After a while, they were high as fuck. Juman opened the McDonald's and gave Savage Keith his order. Both men destroyed their order and settled back to put a plan together on how they were going to go into the house.

Chapter Thirty-One

Monday, 9:24 a.m.

"Change the light to red now, Black Wing. Over," Tha Pope told Dorian. The real armored truck had four vehicles in front of it and the light had turned red at the intersection of Highlander Road and Spencer Road. Tha Pope had the four-foot electric Apple drone hovering fifty feet above the real armored truck.

"Blue Wing, the light is secure," Dorian said, after he changed the light. "Hold the drone steady. I need to see exactly what you see. Over."

"No problem, Black Wing. Over."

It was now 9:25 a.m. "Red Wing, I'm leaving my location to edge closer to the real truck, just in case I have to force a traffic accident. Over." Tha Pope knew that Lesson could not respond and would not have agreed to Tha Pope putting his life in jeopardy, which could ultimately cause him to get knocked, but since Lesson could not talk, Tha Pope felt like he had to do something and take a chance. Tha Pope exited the Taco Bell parking lot and started driving in the direction of the real Brinks truck.

"Blue Wing, hold steady. I can manipulate the traffic light and turn it to green, and I'm certain that would cause an immediate accident with both lights green at the same time. However, if there is not an accident, then you would have to force the accident. Over," Dorian said.

"I copy one hundred percent, Black Wing. That sounds like a great idea. Over."

From the air view from the drone, it appeared that the traffic on the real Brinks side of the light was becoming agitated. It was now 9:26 a.m., and the light still hadn't changed. The driver of the real Brinks truck pulled into the right lane and drove onto the sidewalk and tried to make a right turn to detour his route.

Chapter Thirty-Two

Monday, 9:26 a.m.

Goob had finished loading the last of the bags into the big truck and secured himself into his seat in the back, across from the money in the rear of the truck, and Jameer took one last look around and climbed into the back of the truck and sat in his seat next to Goob. When Jameer looked at Goob, it appeared as if somebody poured a bucket of water over his head. That's how hard he was sweating.

"All right, Mickelson, nice meeting you, buddy. Maybe I will do another run out here to this location and run into you again," Lesson said. Lesson and Mickelson shook hands.

"Lesson, we have a major problem. The real Brinks truck is about to turn right and come to us from another direction. Even if we make it out, we are gonna need a five-minute to ten-minute head start with all this weight on the truck. Lesson, once they dispatch that there's been a robbery, every squad car will have a BOLO—Be On the Look Out—for a similar armored truck, you dig, bro?" Learn asked. Now he was becoming nervous. Everything had gone smooth up until this point, and if a miracle didn't happen, they were on the way to a federal penitentiary somewhere in the boonies.

Mickelson saluted Lesson and said, "All right, fellas."

Lesson climbed into the back of the big truck and looked in the direction of the real Brinks truck. The real Brinks truck was about 240 yards away and in the right turning lane. Lesson knew that the Wal-Mart security team would not go back inside of the building until the big truck left the Wal-Mart parking lot. Lesson also knew that the Livingston County squad car was still somewhere close by. Lesson told himself to calm down and whispered to himself not to panic as he closed the rear door. Everything went black and his eyes needed to re-adjust to the dim lights. He had $4,780,000 staring him right in his face, and he planned on spending every penny of that money.

Chapter Thirty-Three

Monday, 9:27 a.m.

"Black Wing, change the light to green again," Tha Pope told Dorian.

He was hoping to cause the accident. "If it doesn't work, then I'll do it myself." Tha Pope was referring to ramming his rented U-Haul van into the back of the real Brinks truck. Tha Pope was yelling over the radio traffic, because he had started to panic. The entire plan could be blown within minutes.

Black Wing changed the light to green and the traffic immediately started to take off. It appeared as if all of the drivers were irritated from the delay of the light being red for so long and were driving faster than normal, like they were late for work or an important meeting.

When Tha Pope notice the light change, he gunned the van, just like the other cars that were around him in traffic, except he had a motive. Tha Pope was on a collision course to collide into the back of the real armored truck. He was going twenty miles per hour, then thirty, then forty. He was about fifteen feet away, then ten feet, then five feet, then smack... Booooom.

Chapter Thirty-Four

Black Wing was watching the entire scene play out from his monitor. *Wow*, he said to himself, *this is some real-life movie shit, like some* Fast and Furious 6 *shit for real.*

Dorian saw Blue Wing accelerating in the direction of the real armored truck after he had changed the light from red to green. He knew that there would be minimal damage to the armored truck once the van actually collided with the armored truck. However, the accident would buy the lick team the time they would need to get away from the crime scene. The armored truck would have to wait on the police, and that alone would buy time.

Just when Blue Wing was about to hit the armored truck with his rented U-Haul van, a white Dodge Ram ran smack into the rear of the armored truck, causing an explosion sound: *Smack...booooom.* The impact was so severe for the white Dodge Ram that both the back wheels left the ground. There was minimum damage for the armored truck, however. Because an accident had taken place, the armored truck would have to wait on the police to arrive to give a police report.

•••

Tha Pope gunned the rented U-Haul van into the direction of the armored truck. He was bracing himself for a collision. He knew that he needed to crash into the back of the armored truck. Tha Pope was out of options. At the very last moment, Tha Pope swerved into oncoming traffic and almost hit several other vehicles. He was turning the steering wheel left, then right, then back left, barely missing the other vehicles that were going in another direction. Tha Pope was driving the rented U-Haul van as if he was a stunt driver. He merged back into traffic on the right side of the road, never stopping. He kept going.

Chapter Thirty-Five

"Go knock on the door, Juman," Savage Keith told him. "If Rocci answers, she would recognize me, and if she does, this shit could blow up in our faces. Once the door is open, Ima come around from the side of the house and we're gonna force our way inside, and bring her and Ashanti out."

Juman was looking into his rear-view mirror, waiting on the coast to be clear. He was a little nervous, but not too much. He needed to snatch both women in order to put their play all the way in motion. He was paying attention to the traffic flow and noticed there wasn't a lot of traffic at this time of the morning, but he still wanted to make sure that the coast was clear before the snatch happened. He wanted this grabbed to be perfect. Juman did not know how many soldiers Tha Pope had trained to go and he didn't want to find out. Not if he didn't have to.

"Juman, Ima go position myself on the side of the house. When I get in position, go ahead and knock on the door," Savage Keith said. He was going over the plan with Juman while still sitting in the car. "Let's make it happen, my nigga. Remember, we still have fifty bands on our heads. If a muthafucka sees us, that's a hundred bands, my nigga. So that means if we are seen we are sitting ducks. A nigga would kill his momma for that type of paper, so we gotta be in and out. Don't play with Rocci. She's an old gangsta bitch, trust me. If she can get to the strap, that bitch gonna let it holla, my nigga. Her gun would definitely be smoking. Rocci is a thoroughbred, my nigga." Savage Keith warned Juman to make sure that he stayed on point.

"I know, my nigga. I'm from the same hood as you and these are the same muthafuckas who sent both of us outta town," he said. "And if Ashanti or Rocci puts up a fight, I'm gonna pistol whip their asses, no bullshit, my nigga."

Savage Keith exited the vehicle and crept to the side of the house, waiting on Juman to play his role. Juman pulled the Charger into the driveway at Rocci's house. He got out of the car and went to knock on the door.

Chapter Thirty-Six

"Check this shit out," Aunty told Unc. They both had lived on the block for over thirty years and knew everybody in the neighborhood. Everybody loved Aunty and Unc, because nothing went down in the entire neighborhood without them at least being able to talk about drama. Whenever someone needed information, they went to Aunty and Unc. Period. Point blank. That's just the way it was in the neighborhood.

They were not snitches. They would never tell the police anything. They both respected the code of the streets entirely too much to do some shit like that. But they were a hundred percent about that gossip—they were worse than Wendy Williams and TMZ combined. The hood nicknamed them the Neighborhood Watch. If somebody wasn't watching their kids, they would know and talk about it. If kids were skipping school, they would know and talk about it. If somebody's house had gotten broken into, they would know and point them in the right direction for a fee if someone went to them. So whenever something went down, they knew what happened and they would tell anyone if they were asked or paid.

Everybody knew that if they didn't want to get caught up, then don't pull a bullshit stunt on the block, because they would know. And they weren't worried about shit, because Tha Pope put the word out a long time ago that they were not to be messed with, under any circumstances. And all these years later, no one had crossed Tha Pope's order.

Unc used to be a dealer before he sampled his own work and got turned out. Aunty was his wife, which made her a hustler's wife back in the day when Tha Pope was in charge of everything moving in and out of the hood. Unc was one of his top money makers. Tha Pope told him not to ever party using the heroin or coke that he supplied him with, but Unc did not listen. He and Aunty would party all the time and eventually the addiction got the best of them. They still owned their home that they purchased when the money was rolling in. They chose to never leave the neighborhood that they grew up in and respected. They would say they were born in Detroit, raised in Detroit, and would die in Detroit.

Now both in their mid-fifties, all they wanted to do was get high and gossip. It still felt good to be respected in some capacity from the hood they helped destroy, not knowing that the drugs they were selling were actually hurting their community. Honestly, they thought they were just making money like everybody else, and helping people party on the fun stuff. That was until they became addicted and that addiction had now lasted for the past twenty years.

"Say it again, baby. I can't hear you," Unc said. "What's going on? What do I need to see a little after nine a.m. in the morning?"

Aunty was already alert. She had started her morning off at eight thirty a.m. with a ten-dollar rock. She finished it in four full pulls from the stem that she used to suck down the rock. She had already repacked the stem and was waiting on Unc to wake up to give him his first high of the morning from his ten-dollar rock. She passed the stem to him as he got up to look out of the window.

Aunty already had a candle burning. All Unc had to do was hold the fire to the end of the stem and pull.

As he was pulling, every vein in his neck bulged. Unc held in the smoke as his eyes grew bigger, not from the potency of the crack, but from what he saw going down at that very moment.

Chapter Thirty-Seven

Tha Pope couldn't believe that he had barely made it by the skin of his chin. He didn't know how God had allowed him to survive, swerving into oncoming traffic and not having an accident. He knew for a fact that he was done for.

Tha Pope continued to think about what almost just happened. Minutes ago, he saw his life flash before his eyes. He saw himself as a youngster, hustling and marrying Rocci, her giving him two boys who meant everything to him. He thought about all the good and bad times. When he came back to reality, he couldn't believe that he didn't die and realized that the only thing that saved his ass was that he knew how to drive, and of course a little luck.

When Tha Pope was a youngster, he raced up and down the streets of East Outer Drive just for the fun of it. Most of the time, he had a pistol in the whip and couldn't stop for the police. That was a mandatory two years in the state joint for a pistol charge. Tha Pope was excited and still shook up from that wild-ass driving.

"Muthafucking Lesson, my young nigga, you are a fucking genius, boy," he said out loud. Tha Pope was feeling like he was a young nigga again. He lived for moments like this. If only his boys could be inside his mind right now, they would see that he was fired the fuck up.

Out of all the years he had been in the game, Lesson made getting money fun again and worth it. Tha Pope had money, but he wanted to make sure that his boys were not out there taking penitentiary chances while trying to get their own money. Lesson

156

was far from a dummy, and Learn was just as smart, if not smarter than Lesson, from what he was learning from his older brother.

Tha Pope made big money selling heroin, but he spent a lot of that money over the years. Tha Pope realized that selling drugs came with too many chances. Either the muthafucka he was getting the work from could be under surveillance, or the muthafucka he was selling it to could be under surveillance, and that kind of federal indictment could fuck his entire world up, just because they didn't want to do the five-year bid on some shit they got caught doing.

That's the real reason Tha Pope started hitting licks, instead of retiring. Licks were fast money and it kept his bag full. Tha Pope knew that this was the type of lick he could actually retire from, after the completion.

Tha Pope would tell Lesson and Learn that he was now officially retired. He was a hood legend and he raised his boys to honor the code of the streets. He told them both either respect the game or leave the game altogether. Tha Pope planned to cash the fuck out, take Rocci, and move to Arizona and chill out. He had to make shit right with Rocci first. She was his heart and he put her through so much shit over the years. She would not want to leave Detroit, but to have her husband back to herself, she would leave the only place she ever known as home. His connect was from down there, and life was good. He had taken Rocci down there on vacation and they lived it up. Now they would make Arizona their home.

Chapter Thirty-Eight

Tap...tap...tap.

"Who is it?" Rocci asked whoever was standing on the other side of her door.

"Ma'am, there's a gas leak in the area. I am to instruct you not to smoke or light any flames for the next hour, ma'am." Juman was talking to Rocci from the other side of the door, trying to convince her that he was a city worker delivering delicate information, hoping that she would open the door. "And if you can, ma'am, can you sign this form? My supervisor wanted me to obtain as many signatures as I could, letting the city know that we informed the community of a potentially bad situation and the dangers of smoking or lighting fires during a gas leak. I will need you to sign this form." He held up a piece of paper attached to a clipboard to the peep hole.

Rocci looked through the peep hole, positioned dead center on the door. The guy outside holding the paper was a well-dressed young man. To her, he did not look like the everyday city worker. However, he looked more like a spokesperson for the city. Rocci was concerned. This was Detroit and she knew that for the city to send someone out to warn the community, the gas leak must be serious.

Ring...ring...ring...ring...

Rocci's phone was blowing up. She already had her hand on the handle of the door and was in the process of opening it to sign the paper for the young man. Rocci pulled the door open and

THE LICK

Juman rushed inside and knocked the wind out of her. Rocci and Juman both fell to the ground. He pulled out his gun and held his forearm at the base of her throat, almost choking her.

"What the fuck are you doing, nigga?" Rocci asked the young man. *This nigga must not know who the fuck I am to be pulling this stunt, especially at my home,* she thought.

Juman ignored her and said, "Bitch, if you move, scream, or talk, I'll blow your fucking brains out of the back of your head." Juman had his pistol pointed directly at Rocci's head.

Rocci looked up and was now staring into the eyes of a man who did not have a soul. She knew he was serious by the authority in his voice. Somebody had stripped him of his soul. She knew she had to follow his instructions or he would kill her. When she looked up, she noticed another man had come into her home. He bent down and put his face next to hers. She could feel his breath on her cheek and could smell burnt marijuana.

Rocci instantly recognized the man. He was older, but she had no doubt who she was looking at and she peed on herself. This was the same man who shot her son Lesson. Rocci wanted him and Nesh dead, but Tha Pope left that decision up to Lesson if Nesh or Savage Keith should die. When Lesson hesitated about killing either one of them, Tha Pope didn't force Lesson's hand. Tha Pope had simply put a bounty on Savage Keith's head and forced them to leave the city and state.

Rocci knew she could possibly die at this moment. All she could think about were the things she had not accomplished: not seeing her babies anymore—Lesson, Learn, LJ, and Lovely. There was nothing she could do right now except hope that these two men would not kill her.

159

The streets had caught up with her, sentencing her for all the fucked-up shit that she had done with Tha Pope. It was finally time to pay and Rocci was not ready to go. Just a few minutes ago, she was chilling with her grandbaby, playing a game of hide and seek. Only her grandbaby could get her to use that much energy before noon. Now she was about to die.

"Bitch, do not scream or act crazy. Ima ask you a question. If you answer correctly, you will not die or get hurt. You understand?" Savage Keith asked.

"Yyyyesss," she responded. Rocci tried to say yes, but could not formulate her words. Her yes sounded more like she was from the south instead of a city girl. She felt like she had swallowed a bale of cotton, so she nodded.

"Where is Ashanti?" he asked.

Rocci did not respond. She could not tell him that her daughter-in-law was right in the next room, using the bathroom. She also couldn't tell him her grandbaby was hiding somewhere in plain sight. They were playing hide and seek, before somebody knocked at the door.

Juman punched the shit out of her, knocking her semi-unconscious. Rocci's head bounced off the tiled floor. Juman placed zip-ties on Rocci's hands, forcefully behind her back. He pulled on the zip-ties so hard that they cut off her circulation and her hands went numb. Rocci could now feel the pain in her head after being punched so hard.

Juman held her by the door. "Wait for me, Juman. Ima go get this bitch Ashanti and we're gonna blow this spot," Savage Keith said and then moved quickly through the house, clearing each room like he was a part of the Special Response Police Team. He opened a door that led to the bathroom. He caught Ashanti with her pants down, literally wiping the pee from her body.

"WTF, nigga," Ashanti said, shocked by this stranger barging in on her like that. "Who the fuck are you? Get the fuccc—" She was in the process of saying the word, then stopped, finally noticing the pistol in his hand. Something about this nigga looked familiar and the look he had in his eyes told her that she was in danger.

"Yeah, bitch, you remember, don't you? I'm not dead like you thought, bitch," Savage Keith said.

"OMG," Ashanti said. "Savage Keith, please don't hurt me. I'm not responsible. I was not even Lesson's wife when that shit went down. Please don't hurt me or my daughter."

"Where is she at, bitch?" Savage Keith asked.

"Who?" Ashanti asked, realizing that this guy didn't have her daughter yet.

"Who? Your daughter, bitch. Don't play stupid."

"She's not here. She went next door to play with her friends after we arrived," Ashanti said, a little too quickly.

Savage Keith slapped her savagely. "At this time in the morning? Bitch, you think I'm stupid or something? When did she leave? I've been following y'all since y'all stopped at McDonald's."

"I swear she left out of the back door and went next door," she said. "Let me run over there real quick to get her," Ashanti said, hoping that this fool would let her go next door, where she would disappear and call Lesson to warn him. She knew that Lesson would kill this hoe-ass nigga for hitting her like that.

Savage Keith pulled Ashanti off the toilet by her hair. "Bitch, you really do think I'm stupid," he said. He zip-tied her hands behind her back and walked her to the front of the house. "Let's go," he told Juman as he was dragging Ashanti. "This can be easy or hard. If either of them try to run or yell, shoot both of them. My nigga, if any nigga run up, let that gun do the talking. We gotta make it outta here and back to Columbus," he said, as he pulled Ashanti while Juman pulled Rocci.

Chapter Thirty-Nine

Lovely was crying. She was hiding in plain sight in the living room behind the couch, waiting on her grandma to finish talking to whoever she was talking to at the door. Grandma's phone was ringing. Lovely wanted to answer it for her grandma, but she didn't want to lose her hiding spot, so she stayed hidden.

As soon as Grandma opened the door, Lovely could not believe what she was seeing. The man knocked her grandma down and was hurting her. Then another man came in and threatened Grandma, asking for her mom. And when she would not tell him, the first guy knocked her out cold. She was so scared. Where was her daddy? He would stop them.

The second man left to go get her mom and a few minutes later he was pushing her to the front door and forcing her and Grandma out of the house. She wanted her daddy; she needed to call him, because he would know what to do. After they left through the front door, she waited a few seconds until she heard a car door slam and a car drive off. She wanted to get out, just in case they came back to get her, so she ran as fast as she could out of the house. She didn't have on her shoes or winter coat. She was crying, but she just had to run.

Chapter Forty

"They're about to run up in Rocci's crib, baby," Unc said, seeing the play before it had time to play out. He had to react, but what could he do? He didn't want to get shot trying to play Rambo and his little gun was only a .25. It wasn't a match for the two glocks that he saw.

Rocci was family. She had always looked out for him and his wife, even after Aunty and Unc fell from grace and became the gossiping dope fiends. If he could help Rocci or Tha Pope in any way, he would. He didn't know what to do. He couldn't just run down there with this little-ass gun he was holding. These boys meant business, and he knew whoever got in their way was going to end up with bullet holes in their torso and maybe a head shot.

Unc noticed there were only two men trying to get inside Rocci's house. Unc wanted Aunty to call Rocci to tell her not to open the door. He wanted to warn her there were two niggas outside of her house with guns and one looked like Savage Keith. Unc knew everybody and he knew for a fact that Savage Keith was back and about to wreak havoc on Tha Pope and his family. Why else would he be pulling a bold move like this?

"Aunty, are you calling, baby?" Unc asked.

"I'm calling, baby, but she won't answer the phone," she said, while still blowing up Rocci's phone.

"Call Skeet and tell him what's going on. Skeet lives about five minutes away. He will come at the drop of a hat," Unc instructed her.

"I'm calling him right now, Unc."

Just then, Unc saw Rocci and Ashanti being escorted to what appeared to be a new black Charger in the driveway. "Dammit, Aunty, they are taking them. This shit is crazy."

"Yo, what's up Aunty?" Skeet said as he picked up his phone. "What's wrong?"

Aunty was talking a mile a minute and couldn't get the words out. Unc had taken the phone from out of her hands.

"Nephew, Savage Keith just ran down on the family. He broke into Rocci's house," Unc told Skeet.

"What the fuck you talking about, Unc?" Skeet asked, as he was already getting in his 2019 black Escalade.

"I'm watching the play go down right now, nephew. They are taking Rocci and Ashanti," he yelled. "They are pulling off right now in a new black Charger with tints headed toward East 7 Mile. I didn't know what to do so I'm calling you."

"Oh my God," Aunty screamed and took off running.

"What's going on, Unc? I'm on my way right now," Skeet said, flying through the hood, running stop sign after stop sign.

"It's Lesson's baby girl, Lovely. She's running out of the house bare foot and without a coat. Aunty just grabbed her. She's crying, nephew. She must've seen the entire thing," Unc said.

"I'll be there in two minutes. I'm right around the corner. Unc, hold on to her. I'm calling Lesson now," he said.

Chapter Forty-One

"Keep this bitch steady, Learn," Lesson said to his younger brother. They were going north on U.S. 23, headed in the direction of I-96 East. Learn would have to merge the big truck over the ramp. With all the weight from Lesson, Learn, Goob, and Jameer, plus the twenty-four money bags weighting 250 pounds each, the big truck was moving extra slow.

There was nothing Learn could do about it, except drive and think about how he was going to spend his cut of the money. Learn was not stupid. He had overheard Goob talking about how each bag felt like it weighed 250 pounds each and he knew something was off. Either Goob was losing his strength, or there was more money in the bags. He didn't want to put Goob and Jameer up on the game about the possibility of there being more money, but he had to know.

"Yo Jameer, crack open one of them bags and look inside to see what was forcing Goob to struggle. We almost got caught when he was loading the bags," Learn said.

"I got you, bro," Jameer said.

"Fuck you, nigga. Wasn't you sitting on your ass the entire time, while everybody else was working, especially me, nigga? If it wasn't for me hauling them bags, we would still be out there and probably got caught," Goob said.

"Shut the fuck up, Goob. I'm not talking shit to you," Learn said, trying to de-escalate the situation. What I'm trying to figure out is why the weight was so heavy."

Jameer had just ripped a bag open. He had to cut through a couple of zip-ties. As soon as he opened the bag, he realized the problem. H didn't even have to open the bags. If he would've read the outside of the bag, the money breakdown was written on the outside. Twenty of the bags contained $25,000 in quarters, and four bags contained $20,000 in quarters. Which was in addition to the $175,000 in all denominations that each bag contained.

Jameer was writing something down on a piece of paper. "Bro, that's a lot of change," he said, staring at Lesson.

"How much is a lot, Jameer?" Lesson asked, annoyed that this was being talked about as a problem.

"How about $580,000 in coins, problem," Jameer said.

"Tell me again, Jameer. How the fuck is a half a million a problem?" he asked, shaking his head.

To Lesson, it didn't matter if it was $580,000 in pennies— almost $600,000 is still spendable money, no matter what form of currency it came in.

"Pops, you hear this shit I'm hearing?" Lesson asked, talking to Tha Pope. Lesson was the only one who still had in his earpiece from the Red Wing team.

"What's up, baby boy? I hear them ungrateful niggas," Tha Pope said. The team knew he was on joke time with them.

"That was some straight up Jeff Gordon driving you did back there," Lesson said, even though he didn't get to see it in person. He heard it all through his earpiece. Tha Pope was still hyped the fuck up.

"Tell Goob's ass that I got something to show him, just so you can see how a real nigga do it. I got it on video," he said, referring to his recording from the drone. "I could not have drawn the play up any better, my boy. How are all the guys doing?" he asked. "You boys handled your fucking business. When the shit started hitting the fan and things started to spiral, you guys didn't panic and y'all kept at it. Tell big Goob I said good work. He definitely played a hell of a role."

"Goob, Tha Pope said you showed up for the game," Lesson said.

Goob poked his chest out and said, "You hear that, Learn? Your daddy said I was the star."

"You were, bro. I can't take nothing from you, Goob. I knew something was slowing you down, and I wanted to figure out what was the issue back there, that's all," Learn said.

"Pops, make sure you bring that drone down and get rid of it, because of the data that it contains. You know if the feds get it and send it to Quantico, then it's a wrap," Lesson said.

"I got it. I had to pull over a few blocks from the accident and fly it to the van. I got it right here. I already smashed the circuit board, and threw it out the window," he said to Lesson. "So we should be good. I got the video on my Google Drive account. It's in the clouds, baby boy."

"I'm about ten minutes in front of you guys. When you guys get to the location, all we have to do is unload the cash, change clothes and everybody jump into the van. Switch and go. This big old thang is pushing, Pops, but she pushing slow," Lesson said, referring to the big truck. "We should be there in the next fifteen minutes. I just hope that U-Haul van holds up for us. We will be carrying a lot of weight," Lesson said.

Chapter Forty-Two

"Stix, you rode up and down 7 Mile and you didn't see no new black Charger?" Skeet asked over his cell phone. He was pacing back in forth in the living room at Rocci's house.

"That's not what I'm saying, Skeet. This is Detroit. Black Chargers come a dime a dozen," Stix said. I saw a million of them joints, just not any that Unc said they took Ashanti and Rocci in. You sure that the Charger was brand new, Unc?" Stix asked.

"Hang on, Unc. You sure that the Charger was brand new?" Skeet asked Unc.

"Hell, if it wasn't brand new, it was a model that was 2018–2019," Unc said. Skeet relayed the message to Stix.

"Me and this nigga, Mac, was straight running down on every black Charger from Pershing High School, all the way down to the Borne," he said, referring to Osborne High. "Them niggas are gone. We gonna have to wait until they want to be heard from. You know they gonna call," Stix said. "They have to want something, or else they would've killed them at the house. I can't keep riding dirty with the heat like this, bro, or Ima catch a case or get blasted running up on all these niggas, like I'm about to jack their ass. This still is Detroit."

Stix was right. They were out of pocket on some wild shit looking for Savage Keith's ass, but what else could they do? They only had one option and since that option failed, they had to go to the drawing board and figure out something else. Stix was a part of Lesson's crew. The team consisted of six friends: Lesson, Learn,

Skeet, Mac, Fresh, and himself. They had all grown up together. Lesson and Learn were real-life brothers, and Skeet was Lesson's right-hand man. Learn's right-hand man was Stix, and Stix's real-life brother was Mac. Mac's right-hand man was Fresh.

Skeet was now sitting on Rocci's couch, holding Lovely in his arms like she was a baby. Skeet felt like Lovely was in semi-shock. She would not talk to him. All she kept saying over and over was that she wanted her mommy and daddy, and the tears were rolling.

Skeet had been around Lovely growing up all these years. He was like her uncle. Skeet had known Lesson since before he made it to high school. Lesson used to come over to his house and creep with his sister, Nesh. Skeet didn't mind, because he knew how much they were in love with each other.

Lesson used to always have Skeet run to Coney Island to get him and Nesh something to eat, and if he did it, Lesson would buy him food, too. One day, Lesson was playing ball, hooping behind Osborne High when he got into a fight with some guy. His homie jumped in to help. They were getting it, because it was two against one. Skeet jumped in to make it a fair fight and since that day, he was Lesson's right-hand man.

Skeet's sister, Nesh, was Lesson's first baby momma. He was LJ's real uncle. He treated both kids equally, but he had a thing for Lovely. She was his heart and always called him uncle. It was breaking his heart that she was in this situation, but there was nothing at all that he could do at the moment, except make plans to lay Savage Keith's ass down when he caught up with him, for the pain he had caused his niece.

Skeet told Lesson that he was shielding Lovely too much, by keeping her locked in the suburbs. Lesson told his right-hand man that if Lovely never came to Detroit to visit family, then she would never see any foul shit. Lesson thought he knew what was best and didn't really show Lovely the ropes when it came to city life, because he never had plans for her to be an around-the-way type of girl. Lesson would not hear any of it. He wanted his baby girl to be raised in the burbs, but understand the city life from his prospective.

Skeet knew that Lovely definitely understood what life was like in Detroit from a conversation point-of-view, but she physically had no clue what was going on in the city. Today, she saw just what the streets of Detroit had to offer. What she saw today touched Lovely personally, and she would probably never forget what went down—and that's exactly what Skeet feared.

"Ay, Fresh, try hitting up Lesson again," Skeet said. "Damn, I can't believe this nigga is not answering his phone, especially when it's getting blown up like this."

They were also calling Tha Pope and Learn. All three of them were M.I.A.

"Bro, he's still not answering his line," Fresh said. "I don't know what's up with this nigga. You think them niggas got a hold of Lesson before they came out here?" Fresh asked.

Now that was something to think about. Everybody in the living room was lost in thought. Skeet was the first to talk.

"Naw, bro, because why would they come out here to get Rocci and Ashanti? I think they are trying to use them for some type of leverage," he said, and everybody agreed. Snatching the women did not make sense, if they already took the men. Skeet and Fresh were staring at each other. Fresh was shaking his head, while looking at Lovely.

"She shouldn't be hearing and seeing all this, Skeet," Fresh said.

Fresh had his hand resting on the back handle of his MAC-11. When Fresh got hold of Savage Keith, he was a dead man. He wasn't going to let Tha Pope talk him out of killing Savage Keith for violating the code of the streets. The code was never to touch a man's family, unless yours was touched first. Fresh knew that Tha Pope would never agree to going after Savage Keith's family, even in this situation with his family being violated. That was the only reason that Fresh had not gone over to Savage Keith's mother's house to put a bullet in her fucking head.

"Give me the phone, Fresh," Skeet said and tried calling Lesson again.

He got the same voicemail as everybody else. He left a message, telling him what happened, and he hoped that would be enough to get Lesson to hit him up, because Lovely needed him. He couldn't handle too much more of her crying. It was personally fucking him up.

Skeet wanted to call Nesh and have her come get Lovely, but Nesh had changed ever since she started fucking Savage Keith. He accused her of trying to get Lesson and him killed. Once he found out that was not how it really went down, their brother and sister relationship was already damaged from years of being estranged. Skeet wanted to trust his sister the way that he had done while they were younger, but shit, she wasn't the same. He also didn't want to call her, because Lesson had just told him that he had to check Nesh for keeping LJ away from Ashanti and Lovely. And because he didn't know what had sparked the recent drama, he really didn't want to call her.

"Fuck it," he said. Skeet knew that he couldn't keep Lovely around all this mayhem. His sister would have to watch her.

Fuck—Skeet was about to call Nesh when LJ walked into the house carrying a football. He took one look around and knew something bad had happened.

"What's wrong, Uncle Skeet?" he said.

"Where have you been?" Skeet asked. LJ told him he was around the corner, throwing the football with his friend early in the morning. Skeet explained to him what just went down. Lovely snapped out of the mental coma she was in when she recognized LJ's voice. She reached her arms out to her big brother.

"Lessonnnn!" she screamed and started crying harder. He picked her up and held on to her, telling her it was going to be okay.

Chapter Forty-Three

"How much is missing again?" FBI Special Agent Dave Opperman asked the chief of Wal-Mart security.

"Almost five mil," Mickelson said, looking dumbfounded. He couldn't understand how this had happened, and especially to him. Mickelson knew for a fact that this heist wasn't his fault. He had followed the same exact routine that he always followed for the past fifteen years. Now this jerk was trying to blame him for doing his job, just because he had a badge saying he was F-B-fucking-I. *Fucking piece of shit*, Mickelson thought. They were inside the Wal-Mart security room, and this fucker who introduced himself as Special Agent Dave Opperman was trying to interrogate and intimidate him like he was a criminal. *Special Agent Dave must not know that I have handled hundreds of millions of dollars over the past fifteen years*, Mickelson thought.

"Dave, you got a second?" another agent interrupted him.

"Yeah, bud, what's up?" Dave asked.

"The owner of Wal-Mart, Sam Walton, is on his way. The owner of this franchise Wal-Mart #987, Marty Sheener, is making a big deal of his arrival and said Sam is flying in on a company jet as we speak. Sam is supposed to be some big honcho CEO of the company," the agent said.

"No shit, Sam Walton is on the way?" Dave asked, all starstruck.

"Yeah," the agent said, "and he should be here within the hour. Marty said Sam is very important and needs to get ahead of this, before the media makes a field day outta this debacle. He wants to assure his stockholders that this was an isolated incident and that law enforcement is on top of this, and they will do a thorough job in apprehending the suspects. Dave, he also said he wants to be the first person to make a statement, being that this will probably bring national attention to the Wal-Mart corporation."

"Is that all?" Dave Opperman asked the special agent.

"Almost. I just want to inform you that FOX News is outside asking questions and setting up their equipment. We also have word that CNN, ABC, and NBC are on the way," the agent said to Dave, shaking his head.

"Okay," Dave nodded, dismissing his coworker. He turned back to Mickelson. "Show me the security video of this armored truck you say showed up thirty minutes before the original armored truck arrived."

"The system was down and we couldn't just let the armored truck sit out front waiting, because of all the money that the truck could possibly be carrying. Over the last fifteen years, we have been trained to move the armored truck as quickly as possible. Our system was down. That included video feed and data, but we still needed to transfer the currency. We were at capacity for cash storage, because of Black Friday and this being Cyber Monday, the cash flow was bound to continue. We would not have had anywhere to put the incoming cash," Mickelson explained.

"Mickelson, the system was miraculously fixed as soon as the fake armored truck left, is that correct?" Dave asked.

"No, I mean, yes, I mean, I'm not lying, I swear," Mickelson said.

"I'm not saying that you are lying, buddy. What I'm saying is, don't you think it's strange that the system started working immediately after the truck left, and the computer data clearly says pick-up for the currency is for nine thirty a.m.?" Dave asked.

"I'm not a computer geek. I just do the job I'm paid to do," Mickelson said.

"Apparently not," Dave said, "because you let somebody come in here and trick you outta almost five million, buddy. The way I'm seeing this picture, either you are a fucking stupid shit-face, or this was an inside job."

"Noooo, it's not like that," Mickelson said. "I've won company awards for top chief of security of the year. I always do my job. I'm not liable. This was a professional job."

"You're gonna have to give me more than that, Mickelson. I need to know more if I'm going to be able to get all this money back and clear you of any wrongdoing. Every second we lose here, going over your story, makes the chances of recovery slim. So start from the beginning again and tell me something that could help us out, because five million has just disappeared. What would you like to say to me, Mickelson? Because I need answers," Dave said.

Mickelson was now sweating bullets, and he could see clearly how he had been played. All the facts were on the table. He had become relaxed and complacent. Everything he had first thought he had done right was wrong, and his biggest mistake was not waiting on the computer to go live again, especially when it came to that type of money. Mickelson should've known something wasn't right when the regular driver, Riley, was not there. But they had a real armored truck that looked identical to a regular armored truck. Hindsight was a muthafucka. If he could do it all over again, he would do things different, he thought. Mickelson knew that he was in big trouble.

"Yes, I would like to say something," Mickelson said.

"What's that, bud?" Dave asked.

"I want a lawyer," Mickelson said firmly.

Chapter Forty-Four

"Pass that weed, nigga. Damn you over there sucking it up," Juman said. "You should've just rolled two blunts, bro, if you didn't want to share."

Juman reached over, grabbed the blunt out of Savage Keith's hand, and started bobbing his head to the music. They were Listening to Money Bagg Yo's "What You Said, What You Said." He was feeling good. It had taken less than a day being back in Detroit to come up on the big package. Rocci and Ashanti were the package. This script could not have been written any better.

If Tha Pope and Lesson ever wanted to see Rocci and Ashanti alive again, they were going to pay big money for the exchange. They would also have to take the bounty off of their heads. Tha Pope needed to know that this wasn't a game, and no amount of negotiation could stop them from killing Rocci and Ashanti, if their demands were not met.

"Savage Keith, we 'bout to run it up, big dog," Juman said to his nigga from the mud.

Juman had thought about this day for years. He knew that all they had to do was get the ups on Tha Pope and it would be a game changer. Savage Keith and Juman had stuck by each other, and now they were about to get paid together.

Savage Keith kept looking in the mirror, catching glances of Rocci and Ashanti. Rocci was madder about the situation than scared. She kept touching her face where Juman had hit her. Rocci's eye was starting to swell. Savage Keith had told her ass to tell him

what he wanted to know and she would not get hurt, but Rocci had
to be on bullshit, even when her life was in another muthafucka's
hands. So Juman cold-clocked the bitch.

"Where are you taking us, Savage Keith?" Rocci asked him.

"We're headed to a safe house down in Ohio for a while. I have
a cozy little spot that's low-key," he said. "Once we get there, Ima
have you and Ashanti make the call to Lesson and Tha Pope, and
we are gonna see what y'all are worth to them."

"Why are you doing this, Savage Keith? Tha Pope could've
killed you, but he let you live after you shot Lesson. You shot my
son over some hating jealousy shit," Rocci said.

She was reminding Savage Keith of the day that changed his
life. The day that forced him to leave his city—the only place he'd
ever known. Those thoughts alone were fucking with Savage
Keith's head, making him mad.

"Is that what Tha Pope told you, Rocci?" Savage Keith asked.
"My recollection is a little different. We were robbing Lesson's ass,
just Like Tha Pope would get a nigga if the lick was right, or just
like Lesson would get a nigga. All I wanted was the weed and the
ten bands he had in that bitch. I knew he had it, because I played
his bitch, Nesh, into spilling the beans. She was mad about Lesson
getting Ashanti's ass pregnant. She said that this stupid-ass nigga
could not get the bitch to have an abortion. Nesh felt like Ashanti
was gonna use the baby to be a part of Lesson's life, so I played on
that while I was giving her this good dick."

Savage Keith laughed, grabbing his dick, reminiscing about the
old days.

"I can't front. Lesson had a good thing going with that bitch
Nesh. She gave a nigga the best sloppy head I ever had till this day,

and fucked a nigga good. I got her to open up about Lesson making her think he was a fool to fuck around on her, being the queen that she was, and she started trusting a nigga with Lesson's secrets. I would see them in the clubs together and I'd salute her, but Lesson would think I was saluting him. I even videotaped us fucking and would show the movie to my niggas. I was just fucking her, because I knew that she wanted the dick, but one day, she ran off at the mouth, talking about if Lesson's spot ever got raided there were ten bands in that bitch hidden. Then she told me that Lesson was about to hit the hood off with this new bud called Sour Diesel, so I had to get the nigga. To this day, I don't know how Tha Pope found out it was me. Shit, I even took Juman down to Ohio to get treated for the bullet wound. I guess they don't call him Tha Pope for no reason.

"While we were up in the spot, Lesson started stalling, then this nigga, Tha Pope, comes from out of nowhere like he John Wayne and blasted my nigga in the shoulder, and I pulled the trigger by mistake. I never wanted to kill your soft-ass son, Lesson. Shit, I wasn't even trying to shoot the nigga. I was just trying to come up," he said. "I think Tha Pope realized that as well. Why else would he let us live? We were young niggas trying to make some money in Detroit, but he had to save face. He couldn't let the nigga who almost took out his son stay in the city, because the streets talk. So he put a lifetime bounty on me and my nigga's heads," Savage Keith continued. "And I couldn't wait around on him to die to be able to come back home to see my family without looking over my shoulders. What about my kids, Rocci?" Savage Keith asked. I'm not a twenty-year-old punk-ass kid no more, Rocci. I'm coming home and I'm not leaving. Tha Pope made his choice. We both know that the city is not big enough for the both of us. Just like I had to live with my choices, he gonna have to live with his choices."

Rocci never heard this side of the story and it made perfect sense. How could Tha Pope be Tha Pope if the soldier who blasted his son stayed in the hood to talk about it? Now Rocci understood why Tha Pope had to save face.

"Why take us down here, Savage Keith, when you could've kept us somewhere in Detroit?" she asked. "Are you planning on killing us?"

"If I wanted you dead, I would've killed you, but you staying alive is not up to me," he said. "That decision alone is for Tha Pope to make. our life is literally in his hands. I'm not gonna be on any bullshit with you or Ashanti. This is strictly business. Your stay with me can be peaceful or hard. We just want the money that we are gonna ask him for. If Tha Pope doesn't send the money fast enough, then Ima send him a message, showing him I'm not playing. If he fucks with my family, then it will be a life for a life, but I know Tha Pope is smarter than that. Ima make y'all as comfortable as I can, but if either one of you get out of line, try to run, or bring unwanted attention, Ima make you wish you took me up on my offer to just listen and follow my instructions. I won't hesitate to kill either one of you. Ashanti doesn't know why they call me Savage Keith, so she may not believe me, but Rocci, you know what's on my resume, so you betta warn her ass. All y'all have to do is wait on Tha Pope," Savage Keith said. "This is the only advice I can give both of y'all."

"What about my fucking face, Savage Keith? You did not have to let this hoe-ass nigga hit me like I was a nigga," Rocci said.

Savage Keith knew that she was upset about being hit by Juman, but she couldn't say that he didn't warn her beforehand.

"That one is on you, Rocci. You made a decision not to tell me where Ashanti was inside of the house, and let's not forget that Tha Pope shot Juman in the shoulder," he said.

"Where are we gonna be staying, Savage Keith? Will we have a bed, shower? What about food and water?" Ashanti asked. She was definitely scared.

"So her fine ass does know how to talk," Juman interrupted and was staring at Ashanti through the rear-view mirror. He could not deny that she was beautiful. You could tell by how he was looking at her that he was attracted to her.

"It doesn't matter where. Only thing that matters is if Tha Pope wants y'all back," Juman said.

"Yeah, it matters, muthafucka. Y'all are violating the code of the streets by bringing family into a man's beef," she said.

"Bitch, this ain't the mob. Ain't no rules in Detroit. He violated my family when he put that bounty on my head when I was just a twenty-year-old kid doing the same shit that made him Tha Pope," Juman said He was getting upset and Ashanti's mouth had just pissed him the fuck off.

"You know what? I don't give a fuck where you take us. When Lesson finds your hoe asses—and he will find you—you will be a dead nigga, you bitch-ass nigga," Ashanti blurted out with malice.

Whapppp. Juman backhanded her with his right hand. Ashanti and Rocci were in the back seat, and Juman hit her so hard that Ashanti's face hit the window and he almost lost control of the whip for a few seconds, before getting the ride under control.

"Homie, chill. You can't let that bitch get to you. We already won and we got too many guns in this ride to get pulled over by the police. The whip smells like weed and we got the hoes in the backseat tied in zip-ties. They gonna tell the police, because they want out. Don't fuck up the investment, my nigga. Hold it together," Savage Keith said.

Juman shot Ashanti a look like this wasn't over.

Chapter Forty-Five

"After you pull in, back the big truck all the way up so the back of the van and the rear of the truck are interlaced with each other," Lesson told Learn. "We gotta move this cash as fast as possible. Goob and Jameer, y'all stay in the truck and pass the bags to me and Learn. This shit should not take more than five minutes. I want to get this shit over and done with so we can distance ourselves from the big truck," Lesson said. He had given out instructions to everybody. "Pops, check your laptop and see if anyone is on the news talking about the lick."

Everybody started working. They looked like they were in a factory working on an assembly line. When they were finished, they stripped off their uniforms and threw them into the back of the big truck. Tha Pope had clothes for everybody.

After seven minutes, Goob and Jameer were in the back of the van, with sweatpants and hoodies on. They were packed into the van like sardines along with the money. Lesson and Tha Pope were up front. Tha Pope was in the driver's seat, still looking on the internet, waiting on Lesson to tell him to roll out.

"It's quiet on the internet, for the time being. I don't see nothing yet," Tha Pope told Lesson.

Lesson Jumped out and walked up to Learn. "Bro, the drop-off is about a mile from here. You know where it's at." Learn nodded. "Bro, drive this bitch inside of the dilapidated building and close the garage behind you after you go in. There's two red five-gallon gas cans in there. Soak the big truck down real good, along with the clothes. Torch this bitch," he said, rubbing the hood. "She was a good, loyal bitch to us, but this was her last ride. After you finish, you will see a 2010 white Caravan outside. The keys are under the driver's seat mat. Meet us at my house in Clinton Township. Be careful, bro," Lesson said and pounded his little brother's fist. Learn jumped into the big truck and took off.

Chapter Forty-Six

Sam Walton was seated in the back of a black 2019 Chevy Tahoe. He was being chauffeured to the site of Wal-Mart #987. Sam was tired. He was ninety-one years old and still running the day to day operation for the company he started in the 1960s. He loved working and he could not find a replacement who loved the business just as much as himself.

Sam had watched the company grow from just one Wal-Mart to become the biggest national franchise in American merchandise history. Sam's company employed thousands of people. His company went public in the late 1970s and his shareholders were every bit as involved in the franchise as he was. Sam was not a good CEO, he was a great CEO. He was the people's champ, and he was hands on. If there was a problem, all you had to do was put in a request to see Sam. He would talk to you about the problem and what it would take to make the company better.

When Marty Scheener, the franchise owner of Wal-Mart #987 in Hartland, Michigan, called and told Sam that there was a big problem, Sam dropped everything he was doing and called Marty back immediately. He asked him personally what the problem was. It had to be big, being that Marty was a franchise owner. Sam knew that it had to be big for Marty to seek him out. Marty explained that somebody had robbed his store. Sam asked if law enforcement was involved. He had dealt with multiple stores being robbed over the years. Sam didn't think this was a big problem, but thanked Marty for the information.

It wasn't until Marty told Sam the details of the system being hacked and a fake armored truck posing as a Brinks truck, which faked out the entire security team—the same security team who had just won a company award.

Sam realized that he had a real problem on his hands. He knew how unfriendly the media was and how they had been waiting for a story of this sort to portray his company with a bad image to make his stocks fall. Sam flew into Detroit Metro Airport in Romulus, Michigan, on his company jet and was on his way to Livingston County to meet with the new Sheriff Mike Murphy and the head of the FBI, David Opperman, who was running the field office for the Eastern District. Sam was not angry. He was baffled how almost five million dollars could walk away without a trace. How can a regular Joe have access to an armored truck and as big of an armored truck? And how could no one have located the truck six hours later?

Sam came to Michigan to get answers and speak to the media. When he arrived at Wal-Mart #987, it looked like a circus. There were Livingston County Sheriff deputies trying to maintain control, because the incident happened in their county. There were dozens of Michigan State Police, and there were the good ole boys, the FBI. It was obvious that a serious crime had taken place several hours ago.

When Sam stepped out of the vehicle, the cameras started flashing and the film started recording him like he was the main actor who was up for an Academy Award. Sam knew that for the next few days and maybe longer, his face would be all over every news outlet across the country for all the wrong reasons.

Chapter Forty-Seven

"Dad, I'm at Grandma's house with Lovely. Where are you? I'm being a man like you always told me, but my sister is scared and waiting on you to come home. Why are you not picking up the phone? Nothing you are doing could be more important than Grandma and Momma Ashanti being taken," LJ said as he left a message for his dad personally. He thought maybe if he called, his dad would pick up for him. "Please call, Dad. This is important." He hung up and waited on his dad to call back.

"LJ, is Grandma and Mom gonna be okay?" Lovely asked her big brother.

"Yeah, sis. They are gonna be okay. I overheard Uncle Skeet saying whoever took them wanted them alive, or else they would've shot them in the house," he said.

"LJ, I saw the entire thing. OMG, it was so scary. Grandma got hit in the face and I really think she was unconscious for a few seconds. This other man was dragging Mom out of the bathroom. I thought I was gonna scream, but somehow I kept quiet," she said. "What do you think Granddad and Dad are gonna do to the bad men who did this?"

LJ was rubbing Lovely's back to console her. He blew a lot of air out of his mouth. LJ knew more about who his father was than Lovely knew. LJ lived in Detroit all his life and his Uncle Skeet was his dad's right-hand man. He saw firsthand what happened when a person crossed the family. He knew that somebody was going to die; he just hoped that this time it wasn't going to touch his family.

Everybody in the hood had respect for his granddad. LJ never in a million years thought something like this could happen to his family. Who would be foolish enough to try something like this?

"Sis, it's gonna be bad for whoever did this, mainly because they did it in front of you, and I don't think Dad is gonna be able to handle it," he said.

"Why do you think Dad is not answering his phone, or granddad?" she asked.

"I think they are both working and don't have their phones on them, but as soon as they cut their phone on, they will come right over here," he said and kissed her forehead.

Chapter Forty-Eight

Skeet, Mac, Fresh, and Stix were still in the living room. The kids had gone into one of the back rooms. Skeet was thankful for LJ being there to console his sister, because there were a few things that she shouldn't be seeing or hearing. Had she stayed out there in the living room, there was no question some of the things she would hear, she would never forget. The living room was turned into ground zero. Each man had at least two guns spread out before them, fully loaded and ready to go.

They were waiting on Lesson or Tha Pope. They didn't know what to do, because they didn't know where Savage Keith was. Only Tha Pope and Lesson knew that information. Had they known where they were hiding, the crew would've blown down on them.

This shit had just become personal, especially for Skeet. Each man had a certain type of loyalty to one another. That's what made their crew so strong. They weren't just homies—they were friends and some of them were brothers.

"What are we gonna do?" Mac asked.

"Whatever we do, I'm right there with you," Fresh said. Fresh was not gonna let Mac out of his sight. Fresh was still fucked up from Savage Keith robbing Lesson and tying up Mac and Skeet right before he shot Lesson ten years ago. He knew if he would've been there, Lesson would not have gotten shot, because Fresh didn't give a fuck. They would've had to shoot Fresh, because he would've gone for his gun. That's just the way Fresh was.

THE LICK

Tap…tap…tap.

"Grab the door, Stix," Skeet said.

"What up doe, Unc?" Stix said, stepping to the side, letting Unc inside.

Unc left and came back in his war gear. Unc had on all black and was wearing an Army fatigue skully. Unc pulled out his little .25.

"I'm sorry, younguns, this was all I was working with. Them niggas had some big shit. I was over-powered, that's why I called you, Skeet. Shit, if I had a ride, I would've followed them," he said.

"You good, Unc," Skeet said. "If it wasn't for you, then we wouldn't know who took them and it would've been hours until we figured that shit out. Your eyes have always been golden. You and Aunty still got those neighborhood eyes. Y'all still see everything you ain't supposed to see, that's why I'm glad you haven't left the hood, old head. Mac, you still got that half of zip you was shooting out there for the testers?"

"Yep, I was out there trying to get it off when all this shit went down," Mac said.

"Give the rest to Unc," Skeet said. "Unc, this should hold you over until we hear from Lesson, but Ima personally tell Tha Pope what you did for the family, old head," Skeet said, giving Unc a hood hug.

Unc saw the work and had that greedy fiend look in his eyes when he realized how much dope was about to hit his hand. He tried to play it off, but he had a forever habit that needed to be scratched.

"Baby boy, I didn't hip you to what was going down for a big pay day," he said.

191

"I know, Unc, but you still gotta get rewarded for lacing my boots," Skeet said. "It's all love, Unc. Take it."

Mac forced it in Unc's hands. Once his hands touched the work, Unc was not going to let the bag go. He was responsible for Aunty habit as well.

"Thanks, nephew," Unc said.

"We just gotta wait," Skeet said. "They will show up." Skeet was referring to Tha Pope, Lesson, and Learn.

Chapter Forty-Nine

When Learn looked through the rear-view mirror, all he saw was black smoke coming from the dilapidated building that Lesson told him to use. When Learn went inside, the roof was sagging. Learn thought that the roof would cave in on him at any moment. Outside of the building was a sign from the city taped on the wall saying Do Not Enter, Unsafe, Condemned.

Learn used the first red five-gallon gas can to douse the inside of the truck. The smell from the fumes was so strong, he thought he might pass out. Learn used the other red five-gallon gas can to douse the outside of the truck. He even poured gas under the hood. Learn poured a trail of gas leading to the entry of the building and lit a match. He tossed the unused book of matches in the grass.

The fire took immediately, and within seconds, the entire truck was engulfed in flames. It didn't take long for the building to catch. Learn had gotten caught up in watching the flames until he realized the fire had gotten out of hand. Learn walked to the Caravan like he didn't have a care in the world.

Learn called Lesson. Ring…ring…ring…

"What's up, bro?" Lesson asked.

"Touchdown, bro. I'm on my way," Learn said then hung up.

Chapter Fifty

Rocci and Ashanti were inside a finished basement. There was a bedroom, bathroom, kitchen and couch down there. They knew they were somewhere in Columbus, Ohio. That's what Savage Keith had told them while they were on I-75 heading south. Besides that information, their exact location was undisclosed to them.

Juman's attitude had changed for the worse after his encounter with Ashanti. Juman knew that Ashanti meant every word she said about Lesson killing him after he found out about the kidnapping, and that alone had ruffled his soul. Juman knew that they were playing with fire. If this shit went haywire, there was not a question about somebody dying. The question was who would die first. If Lesson and Tha Pope got the ups on him and Savage Keith, they were as good as dead.

What Ashanti didn't know was that Savage Keith was really a savage and he had put a play in motion that would force Lesson into the same position that they had been in for the past ten years. Juman and Savage Keith knew that if they followed the plan, they would come out on top.

Rocci was whispering to Ashanti. "Baby girl, you can't show these niggas your anger. They can do anything to us right now. Just let them think they are in control. Once they get in contact with Tha Pope, he's gonna take care of everything. One thing about my husband is that there is no amount of money worth a life of any of his family members," she said with confidence. "He's gonna pay the ransom and we are gonna be out of here, baby, but don't make these niggas mad. Savage Keith told us in the car he had no problem killing us, and there's no doubt in my mind that he is serious, baby. Just think. They snatched us in broad daylight. They didn't care who saw it. They wanted us and they got us."

Rocci was looking Ashanti directly in the eyes, making sure Ashanti understood the predicament they were in and the seriousness of the situation. Rocci knew that Ashanti was scared, because at times she was shaking uncontrollably, but Lesson had showed her how to play her role and she was playing it to a T.

"How long you think we are gonna be here?" Ashanti asked Rocci.

"I don't know, baby, but as long as we got each other, it don't matter. They can play with our heads, but they can't break us. Just keep telling yourself that, baby, and control the words that leave your mouth for the both of our sakes," Rocci said. "We can both lean on each other."

As they were talking, Juman walked down the stairs. He walked over to Ashanti and grabbed her arm, pulling her to her feet.

"Let's go, smart mouth," he said.

"What the fuck are you doing? Don't touch me. I'm not giving you any problems," she said, trying to pull away from the vice grip Juman had on her arm.

"Bitch, I'm not gonna tell you again, and this will be the last time I explain myself before I start slapping the shit outta yo ass," he said. "It's time to call your hoe-ass husband, or do you wanna stay here and get to know a real nigga on a personal level?" Juman asked, wetting his lips with his tongue.

The look in his eyes told Ashanti everything she needed to know—that this nigga was serious. Ashanti looked at Rocci, and Rocci nodded, telling her to go, because she really didn't have a choice in the matter anyway.

Ashanti and Juman walked upstairs together. Once they got to the top, Juman closed the door and locked it, leaving Rocci to her thoughts. When Ashanti went into the other room, she noticed Savage Keith had his shirt off, wearing only his wifebeater. She could see all of Savage Keith's tattoos. Every inch of his torso was covered in them. He was rolling up some more Sour Diesel and never looked up at her.

"Ashanti, Ima let you call your man. Tell him that Savage Keith and Juman got you and Rocci down in Ohio. Tell him that Rocci will be calling next, and to give Tha Pope the number. Tell him that I will only do business with Tha Pope, you understand?" Savage Keith asked.

"Yes," Ashanti said.

"Juman, give her the burner phone to make the call," Savage Keith said.

Juman positioned himself directly behind Ashanti. Her ass was touching his dick. Ashanti did not care about the gesture. All she wanted to do was call Lesson. If she had to deal with this creep for a few minutes before he died, then so be it. She was going to tell Lesson to kill this bitch-ass nigga nice and slow, for all that he put her through today. She would ask Lesson to let her take the final kill shot. She deserved to kill his ass. She had never killed a soul in her life and didn't know if she could do it, but she wanted to be in a position to try.

Ashanti started dialing Lesson's phone number and only got voicemail. She was disappointed, because she needed to talk to him. "Lesson, baby, please listen. Savage Keith and Juman snatched me and Momma. They drove us to Ohio and said they only want to talk to Tha Pope. They said it's up to Tha Pope if they let us live. Lesson, baby, please pick up. This is serious, baby. I need you," she said, as Juman pried the phone out of her hand and hung up.

Ashanti was shaking. Juman did not let her go. She could feel his dick getting hard, but she didn't want to set this sicko off, so she stayed in his arms.

"Savage Keith, I did what you asked. Can I go back downstairs in the room with Rocci?" she asked.

"Take her downstairs, Juman," Savage Keith said.

"Bro, this bitch acts good when she's not in the same room with Rocci. We may have to keep them separated," Juman said.

Savage Keith ignored him and said, "Grab Rocci while you're down there, so she can call Lesson so he can get in touch with Tha Pope."

Juman and Ashanti reached the door. Juman whispered into her ear, letting his wet lips brush against her earlobe. "This is not over. You betta hope Lesson comes to get your ass," he said and pushed her roughly down the stairs, making her stumble all the way down. When she reached the bottom, she fell onto the floor.

"Let's go, Rocci. It's your turn, and don't try nothing, bitch. I know you still mad about your face," Juman said.

Rocci got up off the bed and walked upstairs with Juman. Rocci turned her head to look at Ashanti and winked at her—a small gesture letting her know that everything will be okay.

Rocci grabbed the burner phone and called Tha Pope instead of Lesson, as she was instructed. Rocci acted like she was talking to her son, but she really was talking to Tha Pope's voicemail.

"Lesson, your sins have caught up with Momma. Savage Keith and Juman snatched me and Ashanti. Tell your father that Savage Keith only wants to talk to him. Hurry son, we need to get this over with," she said and hung up.

Rocci new that Tha Pope and her boys were finishing a job and as soon as Tha Pope picked up the phone, he would move Heaven and Earth to find them.

Chapter Fifty-One

"When we pull up to this muthafucka, don't be making a lot of noise, doing too much talking while we are in the garage. Everybody understand?" Lesson asked.

Everybody nodded in unison. Lesson stared Big Goob down. He didn't want any misunderstandings. "We are gonna unload six bags, that's all. And Ima give Jameer his cut first. After he leaves, then Ima give Big Goob his cut."

Once Tha Pope backed into the garage and Lesson closed the door, it was showtime. They all went to work, pulling out the first six bags. Lesson already had the hockey duffel bags he bought from the sporting goods store lined up against the wall in the garage. Lesson busted open the first three bags and took out Jameer's cut, minus the coins. He packed Jameer's money inside of the hockey bags and walked inside the house, carrying Jameer's bag. He hugged his nigga, telling him he did a good job.

"You did your part, so I put an extra $25,000 in there for you, lil homie. You handled your business like a professional. You earned this $525,000. Make me proud. Go legit, lil homie," Lesson told Jameer.

Jameer hugged Lesson, and said, "Thanks, bro. This shit was smooth as hell. Smoothest half a mil I ever made."

Lesson picked up the bag and pushed it into Jameer's chest. Jameer threw the strap over his shoulder and walked out the front door, heading for his ride. Lesson went back into the garage and opened the last three bags. Lesson grabbed all the cash that was inside of the bag, minus the coins, and repacked the cash into a hockey bag. Lesson was moving fast, because he wanted to take care of Jameer and Goob, then take the rest of the money to his lawyer, Anthony Wise, to be laundered.

"Come on, Goob. I gotta get you out of here," Lesson said, heading back inside the house. Big Goob followed Lesson inside and when they reached the living room, Lesson said, "Good work, my nigga. If it wasn't for you, we might have been in trouble. I dropped an extra $25,000 on you, homie, so your cut is $525,000. Just like I told Jameer, make me proud, homie. You definitely earned this bread," Lesson said, giving his big soldier a hood hug. Lesson pushed the hockey bag into Goob's chest.

"Bro, you changed my life. Thanks, Lesson. I'm about to do my thang, and I'm not talking about buying a new whip," he said, pounding his fist on top of Lesson's before heading out the door.

As soon as Lesson locked the door, he went back into the basement. Tha Pope had all the bags out of the van, lined up on the floor of the garage. Tha Pope was busting each bag open and dumping the money out onto the floor. Lesson started repacking all the money into nine Detroit Red Wing Hockey bags, which were bigger then the original money bags from the lick. Lesson didn't need as many bags for repacking. Lesson also added the coins to three Detroit Red Wing Hockey Bags.

Lesson and Tha Pope were on a mission. They were headed to Wise, Storm, and Associates. When the money was repackaged, Lesson and Tha Pope packed the money back inside of the U-Haul van.

"You ready, Pops?" Lesson asked.

"Never been more ready in my life, son," Tha Pope said and they were out of the garage, headed for the law offices of Wise, Storm, and Associates.

Chapter Fifty-Two

"Stand by. We are going live in five, four, three, two, one. Breaking news! Good evening. My name is Sam Walton. I am the CEO of the Wal-Mart Corporation," he said, standing directly in front of the manmade podium. "Standing next to me today is the store owner of franchise #987, Marty Sheener. Today, store #987 was robbed by a team of professionals posing as Brinks Armored Security personnel. No one was hurt, however, a large amount of money was taken from the Wal-Mart security team. Law enforcement is working diligently to apprehend the suspects and bring closure to this situation. I'm here to tell the public not to worry. I am personally telling all of my associates and customers not to worry. Whenever you come inside of a Wal-Mart, it will continue to be a safe environment to shop for merchandise. We will ramp up security to make sure that this situation never happens again. Thank you. I will only answer a few questions, then turn the investigation over to law enforcement."

"Mr. Walton, I'm Veronica Starr, from FOX News. I'm hearing that a hacker was involved and installed an illegal software into your system that prevented incoming and outgoing data. Is that information true?" she asked.

"Veronica, the investigation just started. We personally do not know how this heist was orchestrated," Sam said, instantly dismissing her question.

"Mr. Walton, Lester Holt here from NBC News. Was an identical Brinks armored truck used to orchestrate this heist?" he asked.

"Again, thank you for your questions," Sam said, "but I cannot truthfully answer these questions without facts to back them up."

"Mr. Walton, Larry King with CNN here. Were all the perpetrators African-American?" he asked.

"Sorry guys, I think I answered enough questions for the day," Sam said. "As soon as we have more information, we will share it with the public. Until that time, we do not want to compromise the investigation with speculation. Thank you."

Sam Walton was stunned as he was walking away from the podium. How did the media know so much about the robbery so fast? He couldn't believe how so much information had leaked to the press. Sam had a lot to think about. He would have to hire a public relations specialist to do an image makeover.

"Sam, you got a moment, buddy?" FBI Special Agent Dave Opperman asked.

"Sure, what's up?" Sam asked.

"You really handled that news conference like a pro. I understand why you wanted to put your face behind the camera. The public needed to see that you are taking this situation serious," Dave said and reached out and shook Sam's hand.

"Dave, just make sure that you put all your resources into apprehending whoever is behind this, okay? Because this heist is a very big deal," Sam said. Dave nodded and walked away.

Chapter Fifty-Three

"If my bitch and daughter-in-law were taken, would you act like you don't give a fuck?" Juman asked himself, talking out loud. Basically, it was a rhetorical question that held a lot of legs. "I mean, this nigga must believe we will kill these hoes or fuck these hoes up." Juman had been angered ever since Tha Pope had shot him. Just the thought of Tha Pope left a bad taste in his mouth.

"Chill, homie. I don't think Tha Pope or Lesson knows about them being taken. Trust me, if they knew that both of their women had been snatched, we would've gotten that call. Trust me on that," Savage Keith said, assured of himself. "Ashanti is Lesson's wife and baby momma and Rocci is his mother. Trust me. They don't have their phones on or something."

"So what do we do just wait and play babysitter?" Juman asked Savage Keith.

"Yeah, that's exactly what we are gonna do. Juman, my nigga, what's the rush? Why does this deal have to go down hours after it happened? Do you think it's better if they sweat a little bit and worry about their family members? If we act like holding them is a problem, then shit is not gonna work out for us the way we are anticipating it to," Savage Keith said. "Chill, homie. Calm down. We are about to get paid. All you gotta do is hold on. We've already made it this far, you dig?"

"Yeah, bro, I'm tripping," Juman said.

"Bring Ashanti in here," Savage Keith said.

Juman got up from the couch and walked to the door leading downstairs and turned the combination on the master lock until the numbers lined up correctly. He pulled down on the lock until it snapped open and went downstairs to grab Ashanti. Ashanti was lying in Rocci's lap and Rocci was rubbing Ashanti's back, quietly talking to her. They both heard the lock open on the door and saw Juman come down the stairs, so they perked up.

Every time Juman came into Ashanti's vision, something turned in her stomach. She regretted starting that argument with him in the car on the way here. If she could apologize, she would, but she could not bring herself to saying anything to these pieces of shit-ass niggas. She could tell that Juman wanted to hurt her.

"Ashanti, get up," he said.

Ashanti instantly walked up to Juman without hesitation. "Hey, what's up?" she asked, looking him directly in his eyes.

"Turn around," Juman instructed her. Ashanti turned around and was now facing Rocci. Juman pulled out a zip-tie and fastened in onto Ashanti's wrist behind her back. Juman turned her around. "Come on."

Ashanti hesitated. "Where are we going?"

Slap. Ashanti fell to the ground. She didn't have access to her hands to brace herself from the fall. Unfortunately, she fell flat on her face.

"Didn't I tell you earlier not to question me again?" he asked, pulling Ashanti to her feet. Her legs felt like jelly. No man had ever hit her before in her entire life and Juman had slapped her twice in one day. Ashanti's eyes instantly became moist.

"Juman, please don't hurt her. She's just scared, that's all," Rocci said, trying to intervene and deescalate the situation.

"She's not scared. She thinks I'm your son, hoe ass. I keep telling her I don't play that talking back shit," Juman said, looking at Rocci, but talking to Ashanti. "Come on, let's go now."

They went upstairs. Savage Keith was sitting on the couch watching The Big Ten Network, watching the University of Michigan play the University of Wisconsin on demand. Savage Keith was agitated just watching the Badgers' running back Jonathon Taylor run all over U of M in the first quarter. He had over 140 yards and two touchdowns.

"They're gonna have to fire Coach Jim Harbaugh's ass. It's been five years and he hasn't made the college football playoffs. This shit is pathetic. I think they sent Lloyd Carr into retirement too fast," Juman said.

Savage Keith looked at Ashanti and saw a fresh, bright red hand print on the side of her face. He knew that Juman had slapped her again. Savage Keith was not about to let Ashanti come between Juman and him. If Ashanti would not listen, then fuck her. She would have to fend for herself. Savage Keith had already warned her.

"Who can you call to find Lesson?" he asked her.

"Umm, I can call Lesson's right-hand man, Skeet."

"Call Skeet and tell him to find Lesson. Tell him that we want $100,000 apiece for both of y'all's asses and hang up. You got it?" he asked.

"Yes," she said, glad to be able to call somebody to tell Lesson that she was in trouble.

Juman positioned himself behind Ashanti again. This time, her hands were tied so he asked her for the phone number. She told him and he dialed it for her and held the burner phone to her ear. After a few seconds, Skeet picked up.

"Yo, who is this?" he asked. Ashanti could tell that Skeet was stressed.

"Little bro, it's Ashanti."

"Ashanti, where are you? We've been waiting on your call," Skeet said. "Unc and Aunty saw the entire play go down and Lovely saw it as well. What do them niggas want? Have they hurt y'all?" he asked.

"They want to speak with Tha Pope and want him to bring $100,000 apiece, and yeah this nigga has put his hands on me twice," she said, referring to Juman.

"Who hurt you, Ashanti, and where are y'all at?" He was asking a million questions as quickly as possible.

"They got us in a basement somewhere in Columbus, Ohio."

Juman hung up the phone. "Bitch, I warned your stupid ass." He slapped her again. She fell on the floor again and he pounced on top of her, wrapping his hands around her throat, choking her.

Please God, don't let me die, not like this, Ashanti was praying as she was losing consciousness. She started foaming at the mouth. Savage Keith knew if he didn't stop, Juman he was going to kill Ashanti right there.

"Juman, chill, homie. That's $100,000 you are about to flush down the toilet," he said.

Juman let her go. Ashanti was gasping for air in big gulps. It was harder for her to breathe, because her hands were tied behind her back. She could not believe she was in this position. OMG, what did I do to deserve this from these worthless-ass niggas? she thought.

BRIAN D. ALI, JR.

Juman reached for Ashanti's black leggings and snatched them down, exposing her red thong. Ashanti closed her eyes shut. She knew he was going to rape her and she just wanted him to hurry up. Juman pulled up her shirt, exposing her red lace Victoria Secret bra that matched her panties. One of Ashanti's nipples slid out of the cup on her bra.

Juman started taking pictures of Ashanti's exposed body from the camera on the burner phone. Juman took about ten pictures, preparing to send them to all three phone numbers that Ashanti and Rocci had called. Juman picked Ashanti up. She started screaming and jerking her body, so Juman body-slammed her like she was a UFC fighter, leaving her unconscious.

Juman stuffed Ashanti inside of a closet between the couch and Lazy Boy. He closed the door and pulled the Lazy Boy in front of the door, locking her inside. Savage Keith just sat there watching his friend go ham on Ashanti.

"Bro, you gonna kill that bitch and fuck up our money," Savage Keith said. Juman was out of control. He could barely breathe and he had a deranged look in his eyes.

"Bro, I'm good," Juman said. "I just needed to teach that bitch a quick lesson. Now she knows that I'm not her nigga, Lesson," he said, pressing send on the phone. "Now when they get those pictures, watch how fast them muthafuckas call."

Chapter Fifty-Four

"Pops, help me unload the van. Ima pull the dolly out and we are gonna stack all nine bags onto it and Ima wheel the cash into the law office and drop it off. I want you to take the van back to U-Haul. I'll catch an Uber and meet up with you later. My legal team is about to clean this money and Ima transfer your money into a fresh, legal account for you. How does $700,000 sound for your cut, Pops?" Lesson asked.

"It sounds like legal retirement money," Tha Pope said. "I need to take a shower and drink me a cup of coffee. It's been a long day. It's relax time, plus I want to watch the news and see what's happening."

He helped Lesson unload the bags and together they stacked the hockey bags onto the dolly.

"Ima pay U-Haul for the dolly. Ima tell them somebody stole it, that way you don't have to bring it back," Tha Pope said and pounded Lesson's fist and drove off.

Lesson was tired as hell. It had been a long day and he still had to deal with this meeting. He knew that Anthony would try to con him before the meeting was over. He hoped that this process would be quick, but you never knew when it came to Anthony. He was a great lawyer, but he was also a greedy muthafucka. Lesson had on a brown Nike hooded sweatshirt with the hood covering his head, and brown Nike sweatpants. He also had on some walnut Timberlands.

Lesson started pulling the dolly into the office. When he came in, Cindy, the receptionist, did not recognize him. The last time he was in her presence, Lesson was dressed professionally in a three-piece Gucci suit.

"Cindy, is Anthony in his office? He should be expecting me," Lesson asked. Lesson was pulling the cart past her desk, heading in the direction of Anthony's office.

"Excuse me, sir. You cannot just walk past me like that. Ima gonna have to call security if you don't stop," she said. All Cindy saw was a hooded Black man barging past her, and she was not going to allow that to happen.

"Huh?" Lesson asked. He pulled down the hood and looked Cindy in the eyes.

"OMG, Mr. Day. I'm so sorry," she said. Her face was as red as a ripe beet.

"It seems like you always get flustered around me, Cindy," he said, flashing her his million-dollar smile. "It's okay. I find that attractive, being that you are a beautiful woman and all. Maybe I can take you to dinner one of these days, off the record of course."

Cindy knew exactly what he was talking about. He wanted to go out with her, and it would stay confidential. "Yes, I would like that," she said. "I'll give you my number on your way out."

Lesson winked at her then walked past her and barged into Anthony's office like he was a partner. Bringing Anthony almost a million dollars, Lesson felt like he was now in control. It wasn't every day that someone earns a million dollars just to transfer funds. Lesson wasn't a partner, but this transaction made him a part of the team, and he considered himself top priority for Anthony Wise at the moment.

"What the hell is this?" Anthony asked. He looked up and when he saw a Black guy dressed in sweats enter his office, pulling the dolly backward. Anthony did not get to see who the guy was, only his back.

Lesson sat the cart upright and closed the door. He turned around and smiled. "Anthony, what's up, buddy?" he asked.

Anthony was shocked. He did not recognize Lesson. The guy pulling the dolly looked every bit like a delivery guy.

"Is that what I think it is, Lesson?" he asked. Anthony knew for a fact that the bags contained money. What he wanted to know was how much was in the bags. Anthony got so excited that he had to sit still for a while, because he had a semi-erection and he didn't want Lesson to think he had been sitting behind his desk masturbating.

"Yeah, it is, and more than we talked about," Lesson said. "That's not gonna be a problem, is it?"

"No, it shouldn't be, but how much more, Lesson? I would really like to know."

"How about $3,730,000 in nine Detroit Red Wing hockey bags. That includes about $580,000 in coins. That won't be a problem, will it?" Lesson asked.

"Hang on real quick," Anthony said. He had his calculator out and was punching in numbers. "You know, Lesson, my fee out of that amount will be...let me see...um... $932,500. That's nonnegotiable. Are you okay with that fee, Lesson?" Anthony Wise wanted to make sure that Lesson kept his word.

"Yeah, I know the breakdown by heart, Anthony. And you will wash $2,797,500 for me, right?" Lesson asked.

"Of course," Anthony said.

"I have a Wells Fargo account that I would like for you to deposit the money into, before I leave. Is that okay?" Lesson asked.

"Well, hold on now, Lesson. I don't know if doing this transaction right now will be possible."

"What, muthafucka? That's not what you said the last time I was in your office, or I would not have come here if you was unsure of your capabilities. Now all of a sudden, you wanna change the rules on me?" Lesson grabbed the cart and pretended to start to walk out.

Lesson was bluffing. Tha Pope had already left and Lesson wanted to see how money hungry Anthony Wise really was to make almost a quick million for doing absolutely nothing.

"Hang on, Lesson. No need for the hostility. Let me see what I can do," Anthony said and reached for his phone and dialed Brittney's extension. "Brittney, I have Lesson in here right now. Yes, he has the money. Yeah, it's over three million and he knows we want twenty-five-percent. Yep, he's okay with that. There is a problem, though. He wants the money to enter his account right now. Yeah, come down, please."

Lesson figured Brittney wanted the money and wanted to complete the deal. Two minutes later, Brittney Storm barged into Anthony's office, leaving a scent of an expensive flower perfume in her wake. She walked up to Lesson and gave him a friendly hug. As she looked into his eyes, Lesson thought he was staring into fresh ocean waters, next to a Caribbean island. Brittney's hair was bleach blonde in a tight ponytail with a red ribbon holding the tail together. She was five-foot-four and 124 pounds—a white man's dream girl. She wore an extremely tight fitting short brown skirt and a white sheer blouse. She had a pointy nose and her makeup was done to perfection.

"Lesson, do you want to close this deal or not?" Brittney said as she took control of the meeting.

"Of course, Brittney, or I would not be here," Lesson said, almost annoyed.

"How much cash do you have in the bags?" she asked. When she had walked in, she saw the Detroit Red Wing hockey bags stacked up on the dolly and knew instantly what was inside.

"I brought $3,730,000 altogether and twenty-five-percent of that amount is $932,500," he said. "I want $2,797,500 deposited into this account right here." Lesson slid her the account information for his Wells Fargo account.

"Lesson, you know this will take a few hours, but I can assure you that the funds will be in this account before the closing of business hours today. Is that fair?" she asked, blinking her long, fake eyelashes at Lesson.

"Sure, that will be fine," he said. He shook hands with Brittney and Anthony. "I will be calling you at the top of every hour until the transaction is complete," he said and headed for the door.

Brittney did not respect men. She respected money and power and she knew at the moment Lesson had both. When he went into the lobby, Cindy was waiting for him with a sealed envelope in her well-manicured hands.

"This is for you, Mr. Day," she said. The envelope contained her phone number. Cindy did not want everybody to know her business. She was okay with Lesson wanting to be discreet.

"Cindy, can you call me an Uber, please?" he asked her.

"Certainly, Mr. Day," she said as Lesson grabbed the envelope out of her hand, brushing her hand, sending shocks directly to Cindy's pussy.

Anthony and Brittney were smiling at each other. Brittney was directly in front of Anthony's desk with both of her manicured hands resting on the desktop. Anthony could see well into her cleavage.

"You know your greed could've almost blown a million-dollar deal, Anthony. Baby, you have to know when to fold your hand," Brittney said. "Now, how much is half of our combined cut, sir? My pussy is super wet just thinking about the money in those bags."

Brittney walked around the desk, standing directly next to Anthony. She then stepped out of her European size thirty-seven Jimmy Choo rose-gold crystal covered pointy toe pumps and was rubbing her feet. She loved those shoes. They had cost her almost five grand, because they came directly from Italy, but they hurt her feet like crazy. Every move she made was turning Anthony on.

"Let me feel how wet your little slit is, Britt. You have the wettest pussy I ever felt," Anthony said and reached a hand up her skirt, trying to feel her wetness. He barely came in contact with her moist spot before Brittney tapped his hand away.

"You bad little boy," she said seductively. Brittney had learned a long time ago how to get what she wanted from Anthony. "First, tell me the amount of my half. Then I'll let you play with my slit for the next fifteen minutes."

Anthony was beside himself. He reached for the calculator, punched in the whole amount and divided it by two, and said, "Your half is $466,250."

THE LICK

Brittney was true to her word and let Anthony rub her slit until she came on his fingers. Brittney was hot and bothered but re-energized. She had just made almost $500,000 for doing abso-fucking-lutely nothing. Now it was time to work. She had three hours to transfer the money into Lesson's account. All she had to do was move a few funds around in some of her well-to-do clients' accounts—those who wouldn't immediately notice—and add the money back later. That was simple and would be a piece of cake.

Brittney's mind was busy thinking about the vacation home she wanted to purchase off of the coast of Alabama. Lesson had come through for her. She would get more money out of this deal than she anticipated. When she finished each transaction and made sure that all of Lesson's money was in his Wells Fargo account, she went back into Anthony's office and let him rub her slit again, because she was so excited.

Chapter Fifty-Five

Skeet had just gotten off the phone with Ashanti. He told the homies Mac, Fresh, and Stix about the phone call with Ashanti and that Savage Keith was asking for $100,000 apiece.

Skeet knew that Lesson did not have that type of money, with all his bills. Lesson owned a couple cars and some property, but he was still paying monthly mortgages on them. If Lesson had to raise that type of money, it would take at least a few days. Lesson could ask his crew how much they could pull together, but everybody was paying bills and trying to make it. Nobody was starving, but Skeet didn't think anybody had that much put aside, except Tha Pope. If anybody had that type of chicken stashed away, it was him. And Tha Pope would spend it all to bring his family home.

Skeet knew that once Lesson found out about his family being taken, he would wild the fuck out. Lesson was a calm dude, but when it came to somebody harming his family, Lesson would not be able to think straight. Skeet figured that was why Savage Keith had told Ashanti to have Tha Pope get the money together.

Skeet's phone was blowing up with all types of images coming in from the same number that Ashanti called from. When he started opening them up, he saw Ashanti—the always happy and joyful Ashanti, his right-hand man's wife—with her face bruised and body exposed.

Skeet was not a dummy. The pictures told their own story of what Ashanti was experiencing. He knew that when Ashanti came home, she would never be the same again. Skeet told himself that under no circumstances would he show his crew the pictures. He would let Ashanti save a little face and keep her dignity. One day, she would want to be treated normally without the homies feeling sorry for her, from what the pictures implicated.

"Ima kill that nigga slow, bro," Skeet said out loud. He was mentally telling Lesson the gory details, even though he wasn't there. He wanted his bro to feel him. Mac looked at him and asked him if he was good. "Yeah, I'm straight, bro. We just gotta get our people back and I feel like I'm letting them down sitting around."

There was nothing any of them could do, except wait, and wait they did.

Chapter Fifty-Six

There were fire engines everywhere. They were trying to contain the fire coming from the dilapidated buildings. The fire chief was on site, instructing his crew on the best way to contain the fire. The chief told the county commissioner that they needed to hurry up and demolish all the condemned buildings in the city of Detroit, because they were target practice for arsonists.

"Hey, chief, got a moment?" One of the fireman came up to him in a hurry.

"Yeah, what's up, Bobby?" he asked.

"There's an armored truck inside the building. It's completely destroyed," he said, "but it looks like somebody intentionally started this fire. We have located an accelerant that we believe is gasoline. The truck was completely destroyed, and half of the building has collapsed, but we should be able to pull the truck out."

"Thanks, Bobby," the chief said. "Is there anything else?" The chief noticed that Bobby had an evidence bag in his hand.

"Yes, we think whoever started the fire used this book of matches to start it with. Unfortunately, we don't know how much evidence can be lifted from this item, because the matches were submerged in water," Bobby said.

"Thanks, Bobby. Send it to Michigan State Police Forensic Unit for processing and attach my name to the order for a rush job, please," the chief said.

Once the fire was completely contained, a tow truck pulled the armored truck from the debris. An unmarked older model black

Dodge Charger pulled up to the scene and a tall white man with good hair got out of the car.

"Who's in charge?" he asked to a passing fireman.

"The chief is right over there," the fireman said, pointing.

Special Agent Dave Opperman walked over to the heavyset chief and stuck his hand out. "Howdy, I'm Special Agent Dave Opperman and you are the chief, correct?"

"Yep, the one and only for the past twenty years," Chief Dingell said. After the handshake, Special Agent Dave Opperman got right down to business.

"So, I overheard radio traffic saying an armored truck was torched," he said.

"Yes, sir. We pulled it out a few minutes ago. It's actually over there, if you want to go check it out. I'll come with you," the chief said.

"So what do you think happened here?"

"Well, we know for a fact that an accelerant was used and we believe it to be gasoline—a lot of it, actually. And whoever torched it apparently did not want to leave a trace of evidence. Except for the metal frame, they succeeded," the chief said. "However, one of my firemen found a book of matches that may contain evidence. Unfortunately, they were submerged it in water. I told him to rush the matches to the Michigan State Police Forensic Unit to see if they can obtain some evidence from the item."

"Well, you've been a big help, Chief Dingell. I may have to buy you lunch in the future," Dave said.

"That would be well received," Chief Dingell said.

"Hey, you mind if I take a closer look at the truck?"

"Not at all. Take all the time you need."

Dave walked around the big truck and said out loud, to no one in particular, "What are the chances of an armored truck being burned less than a day after a major heist that also involved an armored truck? It has to be connected. These are not your regular street thugs. They really knew what they were doing, and the only way I'm going to catch these guys is if they slipped up somewhere, and so far they have a perfect record. Let's hope the chief is onto something with the book of matches."

Chapter Fifty-Seven

"Damn, that shower felt good," Learn said. "Ima have to call Tia over here to give me one of her famous massages."

Learn was acting like he did the major lifting during the lick. His body was stiff from sitting still and worrying for more than five weeks. He was glad it was over. He had a lot of things that he needed to do, once Lesson laundered the money.

Lesson was gonna give Tha Pope an extra $200,000 for a total of $700,000. Lesson had first told Tha Pope that he would give him a cut of $500,000, but Tha Pope had risked his life and freedom for the team and was prepared to crash into the real armored truck. The rest they would split right down the middle.

Lesson had said something to Learn about this big investment that he had going down in Corktown and he wanted Learn to go in with him and invest the majority of the money. If Learn took Lesson up on his offer, that would leave them $97,500 to split. Lesson had told Learn that he wanted to buy his hacker a house out in Taylor for almost $70,000. So that would leave even less money.

Learn didn't know if he wanted to be that broke, knowing he had about one million in clean money in the palm of his hands, but Lesson did say that the property could be sold within a year for five to ten million. Learn knew that he would be stupid if he didn't take Lesson up on that offer. Plus, he wanted to do business with Jessica, Lesson's real estate agent. All of the properties that

Lesson had bought from her were cheap and he could flip them for more than he purchased them for.

Learned picked up his phone and held down the power button to cut the phone on. His phone had been off all day and he wanted to see which of his female friends was thinking about him the most.

WTF! Learn had seventy-five missed calls, thirty voice messages, and ten incoming images. He wanted to see who was sending him pictures. Everything else could wait. Learn started sliding through the pictures and what he saw made his heart drop.

"Is this some type of game?" he said out loud. Why the fuck would Ashanti be sending him pictures of herself tied up and exposed? Learn had never seen Ashanti naked by mistake, so why would she do this?

Then Learn noticed the bruises on her face and he knew that Ashanti was in some type of trouble. He remembered all the missed calls and voicemails and he started listening to the voicemails first, while texting Lesson about the pictures. Stix had left damn near every message on his voicemail, telling him that his mom and Ashanti had been snatched by Savage Keith and his right-hand man, Juman. Learn's head was spinning.

This shit could not be happening, especially right now, when everything was going right for him. If this shit was true, Savage Keith would pay with his life.

Learn thought about a few days earlier, when he had seen his mom. He couldn't believe that a bitch-ass nigga like Savage Keith, who Tha Pope sent away years ago, was back and pulling stunts like this.

THE LICK

Learn called his mom and got voicemail. Next, Learn called Stix, and it broke his heart what he heard. Learn knew that all of the homies were at Rocci's house. He knew that he needed to get there, immediately. Learn jumped into his white 2019 R8 Audi Spyder. The car was built for power, a V10 coupe with 562 HP. He stepped on it and headed to Rocci's house, blowing past everything except the wind.

Chapter Fifty-Eight

Lesson checked his account and his heart almost dropped. What he saw fucked him up for real—$2,797,500 in legal cash was staring right at him.

"Touchdown, baby," he said.

Finally, it was over with. He had hit the lick, finished the lick, paid Jameer and Goob, and washed the money. He lost damn near two million dollars paying all the expenses that he needed to complete the lick and give his crew their cut. When it was all said and done, Lesson's and Learn's cuts would be one million apiece. They would buy the apartment building in Corktown, sell that joint, and either double or triple their money. Right now, Lesson was staring at his bank account and it felt good. He was officially a millionaire at thirty years old. And his money was legal.

He tapped a few keys on his computer and transferred $700,000 to Tha Pope's account. He knew that Tha Pope would be excited to see his balance skyrocket.

Lesson wanted to tell Learn that everything was a go. Lesson picked up his phone and powered it on. He had ninety missed calls, forty-six voicemails and ten images.

"Who the fuck is this blowing my shit up like this?" Lesson said out loud and scanned the images. He saw his wife tied up and exposed down to her panties and bra, and her nipple was showing. Lesson also noticed a bruise on her face. "What the fuck is going on?" Lesson yelled to no one. He knew that something bad had happened, but he needed to find out more. He listened to one of

Skeet's voicemails and almost had a heart attack. He immediately called Skeet.

"Yo, my nigga. What the fuck is going on?" he asked.

"Bro, did you get my voicemails and all my calls?" Skeet asked.

"Yeah, I'm looking at them now, bro. Is this a game?" Lesson asked, even though he already knew that this was serious.

"Bro, the entire crew is at Rocci's house. Learn just pulled up now. We have been here since early this morning," Skeet said. "Lovely saw the entire thing, bro. She's fucked up bad, bro. LJ got her in the room right now. I called my sister, Nesh. She hasn't made it here yet to pick up the kids. I didn't know if you wanted me to, because of what went down ten years ago. Savage Keith and Juman snatched your mom and Ashanti and took them down to Columbus and said they want $100,000 apiece and they only want Tha Pope to facilitate the deal."

"I don't give a fuck what they want. These niggas violated my fam. They touched my family and my daughter saw this shit, bro. I'm on my way."

He jumped into his Dodge Charger and took off. Lesson could not think at all. He was speeding, running red lights and blowing through stop signs, trying to get to his kids and his niggas. When Lesson arrived at the house, he left the keys in the car and ran inside. Mac, Skeet, Stix, and Fresh were all in the living room.

"Where's my daughter?" Lesson asked.

Skeet pointed to the back room. Lesson went back there and saw his little brother holding Lovely. She was crying her eyes out. Lesson saw his son and instantly realized that his namesake had grown up today. Young LJ had a lot on his plate, but he was handling himself like a man and that forced Lesson to respect him a lot more. He was proud of LJ for taking care of his sister during this crisis. Lesson reached his son and hugged him tight, then kissed the top of his head.

"You okay, boy?" he asked.

"Yeah, Dad, I'm good. I tried to be a man while you were gone."

Lovely looked up when she heard her father's voice. She saw her father and their eyes connected. She stopped crying.

"Dad, I knew you would come," she said and reached out to him to be picked up.

He held his baby girl in his arms. What hurt him the most, right at this moment, was that his lifestyle had caught up with him and had touched his family. When he first met Ashanti, he never thought sleeping with her would bring him years of pain. Lesson could not blame Nesh for fucking another nigga, but damn, why did she choose to fuck a nigga who wanted to bring destruction to his life every chance he got?

"I'm so sorry you had to see everything you saw today, baby," he said.

"Dad, they hurt Grandma and forced Mommy and Grandma to go with them. I was hiding. Me and Grandma were playing hide and seek and somebody knocked on the door. Grandma answered it and he knocked her down," Lovely said. "I was so scared, Dad."

Lovely started crying again, to the point that she was hyperventilating. Learn was sitting on the bed. He didn't know what to say. His crew had briefed him about everything that had happened. They were waiting on Lesson and Tha Pope to show up. Learn didn't think Tha Pope knew what was going on. All this news had been sprung on him in a matter of minutes. Learn got up and looked at Lesson.

"Does Pops know what's going on?" he asked his older brother, who was in tears holding his baby daughter in his arms.

"I don't know, bro. You wanna go get him?" Lesson asked, trying to conceal his emotions.

"It's okay, Dad, don't cry," Lovely said.

"I'm going to get Tha Pope. I'll be back, bro," Learn said and tried calling his father again. "Shit, he still hasn't cut his phone on and we are losing time."

Lesson nodded and Learn left the room.

"Where you going, bro?" Stix asked Learn.

"To get Tha Pope."

"We rolling together then," Stix said. Stix wasn't gonna let his right-hand man out of his sight. From this point on, they would all ride in twos, until further notice.

Chapter Fifty-Nine

As soon as Learn and Stix stepped onto the porch, they saw Tha Pope pull up in his 2019 yellow Corvette Stingray. When he got out of the whip, he was dressed in money. Tha Pope had on a black three-piece Armani suit and black gators. Tha Pope looked like money. Most young niggas spent their money on $200 sneakers and $500 jeans. That wasn't how Tha Pope spent his money. Tha Pope spent his money on alligators shoes and expensive suits. Tha Pope wasn't playing when it came to being fresh. When he stepped on the scene, all eyes were on him. When he saw all the familiar cars in the driveway, he yelled to Learn.

"Why didn't y'all invite me to the party?" he asked, smiling. Learn did not return his smile and instantly Tha Pope's street sense picked up on the fact something was wrong. He knew that he just inherited a problem. Learn ran off the porch and stood face-to-face with his father.

"Dad, Savage Keith snatched Rocci and Ashanti this morning. He had Juman with him and he did that shit in front of Lovely. She's fucked up, Dad," Learn said, looking beat down.

"What the hell you mean, they snatched Rocci and Ashanti?" he asked.

"I mean, kidnapped, Dad," Learn said and had a defeated look on his face. "Ashanti called and said they were down in Columbus, and they want $100,000 apiece to bring them home."

"Let's go inside, son," Tha Pope said.

He was a little too calm for someone who just realized that part of his family was missing. The information he heard knocked the wind out of him, but he had to stay calm to figure out how to make this situation right. When he entered the house, Mac, Fresh, and Skeet dapped him up. Tha Pope took a seat and put his face into his hands. He could not believe all the shit that went down today. Twenty minutes ago, he just got conformation that he was $700,000 richer and he didn't have to hide the money in a storage locker, because the chicken was legal.

All day, he was thanking God for letting him walk away from the lick and not be in prison. Now his wife and daughter-in-law had been taken over some shit that he could've dealt with ten years ago. At the present moment, Tha Pope regretted not killing Savage Keith and Juman himself. He had chosen to let them live, because they were young and they had heart. They just robbed the wrong nigga and got caught doing it. Had the police caught them, they would've gotten ten to twenty years in Michigan's Department of Corrections, but Tha Pope gave them a way out. He forced them out of the city, but let them keep their lives.

Now that he thought about the situation, he could've called off the bounty, but last he heard, both boys were getting good money down in Columbus, so he let things stay the same as the had been for years. Now that decision bit him in his ass and there was no telling what Savage Keith had done to his girls.

In the background, Tha Pope heard one of his favorite songs, and it snapped him out of his funk. Yella Beezy's "I'm On My Way Up" was playing and Tha Pope started rapping the lyrics, "These niggas tried to take me down, but I'm on my way up." He got up and looked at all his young thugs, and he could tell that they were waiting on either him or Lesson to tell them what to do.

"Ima show y'all why Detroit called me Tha Pope for so many years," he said disappeared into the back room to face his grandkids and son.

Chapter Sixty

All these cameras and nothing on them. "Everything looks normal," he said. Special Agent Dave Opperman was sitting at his desk, reviewing twenty-four different cameras from twenty-four different locations, all facing Highlander Road. Dave had downloaded these videos on a thumb drive. "There has to be something on these videos that I can use."

Dave was getting frustrated, searching for clues to break the case wide open. He had a map tacked onto the bulletin board of Highlander Road. He had thumbtacks strategically placed in the spots where he confiscated videos. He opened the Taco Bell video to review the outside, facing the parking lot. After a few minutes, he paused the video and called Taco Bell.

Ring...ring...

"Taco Bell, this is Becky. How may I help you?" the employee said.

"Hi, Becky. I'm Special Agent Dave Opperman. I'm working on the heist that happened across the street from your location at the Wal-Mart. I have a quick question. When do you guys open?" he asked.

"We open at ten a.m.," Becky said.

"Do you guys get to work early, like around eight, eight thirty a.m.?" he asked.

"No, sir. The earliest anyone will arrive is at nine thirty a.m.," she said.

"Thanks, Becky. You've been a big help," he said and hung up. "If they don't open until ten a.m., why would anyone be sitting in the parking lot at eight thirty in a U-Haul van?" he said to no one. Then he remembered something from the traffic camera on top of the traffic light at the intersection of U.S. 23, right before the accident with the real armored truck. A U-Haul rental van was driving erratic right before the accident. Dave was looking at the footage and it appeared that the van was trying to force an accident. When the traffic light mysteriously changed from red to green, the van swerved at the last moment, and a Dodge Ram crashed into the back of the armored truck.

"These two videos are connected," he said. "Let me take a look at the Taco Bell video again." Dave rewound the Taco Bell video back, starting at 7:30 a.m., then 8:20 a.m.

Dave saw a man open the door of the van, place a drone on the ground, and close the door. Seconds later, the drone took off and was airborne. "What is this guy doing, flying a drone at eight in the morning?"

Dave went to the traffic camera again and rewound it to the moment that the real armored truck was stopped. *WTF!* Dave jumped and spilled his coffee in his lap. "Dammit," he said. "Is that what I think it is?" At the traffic light, about twenty feet above the armored truck, he was staring at a drone hovering above the truck.

"These guys are fucking professionals," he said. If he had any doubt before, he was certain now that he was dealing with a team that used a lot of resources to complete the heist.

Chapter Sixty-One

"You wanna go get something to eat really quick?" Savage
Keith asked Juman. He felt like his boy was tripping and maybe
needed some air. He was trying to get him to go outside for a while
and smoke a blunt, come back high as fuck with the food, and get
full.

"Naw, man, go ahead. You go, bro. Ima chill here and watch
the girls. I was tripping earlier, bro. I fucked around and I damn
near lost it, fucking with that bitch Ashanti's mouth. She talks too
much, for real, dog," he said. "But it's not really her, my nigga. Just
seeing Rocci and Ashanti, brought back memories when that nigga,
Tha Pope, shot my ass, and I couldn't even move my arm for six
weeks, then I had to do all that physical therapy. I was tripping, but
slapping that bitch felt good, bro. It was like I was getting back at
both of them niggas, Lesson and Tha Pope. I'm good now, bro.
I'm not gonna fuck up our money. A nigga ain't that stupid to
throw $100,000 apiece down the drain. This is our payday. I'd be
stupid to let this type of chicken walk away from us. We gotta get
that bounty taken care of as well. I'm not stupid, my nigga. If I
blow this shit up, then everything we did today would've been for
no reason. When we get back to the city, muthafuckas gonna
respect us on another level. They're not gonna want what
happened to Tha Pope happen to them, you dig?" Juman asked.
He was backtalking rationally and on top of his game. When Juman
was thinking like this, nobody could out-think him.

"Good, my nigga. Stay focused, because we can't be half-stepping shit, fucking with these niggas. Ima need for you to stay on point, just in case one of us goes down, you dig?" Savage Keith asked.

"We good, bro. Trust me. Now go get that food. Where you going to grab it from?" Juman asked.

"I was thinking of getting a carryout from that new Mediterranean restaurant right by Ohio State University. I think the name is Jobos," Savage Keith said.

"That shit is expensive as hell, bro," Juman said.

"I know it is, but money is not the problem. The problem is that I don't know if they do carryout," Savage Keith said.

"Fuck it, go get some soul food from Betty's. Get the hoes some, too. I know they hungry. They haven't eaten all day," Juman said. "I think only spot that's open is the one on the north side. That's about twenty minutes away."

Savage Keith threw on a shirt and headed out. "I'll be back in an hour, bro. I'm taking the burner phone with me, just in case they call."

As soon as Savage Keith left, Juman pulled the Lazy Boy away from the closet and opened the door. Ashanti held up her hand, covering her eyes from the light being so bright. Her eyes needed to adjust.

"Juman...I...I... I'mmm sorrry," Ashanti said, stuttering.

Juman figured he had broken her dumb ass. She had been difficult all day and it made him feel good, like he was making progress with her.

Ashanti was furious. She was going to play this nigga's head game for now, because she didn't have a choice. Her thoughts were consuming her. She had become a darker person in the short time she had been kidnapped. She wanted Juman dead in the worst way. She was going to have Lesson kill this bitch-ass nigga, and if he did it slow that would be even better. Her back was killing her from being body-slammed. Her head hurt from being knocked around and she had a headache that wasn't going anywhere. Ashanti was a survivor. She knew that she would be okay. Lesson would be there soon to come and get her.

"Get up," Juman said and pulled Ashanti up by her arms. He turned her around and cut the zip-ties from her wrist with his pocket knife. "Go in that bathroom right there and wash your face and straighten yourself up."

Ashanti went into the bath room and closed the door. As soon as she got in there, she was disappointed. She was hoping to be able to escape from a window, but there were no windows in this bathroom. *What type of bathroom doesn't have windows?* she thought. She picked up a blue rag from off the towel holder and washed her face. She didn't know whose rag it was, but it had a masculine smell to it. When she first looked into the mirror, she thought her face was worse than it looked from the pain, but after she wiped it, she saw it wasn't that bad. It was just bruised.

"Hurry up in there, before I come in there to get you," Juman said from the other side of the door.

"Okay, one more minute," she said. On the counter right next to the sink, she saw a box of razors, the same kind that Lesson used as a replacement when his razor went dull. Ashanti's hands were shaking as she opened the box. She reached inside and was about to take a razor out when the box fell onto the ground. The contents inside of the box fell all over the floor and made a jingle sound. "Oh shit...oh shit," she said, trying to hurry up and put the razors back into the box.

"What the fuck are you doing in there?" Juman asked as he opened the door, checking on her.

Ashanti was caught red-handed with the empty box of razors in her hand. She was in the process of stuffing razors back inside of the box as fast as she could before he barged in.

"What the fuck are you doing?" he asked.

"It's not what it looks like. I was gonna take a shower and shave my legs, that's all."

"Bitch, you think I'm stupid? I know what you were thinking of trying, but if you think I'd let you cut me, then you are more stupid than I gave you credit for," Juman smirked. "That's why I can't trust a bitch."

Juman tried to grab the razor out of her hand, which turned out to be a big mistake. Ashanti sliced his hand wide open.

"Uggghh, you stupid bitch!" he said.

Blood instantly began rushing from the wound. He took a step back, trying to look for a way to get a better grip on the situation and make sure that she didn't have enough room to cut him again.

Ashanti was standing next to the toilet, holding the razor out in front of her in her hand. She was in attack mode—survival mode. "Do not come near me, muthafucka, or I'll cut your ass again," she said. She was angry and serious.

"Oh yeah, bitch?" he said. That was all he needed to hear. Juman grabbed a towel and wrapped it around his hand. He punched Ashanti directly in her nose, knocking her into the shower. She tried to grab the shower curtain, but it ripped. She tumbled into the shower and onto the floor. Ashanti dropped the razor, blinded by the tears in her eyes from the punch.

Juman pounced onto her slapping her with an open hand, then his backhand multiple times. Then he picked Ashanti up in a tight bear hug. She was screaming and kicking her legs. He walked her into one of the rooms. Juman threw Ashanti on the bed and as soon as she hit the bed, she tried to jump right back up and darted for the door, but her legs were too shaky. She wanted to get out of the room, but as she reached the door, Juman caught her by the hair and yanked her backward until she fell onto the floor.

Ashanti felt locks of her hair being ripped from her scalp. When he opened his hand releasing her from his grip, strands of her hair fell from his hand. Juman picked her up and threw her onto the bed. He turned her around to where her stomach was flat on the bed. He pulled out another zip-tie from his pocket and tied her hands back up.

Ashanti was hysterical, screaming. Juman reach inside the dresser drawer and pulled out his thumper. When Ashanti saw the gun, her eyes got big and she became silent.

"Yeah, I thought this would quiet your ass up, bitch," he said. "I told your stupid-ass not to fuck with me, didn't I, bitch?"

Ashanti looked into his eyes and saw a man possessed. He had turned into a demon. Blood was dripping from the towel onto the grip of the handle of the gun, down onto the carpet, making red stains on the brown carpet.

"Bitch, you cut me good, didn't you? Ima make your ass pay for this shit this time," he said, walking toward her. He leaned over the bed and whispered into her ear, "If you scream or yell, I'm killing your ass. Fuck that $100,000. You think your ass is worth it?

I'd rather kill your ass and make that nigga Lesson suffer, like we did for the past ten years. You understand?" he asked her, licking her ear, leaving a trail of saliva. Ashanti did not say anything. "Answer me, bitch," he yelled. "I said, do you understand?"

"I understand. Please, I will not say nothing," she said. Ashanti knew that she had crossed the line. When she cut Juman, she had no doubt in her mind that he would now try to hurt her. She just didn't know how he would hurt her, or how much pain he would cause.

Juman put the gun back inside the dresser drawer and snatched Ashanti's leggings all the way off. "I know that you want it, that's why you've been giving me so much attitude all day. Lesson hasn't fucked you good in a long time, I can tell, but you don't have to worry about that anymore."

Ashanti knew that this wasn't about taking pictures. She closed her eyes as tight as she could as he ripped off her panties. Ashanti was completely naked from the waist down. Juman shoved his middle finger all the way inside of her pussy, violating her.

"Tell me that you like it," he said.

Ashanti would not speak. She wouldn't give this rapist the satisfaction he sought. If he was going to rape her, then he would have to do it without her participating. He could force her to have sex with him, but he could not force her to play along with his sick-ass game.

Juman pulled down his Rockstarr jeans, pulling his dick out. His dick was rock hard. He forced Ashanti into the doggy-style position and forced himself inside of her. He was holding her thighs, pulling her back into him and pushing her away from him, picking up speed as he got a better grip on her thighs. Juman felt

Ashanti getting wetter and wetter. Ashanti felt like he was ripping her into pieces. Juman was beside himself. He was fucking the shit out of her.

Ashanti felt like the world was over. She had not slept with another man in over ten years and now she was being forced to. She thought about Lesson and wondered if he would understand, wondered if he would he still want her after he found out what Juman had done to her, and forced her to do to him. Ashanti knew that she could never tell Lesson about tonight. She would take this to her grave. The entire time Juman was raping her, the only sounds heard in the room was Ashanti's muffled cries and Juman panting.

After about ten minutes, he nutted inside of Ashanti. He stayed inside of her until he regained his composure, then he pulled out and went into the bathroom to wipe himself off. When he came back inside the bedroom, Ashanti was curled up into the fetal position. Her hands were still tied behind her back, but she managed to pull her knees up to her chest as close as they would bend.

Juman cut the zip-ties and pulled Ashanti to her feet. "That wasn't so bad, was it? I know you liked this dick, baby. I felt your pussy became super wet, and you was getting into it. I should've cut your zip-ties and let you have a little more fun," he said. "Just think, if Lesson don't come and get you, we can fuck like that every day."

He was making her sick to her stomach. His smell and the way he talked completely grossed her the fuck out.

"Go take a shower. You got five minutes—and don't fuck with those razors. If anything is missing from the bathroom, I'm gonna kill your ass."

She knew he was serious. She wouldn't try anything this time. She needed to live for her daughter Lovely.

While Ashanti was in the shower, she washed her body three or four times to get Juman's smell off of her, but no matter how many times she washed herself, she kept smelling him and seeing visions of him raping her. She tried to think of something else, but her thoughts kept coming back to Juman.

After her shower, Ashanti put all her clothes back on, minus her thong. She had a blank look on her face. She would not talk to Juman, unless he asked her a direct question.

Juman walked Ashanti to the door leading downstairs to the basement and unlocked it. "Don't tell Rocci that you fucked me. She'll treat you the way she treated Nesh after she found out that Nesh betrayed her son for fucking Savage Keith," Juman said, planting a seed inside Ashanti's head so she would not say anything to Rocci. He opened the door and tapped Ashanti on the ass, and she walked downstairs to meet Rocci.

Chapter Sixty-Two

They were all in Rocci's basement, standing around the pool table. Lesson and Skeet stood next to each other on the left side of the table. Learn and Stix stood next to each other on the right side of the table, and Mac and Fresh stood next to each other down on the end. Tha Pope positioned himself at the head of the table. He placed a bag on the tabletop.

"Everybody in this room is family. I watched all you guys grow into men, and y'all watched me retire and let Lesson run the family business. Most of my older homies are either dead or in prison. We have a small problem that turned into a big problem. After we deal with this problem, we can never let nothing like this happened to none of our families again. I'm gonna personally kill Juman and Savage Keith for violating the rules of the streets. Never bring another man's family into a street beef," Tha Pope said.

"Since they already violated, we can blow down on both of them niggas' families. I have all their addresses right here," Stix said.

"No, we are not gonna hit them back like that. We aren't bringing nobody else into this and we don't want the retaliation to spill over and get Rocci and Ashanti hurt," Tha Pope said. "Since Savage Keith wants to speak with me personally, that's what he's gonna get."

Before Tha Pope entered the meeting, he was upstairs placing $10,000 stacks into a bag. He pulled out twenty $10,000 stacks that

Rocci and he had stashed in case of an emergency. This was a big-time emergency. He poured the contents onto the table.

"These niggas want $200,000 and that's what I'm gonna give them," he said. "These boys don't know who they are fucking with. Two hundred thousand ain't shit to me. We gonna get our women back tonight. Ima make the call. After that, Ima make the drop and we will catch up with them later. The most important thing right now is for us to bring Rocci and Ashanti home and rebuild our family, but after I do that, Ima put $200,000 apiece, on both of them niggas' heads," Tha Pope said. "Lesson, make the call and put it on speaker for everybody to hear. I don't want nobody to say anything while I'm talking."

Everybody at the table nodded.

Chapter Sixty-Three

"Damn, boy, this food is good as fuck," Savage Keith said as he and Juman were eating pork ribs, macaroni and cheese, and greens, with butter biscuits. "Ain't nothing like that good ole soul food from Betty's."

Both men loved Betty's because she was from Detroit, and eating her food was like being home. When Savage Keith first came back with the food, Juman called Ashanti upstairs to grab the food for her and Rocci.

Savage Keith was surprised that Juman let her go back into the basement. He also noticed that she had a distant look in her eyes, like something bad had happened to her. Ashanti would not even look at Savage Keith or challenge anything he said to her. She followed every instruction Juman gave her without a problem. When Juman reached out to touch her arm, Ashanti drew back, like she was traumatized.

Savage Keith didn't give a fuck. He was happy that she wasn't setting Juman off anymore. After Ashanti went back downstairs and they were eating, Savage Keith noticed Juman had a bandage on his hand.

"What happen to your hand, bro?" Savage Keith asked, looking concerned.

"Shit, ain't about nothing. Just a little scrape," Juman said.

"You sure, bro? That shit looks like you downslid down a razor blade and landed in an alcohol river. That shit is bleeding bad. You might need to stitch that thang up. You got blood soaking through the bandage, and I don't want all that blood leaking onto the carpet," he said.

"Naw, I'm good, Savage Keith. Don't worry, it'll be all right and I'm not gonna let it leak on your shit," Juman said. He didn't want to talk about it and wanted to finish eating.

Ring…ring…ring…

Both men were caught off-guard by the phone ringing. It was like the world had just stopped. They had been waiting on this call all day and it had finally come.

"You gonna get that?" Juman asked.

"Yeah, I was letting it ring a few more times first, just to let them know that we ain't pressed," he said. Savage Keith answered the phone. "This better be Tha Pope."

"The one and only. You got my attention, Savage Keith. It didn't have to come to this. All you had to do was ask for a meeting," Tha Pope said. "Now you done involved innocent people and brought family into a man's beef."

"Fuck all that extra talking. I got both of your bitches. What are they worth to you?" Savage Keith asked. "And the number better be correct, because neither one of them is worth shit to me."

"I got your message and I believe you asked for $200,000 for the exchange, is that correct?" Tha Pope asked.

"Yeah, that's all we want. I could've hit your hand for a little more, but $200,000 seems fair, and a fair exchange ain't a robbery, you dig?"

"So how do you want to handle this transaction?" Tha Pope asked.

"It's simple. I want you to come alone with the money and we will do the exchange like that. I don't want none of your sons or their crew to come. I will give you exactly five hours to get here and I know how y'all operate, so I know you got the whole crew at her crib. I need to see them on video STILL in her crib while you making the trip. If either one of them leave the video before the exchange, I'm killing both of these bitches," he said. "Do you understand the rules and regulations? Because the penalty of a violation is death and that death will be on your hands, not mine."

"Yeah, I hear you loud and clear. You don't have to worry about my boys coming. They will listen to my directions when I instruct them to do something," Tha Pope said.

"All right, since we have an understanding, I want you to get in your car and head this way. Within three hours, I'll call you back with the address for the location," Savage Keith said.

"You still in Columbus, right?" Tha Pope asked.

"Ain't no better place else I'd rather be right now."

Tha Pope got up to leave. He was rushing; he didn't say nothing to nobody. He jumped into his 2019 yellow Corvette Stingray, not realizing that it was a two-seater, and Rocci and Ashanti weren't going to both be able to ride back. Tha Pope left and headed for Ohio.

Lesson called his phone within fifteen minutes and started whispering, because he didn't want the video chat to pick up his conversation. Lesson was angry that he was forced to stay put. Anything could happen and he was leaving his father, mother, and wife out to dry.

"Pops, I'm going with you. Fuck that nigga. You can't go by yourself," Lesson said.

"Son, he just told you that he won't give me the rest of the directions for the next three hours, so all I know is I'm headed to

Ohio, in the direction of Columbus. Plus, he wants to video chat with all six of y'all at Rocci's house. Ain't no way to get around that, my nigga. Ima go get my girls, give these niggas this money, and bring them home. I love you, son. I have been in worse situations than this before. I can handle this, son," he said, trying to assure his oldest boy that they called him Tha Pope for a reason. "Ima keep you updated on the progress."

"But, Pops…" Lesson was breaking up, becoming emotional.

"Don't 'But Pops' me, Lesson. This shit is serious. Don't risk our family life, just because you want to be there," he said. "Lesson, I know that you would give up your life for your family, and I would do the same," Tha Pope said.

"I love you, too, Dad. Be careful, my nigga," Lesson said and hung up.

Chapter Sixty-Four

Ring...ring...ring...

Who the fuck is calling me? Lesson thought, while sitting on the couch. If it wasn't about his family, he really didn't want to be bothered. Tha Pope had been gone for an hour and a half. Lesson looked at the caller ID and noticed it was Dorian calling. He felt obligated to answer for him, considering all the help Dorian had given him over the past couple of weeks, especially today.

"Hey, Lesson, what's up?" Dorian asked.

"Hey, young fella. How's things going?" Lesson asked dryly, not wanting to let on that this was the wrong time to be calling.

"It's going okay. I was wondering if you were busy right now," Dorian said.

"Yeah, I'm pretty tied up right now," Lesson said. "But you are one of my guys. What's on your mind, kid?"

"Well, honestly, you remember the house you said you would buy me?" Dorian really didn't want to ask Lesson. He wanted Lesson to keep his word and do it on his own time, but the real estate lady had called and said that there could be a bidding war on the property next week, if they had to hold an open house to sell the property.

"Yeah, what's up with the house, buddy? I'm still gonna get it for you, I just ran into a family crisis, that's all," Lesson said. "Is the house still available?"

"Well, yes and no," Dorian said. "I can purchase it for $68,000 right now, but next week, there will be a bidding war, and I may not be able to get it."

"Oh shit, my bad, buddy. I'm sorry on the wait. I know how much that house means to you. Text me your bank account information and I'll transfer the funds right now, and you can purchase the house in the morning. How does that sound?" Lesson asked.

"Perfect," Dorian said. He texted Lesson his account information and within the next ten minutes, $70,000 was pending. Lesson had given Dorian an extra $2,000. When Dorian saw the transaction pending, he thanked Lesson.

"Lesson, I know you said that you were going through a personal family crisis. I was wondering if it has anything to do with computers. You know I can help," Dorian said.

"Not this time, buddy. I don't think you can help," Lesson said and started thinking about the situation. "Hang on for a second, Dorian. Let me think about this really quick."

After a few seconds, Lesson didn't know why he didn't call Dorian as soon as Tha Pope had left. Lesson explained to Dorian how his wife and his mom were kidnapped, and how the kidnappers told him and his crew that they had to sit in front of the video chat camera for five hours, until the completion of the exchange.

Dorian was thinking of ways that he could help Lesson, but he kept drawing a blank. He wondered how he could force the video to show Lesson and his crew sitting at their current location, but really not be there. Then it hit him. Just record thirty minutes of video and keep rewinding it over and over, forcing it to play as the original video. The only problem was if they lost the connection, then they would be busted. Nobody would be able to answer the phone and reset the video. But if that was a risk that Lesson wanted to take, then he could do it for him.

"Hey, Lesson. How many times has the video dropped since you guys have been on the video chat, because of a bad signal?" Dorian asked.

"Not one time, little buddy. We have a great connection at my mom's house," he said.

"Okay, Lesson. I will tell you the risk of this operation first, to make sure that you want to proceed and take the risk, okay?" Dorian asked.

"What are the risks?"

"Well, the only risk would be if the call drops, then you are in big trouble, because I'm not gonna be able to reconnect you, unless somebody stayed there at your mom's house, you got that?"

"Yeah, I got it and I trust your skills, Dorian. So tell me your plan," Lesson said.

"Okay," Dorian said, perking up in his chair and readjusting his headset. He was ready to see if Lesson would go for his plan. "For the past ten minutes, while we have been talking, I have been recording you guys. Tell the guys to sit still and act normal for the next twenty minutes, okay?" he instructed Lesson, and Lesson relayed the information to his guys. "So after I finish recording the video, I'm going to save the video and insert my connection into your video chat software, and I'm going to play it over and over again for the next five hours. You don't have to worry about sound, because everybody knows that these videos have a delayed reaction, after talking a few minutes. That should give you enough time to get there and help your father."

"Yeah, that's exactly what I want you to do, and when you say insert, does that mean hack into the system?" Lesson asked.

"Lesson, you know we don't use that word," Dorian said. "And another thing, do you have the address to the location?"

"Not yet. I'll have to wait on Tha Pope for that information," Lesson said.

"Well, Lesson, if the location is connected to the phone number you have given me, which they are using for the video chat, I have the address for you right now. I ran a trace on it as soon as you told me your family was missing. I thought that maybe it would be helpful. I installed illegal software onto my hard drive that can track government agents, and I'm texting you that information now," Dorian said.

Lesson was amazed by how smart this young man was. He had a special talent that should've made him a CEO somewhere in Silicon Valley, or at Quantico, working for the government.

Lesson received the text and said, "Bingo! Thanks, Dorian, you have saved my ass twice in one day, and now I'm in your debt again."

"Well, Lesson, I can't ask you for anything else. You have always been a great friend to me," he said, smiling to himself. "However, I may need some new furniture in the future," he added, thinking about his new house and how bare it would be for a while.

"That's nothing, little buddy. I will have your home completely furnished for you before the week is out. And if I don't, just call and remind me," he said. Lesson was laughing and feeling a little better. He was so happy that he answered the phone for Dorian.

Things were completely different than thirty minutes ago, when they had no hope. Dorian had figured out a way for them to leave the house.

"Okay, Lesson, your thirty minutes is up. You can leave now," Dorian said.

Lesson was not wasting any time. He was in a rush, because he was now almost two hours behind Tha Pope, and he was about to drive over 100 mph all the way to Ohio.

Chapter Sixty-Five

"We got a rush on that print from the book of matches that the fire chief sent into forensics," Special Agent Rick said to Special Agent Dave Opperman, who had been napping good. He had dosed off, but this call had woken him up. It had been one hell of a day.

Once Dave came all the way to his senses, he figured either this was going to be good news or bad news, and he would welcome both. Good news meant a break in the case; bad news meant more sleep.

"What do you have, Rick?" Dave asked.

"Well, forensics got a call from Governor Gretchen Whitmer. Apparently, she had spoken to the fire chief and she owed him a favor. So she reached out to forensics and she told them to rush everything. That was her orders, so these guys dried the matches out and guess what they found, buddy?"

"A fucking million dollars?" Dave asked sarcastically.

"No, not a fucking million dollars, Dave, but better. They pulled a partial thumbprint from item #243356-19 and ran that into the computers nationwide and we came up with a possible 467,005 possible suspects," Rick said.

"So how does almost half a million people help me?" Dave asked.

"Well guess what, smart-ass, smarty pants, Mr. Fucking Grumpy? We narrowed the names down to the state of Michigan, and guess what? There are only ninety-eight names on the list and we are sure that whoever torched that building is one of the ninety-eight names on the list."

"Well, I'll be damned," Dave said. "You finally have earned your check for the week that I was convinced the government was paying you for doing absolutely nothing. I was jealous, because I always wanted to know what it felt like to sit on my fat ass all day and make $100,000 a year," Dave said, getting up while yawning and stretching. "Can you send me a copy of that list please, Rick?"

"Of course I can, because even you know that you can attract more bees with honey," Rick said, hinting at Dave being nice to him.

Chapter Sixty-Seven

Lesson and the crew were inside Ashanti's Chrysler Town and Country minivan and every seat was filled. Lesson was driving as fast as the van would go. At times, he would hit the limit of up to 140 mph, and when he thought he was in an area where highway patrol would frequent or hide to patrol for speeders, he would slow down to 100 mph, but he never went below that. He needed to catch up with Tha Pope and he could not do that following traffic rules.

Lesson had caught up with Tha Pope somewhat. He was only one hour and fifteen minutes behind him. Tha Pope would be there within the next hour and Lesson would arrive within thirty minutes behind his dad. The way he was driving, it was definitely possible. It was now three a.m., so this deal would be done before the sun came up.

Lesson didn't care about fucking Savage Keith up today. He just wanted to get his mom and wife back into safe hands.

Lesson knew that Ashanti would never forgive him for putting her in this type of situation. He would vow to do everything he could to make it up to her. Lesson also knew that any chance of Ashanti and Nesh working out their difference was now out of the question. Ashanti would hate her for the rest of her life. Lesson knew that Ashanti would blame Nesh for getting involved with a person like Savage Keith in the first place.

He would stop trying to play peacemaker between the two women. What was done, was done, and he could not blame

Ashanti. He would try to tell her to blame him for this situation. He was responsible, after all. Lesson had a chance to kill Savage Keith and he didn't do it. Now he would regret that decision for the rest of his life. All this pain from one simple decision.

Lesson had been up since four a.m. the previous day, which meant that he had been up for the past twenty-three hours, and he wasn't the least bit tired. He wouldn't be able to rest until he had his family back home and safe.

"Bro, how much longer until we get there?" Learn asked.

"Probably a little more than an hour. I'm trying to push this muthafucka at least 120 mph all the way there," Lesson said.

"You think Pops is gonna have them with him when we get there?" Learn asked.

"I hope not, for real," Lesson said. "But then again, I don't know. Dealing with them hoe-ass niggas, we need to be there with him to have his back, just in case. But Tha Pope is smart. He won't make a crazy decision and won't go in unless he thinks things are copacetic, especially knowing that we are right behind him," Lesson said.

In the back seat, Stix and Skeet were wide awake and had their pistols in hand. Mac and Fresh were asleep. They would be ready once everybody arrived.

Chapter Sixty-Eight

"Your husband is on his way to bring me my money," Savage Keith said, standing at the bottom of the stairs facing Rocci.

He felt good about how everything had turned out. He put a plan together and followed the plan to a T. He was gonna take the $200,000 that he was getting from Tha Pope and try to find a connect. Savage Keith figured if he went to Arizona with that type of cash, he could find exactly what he was looking for. The quality would be off the charts, being that Arizona was on top of the border.

He thought about the cash flow in Columbus, but it wasn't like getting money in Detroit. He had made a lot of money down here, but it wasn't home. Tha Pope had stripped him away from his hometown, like the white man stripped Africans from their homeland and made them slaves in America. The slaves learned how to survive and Savage Keith was no different. He not only survived, he thrived out here in Columbus. He had made a name for himself, and in a low-key type of way he would miss Columbus. He figured that he made a lot of connections down here to keep a few spots jumping.

"What time is they coming to get us?" Rocci asked Savage Keith.

"They are not coming. I made your boys and their crew to stay at your home, to prevent any John Wayne-type shit from jumping off. I have them on a video chat. I told them if they leave before I get my money from Tha Pope, then I would kill both of y'all.

Ashanti, you know I'm not bluffing. Juman wants you dead for whatever reason, so it would be in everybody's best interest that my instructions are followed to a T," Savage Keith said and looked at Ashanti, who seemed extremely uncomfortable at the mention of Juman's name. She kept her head down. "Tha Pope should be here any minute. We are waiting on him. Juman is watching from outside, just to make sure he doesn't have any crazy ideas inside his head." Savage Keith lifted his phone up so it was in view of Rocci and Ashanti. "Y'all wanna see Lesson and Learn live in the D?" he asked them, smiling.

Ashanti perked up. She needed to see Lesson, just to make sure that he was real. She wanted to talk to him. Savage Keith showed them the video and they both saw their loved ones: Lesson, Learn, Skeet, Stix, Mac, and Fresh. Ashanti started crying. She wanted to touch Lesson so bad. She wanted him to save her. She would do anything to be in his embrace, because she felt lost.

Rocci's heart was instantly broken. She thought about how Tha Pope having to deal with these maniacs by himself could pose a problem. She wanted her boys and their crew with Tha Pope, but they weren't here, and somehow Savage Keith had won. Savage Keith thoroughly thought out a plan that was foolproof. She hoped that they would just take the money and release them. That was the only thing that she would be able to hang on to—that Savage Keith would keep his word.

"Can I talk to them?" Ashanti asked.

"Go ahead. It ain't like they can help you from five hours away," Savage Keith said.

"Lesson, baby, what's up? Can you hear me?" Ashanti asked. She was waving her hands at the camera and trying to get Lesson's attention, but he ignored her completely and sat in the same spot on Rocci's couch like she was invisible. "WTF! Why are they not answering?" she asked Rocci.

Savage Keith yelled into the phone. "Ay, I got y'all's momma and your bitch right here. They trying to get your attention," he said. Savage Keith was shaking the phone. "Damn, it must be a bad connection or something. Let me hang up and call them back so y'all can talk to them for a minute. As long as they can see that both of y'all are okay, it will make this final stage go by smoothly," he said and hung up.

Chapter Sixty-Nine

Tha Pope was speeding down University Boulevard in Columbus. He was right around the corner from where Savage Keith told him to meet them. He wanted to ride past one time to get a quick view of the layout of the house, just in case shit went haywire. That way, at least he would know how to get out of that bitch with his girls.

Savage Keith told him not to bring a pistol. Tha Pope would not bring a pistol inside of the spot where the girls were being held, but he refused to be vulnerable. He had to have a pistol close by. Anything could go wrong. What if he got robbed before he could make the drop?

Ring...ring...ring...

"Yo, Lesson, what up, son?" he asked, as he pulled up in front of the address Savage Keith had given him.

"Pops, I'm thirty minutes behind you. Stall for a few minutes if you can. I'm still driving at 120 mph. I'll be there in fifteen minutes. I'm out here flying like a ghost, cutting time in half. Just wait before you go in," he said. "We are gonna creep up while you are inside, that joint."

"I can wait about five minutes, son, but that's all. Rocci and Ashanti have been with both of them niggas all day and it's no telling what has happened to them, since they have been gone," he said.

Lesson's stomach turned. He knew the dangers of something foul happening to them, but he didn't want to think about it.

Lesson wanted to believe that all Savage Keith and Juman wanted was the money. He was going to kill both of them anyway, but if they hurt his mom and wife, he would torture them.

"Okay, Pops. I'll be there in fifteen minutes or less," Lesson said and hung up.

Tha Pope waited a few minutes and got out of the yellow Corvette. He had his phone in his hand and a duffel bag full of money. He starting walking up the walkway, heading for the door.

Chapter Seventy

"Damn, this shit ain't working," Savage Keith said to Rocci. He could see the disappointment on Ashanti's face. It was like she was depending on talking to Lesson, for the sake of her sanity. Fuck it. Let me just call this nigga and tell him we good on the video. Ain't no way he can make it down here before we are out of here and headed back to Detroit, he thought.

Savage Keith tried calling the video phone multiple times and it just kept ringing, so he tried one of the numbers that was in the phone from earlier, when Ashanti and Rocci used the phone upstairs.

Ring…ring…ring…

"Yo, what's up?" Lesson asked.

"Why the fuck are you not answering the phone, my nigga? Didn't I tell you not to let the line die?" Savage Keith said, trying to place fear into Lesson to let him know who was running shit.

Lesson had to be quick on his toes and think fast. He didn't know how much Savage Keith knew at the moment about the video chat, but he was sure that Savage Keith didn't know about Dorian hacking the phone and set the video on a thirty-minute repeat.

"My bad, homie. The phone lost the signal and I can't find a good spot right now for that phone," Lesson said. "You know how Metro phones are, homie. But we listened to you just like you told us to and stayed, you know that. You saw us sitting down, waiting on the transaction to be complete," Lesson said, driving faster.

"Bro, just let my family go. Tha Pope never goes against his word. He told me that he just wants the family and he won't retaliate."

"Bro, you know I'm not a dumb nigga, so miss me with that fast-talking bullshit, nigga. We definitely gonna get it on in the future, unless you lay the fuck down, but right now, it's all about the money, and guess what, my nigga?"

"What up, bro? You holding the best hand?" Lesson asked.

"Ima leave you with a surprise after I get my money, you dig? It's gonna be memorable," he said. Savage Keith noticed Juman calling and knew that Tha Pope had arrived. It was showtime. "Lesson, your daddy is here," he said and hung up.

Chapter Seventy-One

Tha Pope was walking up the stairs, carrying the duffel bag over his left shoulder. He wasn't scared, but he was nervous. He didn't know what he would encounter on the other side of the door. He had the cash and he was doing his part, as instructed, but these young boys had a hard-on for him and his family. Why else would they go through so much trouble to bring pain to his family, by bringing them all the way out to Columbus?

Tha Pope knew that they heard stories about him from his past, and they knew that he would move Heaven and Earth for his family. Tha Pope hoped that Savage Keith would remember the mercy he showed to him when he was twenty years old and out of control. Savage Keith played his role to a T, and Tha Pope could not figure him out.

Ring…ring…ring…

Tha Pope answered the phone and put it up to his ear.

"Yo, Pops, I'm eleven minutes behind you. Just take it easy and I'll be there," Lesson said to his father.

"Okay, son. I'm going in now. Whatever happens, I want you to know that today you made me proud. You figured it out and brought success to the family and your team. I enjoyed today. The lick went down perfectly. We walked away with almost five million, and we didn't have to pull out a pistol. Them stupid muthafuckas gave us the chicken. I know they are madder than a muthafucka. I watched the news conference and they are saying this was the best heist in over twenty years, son," Tha Pope said proudly. Lesson laughed on his end. "We are in a situation that we have to take seriously, son, and no matter what happens after I go inside to get the girls, you are responsible for the family, just as I have been responsible for y'all for all these years. I passed the torch to you, son, and you got big shoes to fill. It honestly wasn't fair for me to be your father and bring you into the life, being that I'm a hood legend. I'm proud of you and your brother."

"Pops, I'm eight minutes behind you," Lesson said. "Hang on. I'm on my way," he said, his voice cracking.

Tha Pope hung up and knocked on the door.

Chapter Seventy-Two

"Yo, my nigga. Who was you talking to?" Juman asked.

Tha Pope jumped. He didn't notice Juman creep up on him like that. He no doubt slipped while talking to Lesson. The man he was talking to had to be Juman, the kid he shot about ten years ago.

"I was talking to my son," he said.

"That shit was real sentimental. If I had a father like you, maybe I could've stayed in the city for the past ten years."

"Listen, son, I didn't know who you were when I shot through the door. I'm Lesson's father and he was in trouble, and I had to save my son's life. I didn't know what you young niggas had planned. I just had to help my son," Tha Pope said, trying to reason with Juman.

Savage Keith opened the door, looking Tha Pope directly in the eyes. "Nice to finally meet the man who put a bounty on my head for over ten years," he said. "Is that luxury bag for me?" Savage Keith asked, smiling, reaching for the bag. Tha Pope handed it over with no problem. "Come in. We have a lot to complete in a short amount of time before we leave and I let your women go."

Juman had his 9mm in hand and nudged Tha Pope in the center of his back with the gun, moving him along. They led him down to the basement. Tha Pope was silent. Something didn't feel right, but he stayed calm. He had to remind himself that this wasn't about him. It was about getting the women to safety and home.

As they made it downstairs, Rocci and Ashanti saw Tha Pope and ran up to him, hugging him like the scene at an airport, where a soldier was coming home from a three-year tour in the Middle East.

"Oh my God, baby. I love you," Rocci said. "I will never leave your side again. I don't care about those other bitches. I just want my family back together."

"Ashanti, are you okay?" he asked, hugging her.

"Yyyesssss…I'm okay. It's been a long day. I'm so glad to see you. We need to get out of here. Please, can we go?" she asked.

Tha Pope had never seen her like this. She was really broken up. Tha Pope was not a psychologist, but he noticed that something bad had happened to her today.

"I'm gonna get y'all out of here, once I hear Savage Keith out," he said.

Chapter Seventy-Three

Lesson was speeding. He would be there in four minutes. He knew that his father was inside the house with Savage Keith and Juman. He wanted to be there—and he was almost there. He was flying through Columbus like he had flashing lights on top of the van and it was legal to drive that fast. All he could think about was more than half of his immediate family members were inside of that house with two madmen who wanted revenge over some shit they started in the first place.

He didn't want to lose anybody in his family. He wanted to be there to help his father. Tha Pope had told him that he was responsible for his family, so he needed to bring an end to this ordeal, one way or the other. Lesson did not trust Savage Keith or Juman. He trusted that his father would hold onto his end of the bargain, but those two niggas were grimy Detroit niggas, who had been forced to live in a hole in the ground.

"Lesson, calm down, bro," Learn said. "We are gonna get there in time. You can't stress this shit, bro. We are almost there and Ima need you to be thinking clearly. We can't just run up in there like we are a Navy Seal team. We don't know what's gonna be on the other side of that door."

"I'm cool, bro. Ima call Pops, and hopefully he answers the phone and gives us a few details that we can work with," he said.

Chapter Seventy-Four

"You didn't have to take advantage of us the way you did," Savage Keith said. "We were kids and were trying to come up the same way you came up, and you threw us away, simply because you had the power. You didn't want us around, because the hood would not respect you knowing the little nigga who shot your son was living right around the corner."

"You're right, Savage Keith. You are just like me. You came up hard, but you put a play down on the wrong nigga and family. I couldn't let that slide with me being involved in the streets the way I was back then, but I didn't kill you, because of your age. I sent you away and I knew where you were at the entire time. I wanted you to live and be successful, but you couldn't do it in Detroit," Tha Pope said.

"What about my family, Pope? And Juman's family? We had baby mommas and kids. We was robbing, because we was broke. When you pulled that little stunt, we left our families without money. We couldn't move our families down here. And on top of that, you never considered taking the bounty off of our heads. You said, fuck us," Savage Keith said.

"Look at me," Juman said, forcing Tha Pope to look the other way. Juman was taking off his shirt, exposing his massive shoulder, showing Tha Pope his scar. Tha Pope could see where an old incision had to have contained at least forty-two stitches. The skin had keloid. "This wasn't enough," Juman said. "You shot me for

trying to make money, then you ran us from our neighborhood."
Spit was flying from his mouth as he talked. "We were kids."

"I know I hurt you guys, but I had to make a decision, just like
you made the decision to fuck Nesh," Tha Pope said, turning to
Savage Keith. "Just like you made the decision to stand in the
doorway of my son's spot, holding a gun to him and his friends.
Juman, you didn't have to shoot my son. Savage Keith, you are not
innocent. You chose to hold a gun to my son," Tha Pope said,
staring back and forth between them. "I did not come after y'all's
families like you did mine, and even now, you think I'm gonna kill
you. I'm not, because you're right. I should've taking the bounty
off years ago. I'm giving y'all this $200,000. I'm retired. I'm going
to tell Lesson to let this situation slide, so no more blood has to be
shed. All you guys have to do is walk away with the money and
leave well enough alone," Tha Pope said, meaning every word.

Tha Pope was tired of the lifestyle that he led, and his sons had
enough money to walk away from the hood. Lesson had proven
that he wanted out when he moved his family to Chesterfield
Township. Learn would follow his older brother to the end of the
world.

"Naw, my nigga. Ah, it ain't that simple," Savage Keith said.
"You won't let this go, because I wouldn't after some niggas
violated my family. We either will have to run for the rest of our
lives, hoping this shit don't catch up with us, or look over our
shoulders, waiting on the worst," he said. "So Ima give you a
choice. A choice that you didn't give us. You will have one minute
to make the decision, or Ima kill everybody in this bitch."

Tha Pope knew that this wouldn't end well. Savage Keith had
his mind set on blood being shed and somebody dying. Tha Pope

was sweating. He hoped that Lesson and the crew would arrive. They should be here, if his math was correct, in a few minutes.

"What's the choice?" Tha Pope asked.

Savage Keith pulled out a snub nose .38 from the small of his back. He opened the barrel and placed a single bullet into the barrel, and closed it. The bullet was lined up to be the next shot. Savage Keith pulled his 9mm handgun from his hip and pointed the gun at Rocci.

Rocci started crying. She knew that someone was gonna die. They had followed all these niggas' instructions and he used them to kill them all. Her tears were rushing from her face like a river flowing downstream.

"Noooo," she said. "Please let us go."

"Who do you want to live the most?" he asked Tha Pope. "Is your life worth two lives, or will you be selfish and save your life at the expense of their lives?"

Ashanti fell onto the ground and closed her eyes. She could not watch. If she died, she did not want to see it, hoping not to feel it either. If Tha Pope died, she could not watch. She loved him like her blood father. He had been there for her for the past ten years. How could she tell her husband that she saw his father die? Why would God force her in this position to have to tell Lesson exactly what happened, when it happened, and how it happened?

"Take my life and spare theirs," Tha Pope said.

"No, Pope. Do not do this. Please," Rocci said, getting up and hugging and kissing him. "Please do not do this to me...please. You are the head of our family. We cannot live without you. Give him more money, Pope."

"Baby, look into their eyes. It's not about money. That's not what they are after. They are out for blood. They want to make sure that nobody will come after them, once this is over. And with me gone, they feel like they are on even ground," he said, holding on to Rocci. She meant the world to him. She would never know that those women meant nothing to him. They were just a quick fuck. Rocci was his everything, his lifeline. "I'm so sorry for what I put you through, baby. I fucked up in a major way all these years. The lifestyle of a hustler is never easy on a hustler's wife, and now he realized that. He always runs out of time. I can't believe that it's gonna end like this," he said. "When I woke up this morning, I wanted to surprise you and bring good news that would change your life."

They stood face-to-face and stared into each other's eyes, understanding the love that they always felt for each other. The streets were breaking them apart. Juman pointed the pistol at Ashanti. Ashanti was crying so hard, she felt like she would die from a heart attack if not from a bullet.

"Here, Rocci," Savage Keith said and held the gun out to her. Rocci looked at the gun like it was a snake. She would not touch it. "Pope, tell your bitch that if she don't take the gun and follow my instructions, everybody dies."

"Take it, baby," he whispered. "I'm saving y'all's life. Give me that glory to take back to my sons."

Rocci took the gun from Savage Keith. She held it to her side. It felt like it weighed a million pounds. She was staring at Tha Pope with so many emotions.

"Rocci, Tha Pope made his choice. He is giving up his life and sparing your life, and Ashanti's life. Because Ima a good nigga, Ima give you ten seconds to shoot him in the heart, or I will shoot all three of y'all, as soon as the count get down to one second," he said. "Ten…nine…"

"Rocci, I love you. Don't let him kill y'all," Tha Pope said.

"Eight…"

"Please, baby, shoot me. It's okay."

"Seven…six…"

"I don't want to die by another man's hands."

"Five…four…"

"I'd rather you do it, baby."

"Three…"

"If you don't do it, you will kill Lovely's mom as well."

"Two…"

"Now, Rocci, please do itttttt."

Boom!

The entire basement rocked from the explosion from the gun. Rocci still held the gun in her hands with her eyes closed. She had shot her husband at close range, in order to save her life and Ashanti's, only because Tha Pope had made her. Rocci knew that she could not live in this world without him. They had wasted all these years trying to figure out who was right and wrong, and now Tha Pope was dying.

He was lying on the ground, his eyes wide open, panting, breathing deeply, trying to suck in as much air as possible. Tha Pope had a gunshot wound on the left side of his chest. Blood was now forming in the corners of his mouth.

Savage Keith and Juman rushed up the stairs, taking two at a time, and ran out of the house, never looking back. Rocci could hear a car start up outside and speed off, tires screeching.

Rocci was screaming Tha Pope's name, over and over. She rocked back and forth, looking at her baby's father dying. She reach down and bear hugged him. There was nothing that she could do. Tha Pope's phone rang and Rocci reached inside his pocket, grabbing it. She had Tha Pope's blood all over her hands. She wanted to call for an ambulance, when she noticed it was Lesson calling.

"Lesson, I had to shoot Tha Pope. I had to," she said, sobbing. "They made me and then they left," she screamed.

"Mom, we are outside. Where are they at in the house?" he yelled.

"They are gone, baby. They left a few minutes ago. We are in the basement."

All six men came rushing down into the basement. Rocci told them that they made her choose his life or theirs and Tha Pope made her shoot him. She was hysterical.

"It's okay, Mom. We are gonna get him to the hospital. He's still alive and he's gonna make it."

Mac, Skeet, Stix and Fresh were carrying Tha Pope to the van. When they reached the van, they laid him down onto the back seat and stretched him out. Lesson and Learn grabbed Rocci and Ashanti, and they all jammed inside the minivan. Skeet, Mac, Stix, and Fresh said they would meet them at the hospital.

Tha Pope was trying to talk, but no words would come out. Rocci was on her knees in the van with her hand on her husband's chest. She had opened his shirt and saw the entry wound. Blood oozed from the hole in his chest. She held a piece of cloth that she had torn from her shirt against his wound. She could still feel his heart beating. She knew he was alive.

Tha Pope was still trying to talk. Rocci kept trying to shush him. Blood was leaking out of his mouth with every word he tried to say.

"I love you," he said. "Family first."

Rocci could not stop crying. She hoped and prayed that they would make it to the hospital in time. Tha Pope was hanging on by his last leg. Rocci felt if they could make it to the hospital, Tha Pope would survive.

Chapter Seventy-Five

"Good morning, sir. How may I help you?" a little white woman doing lobby management asked.

The man who was standing alone in line was short and had a stocky build, with smooth, creamy black skin. She thought he had to be either an athlete or hustler. He was wearing a faded blue Rockstarr jogging outfit. It was easily $150 for the jacket and $150 for the jeans. He also had on gray Timberlands. He wore a faded gray snap-back Detroit Pistons baseball cap and a $10,000 Rolex on his left wrist. He was carrying a Detroit Red Wings hockey bag over his shoulder.

"Um…yes, you can help me," the man said to the little white woman. "I need to speak with your manager. I'm trying to make a rather large deposit," he said, showing her a mouth full of teeth. "The amount is kinda large. I don't think we can do the transaction at a teller window."

"One moment, sir. Let me see if she is available right now," the woman said and walked away quickly.

As the man scanned around the bank, he noticed that most of the tellers periodically glanced at him. He didn't understand why, so he just smiled at each of them.

"Hey, Becky," the little woman said to her supervisor as she was walking into her office. "There's a short, stocky-built African-American man asking to see the branch manager. He said he wanted to make a rather large deposit," she said. "He's carrying a bag with him that could contain money or could be expecting for

275

us to put money into it," she said, concerned. "I think he's a drug dealer, Beck, but I could be jumping the gun. Or he's an athlete. He's dressed like one of those guys who's usually on the Black entertainment channel. Would you like to see him?"

Becky viewed the man on her video monitor and he did look rather strange, compared to her typical customers. However, he did not look like he was there to commit a crime. Just in case, she called a number, telling security at corporate of a possible situation.

"Well, Susan, you definitely profiled the man. Didn't you, darling?" she said.

"Well, honey, I think you did the same, calling corporate security," Susan said.

"Yes, I would like to speak with him. He could be a potential client," Becky said and walked out of the office.

About a minute later, a long-faced, well-dressed white women in her mid-forties walked up to the man with her hand extended. She was not an ugly woman, but she was not attractive either. However, she was well put-together and had a pancake for an ass. The short stocky-built man accepted her hand.

"My name is Becky Vorisky. How may I be of assistance for you today?" Becky asked him.

"I would like to make a rather large deposit and I'm looking for a bank that I can be associated with for a long time. I want to start a business account," he said.

"How big of a deposit? I'm assuming cash?" she asked, looking at the hockey bag while raising an eyebrow.

"Well, about $250,000," he said. "And yes, cash, of course."

"Follow me inside my office, sir. Can I ask you your name?" she asked.

"It's Mr. Maggetty."

Once inside the manager's office, the woman pressed a button that was connected to the blinds on her window, closing them, giving them a little privacy.

"Let's get down to business, shall we?" she asked.

Jameer opened the bag and placed multiple bundles of currency onto Becky's desk. Once he finished, Becky got up and grabbed an electric money counter and started counting the money. After about an hour, Becky confirmed the total amount was $250,000 exactly. She began drawing up the papers for a deposit, when her phone rang.

"Excuse me for a minute. I have to take this call. I will be right outside the door," she said and answered the phone on the third ring.

"Is everything okay?" a man asked her.

"Yes, we are doing a rather large deposit," she said. "No worries."

"How large is a rather large amount?" the man asked.

"Umm... $250,000."

"Whew, that's an extremely large amount of money."

"You know, I thought so, too. He says he wants to open a business account and place the funds into it," she said.

"Okay, after you complete the transaction, I'm gonna place a red flag onto the account, just in case, okay? And I will be talking to my supervisor. That's an extremely large amount of money," he said and hung up.

Becky went back inside of the office and completed the transaction. After two and a half hours, Mr. Maggetty was a part of the Chase banking family.

Chapter Seventy-Six

It was nine a.m. All of Tha Pope's loved ones were standing inside a waiting room at Ohio State University Hospital. Tha Pope was in an operation room. He had been in surgery for the past four hours. Every hour, a doctor would come inside the waiting room to give the family updates on his status. Every time a doctor would come in, they would say that he was in very bad shape, and every hour that he fought death, his chances for survival improved greatly.

Finally, the surgery was over. Tha Pope sustained a gunshot wound to the chest cavity that pierced a vital artery that connected to his heart. The doctors operated and reattached the artery, and it was up to Tha Pope now. They sewed his chest back together, trying to get him out of the operation room to start recovery as quickly as possible. Multiple doctors surrounded Tha Pope, tending to his wound, checking his vitals, and making sure that they were doing everything in their power to keep him alive.

A pudgy Arabic doctor in his early fifties entered the waiting room and saw a familiar scene that he had become accustom to. Family members were crying, upset, and hoping for a miracle. Dr. Hassan was not God, however, he was a damn good doctor and people expected him to play God during a crisis. Hassan believed in telling it how it was to ensure that a family did not have false hope. He had seen so much death since he had become a doctor. He didn't get choked up when it came to a human being passing away. What disturbed him the most was family. The sight of

278

mothers, fathers, siblings, and children crying tore at his soul. He did not know how gunshot wound victims could do this to their families.

"Hello, may I speak to Mr. Day's wife and children first, please," he said.

"Yes, I'm Mrs. Day, and these are my husband's children," Rocci said. Both of her sons were standing on both sides of their mother, each holding an arm, supporting her the best way that they could in case bad news followed, and they had to physically support her.

"I'm Dr. Hassan. I'm the ER doctor who performed the surgery," he said. "We have been working extremely hard to try to stop the bleeding and stabilize Mr. Day. Your husband is very strong. He has hung in so far, but there's a long way to go before I can say he's gonna survive. This situation is not in my hands anymore. I've done everything possible. It's now completely in God's hands, if you believe in God. I hope that you are praying for Mr. Day to recover. I have done all that I can do. This was a very serious gunshot wound and he could've been dead on arrival," he said. "Time will tell if he pulls through," Dr. Hassan cautiously explained. "I don't want to give you any false hope, that's why I can only be very blunt with you."

"Doc, in your opinion, do you think he will pull through, based on similar gunshot wounds you have seen in the past?" Lesson asked.

"Sorry, Mr. Day. I can't answer that question. People are different. They are not vehicles. When a part goes bad on a vehicle, it can be replaced immediately," he said. "That's not always the case when it involves human bodies. Only thing I can tell you is that every hour that he is alive, his chances are better for survival."

Nobody wanted to ask a stupid question. It was apparent that this doctor would simply tell it how it was. The doctor was right. There was nothing he could do that he hadn't done already. Lesson, Learn, Rocci, Ashanti, Fresh, Stix, Mac, and Skeet were all praying for Tha Pope. Everybody wanted him to pull through for their own selfish reason, on top of him being family and a legend in the city of Detroit. They would wait it out, because in their hearts, Tha Pope couldn't die on them, not like this. Tha Pope was immortal.

Chapter Seventy-Seven

"Can you drive down to Columbus and bring the kids with you, big sister?" Skeet asked Nesh. "We don't have anyone else to bring them down, and Lesson wants them here, just in case Tha Pope doesn't pull through."

It had been a few days and Tha Pope wasn't getting any better or worse. It appeared that his body was simply in limbo.

"Is it that serious that he won't make it, Skeet?" Nesh asked her brother.

"Yeah, it's pretty bad. You know Tha Pope. He's a fighter, so in our hearts, we honestly believe he will make it, but the doctor told us to take this situation very seriously, because it could go either way," he said. "Lesson wants his kids here with him."

"I love Tha Pope. He was like a father to me before that situation went down, involving Savage Keith," she said. "Bro, I know what I did was wrong, but it wasn't supposed to go down like that."

Skeet was in between a rock and a hard place. Nesh was his older sister. He heard her side of the story. He knew for a fact that Lesson had a roaming eye back in the day, and he strayed a lot—to the point that it got his ass caught up with Ashanti getting pregnant. It was only fair for Nesh to try to hurt Lesson by cheating on him.

Unfortunately, her cheating caused Lesson to get shot. Skeet and Mac got tied up, and now ten years later, Rocci and Ashanti got snatched. Somebody had to take the blame for these events, and the easiest person to blame was Nesh. Skeet had told Lesson that it was not fair for him to be in the middle of a beef between his sister and right-hand man. Even Lesson agreed that if he hadn't cheated on Nesh, they would probably still be together to this day.

"I know, big sis, but unfortunately, shit has snowballed, and look how shit keeps happening. Now Tha Pope is in the hospital, because of Savage Keith," he said.

"But how is that my fault? This nigga Savage Keith is doing this shit on his own. What if it was something that Lesson or Tha Pope has done that triggered him, that's making him retaliate ten years later, while everybody's guard was down?"

Skeet thought about what Nesh was saying, and he now viewed the situation differently. He knew that his sister wasn't a dummy. Her street smarts were what attracted Lesson to her to begin with, and what she said to him made all the sense in the world. He needed to talk to Lesson and ask him a few questions.

"Bro, can I tell you something that's only between me and you?" she asked Skeet.

Nesh and Skeet had been closer than twins. When the robbery situation went down ten years ago and he was almost killed along with Lesson by Savage Keith and Juman, their relationship took years to repair. Nesh just couldn't get through to him, because he felt betrayed. She tried to tell him that she didn't try to set Lesson up, but the way it looked to everybody, Nesh was behind the entire plot.

It took almost five years for Skeet to finally sit down and talk with her, regarding the situation. By then, both brother and sister had changed. Nesh wasn't the same big sister he had grown up with, and Skeet had outgrown his youth. He was a major player in the streets, who was being talked about on both sides of town.

"You know you can talk to me about anything, sis."

"Me and Lesson got together back in July after the family barbecue. We were both drunk as fuck, but I remember him telling me how much he loved me, and I thought that maybe we could go at it again," she said, baring her soul to her brother. "Then this nigga started acting like I don't exist and ignoring me like we didn't just fuck. I swear, bro, it was like we never missed a beat, like when we were younger. I asked Lesson if we could talk. He said he was working a job and it would be a couple of weeks, but too much shit has happened over the last week, and I just need to talk to him."

"Sis, I know you still love that nigga and I know that he still loves you, but he's married to Ashanti, and has moved on with her."

"I know, Skeet, but...but...but..." Nesh couldn't get the words out. She started crying. "But I'm...I'm..."

"What's up, Nesh? You can trust me, for real. Tell me, Nesh I won't say nothing."

"I'm pregnant, bro. I'm five months pregnant," she said. "Lesson is the father. I just wanted to tell him, and I want my family back."

Damn, if Skeet thought a nigga's day couldn't get any worse, it just became that. How could he keep his sister's secret, as he just promised her? And how could he not tell his right-hand man about something that could potentially blow up in his face at any moment?

"Are you gonna tell him, Nesh?" he asked, already knowing the answer to the question.

"Yeah, as soon as I get down there. I want to see Tha Pope and I want the kids to see him as well, just in case he don't pull through."

It was so hard for her to say that, because she knew how strong Tha Pope was. She just wanted to be there for him and show her support. She was still a part of the family she created with Lesson, and his recklessness forced her to make a life-changing decision by fucking Savage Keith. One way or the other, she vowed to change things for better, not for worse.

Chapter Seventy-Eight

"Page Dr. Hassan," yelled a nurse in the ICU, who was servicing Tha Pope.

He was having his second seizure in three minutes. This one was massive and lasted about four minutes. Tha Pope's body was convulsing and looked like he was possessed, similar to when a priest holds an exorcism calling out demons.

Rocci tried to hold on to his arms, but Tha Pope's strength was amazing. It took Lesson, Learn, and two male nurses to hold him down. Dr. Hassan entered the room and immediately inserted a syringed into his IV port to stabilize Tha Pope.

"When did this seizure first occur?" he asked the nurse assigned to Tha Pope.

"Sir, he had a seizure about three minutes ago and I charted it and sent you a page. I thought it was random, then exactly three minutes later, he had another seizure. This time, it was a massive one."

"I'm ordering a CT scan immediately to check for problems and brain activity," he said.

Rocci was staring at the doctor, lost. Both sons were huddled next to their father. Lesson approached the doctor and asked why he was ordering the procedure for brain activity.

"Your father has just had two massive seizures in less than ten minutes. I'm not certain, but I think something is going on inside his head. And science will determine certain things in a way where I won't have to guess. Honestly, I would like to look at scans of his brain. Listen, son, I know this is hard for your family and I'm doing everything I can to save your father, but there's only so much I can do. Your father will have to fight on his own for me to help him recover," he said. "I honestly want to bring him out of this ordeal, but something has caused him to have those seizures, and I need to look at his chart to make sure that he is okay and has activity."

A transport nurse technician came inside the room and immediately started to transfer Tha Pope, with the help of another nurse, onto the transport bed. The room was completely silent. Everyone was watching the nurses tend to Tha Pope. Once they finished, Rocci kissed Tha Pope on the forehead and whispered into his ear.

"Hold on, baby. Ima be with you every step of the way," she said.

They rolled him out, heading in the direction of the CT scan. As they were standing in the room, Nesh walked in, holding Lovely's hand with LJ following them. Lovely immediately ran up to her mom, and LJ to his grandma. All four of them formed a bear hug: Ashanti, Lovely, Rocci, and LJ.

"Grandma, are you okay?" Lovely asked, hugging her next. "I saw that man hurt you pretty bad. I wanted to help, Grandma, but I was scared. As soon as you left, I ran outside and Aunty ran up and grabbed me. She took me to her house and then she called Uncle Skeet to come get me. And, Mom, I saw them take you, too. I don't know why those men would want to hurt you. Can you tell me why they took you like that from Grandma's house?"

"Baby, those men were bad. They are in serious trouble for what they did, okay? That's all you need to know," Rocci told her granddaughter, while rubbing her back.

Lesson was waiting on his children to finish reuniting with their mom and grandma. When Lovely saw him, she came over to him and he picked her up. She laid her head on his shoulder like she was still a baby.

"Dad, can I ask you something, and you promise you will do it before I ask you, so you can't change your mind after I ask?" she asked her father.

"Yes, baby girl, you know I would do anything for you," Lesson said.

"Dad, when you find out who hurt Grandma and Mom, can you hurt them for hurting them?"

Lesson tensed up. Just two days ago, his daughter would never have said something like this to him. What he realized was that his daughter saw more than she was supposed to see during the kidnapping, and it hurt her to the point where she wanted somebody else to hurt. Lesson felt his daughter's pain.

"Yes, baby. Whoever has done this to all three of my ladies, I will get them back and it's gonna hurt, trust me," he said.

Lovely did trust her father and she let the situation go. "How is Granddad doing? Is he getting better?" she asked him.

"I don't know if he's getting better, baby. What I do know is that he's not doing too well, but I think he will pull through. Your grandfather is strong," Lesson told her.

Chapter Seventy-Nine

Knock…knock…knock…

Jameer looked outside of the window in his living room and noticed two white men dressed in bad suits, standing at his front door. Jameer looked beyond them, up and down the street. He noticed that he was not in any immediate danger of a raid.

"Who is it?" Jameer asked through the door. Jameer was standing in his entrypoint and he had on his Detroit Lions housecoat and matching house slippers.

"We are the IRS. Do you have a minute to spare, Mr. Maggetty?" said one of the men.

"Sure," Jameer said and opened the door. "What's up? How can I help you?"

"Can we come in, sir?" asked a pale, chubby white agent, who introduced himself as Billy Wagner. Jameer couldn't take his eyes of Billy's balding spot. It was a perfect doughnut.

"I'm Dawson O'Reilly," the other guy said. He resembled a meth head. He was underweight and his suit hung off of his body, like he had recently lost a lot of weight. "I don't think you would want all your neighbors in your business. This seems like a very decent area."

Jameer offered them in and they accepted. He gestured them to the couch and they sat down. "So what's this about, gentleman?" he asked, using his white voice. "It's kinda early, you know."

"Well, sir, your account at Chase bank was red flagged and I spoke with branch manager, Becky Vorisky, and she told me that you deposited a large amount of cash into her bank," he said. "So we ran your bank account history, your taxes, and your credit. You know what we came up with, son?" Dawson asked Jameer, who was becoming nervous.

"What's that, buddy? I thought you wanted to talk. Now you got me answering questions," Jameer said.

"Nothing. We found absolutely no history," Dawson said.

"So if you came up with nothing, then why the fuck did you wake me the fuck up?" Jameer asked, feeling back in control.

"Nothing meaning you don't work. You don't have a bank account, and you never had a banking account. You pretty much didn't exist on paper financially, until now. You have a criminal record, though. Can you explain how you obtained a quarter of a million dollars without a trace of where it came from?" he asked.

"I...I...I...have my ways of making money and have been saving my money for years," Jameer said. "I also don't have to answer these questions."

"Come on, slick. We are not buying that either, son. If you make money legally, why haven't you claimed any money on your taxes? You haven't even filed...ever, sir."

Billy Wagner had inserted himself into the conversation. They were playing good cop and bad cop.

"I'm not your son," Jameer said.

"There's two ways for you to come in contact with that type of cash," he said. "Either you are a drug kingpin," Billy said, making it sound good, "or you are a...let's let that question hover in the air for a minute, because I think we both know what you are."

"Hey, Mr. Maggetty, can I use your toilet?" Dawson asked, feeling the need to urinate from all the coffee he consumed that morning.

"Yeah, go right around that corner. It's on the left," Jameer said.

He wanted to break these muthafuckas up. They were tag-teaming him and he needed a quick timeout, because he was off balance, a little bit. Dawson immediately disappeared. Jameer picked up a bottled water he had sitting on his table, twisted the top, and took a gulp while Billy continued talking.

"Or you could be a part of that major heist team that took all that cash from that Wal-Mart not too long ago in Livingston County," Billy said, pulling Jameer's leg.

He knew that Jameer was probably a drug dealer and he was having a little bit of fun with him. That was, until Jameer spilled water all over his housecoat. From that reaction, Billy knew that he probably struck a nerve, and maybe Jameer at least knew something about the heist. Why else would he spill his water? He would call his buddy Dave Opperman, and have him look into this situation a little closer.

"Put your hands on top of your fucking head," IRS Agent Dawson O'Reilly said with his gun pointed at Jameer.

"What the fuck, man, is your problem? You are in my fucking house," Jameer said.

"Special Agent Wagner, there's a loaded 9mm in the bathroom. Take photos with your company phone and bag it for evidence."

"I thought you guys were IRS agents. You can't arrest me," Jameer said, trying to put his hands down.

"I said, put your fucking hands in the air, before I shoot you in the forehead, and that will force you to drop your hands."

Special Agent Wagner went into the bathroom and returned with the evidence in a bag.

"Call it in, Billy. We are bringing this scumbag in. I ran your name and you have a prior conviction for assault, so I know that you do not own a gun permit," he said. "We are the IRS, investigating you for money laundering and tax evasion. The loaded pistol will also become a part of your indictment. For the gun alone, you will probably get sixty months in the federal system," he said. "Now stand up and turn around."

After Jameer complied, the agent handcuffed him and all three men walked out to the patrol car. They placed Jameer into the backseat and Billy told Dawson about his line of questioning in the living room, when Dawson had gone to use the bathroom.

Interesting, Dawson thought. He knew that once he got back to the office, he would call Special Agent Dave Opperman, whom he had trained with in the academy.

Chapter Eighty

"Can this wait, Nesh?" Lesson asked her.

They were both standing in the Buckeye Cafeteria, grabbing refreshments and coffee for everyone who was there to support Tha Pope.

"No, Lesson. I told you when you called that I wanted to talk to you. I also tried to talk to you when I dropped our son off at Rocci's house, before them niggas ran up in that bitch. You know, Lesson, besides everything we been through, I was good to you," she said.

"Nesh, this is not the time for that. My father is upstairs in this hospital, fighting for his life," he said.

"This is the right time, Lesson," she said. "We been through some shit and you threw me away over some shit that you kicked off. How many times has your mother told Tha Pope that if he wasn't fucking so many bitches, they would still be together right now? It's the same with us, Lesson. You know my son, our son, could've been inside that house, don't you?"

"Bitch, it's your fault that these niggas are still fucking with my family," he said, becoming angrier at her by the second. "Nesh, you are the one who chose to fuck a nigga like Savage Keith in the first place."

"Nigga, have you forgotten what drove me into that nigga's arms?" she asked. "It was your recklessness. Nigga, at least you could've worn a condom, and now the bitch you cheated on me with became your wife. Yeah, that shit still hurts, Lesson," she said.

Tears started streaming down her face. Lesson knew he fucked up ten years ago, but he couldn't take it back now, and he really thought that Nesh had set him up. Once he found out what really happened, it was too late. His heart still ached for Nesh, but fate had a say in the matter and had spoken.

"Come here, Nesh," Lesson said and hugged her tight. This was his first true, real love, and over the years, he had dogged her out over the shit he started.

"What did you need to tell me?" he asked.

Chapter Eighty-One

Ashanti had to get out of the waiting room. Too many people kept asking her if she was okay like she was crippled and needed help. They could not help her with what happened between her and Juman. Eventually, she would have to tell Lesson, but right now was not the right time. Too much had happened.

She was walking to the cafeteria to get some air and be next to Lesson. As soon as she made it off of the elevator, her heart fell out of her chest. She saw Lesson holding Nesh in his arms the way he held her. Or was she tripping? Could it just be that her emotions were way too fucking high?

Maybe Lesson was consoling her. Tha Pope was like a father to her as well, and she was Lesson's first baby mother. She could not be mad at Lesson. She trusted him. She just didn't like them hugging.

Ashanti walked in their direction at an angle that they did not notice her coming from. Ashanti would never be able to rationalize what she was about to hear.

Chapter Eighty-Two

"You remember that night we spent together after the barbecue in July?" Nesh asked, tears still streaming down her face.

"Yeah, I remember, Nesh. We were both drunk, but I remember."

"And do you remember the things you said to me, Lesson?"

"Nesh, I was drunk, but yeah I remember, and I didn't lie to you, baby. You were my first love and I do still love you, but I've moved on. Things wasn't meant to be and I'm responsible for that. I have to leave it with that. It was my roaming eye that got Ashanti pregnant. I thought that you would've understood that getting Ashanti pregnant was a mistake. I wanted us to get past it, but you couldn't let it go and leave well enough alone, Nesh," he said to her. "Nesh, you pushed me into her arms."

"Just like you pushed me into Savage Keith's arms."

"Exactly the same way," he said, agreeing with her for the first time.

"Lesson, feel my stomach."

"What, Nesh?"

"I said, feel my stomach," she said seriously.

Lesson felt her stomach and was shocked. It felt like Nesh was pregnant.

"Are you pregnant?" he asked her.

"Yes, Lesson. I'm five months pregnant. It happened in July."

Lesson's face fell all the way into Nesh's neck. He felt like his legs were about to give out on him, but to the onlookers, it looked like an intimate embrace between a couple. He already knew the answer to the next question he was about to ask.

"Who is the father, Nesh?" Lesson asked.

"You know I wouldn't play with you, Lesson. You are the father. Why do you think I have been asking to see you? At first I wanted to abort our baby, but I couldn't. Even if you don't want to be with me, I'm not killing our child," she said.

"Damn" was all Lesson could say, and his eyes got big.

Chapter Eighty-Three

Ashanti felt sick to her stomach. She felt like she had to throw up. She could not believe what she was hearing. She had almost lost her life today, was beaten, slapped repeatedly, and raped, because Lesson could not keep his dick in his pants ten years ago. Back when he belonged to another bitch, had Ashanti known that he had a baby and a woman, she would've never slept with him that night. She wasn't messy like that.

He had just confirmed that he made the same exact mistake again, exactly ten fucking years later, only this time, it involved her as the victim. Ashanti wasn't just his girl; she was his wife.

She wasn't trying to eavesdrop, but as she got closer to Lesson and Nesh, she heard a conversation that she feared. She had become entirely too cocky over the years. She trusted her street nigga too much, and he broke her heart.

Nesh had just told Lesson that she was pregnant and from the look of it, Lesson was acting like that was the best news that he heard all day. Lesson looked up and saw her standing right there in his view a couple feet away. He had a bizarre look on his face, wondering how much had she just heard.

He immediately broke his embrace from Nesh and turned to Ashanti. He took a step toward her, and she took a step backward like he was a viper snake ready to attack her.

"How much did you hear?" he asked Ashanti.

"Does it matter how much I heard, Lesson? I heard enough," she said. Ashanti dry heaved for a few seconds. After she got herself together, she said, "You know, the only thing that matters is the position you have placed me in. It's the same position you placed Nesh in years ago. Savage Keith explained to Rocci and me what really happened all those years ago, and why, so I know the truth. Now I know that for the past five months, you have been lying to me, saying you would never cheat and have never cheated. I have been here for you, Lesson. I was your rock, and you pull this on me? Rocking my world with a baby on the way, by someone who you suppose to hate."

Lesson was smart. He was a leader and a great man, but when it came to pussy, he acted like any other man. He jumped in and out of bitches' pussies and didn't think twice about the repercussions. Now he would have to choose, and this choice would not only affect Nesh and Ashanti, but also LJ and Lovely.

"You ain't shit, you hoe-ass nigga," Ashanti said. She had raised her voice she became outraged. "All the shit I went through for your bitch-ass today, getting beat on and kidnapped. You don't even have a clue of what Juman did to me. I hate you," she slapped the shit out of Lesson and took off running.

Lesson tried to run after her and Nesh grabbed his arm firmly, holding him in place. "Let her go, Lesson. She needs a minute to get herself together. Didn't you hear what she just said?" Nesh said.

Skeet walked up and saw the scene for what it was. He knew that his sister had told Lesson. He also knew she wasn't a messy chick, but somehow, from what he just saw, he knew that Ashanti also knew about his sister being pregnant. *Once again, Lesson's dick had got him caught up at the wrong possible time*, Skeet thought.

Chapter Eighty-Four

Rocci was rubbing Tha Pope's head and kissing him. For some reason, he looked exactly the way he had when they had first met more than thirty years ago. She had thought Tha Pope was the finest brother she had ever laid eyes on, and he spoke using the smoothest words. She honestly could not believe, all those years ago, that he was talking to her and telling her that he thought she was the one who would have his children one day. Rocci told Tha Pope that he didn't have to tell her all those lies, because she had planned on sleeping with him anyway.

Tha Pope had everything: a nice, big red Cadillac, his own house, and a bunch of niggas who would listen to him before they would listen to their own mammies. She had given Tha Pope two boys. She never interfered with how he wanted to raise his sons. She did not want her children in the lifestyle, but she let them choose, and they both wanted to be like their father.

She told Tha Pope to teach them how to be a better man than he was, and to never let them go to prison. He succeeded, for the most part. Only Learn had ended up in handcuffs and gotten himself fingerprinted, about five years ago when he was pulled over for driving 90 mph on a 30 mph street. After a sobriety test, Learn was arrested for drunk driving and given a misdemeanor. That was the only time her boys ever had any trouble with the law, thanks to how they were raised.

Tha Pope's only downfall was the fact that he was a pussy chaser, and he passed that shit down to Lesson. Regardless, Rocci loved his dirty drawers, and would ride anything out with the only man she ever loved. She would not leave his side, until he was released from the hospital.

There was a knock at the door and Dr. Hassan entered. He had on a serious face. "Can I speak with you privately, Mrs. Day?"

"No, sir, you can't. I want everyone to hear the results," she said. Besides herself, there were eleven people in the hospital room. The nurse wanted at least seven people to leave the room, but they thought about upsetting so many young, angry Black men, so they let them all stay, hoping they would tire out. However, they didn't. These people had been there for days without changing their clothes, only leaving to eat in the cafeteria. It was like they were standing guard over Tha Pope.

"I will do as you wish," Dr. Hassan said. "I have serious news to share with you, and you are going to have to make one of the toughest decisions in your life. I'm sorry to inform you that your husband does not have any brain activity, meaning his normal functions are not working. Your husband is breathing on a ventilator, and without it, he will die. I have been a doctor for a long time, and I would recommend that you gather your family and say your goodbyes to him and pull him off the ventilator. It is my opinion that he is in pain being forced to live. However, if you can afford to keep him on a ventilator, we cannot stop you. But you will have to make arrangements to hire a full nursing staff to try to keep him alive. As I just said to you, that would only hurt him by forcing his body to stay alive," he said. "I'm so sorry we did the best we could do here at the university hospital. When Mr. Day experienced those back-to-back seizures, he took a turn for the worse and never recovered. If there is anything I can do, please ask, and I will try my hardest to accommodate you."

The doctor went around the room, shaking hands and hugging everyone.

"Nooooooo...please, Pope. Don't do this to me. Don't leave me like this...nooooooooo," Rocci yelled out loud from somewhere deep down in her soul.

Savage Keith and Juman had ripped her heart out of her soul when they forced her to shoot her husband. Now, with the reality that he was dying, she wondered how she could live with herself for the remainder of her life, knowing she killed the only man she ever loved. What she wanted most right now was to die, along with Tha Pope, if they pulled the plug.

Chapter Eighty-Five

An hour later, Lesson asked for everybody's attention inside the room. "Everybody, stand around the bed," Lesson said to his family members and friends. "Everyone here is family, and Tha Pope loved each of you in his own way." Lesson looked like he was hurting, but he was holding on to what his father had told him before he was shot—that he would have to be the head of the family if something was to happen to him. Lesson had been the head of the family for years, but he always had Tha Pope to fall back on to help guide him, if there was ever a situation that he needed counseling about.

Learn was a wreck. He loved his father in a major way. They held a special bond. Learn knew that Tha Pope never wanted him to be in the streets, but he couldn't keep him out. All he wanted in life was to be like his father and brother. Rocci was in the hospital bed, right next to Tha Pope, literally. She couldn't lose any more time with him. She knew that in a few minutes, he would be dead forever. She could not believe her luck. She had seen with her own eyes how Tha Pope had cheated death, and came out on top when he was supposed to be dead twenty-five years ago. And she saw him cheat prison.

Tha Pope was too young to die. He was only fifty years old. He told her that after the lick with Lesson, they would retire, and he was thinking of going down to Florida or Arizona. All he needed was her to go down there with him, and help him choose the location.

Tha Pope's two grandbabies were standing close to the bed, touching him. Lovely was next to her brother. Skeet, Mac, Fresh, Stix, and Nesh were all looking at Tha Pope, holding on to him or touching him in some sort of way. The only person missing was Ashanti.

Lesson opened a Bible and laid it on his father's chest. He started by telling everyone that Tha Pope would die in a matter of minutes. He didn't want his father to suffer. He wanted him to rest in peace.

He started by saying, "The Bible says to be absent from the body, is to be present with the Lord, but we just thank God together, as a family, to be able to come together in prayer. No weapon formed against Tha Pope shall prosper in the afterlife."

Everybody was crying. They were all fucked up. Lesson had only said a few words and they were the right words for the moment.

Lesson nodded to Learn and he turned the power off of the ventilator. Learn didn't care that all of his homies were in the room. He was crying like a baby, and when he looked around, all his homies were in tears as well. Tha Pope's body started shaking. He was suffocating.

Rocci yelled for Lesson to cut it back on. "We can't kill him like this! I can't handle him dying like this! Please, Lesson, cut it back on," Rocci said, referring to the ventilator.

Lesson hugged his mom tight for a few minutes, and whispered, "Mom, it's gonna be okay. I promise. We all will get through this, and if you don't, we will be here with you and for you."

Lesson walked into the bathroom inside of the room. He needed to wash his face. Everybody eventually, one by one, said a prayer for Tha Pope, kissed his forehead, and filed out of the room. Rocci was the hardest to get out of the room. Learn and Stix had to literally carry her out. She was calling them all types of names, scratching them and punching them.

After they got her out of the room, Dr. Hassan told Learn that he wanted to give her a sedative and an anti-depressant to calm her down. Learn agreed. Learn and Stix held her as a nurse administered the shot into her arm. Rocci immediately relaxed.

When Learn looked up, he noticed Ashanti enter his father's room and close the door behind her.

Chapter Eighty-Six

"Hey, Dad. I'm so sorry how this ended up," Ashanti said to Tha Pope. "Thanks for saving my life. I will never forget what you did for me, and not even questioning the decision. You laid down your life for us, and I will never forget it."

She kept staring at Tha Pope. He looked so peaceful and so handsome. She could not believe this man was dead. He meant so much to so many people.

"Why did you have to kill him, God? Why him?" she asked out loud. "Pope, I never told anyone this. I was gonna take it to my grave. I'm telling you now, because I just need to tell someone, or it's gonna kill me. While I was with Savage Keith and Juman, Juman kept getting mad at me and was slapping the shit out of me and putting his hands on me. You know that no man has ever hurt me physically, not even Lesson. Juman had let me use the bathroom to clean myself up after he hurt me, and I saw some razors. I was trying to steal one when he came into the bathroom and started punching on me, so I cut him on his hand. Pope, I was so scared. I wanted to kill him. He beat me for slicing him and threw me on the bed and raped me." Ashanti was crying a river; tears were flowing down her face freely. "I want him dead, Pope. I don't think Lesson can do it. I know you would've done it without me telling you what he did to me. My head is so fucked up and my marriage is over. Your son has been fucking Nesh and got her pregnant again, Pope. How can I live with that?" Ashanti reached over the bed and hugged Tha Pope. "What am I to do now?"

She kissed Tha Pope, made the cross sign on his forehead, told him goodbye and walked out.

Lesson came out of the bathroom with his head down, hearing every word his wife had spoken to his father. He was under more pressure than anyone could imagine. His entire family would never know what it was like to be responsible for so much. When he looked up, he had tears in his eyes.

He walked to the bed and told his father, "Them niggas are gonna pay, Pops. Goodbye, big homie. Watch over me," he said and then he turned and walked out of his pops' presence forever.

Chapter Eighty-Seven

The streets were not only watching, but they were talking about Tha Pope, and how a legend got slain by two niggas he should've killed ten years ago. And to top it off, word on the street was that Savage Keith forced Rocci to kill her husband, a legend, by a single shot to the chest.

Savage Keith and his right-hand man were flexing. They hit the streets of Detroit like they never left. Everybody was paying homage to them like they were legends. Tha Pope had only been dead for ten days. His body wasn't even in the ground yet, and the city had crowned a new king.

Savage Keith was supplying the young life, who hustled all over the city with top-notch dog food. His heroin was the best in the city. Savage Keith and Juman went out to Arizona with the $200,000 they took from Tha Pope, plus the $100,000 Savage Keith had saved and found a connect. His connect told him if he shipped his own work from Nogalas, Arizona, he would give him each key for $32,000.

Savage Keith asked Julio if he could he get ten for $300,000 and Julio told him of course, with the conditions that he front Savage Keith ten extra keys for $350,000, paid on pick-up for his next shipment.

Savage Keith accepted his offer. When he arrived back in the D, Savage Keith turned twenty into twenty-five and set the city on fire. The young life were too young to give a fuck about who Tha

Pope was. They only wanted to make that chicken and drive SRT Chargers, Hellcats, Challengers, and Demons.

•••

Lesson, Learn, and Rocci were planning a private wake and a private burial for Tha Pope. The plan was to drive Tha Pope down East 7 Mile all the way to West 7 Mile and back in a Rolls Royce hearse with seven black Cadillac Escalade stretch-limo-trucks following him. They wanted to let Tha Pope take his final ride, and let the city pay their final respects to a legend.

Everything was set for Saturday. The radio station was promoting his final ride, as well as the internet. Swanson Funeral Home on East 7 Mile was handling the body. Lesson had dropped off a triple-breasted black and white striped Gucci three-piece suit and a pair of gator shoes. On one foot, a black gator, on the other, a white gator. He had a black and white Dobb from Harry the Hatter and a pair of Buffs Cartier glasses that cost $3,600. He would also be buried in his presidential Rolex. Lesson would make sure that his father's sendoff would be on point and memorable.

Chapter Eighty-Eight

His body lay on a metal slab, stiff and cold, from being in the freezer for days. The mortician pulled the body out of the freezer exactly one hour ago. It was his job to clean the body and dress the corpse up for viewing.

Tha Pope's body had already been embalmed for almost two weeks to preserve his flesh from rotting, just like any other meat. The mortician had performed thousands of viewings for regular Janes and Joes. The funeral business was one of the more lucrative businesses in the world. One thing was for sure, and two things were for certain. People were born to die. Nobody lived forever. It didn't matter the cause of death—whether it was cancer, old age, or a gunshot wound, his job was to turn a bad situation into a decent situation, or a closed casket into an open casket for the final viewing.

The undertaker had seen it all and nothing unnerved him. There was no type of death that scared him or turned his stomach. He didn't care if the flesh was rotting or the body was freshly deceased. He could stomach it all. He was sixty-five years old and he had inherited his father's business after he had passed away years ago.

His father had first introduced him to the family business when he was the tender age of seven years old, and for the next fifty-eight years, the undertaker had given his heart and soul to the funeral business. This was his chosen profession. He loved his job so much that he expanded his business. He opened a crematory in the basement of his funeral home. He had two full-body furnaces down there.

The undertaker was popular with a few hitmen from around the way. For $10,000, he would turn a body into ashes without a death certificate from the medical examiner. He managed his funeral home alone and employed no help, whatsoever. Whenever a potential client called Swanson Funeral Home, the undertaker became excited. He loved making money, but more than money, he enjoyed servicing the dead. He loved to look into lifeless eyes. The dead ones never caused problems. They never put up a fuss and they let him treat them however he wanted to treat them.

Sometimes the bodies would sit straight up and stare at him. Sometimes the perfect corpse would roll into his funeral home and he would temporarily fall in love. During those times, the undertaker did his best work.

The undertaker had performed the viewing of the late Aretha Franklin. He did such a great job that his funeral home received a lot of notoriety nationwide. The late great singer was a known figure around the world, and he had received many accolades for the great job that he performed.

The undertaker had known Tha Pope from doing business with him over the past ten years. Whenever Tha Pope needed to get rid of a body, he brought the body to the undertaker. He knew that Tha Pope was a Detroit legend, and he also knew that one day he would prepare his viewing, because of the life that Tha Pope had lead over the years. Almost two weeks ago, the undertaker had been watching FOX News and saw a segment on Tha Pope. They had talked about him for days on end, and he knew that once the medical examiner released the body, he would get the contract.

Now Legend Day was sitting on a metal slab, waiting on the undertaker's professional hands to get him ready for his going home. Both of Tha Pope's sons had already brought their father's last resting clothes to the funeral parlor. They wanted their father to go out like the legend he was. Everybody knew that the final viewing of Tha Pope would be memorable.

The undertaker rolled Tha Pope's body to the tub and washed him with Gucci body wash and sprayed him down with a full bottle of Gucci cologne. While his body was still wet, the smell was overbearing. The undertaker did not dry the corpse off. He wanted it to air dry.

He then rolled Tha Pope back to the finishing table. He put on his Gucci silk boxers and Gucci silk socks on Tha Pope's feet, then he began to dress Tha Pope in a Gucci undershirt, a black and white Gucci suit, Gucci belt, and black and white alligator shoes. He put the presidential Rolex on his left wrist and Cartier frames on his face. Finally, the undertaker placed Tha Pope's body into a mahogany and cream-colored casket, and finished brushing off a few lint balls.

He looked over his work and was satisfied that the job was perfectly complete for tomorrow's viewing. He rolled the body into the wake room to await the family. The undertaker was tired from a full day of work. He needed a full night of sleep to be re-energized for tomorrow's service. He would watch from afar to pay his last respects as well. The undertaker cut off the lights and left the room.

Chapter Eighty-Nine

"Yo, nigga, where the fuck is they holding that hoe-ass nigga's body at?" Savage Keith asked Juman.

"They got that nigga's body on a slab at Swanson over on 7 Mile," Juman said.

"Did you get the camera?"

"Yep, I got it right here. I got that thang from Best Buy. It's real exclusive, and they said that we could shoot a movie with this muthafucka right here, if we wanted to."

Juman pulled the camera from out of his bag and was stroking it in a way that he would rub a pet.

"So, how are we gonna put this play down?" Savage Keith asked his right-hand man. "As they pulling up to Swanson Funeral Home?"

"I can't tell you right now, bro. It's a surprise, my nigga. We gonna be legends after this play," he said. "I just want you to ride with me and trust a nigga," Juman said, looking goofy, his smile stretching from ear to ear.

"We live together, ride together," Savage Keith said.

"And when we die, we gonna die together," Juman said, finishing Savage Keith's sentence.

Twenty minutes later, Savage Keith and Juman were at the side door of the funeral home, looking for an opening to gain access. Juman had the camera in his hand and Savage Keith carried a big-ass moving box.

"Yo, Juman, what the hell you got in this heavy-ass box, doggy?" Savage Keith asked.

"Chill, bro. You're about to find out in the next ten minutes," Juman said.

Juman pried the door opened using a screw driver and they gained entry. Once inside, they had no problem locating Tha Pope's body. They opened the casket and was taken aback by how fresh Tha Pope looked. Rocci really was trying to send her husband home the right way. Both men were impressed. Tha Pope's suit alone had to be worth at least five bands, Juman thought. Looking down at Tha Pope's wrist he noticed a presidential custom Rolex. Juman unlatched the watch, snatching it from his wrist, and put it on his own.

"Here, put this on, Savage Keith," Juman said and handed him a ski mask. "I only want our voices heard, but not our faces shown."

Juman positioned the 454 Triple Blast wireless LG camera onto the wall and mounted it. The wireless camera was transmitting data to another device. It had a battery life of forty-eight hours and it only started recording when the motion sensors were activated. Juman got the angle perfect and clicked the power on.

"Yo, hand me that box, doggy," Juman said. "Bro, when we do this, we gotta hurry up, because this shit is recording." Juman pulled out two eight-inch knives from his belt.

"Yo, what the fuck is that?" Savage Keith asked. "You think you Rambo or something?"

"Yeah, something like that. Here, take this one," Juman said as he held one of the knives out to Savage Keith.

Both men gripped their knives and started stabbing Tha Pope's corpse repeatedly. They went psycho on his already dead ass. Tha Pope was stabbed in his face and body over one hundred times. The camera recorded both men putting in major work on Tha Pope's body. When they finished, Tha Pope's face was unrecognizable, as congealed blood oozed from his face and wounds.

Juman look at the camera, and with his mask on, said, "Watch this."

Juman pulled two gallons of spoiled milk from out of the box and proceeded to pour it all over Tha Pope's corpse. The smell was so bad that both men wanted to gag. Next, Juman pulled a taped shoebox out and started shaking the box.

"Yo, my nigga. What the fuck you got in that box?" Savage Keith asked his right-hand man.

"Step back, big homie, and hurry up and close the casket when I turn this muthafucka upside down."

Juman emptied the contents from the box and Savage Keith closed the casket immediately. Juman walked up to the camera and spoke directly into it. "Tomorrow, during the wake, the city is gonna see the bitch Tha Pope really was. Even in death, we still are fucking over his ass." Juman laughed an evil laugh and exited the wake room.

•••

Only Tha Pope's closest loved ones showed up for his private wake. In attendance was Pastor Rudy Ellis, Rocci, Lesson, Learn, Ashanti, Lovely, Nesh, LJ, Unc, Aunty, Skeet, Stix, Mac, and Fresh. Rocci wanted to have a small wake and then drive Tha Pope's body up and down East and West 7 Mile in a Rolls Royce hearse for Tha Pope's final ride.

The city was expecting to see him take his final drive. People were lined up on both sides of the road, waiting to wave at the passing Rolls Royce.

It had been a long two weeks. The day had finally come to send Tha Pope home to Heaven. Rocci wanted Tha Pope's homecoming to be memorable. The radio stations were advertising Tha Pope's final ride in a Rolls Royce hearse. Everybody was dressed in all white clothing, for an angel was coming home. Aunty sang a couple soulful songs. The first song was "Coming Home" and she finished with "See You Soon," which brought tears to everyone's eyes. No one was holding back their emotions.

Tha Pope meant everything to everyone in attendance. One at a time, everyone got up to tell a story about Tha Pope during his time alive. Everybody who spoke brought on a different emotion. Tha Pope had touched everyone in the room personally.

Rocci wanted to wait until everyone had spoken, before she personally opened the casket for the viewing. She didn't want everyone breaking down before they were able to speak. She knew that once the casket door was raised, there would be a flood of emotions inside the service. Behind them, no one noticed the blinking red dot on the camera that was mounted to the wall, recording.

"How long do you think they are gonna be in there? Everybody in that muthafucka is crying and shit," Savage Keith asked Juman, impatiently. They both were sitting across the street from Swanson Funeral Home, watching the wake on Juman's phone.

"Shit, not too long. It shouldn't be more than two or three hours," Juman said, still recording the entire event.

"Dog, this shit is gonna have the book jumping like a muthafucka," Savage Keith said, referring to Facebook. "Did you already add the part where we stabbed his ass the fuck up?"

"Yeah, I already pasted that video together. We have a before, during, and after video for the book," Juman said. "Wait until these muthafuckas open that casket. It's gonna be primetime TV," he continued. "My nigga, you don't even know what I put in the casket before I had you close it. It's gonna fuck you up, my boy."

"It can't be no worse than how we fucked up the body," Savage Keith said.

"Nigga, that's what you think. I put a little surprise in there for all to see," Juman said with a devilish grin.

•••

"Take your time, momma. Make sure you spend all the time you need with Dad," Lesson told Rocci.

"Y'all come up here with me. I need all y'all around when we open the casket," Rocci said to everyone.

Pastor Ellis unlatched the casket. Everyone was standing around, wanting to see the man who was loved by everyone in the room. These were Tha Pope's final hours above ground. Pastor Ellis made a cross over his heart and opened the casket.

Instantly, Rocci screamed from deep down in her soul, dropped to her knees, and fainted. Ashanti started throwing up, then went into shock. Nesh grabbed LJ and Lovely, and tried to pull the kids away before they could see what was inside the casket.

Pastor Ellis was praying to God. A demon had committed this heinous act. Lesson's crew pulled out their guns and started looking around for potential enemies. Lesson fell to his knees. He could not believe that this would be his final memory of his father. Once again, his family was in shambles and he didn't know what to do. However, Lesson knew who was responsible. It could only be two people.

The wake had turned into complete chaos. It was like a war was going on inside the room. Tha Pope's body rested inside the casket. His suit was completely tattered, two opossums lay dead next to him. His face was partially chewed off. His eyes and eye lids were gone. Parts of his bones were exposed and it was hard to tell where his nose had once been. And there was a spoiled stench coming from the body.

This was not Tha Pope. The corpse that lay before them was a monster. He had been mutilated. Learn ran out of the room and immediately came in contact with the undertaker, who was in a state of confusion. Before the undertaker could explain, Learn jumped on him, assaulting the old man with his fists, beating the old man into the ground, nearly killing him. If it had not of been for Stix pulling Learn away, he might have killed him.

•••

"You catching these Oscar performances?" Juman asked Savage Keith, laughing hard as hell. "The Day family's reign has officially ended, my nigga. We run the city now."

Both men had singlehandedly destroyed Tha Pope's family in less than one month. They would always regret not killing Savage Keith and Juman.

After the casket was raised and all hell had broken loose, Juman had saved the recording and uploaded it to his fake Facebook page.

Juman and Savage Keith pulled off from in front of the funeral home and headed back to the hood, as the new kings of Detroit.

After a few hours of the video going live, Facebook deleted the video and suspended the fake page. Next, Juman uploaded the video to YouTube. He wanted the world to see his handiwork.

Chapter Ninety

Nobody in the city could believe what was happening. A video had been recorded of Tha Pope's private wake. Only Tha Pope's closest family members were invited to attend. However, the service had become a public spectacle. Somebody had created a fake Facebook page and posted a live video of Tha Pope's memorial service. They made the video public for the world to see. Everybody across Detroit had shared the video, over and over. There were at least 100,000 views within the first two hours, adding another 20,000 views per hour. The video was simply blowing the fuck up.

All the major news outlets such as ABC, NBC, FOX News, and CNN were showing censored video clips of the wake. There was a public outcry wondering how someone could be so ruthless and disrespectful, by going into a funeral home, damaging a corpse, and posting it publicly. News outlets were saying that the federal government was involved and looking for suspects.

Chapter Ninety-One

January 2020

"We are gonna get them niggas, bro," Skeet said to Lesson, who had been laid up in a funk for the past few weeks. Lesson knew that he was going to kill Savage Keith and Juman eventually, but right now, he was still mentally fucked up. He had been through a lot in the past couple months. His mind was working on overdrive. He simply needed to chill and regroup. He needed to put a major play together in order to avenge his father and family name, and he didn't want to go the route that his father always warned him not to take.

Lesson didn't want to force Savage Keith's family to bring him out in the open, because Tha Pope always told him never to involve family members. But how could Lesson follow those instructions, when that's exactly what Savage Keith and Juman had done to his family? On top of disrespecting the Day family in public with what they had done to his father's wake? Lesson knew that once he got out of his funk, if he did not find Savage Keith and Juman quickly, then he was going after their families. His mind was already made up, and nothing would change it.

Chapter Ninety-Two

Ashanti rushed out of her doctor's office in tears. She reached her car and got inside. She gripped the steering wheel tightly, slamming her hands against it until her hands became sore. She then rested her forehead against the back of her hands. She could not stop the tears that ran freely down her face.

How could this have happened? She had taken precautions. She had an IUD installed years ago. Now her OB/GYN was telling her that she was almost thirteen weeks pregnant and her IUD had become knocked loose, possibly from having rough sex.

Ashanti was in a state of confusion. She knew that she had slept with Lesson almost a week before she was raped by Juman. Ashanti was not stupid. She knew from the force of how Juman raped her that he had more than likely knocked her IUD out of place from him being so forceful. Ashanti was in the worst position possible. What if she was carrying the baby of the man who raped her, and who caused her father-in-law's death?

Juman was the same man responsible for mutilating Tha Pope's body after his death. Ashanti knew what she should do. She needed to abort her pregnancy immediately, before anyone found out.

She had promised herself, and Tha Pope after his death, that she would never tell Lesson about being raped, because she didn't want him to look at her in the worst way like she was disgusting— as Juman had told her after the rape. On the other hand, how could she kill her innocent unborn baby for nothing? Especially when Lesson was not forcing Nesh to kill her unborn child, whom

Lesson believed he was the father to. How could she kill LJ's or Lovely's sibling, when Lesson really could be the father? What Ashanti knew in her heart was that her unborn child was innocent and did not have a stake in the deadly game that was being played by Savage Keith and Juman.

Ashanti told herself that she did not asked to be raped, and she knew in her heart of hearts that she was responsible for the life of her unborn child—the child who God had given her. Ashanti could not kill her baby and go on living her life like she had not taken an innocent life in the process. She had a lot of thinking to do; however, her mind was already made up.

Chapter Ninety-Three

"We been camped out all week over at this nigga's baby momma's house, and this nigga, Savage Keith, hasn't showed up once," Lesson said to Skeet.

"Yeah, I know, bro. What do you want to do?" Skeet asked him.

"If he don't show up soon, we gonna snatch his bitch up and make her bring his ass out of the dark. If he loves that bitch, like the streets say he do, he will come to her rescue," Lesson said. Lesson had reached a boiling point, where the water was spilling over the sides of the pot. "Fuck the rules," he said, and was about to be on some wild shit in these streets.

Lesson thought about how it all started and was shaking his head. He had not handled shit the right way from the jump, realizing he should've killed Savage Keith and Juman. First, this nigga Savage Keith started fucking his baby momma, Nesh. Then he was clowning him in the clubs, shooting bottles over to his table for Nesh, which Lesson thought was for him. Then he robbed his trap house and shot him up. Next, he kidnapped his mom and wife and forced his mom to kill his father. Then he put Lesson's dad's memorial on YouTube after he mutilated Tha Pope's body. To this day, the video had been viewed over ten million times, and had been a complete disrespect to his family, in a city that once showed them love.

"Skeet, when I kill these niggas, it's gonna be bad, bro, to the point that I'm not gonna give a fuck if I go to prison behind it," Lesson said.

"Bro, I'll never let you waste away in the joint. We are about to put this work in and run the city again," Skeet said.

"Bro, I don't want to run the city. I didn't tell you, but I was in the process of going legit before all this shit went down," Lesson said. "I bought an apartment building in Corktown. You can have the city, bro, and I'll support yo ass. I'll give you all of the assistance you need to win, homie."

"You just caught up in the moment. Once we fuck these niggas over, Ima make sure you are sitting in Tha Pope's chair," Skeet said.

Forty-five minutes later, they noticed a used expensive Bentley turn onto the block and knew instantly who was behind the wheel. They were hoping that Savage Keith and Juman were together inside the vehicle. The green Bentley Flying Spur pulled into the driveway of Savage Keith's baby momma's ranch-style home. Savage Keith and his fifteen-year-old son, Lamichael, got out of the whip and started walking up to the house without a care in the world.

Chapter Ninety-Four

"Sit down, son," Special Agent Dave Opperman told Jameer. "Would you like something to drink while we are here?"

Both men were inside a visiting room at the federal court building in downtown Detroit.

"Yeah, I'm thirsty as hell. Can I get a Coke?" Jameer asked.

Dave pulled his company-issued cell phone from his hip and sent a text message. Within minutes, another agent appeared with a cold can of Coke.

"So, Mr. Jameer Maggetty, I'm reading your file and it says that you have been locked up in detention for a few months now. How are you enjoying your stay?" he asked, but before Jameer could answer he continued. "From the looks of the photos taken of your crib, it looks like you went from Heaven to Hell in a matter of months."

"Life is bad right now, Mr. Opperman," Jameer said politely.

Dave cut in and told Jameer to call him Dave.

"I was denied bond for no apparent reason and my judge, the Honorable Blake O'Neil, seems to have it out for me," Jameer said.

"Well, you are facing some serious charges, son. You have a possession of a felony firearm and a money laundering charge of over $250,000. You are facing a mandatory minimum of a potential ten-year sentence," Dave said. "You know I can pull you from Hell and send you back to Heaven, if that's what you want," he finished, smiling.

"So what do you want to talk with me about?" Jameer asked.

Chapter Ninety-Five

"Grab the little nigga, Skeet, and Ima grab Savage Keith," Lesson said. "Once I get Savage Keith to go with me quietly, let the little nigga go."

"Okay, bro. Let's make this snatch quick," Skeet said.

Both men got out of the car in stealth mode, with 9mm Berettas in their hands and creeped up on Savage Keith and his son.

"Yo, let me holla at you, my nigga," Lesson said to Savage Keith.

Savage Keith realized that he had got caught slipping, thinking he had run Lesson out of the city after the video was posted. He realized that he never should've let his guard down.

"Yo, my nigga, I got my son with me. Don't do anything stupid," Savage Keith said, thinking about the life of his shorty.

Lesson pulled the zip-ties from his pocket and zipped Savage Keith's hands together behind his back. Skeet was holding the gun to Lamichael's head. He was going to let the kid go, once Lesson had Savage Keith situated in the backseat of the car. Skeet just wanted to scare Savage Keith into not trying anything. After noticing that Lesson secured Savage Keith into the back seat, Skeet started walking away with his back to the kid, not worried about him.

Lesson noticed Lamichael reaching for something and kept his eyes trained on him, thinking he was grabbing his cell phone.

Lamichael pull out a glock .17 and was raising his arm to shoot Skeet in the back. Lesson yelled for Skeet to duck.

Skeet heard an explosion and immediately dropped to the ground. All hell had just broken loose. Lesson pulled the trigger from ten feet away. The left side of Lamichael's face exploded, sending brain matter flying in several directions. The kid died instantly, before even hitting the ground.

"Nooooooo...please, that's my son, Lamichael. Why you kill him? Noooooooo," Savage Keith yelled, crying.

Skeet jumped up from the ground and hopped into the backseat with Savage Keith. Lesson jumped into the driver's seat and sped off.

Chapter Ninety-Six

"Jameer Maggetty, you have a right to remain silent. Anything you say can be used against you in the court of law," Dave Opperman said as he finished reading the Miranda Rights to Jameer. "If you want to continue talking to me, sign this." Dave reached over and slid a small piece of paper and a pen to Jameer. After securing Jameer's signature, Dave said, "I want you to detail for me who was responsible for the heist at the Wal-Mart in Livingston County on Cyber Monday, November 2019."

Jameer sat straight up and looked into Special Agent Dave Opperman's eyes, and said, "Before I speak with you any further without an attorney, I want two things. I have two requests."

"What's that, son? What can I do for you?"

"First, I want a big man corned beef sandwich, some curly fries, and a milkshake from Asian Corned Beef. And I want you to bring the assistant United States attorney into this meeting for me to sign an agreement, stating that I will get one hundred percent immunity, if I cooperate," Jameer said.

Special Agent Dave Opperman stood up and told Jameer he would be back tomorrow with the food and the assistant United States attorney. He walked out, smiling.

Chapter Ninety-Seven

BREAKING NEWS: FOX News Veronica Starr is reporting that former Wal-Mart chief of security, Stanley Mickelson, has committed suicide. Police located Mickelson's body after doing a welfare check. Authorities have confirmed that Mickelson has died in his home from a self-inflicted gunshot wound to his head.

Authorities say that an investigations is still pending, however, it should be wrapped up shortly. Mickelson was the chief of security at the time when several men robbed a Wal-Mart in Livingston County while using an armored truck. Authorities believe that the heist was an inside job. Authorities considered Mickelson a suspect, and have yet to clear him of any wrongdoing. Mickelson is survived by his estranged wife, Pamala Mass, and his two young daughters.

Chapter Ninety-Eight

"Get that nigga up," Lesson said as he and Learn took turns savagely punching Savage Keith all over his body. The entire crew stood around watching, including Fresh, Skeet, Mac, and Stix. They all wanted a piece of Savage Keith, but they let Lesson and Learn get everything off their chests from the pain that both brothers felt from losing their father and being forced to look at his mutilated body, whenever Tha Pope's name was typed on the internet.

"Okay, okay," Savage Keith said. "You killed my son. he was just a young kid," he said, expecting sympathy.

"Fuck yo son, nigga," Learn said and continued to beat Savage Keith senselessly. "You had my mom kill my father." Learn hit him in the face again, breaking his nose. Blood was leaking out.

"Skeet, give me the sewing needle," Lesson said, while reaching over and getting it out of Skeet's hands. "Hold that nigga, Fresh." Lesson inserted the sewing needle into Savage Keith's ear cavity.

Savage Keith had never felt pain like that before. He knew he was going to die. He just wanted them to hurry up and kill him. Blood started leaking from his eardrum. He didn't know how much longer her could take the torture.

Fresh grabbed a horse whip and repeatedly whipped Savage Keith's legs. There were thick four-to-six-inch cuts all over his legs. Mac and Stix poured ammonia onto Savage Keith, causing him to pass out. Fresh cut his zip-ties to set his hands free.

"Learn, hand me the can," Lesson told his little brother.

Learn gave Lesson the can that was filled with gasoline, and Lesson poured it all over Savage Keith's head. He instantly woke up in a daze.

"Go ahead, bro. Strike the match for Pops," Lesson instructed Learn.

Learn lit the match without any hesitation and threw it in the direction of Savage Keith's face. Instantly, Savage Keith's head burst into flames. He tried to run, but Mac hit him in the head with a baseball bat, knocking him out completely, his head still burning.

Savage Keith burned to death.

Chapter Ninety-Nine

February 2020

"Lesson, I need to talk to with you," Ashanti said.

Lesson came into the living room and sat down next to his wife. Lesson had changed a lot since Tha Pope died. It wasn't just that his father had died, it was how he died. And even after death, Savage Keith and Juman were still disrespecting his family by going on Facebook, showing the wake and Tha Pope's mutilated corpse.

Lesson's head was still fucked up, and all he could think about was the safety of his family. He had already dropped Savage Keith and his son, Lamichael. The streets were talking about the Day family reign not being over in the city of Detroit.

Lesson knew that Juman was still somewhere out there, lurking, waiting on an opportunity to get Lesson back for killing Savage Keith, and his son. Lesson had to protect his family by any means necessary. Lesson reached over and hugged his wife.

Ashanti felt like Lesson had been relieved of some of the pressure that he was holding inside of himself, but she had to tell him about her pregnancy, because the child she was carrying had an impact on both of their lives.

"Baby, what's on your mind?" Lesson asked. Ashanti started crying. "It's okay, you can tell me, baby." He was rubbing her cheek affectionately.

Ashanti blurted it out. "I'm pregnant, Lesson. My OB/GYN told me this morning."

"I thought you have an IUD?"

"I did, but somehow it got knocked out."

"Us being pregnant is not a bad thing, Ashanti. We lost Tha Pope and are gaining a new life," he said. "Maybe you will give me another son." This was the best news that Lesson had heard since before his father was killed. He instantly started thinking about his family's future. "Baby, how far along are you?" he asked, reaching over and touching her belly, noticing a pudge in her midsection. He could not believe that he was so out of it that he had not paid attention to his wife's weight gain, or her appearance lately.

"My OB/GYN said that I'm twelve to thirteen weeks," she said, looking at the ground.

Lesson didn't know why she wasn't excited. Maybe it was the fact that Nesh was also pregnant and due to give birth to a son in April 2020, which was two months away.

Ashanti had decided to keep her baby and she wasn't going to tell Lesson that the unborn child could possibly not be his baby. If she did that, then Lesson would know that another man had slept with her. Ashanti felt like Lesson had put her in a trick bag by getting Nesh pregnant, and she felt it was Lesson's fault that she had gotten raped. She was not killing her child.

Ashanti would keep her promise and never tell a soul about being raped by Juman in November 2019.

Chapter One Hundred

March 2020

"So here's how this situation will play out," Special Agent Dave Opperman said to Jameer. "You will be released today on a secret bond. It is my understanding that no one has any idea that you have been incarcerated, and we plan on keeping it that way. The government needs to build a solid case against Lesson Day. Right now, all we have is your statement and that's not good enough. That's only good enough to bring down an indictment. However, it's not enough for the United States Attorney's office to obtain a conviction."

"So what do you need me to do, Dave?" Jameer asked his new employer.

Special Agent Dave Opperman gave him details of the operation that was approved to take Lesson Day down.

"For the next six months, every time you meet with Lesson, I want you to wear a wire," Dave said.

"I can't wear a wire, Dave. Lesson is not gonna go for that. He might even become suspicious," Jameer said.

"Son, these are not the old days. Everyone wears a wire daily," Dave said.

"What do you mean?"

"Son, this is the year 2020. I'm going to give you a government-issued phone that's been approved by the Secret Service in Quantico," he said. "The settings will be set to record on voice command. So whenever the command is said, it will instantly start recording," Dave said. "Lesson will have no idea what you are doing." Jameer sat there stunned by the type of technology that the feds were using. "Son, we are not too concerned with the other suspects right now. Right now, we want the mastermind," Dave said. "Once we get Lesson in custody, we will see how the cookie crumbles."

"What do you mean by that, Dave?" Jameer asked.

"Jameer, listen, son, when you break a cookie in half, you never see the crumbles until the cookie breaks into pieces. Lesson is the cookie. He's the mastermind. Once we take him down, if he ever wants to go home again before he's sixty-five years old, he will snitch on the crumbs. That would be the only way to save himself, exactly how you did," Dave said.

"So, are you saying that the crumbs are the other suspects?" Jameer asked, trying to understand special agent terminology.

"Exactly, my boy," Dave said, smiling.

Chapter One Hundred One

April 2020

"Just go, Lesson. I don't care anymore," Ashanti said. "If you think it's okay to leave your family on Easter morning for another bitch and her problems, then go ahead and leave, Lesson."

Ashanti was fuming. Her hormones were already on a million from being five months pregnant. She was getting bigger by the day. She stayed hot and bothered all the time. Any little thing would irritate her. There was only one person in this world right now who she felt understood her pain, and that was her now-eleven-year-old daughter, Lovely.

Over the last five months, ever since Lovely witnessed her mom and her grandma being abducted, their relationship changed for the better. The ten-year-old girl from last year, who always seemed to have an attitude with her mom about something, had disappeared. Her mom had now become her idol. They were inseparable, and Lovely now adored her mom.

"Ashanti, you have to stop tripping and try to make peace with the fact that I have another son on the way," Lesson said. "He will be born any minute today, and you are holding me up. What would you like for me to do, miss my son's birth, Ashanti?"

"You are missing the point, Lesson. You are about to miss being home Easter Sunday with your pregnant wife and daughter. What about *our* family, Lesson? Which family is more important to you?" Ashanti asked.

"He's my son, Ashanti. He's a part of me and he will be LJ's and Lovely's baby brother."

"So fuck me and our family, just because you fucked up and got your baby momma pregnant?" she asked.

"It's not like that, baby."

"Don't 'baby' me."

"I'm not about to beat myself up over my son being born today," Lesson said, his voice starting to rise.

"Fuck you, nigga. Get the fuck out and go be with your other family," she said.

Lovely heard the commotion coming from her parent's bedroom. She entered the master suite and stood next to her mom, clinging on to her arm. Lovely was not a dummy. She knew there was a lot of tension between her mom and her dad lately.

Her parents didn't know, but she knew why they were arguing. Lovely had been hearing pieces of the story over the last couple of months, and had pieced the puzzle together. What stood out the most to her was the fact that her father was acting like her mom was not pregnant, and had not been recently abducted. Lovely also knew that her father was the real reason her mom had been kidnapped, and her father was the reason that her mom and Nesh were enemies.

"Lower the fucking volume of your voice, Ashanti," Lesson said as he checked Ashanti's temperature really quick. Ashanti, ignoring him, continued to scream.

"Why should I, Lesson, when your other baby momma is having another one of your kids today, while we are married? Don't you realize that this affects our daughter as well?"

Lesson knew that she was hurting, and she was right about everything that she had said concerning the situation. Lesson had placed his wife in a bad spot, but he couldn't believe that Ashanti had hit him with a low blow in front of his daughter, who adored him.

However, the way Lovely was looking at him made Lesson feel like an outsider in his own home. Lesson felt like he could make Easter up, but he would never get another chance to see his son being born again. He knew that if he wanted to make the delivery, he had to leave now, and he had already become tired of explaining himself to her.

Frustrated, he said something that he would come to regret. "Either you are gonna deal with my son being born, or you will not. It's up to you." Lesson put on his jacket and vanished through the door, leaving his pregnant wife and daughter speechless.

Chapter One Hundred Two

He couldn't get past how his right-hand man had been killed. Lesson and his crew had savagely beaten Savage Keith to death, causing major trauma to his body, on top of setting his head on fire with gasoline to ensure that he would have a closed casket funeral.

Juman had been sick, crying for months. He was fucked up behind Savage Keith being gone. They had finally built up an empire together and were supposed to get rich together. Juman couldn't fathom that this was the end of a chapter for him and his dog. They rode together for years, during the good times and the bad times. Juman knew that if he was with Savage Keith when Lesson and his crew caught Savage Keith slipping, either Savage Keith would still be alive, or Juman would've been dead, right along with his right-hand man.

He had made a promise a long time ago with Savage Keith that when it was time to die, they would die together, and he broke that promise, because he was still here, alive and breathing, while his homie was gone. He knew that he would be fucked up behind this for the rest of his life. Juman felt that he let them niggas torture his friend in the worst way.

Lesson even made a point by killing his nephew, Lamichael, who was just a kid. Juman tried to place $50,000 on Lesson's head, but nobody would take the contract. He even offered a kilo of heroin, but no one wanted to get involved in the beef between Lesson's crew and Juman and his new crew, called the Savages.

Even without Savage Keith on the scene, Juman was still running the city. He was the new king. He had top-grade heroin that nobody could compete with and the entire young life was coping work from him daily. Juman vowed not to let the money cloud his mind. He was going to kill Lesson, even if it cost him his own life.

Chapter One Hundred Three

August 2020

Lesson and Ashanti welcomed a new baby boy, who they named Life Day. He was dark-skinned, had black eyes and a head full of hair. Lesson was extremely excited to become a father for the second time this year. He was taking photos with his phone and parading his newborn around the room like the proud father he was.

Everyone had come to visit Lesson and Ashanti to congratulate them on welcoming a new addition to their family. Ashanti was in one of her regular funks. Her mood casted a dark cloud over the entire room. Everyone thought that she was experiencing post-partum depression from just giving birth, and she would get over it after a few days.

What nobody understood was that Ashanti was secretly dealing with the fact that Lesson's other baby momma, Nesh, had delivered Lesson's other son four months earlier on Easter Sunday, whom together they named Lucky Day.

LJ and Lovely took turns holding their new baby brother. Both were happy to have two younger brothers. Lesson grabbed for his son. He could not get enough time with little Life. As soon as Lesson started holding his son, Life instantly started to cry. The faces that Life was making while he cried turned Lesson's stomach. Lesson almost dropped his son. Lesson had seen that face somewhere before and something didn't feel right.

Ashanti snapped out of her funk and took her child away from Lesson protectively, and Life instantly became quiet.

Something was wrong, and Lesson could not put his finger on the problem. He wondered where all these emotions were coming from. He had to find out. Lesson looked and his wife, who was paying close attention to the baby. He looked at Life again, then he looked and LJ and Lovely, then back to Ashanti. Tears formed at the corners of Lesson's eyes as he walked out of the hospital room.

Epilogue

November 2020

Twelve weeks after Life Day was born, Lesson was holding two envelopes in his hand. Both contained the results for the secret DNA test that he had performed on both of his newborn sons, Lucky and Life Day. Lesson dreaded opening the envelopes, but he had to know the results for both kids.

Lesson had his reasons for performing the test on both kids. Lesson opened the results for Lucky Day and to his surprise, he realized that Nesh had been telling the truth. He was 99.9% the father of Lucky Day. Lesson exhaled. Then he started praying as he ripped open the second envelope. He already knew what the answer would detail. Life Day did not look like him or his other children.

Lesson thought about the conversation he overheard his wife having with his deceased father. Ashanti had told Tha Pope that Juman had beat her and raped her during the abduction. Lesson had not thought about that conversation until recently. He chose to block it from his mind, until he had gotten revenge on both Savage Keith and Juman.

Lesson pulled the papers from the second envelope and read the contents. Life Day not only looked like his wife Ashanti, he also looked exactly like Juman. Lesson had .05% chance of being the father.

•••

Juman had on all black. He had been sitting in the work van he had purchased just for this occasion. It was an older Ford commercial van, well cared for and clean. When he purchased the vehicle, it only had 128,000 miles on the dash and it ran like a champ. Juman had a large decal fixed to the side of the commercial van, using the company name Top Carpet Guys. Anybody who saw the van would think that it was a parked work van.

Juman had been sitting in front of Rocci's house for the past two hours, waiting in the same spot that him and Savage Keith were sitting at a year earlier when they kidnapped Rocci and Ashanti. Juman thought he saw Lesson and Learn go inside hours ago. Since nobody wanted to take the fifty bands he put on both Lesson's and Learn's heads, he figured he might as well save the money and kill both of them on his own. Juman could not move on with his life until he avenged the death of Savage Keith.

Juman was sitting out front in the van with a fully loaded AK-47 assault rifle. He had murder on his mind and in a matter of minutes, he would have blood on his hands.

Juman looked up and saw Lesson and Learn walking out of the house to a car. As soon as they got inside the car, Juman snapped a round into the chamber, jumped out of the van and ran up to the driver's side of the Dodge Charger, and in a matter of seconds, he emptied the entire clip, spraying everything inside the car.

•••

"Come on, nephew, you ready to go, before I change my mind?" Learn asked LJ. "I still owe you a drive for beating my ass in the game."

"You know I'm ready, Uncle Learn. How long you gonna let me do my thang?" LJ asked his uncle.

"I don't got shit to do. Let's go do our thang and ride around."

Both men were walking out of Rocci's house. LJ got in on the driver's side of Learn's Dodge Charger SRT, and Learn headed to the passenger's side. LJ cut the music on blast and started backing out of the driveway.

BOOM…BOOM…BOOM…BOOM…BOOM.

The car inched backward, out of control, and smashed into a tree.

•••

November 2020

Lesson and Ashanti were seated in the living room of their suburban home, drinking an expensive Chardonnay, talking about their kids and the future. Lovely was holding her little brother, rocking him back and forth, lightly patting his back, trying to make sure that he stayed asleep. The past year had been a hard year for the family, but together, they promised to bring in the new year the right way.

"Look at this, Ashanti," Lesson said and pushed his cell phone into Ashanti's line of sight, showing her the balance from an account that she never saw before. Ashanti looked at the balance on a bank account, and realized it was in her name.

"OMG, Lesson! Is this a game?" she asked, not believing what she saw. "Does that say four million fucking dollars?" She fanned herself, about to faint.

"Yeah, baby, Learn and I bought an apartment building in Corktown before Tha Pope died and waited a year to resell it, and guess how much we sold it for?" he asked.

"How much?"

"A whopping $8,800,000."

"So we are millionaires, baby?" she asked excitedly, thinking about the vacation that they would take.

Lesson's phone vibrated and Ashanti answered it. After several seconds, Ashanti dropped the phone into her lap, and looked off into space, shaking her head, back and forth, whispering, "No…please, God. No…not again."

"What's wrong, baby?" he asked, concerned, wondering who had called, upsetting his wife. Ashanti started crying a river.

Lesson picked up the phone, and asked, "Who the fuck is this?"

Unc from the block was on the line. He called him as soon as he got word on the situation. LJ and Learn had just been shot in Learn's Dodge Charger leaving Rocci's house. He told Lesson the details of what he knew so far. Word on the street was that his son, LJ, had died on the way to the hospital, and Learn was in critical condition at Henry Ford Hospital.

"NOOOO! God, please not my son! Not LJ!" he said loudly, rocking back and forth, trying to regroup from the news.

Lesson heard voices outside of home near his front door. Someone was counting loudly. Lesson started to get up, but before he could fully stand on both of his feet, he heard an explosion.

•••

Multiple U.S. marshals were positioned in a full circumference around the perimeter of Lesson's home. They wanted to make sure that there was no possible way to escape. They were readying themselves to knock his front door off the hinges. Several U.S. marshals stood facing each other with a battering ram, swinging it back and forth, counting.

"One…two…three…"

THE LICK

They banged the front door and it burst into pieces. Multiple U.S. marshals rushed into Lesson's home with their guns already drawn, looking for immediate danger, yelling, "Get down on the ground," taking Lesson by surprise.

Acknowledgements

First of all, I would like to thank the man upstairs. Without him watching over me, I know for a fact that I would not have made it past the age of nineteen.

Secondly, I would like to thank my lovely wife, who has put up with a lot, just being married to me. When I first told you that I was writing a fiction book, you supported me. Thanks for being my manager and research partner. I was buried in the county jail for over three years and I had lost touch with the world. You kept me sane.

Next, I would like to thank my momma. Man, oh man, you made me strong, all my life, and you help me get through so much. I know I hurt you and I'm sorry, but thanks for staying in my life. Without you, the system would've swallowed me up. I have always needed your love.

To my legal team, Andrew Densemo, Brandy Robinson, and Laura Mazor—y'all three are amazing human beings. Nobody fully appreciates the work you guys have done for free in the Federal Community Defenders Office. I have a deep appreciation for you. I understand that without people like you, people like me would be forgotten. That's the real reason why we have been a team for so long. Laura and Brandy, please get ready, because one day soon, you both will be my business attorneys.

To the deputies and staff in Livingston County that escorted me to the computer room daily: Deputies Daniels, Barry, Kourt, Brown, Haggerty, Anderson, Sin, Housler, Murto, Murphy, Powell,

Schmit, Linden, Gust, Bullock, Saunders, Boyer, Crain, Click, Hattfield, and Sutherman; and Sergeants Pengelly, Rosenburg, Davis, Knapp, Carter, and Asquith. Without you escorting me to the computer room, this book would have never been completed.

Thanks to everyone else who helped me along the way. For my favorite Livingston County book club teacher, Mrs. Laura: When you allowed me to join your class, I knew that one day I would write a book, because I was so inspired by all the books we read together. I can't wait for you to read mine.

I would like to thank my first readers who took time out of their day to read my manuscript: CJ Robinson of Ypsilanti, Earl Pitts of Detroit, and my wife's good friend, TyYuana Coates of Eastpointe. Without the feedback that I received during my writing stages, I probably would've quit.

To my lil brother, Randall "Worth" Ali, when I told you that I was writing a book, you told your big bro that you were proud of me. You know, to me, you are the real star in our family and your star still shines bright.

And finally, a special thanks to all my readers and fans. I just introduced to you a special character named Lesson Day. Through him, I have several more books coming soon. Next will be *Predaceous*.

Almost famous,
Brian D. Ali Jr.

Read on for an excerpt of *Predaceous*, the sequel to *The Lick*!

Predaceous

Chapter One

Juman couldn't help but to smile. He knew he was the nigga in his city. He came from nothing and he felt like he made something out of nothing. Those odds left him with a lot.

Juman was a consistent player in the drug game in the city of Detroit. He still had the best heroin in the city, and he had it for the low. He wasn't rich yet, but he could be in the next year or so, if things continued at the pace they were going. Juman wanted to be the plug, and he felt that he could be, if he played his hand right.

His Mexican plug out in Arizona—Julio—loved him and was about to seriously connect him, once he proved himself a little while longer. Everywhere he went, muthafuckas showed him love like he was Mekhi Phifer's character, Money Making Mitch, from the movie *Paid in Full*.

He was riding south down Gratiot Avenue in his new 2020 Lexus two-door LC, heading toward downtown to his new club called Pressure. Sitting next to him was his money-making bad bitch, Tia. Together, they were about to turn the fuck up and get lit.

Every Saturday night, Juman and Tia would arrive at the club to make an appearance. Tonight was a big night. Juman had secured a contract with city promoters and booked the long-time successful rapper, Young Jeezy, along with a local rapper, Payroll Giovanni, who was opening up for him.

Juman was running a little late and stepped on the gas. The powerful coupe glided smoothly in and out of traffic. Every driver who pulled up next to the Lexus admired all of its luxurious details. Juman had paid over $93,000 for the coupe and had put another $15,000 into it to make the coupe extra special. The car had a powerful V8 engine and 471 HP. All the dope boys admired the ride. He wanted to be different and have a ride that only a few people could afford in Michigan.

When Juman pulled up to the entrance of Pressure, the valet took his car and his doormen cleared the way for him and Tia to walk in without interruption. Juman was brown skinned, five-foot-ten, muscular built with shoulder-length dreads, wearing a new Burberry gray checkered three-piece suit that he paid over $2,400 for.

He wasn't handsome at all, but the money he was now making made him attractive to most of the women in the city who knew his occupation. Tia strongly held on to his arm. She was a bad bitch and even a blind man could see it, but she wanted to let all these thirsty hoes, who were watching Juman, know that he was taken. She did not have to compete with any bitch, but Juman had a wandering eye, so she let her position be known to all who were watching.

Tia was more than fine, she was simply breathtaking at five-foot-seven. She was what the hood considered an extra thick, dark-skinned big girl with beautiful curves. She was wearing a Chanel dress that was hugging her body so tight that it was showing off each and every curve on her body.

"Yo, what up, Juman?" someone in line asked.

When he looked up, several other people started calling his name like he was a celebrity. He nodded and wrapped his arm around Tia's shoulder, pulling her tightly toward his body. Juman couldn't believe how many people had shown up. The line was wrapped around the corner. Pressure's capacity was a maximum of 220 people. Juman felt like he could possibly fit another forty to fifty people inside, but that was about it, unless he wanted to deal with the fire marshal. Several photographers were standing next to the entrance, taking pictures. Juman turned toward the camera as it flashed and then walked inside the club.

Chapter Two

Juman and the Savage team were seated in VIP, popping expensive bottles of champagne, having a good time. Besides the hired security, his crew members were the only people inside the club strapped. Juman was able to relax. The crew consisted of Juman, plus four other young members: Ice, 40oz, Pistol, and Jungle. Juman had constructed the crew after his right-hand man, Savage Keith, was killed by his long-time nemesis, Lesson, and his little brother, Learn.

Juman named his crew the Savages, because that's exactly how they carried themselves. They were all violent, dangerous killers, and they held the utmost respect for Juman. He was their leader and big homie. He had taken each of them under his wing personally. They all knew each other for years before Juman came along, and each member had his own sad story. All of their parents were dope fiends, and didn't give two shits about them. The boys were running the streets, wild, getting into all types of bullshit before Juman came along and gave each member a purpose to live life to the fullest, or die in the process trying. No one could deny that their loyalty was to each other. Their motto was "live together and die together."

"Yo, Ice. What time is Jeezy gonna rock the stage?" Juman asked, while nodding his head to Payroll Giovanni's hit "Turn Yo Phone Off."

"Shit, I think he's about to hit the stage in a few," Ice said. "He is supposed to do a six-song track. After that, he said he had to roll out to catch a red eye flight," Ice said, nodding his head to Payroll as well.

Juman didn't want to get too tipsy waiting on Jeezy's performance, and miss out on his club cutting the fuck up. He knew with Jeezy being in the building, his club was going to be the talk of the town, and social media in Detroit was about to blow up. His club was about to get free promotion, because of the star on the stage.

Chapter Three

"Baby, that nigga, Jeezy, fucked the club up and put on for our city," Tia said to Juman.

"Yeah, fasho. He did the damn thang tonight," Juman said.

Juman and Tia were in their office in the back of Pressure, counting piles of large and small bills. They had a sold-out show and they ran through seventy-five-percent of their bar alcohol. After they paid the city promoters, the club profited $95,000.

"Not bad for one night, daddy," Tia said.

She was sitting comfortably with her legs open, showing off her panty-less bald, pink, glistening pussy, and Juman could not stay focused. He was wrapping the bills in money wraps, and she was logging the funds in her ledger. She wanted to keep things on the up and up, just in case they got audited for being a new establishment.

"Not bad at all. I can't complain, baby girl. This is what I was talking about when I told your sexy ass let's go into business together. You get the liquor license and let me get the club," he said. "I knew we would make good, legal money together."

After a while, Tia placed all of the money inside of the safe on the wall, twisted the combination lock, and closed it shut.

"You ready to leave, baby?" she asked.

"Yeah, let me get a shot of that Rémy 1738 really quick and we are out of here," he said, reaching for a shot glass from his mini bar, then pouring himself a hefty shot.

"You wanna go over to Motor City Casino for the night, daddy, and grab a hotel room?" she asked him.

"That depends on if you are trying to stay up with me for the next few hours and shake that ass on this dick," he said, grabbing his dick, making it semi-erect. The small bulge in his pants showed her that he wanted to fuck her.

"Don't start nothing that you ain't gonna be able to finish, nigga. You know how you like to answer your phone and get sidetracked. After this pussy is good and wet, I'm not letting you leave tonight, daddy," she said.

Tia was looking at him with lust in her eyes. She wanted her nigga to know that she was horny for him as well. It had been a while since he beat her pussy up really good. She tried to make him feel like he was the only man in the world while they were together. She loved him for what he was doing for her, but she wasn't in love with him. She had him and wanted him to believe, since day one, that she had his back, but she wasn't side-chick material. Nevertheless, most of the time he believed that she would do anything for him, and that's all that mattered. He wanted her to be his ride or die, but a nigga like Juman came with conditions, so Tia always took care of herself first.

Juman walked up to her and wrapped his hand around her throat and squeezed lightly, until Tia moaned. He knew that she loved rough sex. He released his hand, palmed her ass, and started kissing her roughly.

"Don't play with me, bitch. You know damn well how much I love this pussy," Juman said and reached under her dress and started rubbing her pussy. He pulled his hand back and showed her wetness between his thumb and index finger. "When the kitty is wet like this. I can't leave her."

"Umm...yesss...like that. Play with her some more, daddy," Tia said though she could barely talk. She wanted to hurry up and get to the hotel.

"Let me show you something," she said and pulled away from him. She walked out of the office seductively, leading the way for Juman to follow the pussy. And of course, he followed.

Chapter Four

"Yo, 40oz, I need you and Pistol to follow Jungle and Ice in the GT Mustang out to the trucking station and pick up that shipment that Julio sent," Juman said.

All the men were positioned around a pool table in 40oz's basement, listening to Juman give the rundown on the play that was about to happen within the next hour or so.

"What's in it package, big homie?" 40oz asked.

"We got six kilos of top-grade uncut pure heroin in there. The eighteen-wheeler has about thirty-five assorted washing machines and dryers in the back trailer. Ours is the one with the black and white tape on it. You can't miss it when you see it," Juman said. "You may have to use the dolly. Make sure that you grab the right load, my nigga, so you don't have to be back there forever." Juman was talking directly to 40oz because he was in charge of the crew. Juman trusted him the most, almost as much as he had trusted Savage Keith. "I want Jungle to grab the package. You and Pistol need to be on point and watch what's going on from a distance, you understand?" 40oz nodded. "40oz, this too much work to lose. I paid $45,000 a key from Julio, so stay on point. I can't be losing $270,000. If y'all feel like something is off, leave the load alone and try to grab it on the next stop. You understand?"

"No doubt, big homie. We got you," 40oz said.

"Ice and Jungle, y'all take the van. Ice, you drive and stay on point, while Jungle is loading up the work. Once that's down, stash two kilos a piece into the three stash spots," Juman said.

"We got it, big homie," Ice said. "We have made this pick-up a million times already."

"Yeah, but not with this much work, and all my money tied to one shipment," Juman said seriously.

"Stop worrying, big homie. We got this. Everything gonna be all right," Pistol said, trying to assure Juman.

"40oz and Pistol, y'all keep your distance. 40oz, you drive, and Pistol, you stay on point. Use that 20/20 vision you got. Nobody should know that y'all are watching," Juman said. "Once we breakdown the bag, I got a little something special for everybody."

Juman had that look in his eyes and everybody knew exactly what he meant. After they successfully brought the package home, Juman was going to pay them for a night's worth of work.

Chapter Five

Pistol and 40oz were sitting across the street from the truck stop in the Mustang, watching the comings and goings of traffic. They had been there for twenty minutes. They had their eyes glued to the eighteen-wheeler. Nothing seemed out of place. The coast appeared to be clear.

"Yo, Pistol, call Jungle. Tell him and Ice to pull up. The coast is clear," 40oz said.

"Fasho, I'm on that right now, homie," Pistol said, dialing Jungle on his phone.

"Yeah, what's happening?" Jungle asked, already knowing that it was Pistol.

"Showtime, my nigga. The coast is clear. Pull up and make it happen, and hurry the fuck up so we can get back on the road," Pistol said.

"No doubt. We will be there in three minutes," Jungle said and hung up.

A few minutes later, Ice and Jungle pulled into the truck stop, directly behind the eighteen-wheeler.

Chapter Six

Jungle got out of the van and cautiously approached the driver's side of the truck. A dark Mexican was seated behind the wheel.

"My friend," he said with great English, smiling, noticing Jungle, his long-time buddy.

Both men instantly recognized each other from previous dealings. The Mexican's name was Javier.

"Yo, Javier, how have you been?" Jungle asked.

"Good…good, my friend," Javier said, nodding his head up and down.

"You ready to let me do my thang?" Jungle asked, referring to him going inside the trailer alone to find the package.

"Yeah, go ahead, my friend. Ima go inside and grab a bite to eat really quick, and you should be finished around the time I'm done eating, okay?"

"Yep, I'm gonna be out of your way in ten to fifteen minutes," Jungle said.

Javier nodded and stepped out of the truck and headed inside the truck stop. Once Javier made it inside, Jungle instantly went to work. He went to the back of the trailer and opened the double doors, found the dolly, and started searching for Juman's package, moving multiple washers and dryers around. After several minutes, he located the washer and dryer with black and white tape on it tore both boxes open. He found six tightly wrapped kilos of heroin inside.

Chapter Seven

Pistol and 40oz were watching everything moving from across the street from the trucking station. Everything was going as planned. Nothing looked out of the way and Jungle was moving at a good pace. Within a few more minutes, 40oz knew they would be on the road, on their way back to his house to meet up with Juman. He felt his phone vibrating on his hip and answered it.

"Yo, what's up, big homie?" he asked.

"Everything straight?" Juman asked, checking on the situation.

"Yep, we should be in traffic in the next few minutes. Jungle is almost finished loading as we speak."

"All right, 40oz. Hit me up when y'all are a block away from your spot," Juman said and hung up.

Chapter Eight

Jungle had locked the last of the six kilos into the final stash spot. He was rechecking everything, just to be on the safe side. After he completed the check, he told Ice that they were all set and ready to go.

"Let's hit the road," Jungle said. He was semi-tired.

"Call Pistol and tell him that we are getting ready to pull off," Ice said. Jungle nodded, picked up his phone, and dialed Pistol.

"Yo, Pistol, we are about to pull out. Everything is locked and tight on our end."

"All right, homie. 40oz is gonna be a few cars behind you and we are gonna keep a safe distance, watching your back. Make sure that you tell Ice to drive regular, and everything should be fine, you dig?" Pistol said.

"I got you," he said and hung up.

Chapter Ten

"Stay with them, 40oz. Don't let them get too far ahead of us," Pistol told him.

"I don't know where all this traffic came from," 40oz said.

They were following the van, trying to keep a safe distance, but because of the increase of traffic, they had fallen five cars behind them.

"Stay on them, 40oz. Don't let any more cars come between us. Five cars is too many," Pistol said.

"I already know, homie, but I keep getting cut off, and I'm not trying to make any sudden moves. That would draw too much attention," 40oz told him.

"You see that light up ahead?" Pistol pointed.

"Yeah, Ima try to make it before it turns red on us," 40oz said.

"Ima call Jungle and tell them to slow the fuck down," Pistol said. "I don't want him to run through that light without us."

As he was dialing the number, Ice went through the yellow light and the car behind him went through the light as well. However, 40oz had to stop, because the light had changed to red. Both cars ahead of him had stopped and there wasn't any way around them. They were blocked in completely.

"Jungle, y'all need to pull over and wait on us. We got caught in the light, and we didn't want to blow through it," Pistol said.

"All right, we are pulling over right now," Jungle said.

Chapter Eleven

"Man, why the fuck are we waiting on them?" Ice asked. "We are riding around dirty, with a fed case in the ride."

Ice was referring to the amount of heroin that was stashed inside of the van. He knew that if the DEA or the feds pulled them over, they were getting a life sentence.

"Yeah, I know, but we might need them, so we gonna wait on them," Jungle said to his crime partner.

"Damn that was fast," Ice said as he noticed a vehicle behind them. "That should be them."

"Na, I don't think so," Jungle said, noticing that the vehicle was a van instead of a car. "Whoever the fuck it is, they are pulling up right beside us," he said nervously, thinking it was undercover police.

"Maybe somebody thinks we're stranded or something," Ice said, trying not to panic.

"You see that, Ice?" Jungle said, looking into the passenger rear-view mirror.

"Yeah, I'm hip. I was already looking."

"It's another car pulling up behind us. Something is off," Jungle said. Paranoia had instantly set in for Jungle. "Dog, pull off," he said a little too quickly. "I don't like how this shit feels."

Before Ice could pull off, the van pulled up in front of them and cut them off. They were blocked in.

"Hurry up and put it in reverse," Jungle yelled at him.

As soon as Ice put the car in reverse, the car behind them slammed into the rear of their van, forcing them to stop. The doors on the side of the work van slid open and two masked men with AR-15s jumped out and approached the van with their guns pointed at them.

"Put your hands up and don't move, or we are gonna to air both of y'all niggas out," one of the guys yelled.

Ice and Jungle had no choice except to listen. They knew that if they didn't, they would die.

Chapter Twelve

"Pull over to the curb. Ain't that Jungle right there, standing over Ice?" Pistol asked. "And where the fuck is the van at?"

Both men jumped out of the Mustang with their glock .23s ready, looking around for the van, already knowing that somebody had robbed their homies. However, shit wasn't making sense. Jungle had his 9mm pistol in his hand, talking to Ice, who was on the ground knocked the fuck out.

"Yo, what the fuck just happened? Where is the van?" 40oz asked both men, even though Ice was still fucked up. Pistol was helping Ice to his feet. Jungle had pulled his shirt off and was applying pressure, holding the shirt to his head, trying to stop the bleeding from the gash.

Jungle spoke first. He couldn't believe what had just happened, and worst of all, he didn't know how he was going to tell Juman that they lost everything when the two masked stickup men took the van with all the work inside.

"I don't know what the fuck just happened," Jungle said. "We pulled over like y'all told us to do, after y'all didn't catch the muthafuckin' light," Jungle said, talking a mile a minute, using expressions with hand gestures. To 40oz and Pistol, he seemed super nervous. "A work van with sliding doors on the side pulled up next to us. Then another car creeped behind us. Something didn't feel right when the work van cut us off, so I told Ice to back the van up, and as soon as he tried to put it in reverse, the car behind us slammed into us. It was a setup, 40oz. These muthafuckas jumped out of that bitch with AR-15s and ran down on us," he said, "forcing us to get out of the van and get on our knees. When we got on our knees, they pistol-whipped us and jumped into the van and pulled off."

Jungle looked at Pistol and then at Ice, who was finally coming to. Ice was probably going to have a concussion and a big-ass bump on his head, but besides that, he would make it.

"Ice, what happened?" 40oz asked him, upset that he didn't try to pull off.

"I don't know, nigga. Them niggas had the drop on us from the jump," he said. "Nigga, you asking all these questions. Where the fuck was y'all at?" Ice asked.

"You hoe-ass nigga, don't try to put yo fuck-ups on me. You fucked up. You was driving, nigga," 40oz said.

"Yeah, but y'all told me to pull over. How do we know y'all didn't set us up?" Ice asked.

With so much money being lost, they were all blaming each other, because nobody knew who was responsible. They only knew that Juman would find out who was behind this shit. He had just lost $270,000 in a matter of minutes.

Chapter Thirteen

"So let me get this straight," Juman said, standing in the living room at 40oz's house, talking to all four members of the Savages, who were sitting next to each other on the sectional couch.

Before the Savages came back from the pick-up, Juman went to pick up Tia. He wanted her to put a cut on one of the kilos of heroin, so he could have some new work ready to flood the streets. Tia's father had given her a hustle by showing her the ropes on how to cut dope before he got killed. She used to make money around the city, fucking with multiple dope boys, cutting their work for them over the years.

All that was before she met Juman and became his bitch. Now they were making money together, and her services were off limits to anyone, unless they were a part of the Savages. Niggas from around the city felt some type of way, but didn't express their true feelings about Juman shutting her down and fucking up their money.

Nobody was stupid enough to feud with the Savages. The entire city saw on Facebook what happens when you become an enemy of Juman or the Savages. A while back, Juman and his now-deceased partner, Savage Keith, had taken a legend out of the game overnight, and they did it in a way that was talked about still to this day. They forced a hood legend's wife to kill him, and after the murder, they mutilated his body. Niggas all over Detroit knew how ruthless Juman was and weren't about to get caught on his sick-minded side.

Juman was walking back and forth, bouncing on his tippy toes holding a twelve-gauge shotgun in his hands, smiling on the outside. However, he was fuming on the inside. He was mad as fuck. He was fucked up and he didn't want his little niggas to know how bad he was taking this loss financially. Juman wasn't broke, but with his latest investments including the club and the Lexus coupe that he recently purchased, Juman was basically starting over. He hated getting fronted by Julio, because he wanted to show his connect that he could come up with whatever he needed, and when he paid his ticket, all of the proceeds were his to keep.

Juman didn't like being on a time schedule, moving the work. He liked to take his time, that way he didn't make too many mistakes selling work to the wrong muthafuckas. He knew that Julio was a fair man and would front him whatever, and he also knew that whatever was fronted to him, he was going to be in his debt more than just money. He would owe Julio a favor for a favor.

"Who fucked up, 40oz?" he asked the nigga who he put in charge.

40oz was nervous as fuck, but he didn't want to throw any of his homies under the bus. He was a real nigga. So he told Juman that he personally fucked up.

"I was driving and cars kept cutting me off. Now I realize that it was a play from the jump. I got caught at the light and I had Pistol call ahead to Jungle and tell him to pull over until we catch up, so all this is on me, big homie," 40oz said.

Juman just nodded his head, liking how real 40oz was, willing to get in front of the gun for his crew.

"Ice, why didn't you pull off? I know you saw the play shaping up. You was driving, nigga," he said.

"Dog, I just got pistol-whipped over yo shit. My head is still throbbing. I don't got time for this shit right now. We need to figure out who knew what was really going on," Ice said.

"Oh yeah, nigga you lose my muthafuckin' work and you think you gonna tell me what to do?" Juman asked Ice, and he wasn't going to forget that comment Ice made either. "How the fuck can four niggas lose six kilos of the best heroin coming into the city? And how did them niggas have the drop on us?" he asked everybody.

Nobody said a word. Everybody was looking at each other, trying to figure out the same thing.

"Baby, you smell a setup in this bitch?" he asked Tia.

"Of course, daddy. Even a nigga who can't smell shit, can smell that somebody in this room set you up," she said, seriously. "Six keys don't just walk away, and that setup was premeditated."

"That's exactly what's going on," he said. He thought the same thing, and Tia was confirming his thoughts. Juman started walking toward the couch and was in front of Ice. "Somebody gonna pay for my loss."

Once he got close enough, he leveled the pump to his chest and pulled the trigger. Ice's body jerked hard into the back of the couch with so much force, if it wasn't for the back rest, the pump would've knocked Ice to the ground. Blood splattered onto the other three men seated on the couch, and they all panicked, because they didn't know what Juman would do next or what was on his mind.

From the looks of things, he just lost his fucking mind.

"Breathe, you bitch-ass nigga," Juman said to Ice. He put his lips inches from his ear and whispered, "I told you that I was a genius. Remember when I told you yo mouth was gonna get yo ass popped one day?"

Ice was wheezing, trying to take big gulps of air. Juman had pumped buck shots into his lungs and he was on the couch, dying. Ice was looking at Juman like he couldn't believe that his big homie could do this to him. However, at the moment, Juman didn't give a fuck about Ice. He only gave a fuck about all the money that he had just lost, and Ice paid for the loss with his life.

Chapter Fourteen

"You think he's gonna try to smoke one of us?" Pistol asked 40oz. Pistol knew that out of the three remaining members in the Savages, 40oz was the closest to Juman.

"Naw, man. Everything is cool. We need to find out who was responsible," he said.

"Juman seems to think Ice was the thief," Jungle said.

All three men were in a stolen U-Haul truck. They had wrapped Ice's body up in an old rug and Juman told them to wet the body with gasoline and set the entire truck on fire in front of Ice's mother's house, so she could suffer along with her traitor-ass son.

They all hated to fuck over Ice like that, since he was one of their day-one niggas, but they were not about to go against Juman. He also instructed them to put the couch that Ice was killed on into the back of the truck so it could burn when the truck went up in flames.

Before they left, Juman made Tia go to Wal-Mart to get ammonia, baking soda, and fresh towels to clean up the blood. When they took Ice's body out of the house, no one could tell that someone had just been killed hours before.

"If Ice didn't rob us, then who did?" Pistol asked 40oz.

"For now, we are gonna go with the theory that Ice did it and we will keep our eyes and ears to the streets," 40oz said.

"You know the streets can't hold water," Jungle told the group.

"Six kilos of pure heroin. All we gotta do is wait and see who comes up in the game next," Pistol said.

"Somebody had to set us up, and it had to be Ice," 40oz told his crew. "You see how that nigga always was trying to check Juman, or talk shit to him?" All 40oz could think was, how did shit get so bad so quick, when everything was going right for so long? He couldn't believe that Juman had killed one of his best friends.

Chapter Fifteen

"You know one of them niggas robbed you, baby," Tia told Juman.

She was sitting on his lap, rubbing his chest. They were at Juman's condo in Plymouth Township, Michigan. He could not believe that somebody in his crew had fucked him over. He had taken these little niggas from nothing, and given them everything that he could. All he expected in return was that they didn't hesitate to bust their guns.

"It had to be Ice," he told her. "I know for a fact that it was." Lately, he noticed several things that were off about Ice and when his gut told him something wasn't right, he didn't question himself.

Tia couldn't let it go, though. "What if you are wrong and you killed the wrong nigga, and you still have the nigga who took the world from you, in your inner circle, playing you every day?" she asked.

"If that's the case, baby, before it's all said and done, that nigga is gonna show his face," he told her. "Once he put that work out in these streets, Ima let the streets lead him to me."

Juman was certain that nobody in the city or surrounding cities would be able to put the brakes on that type of quality of heroin, and if it wasn't Ice who robbed him, then whoever it was, was about to feel the wrath of the devil in the flesh, known as Juman.

About the Author

Brian D Ali Jr. is a reformed career criminal who has been incarcerated multiple times for more than half his life. After a disastrous near-death clash with the law in 2016, he renounced crime life in order to be a better more productive member of society and pursue his talents of writing. Although a native of Detroit, Michigan, Brian also spent many years in Arizona and Pennsylvania. He has been married for over a decade and is the father of two sons. He is currently working on a follow-up to his debut novel, which will be released early 2021.